TEMPERED BY CONFLICT

BOOK TWO OF NATONUS REFUGE

MATT LEVIN

For all the folks who have taught me
that not everyone can be convinced

CHAPTER I

A digital display in Isadora Satoro's office, nestled in the government district of the Obrigan City megalopolis, constantly reported the number of cryo pods left aboard the *Preserver*. As of the
most recent settlement endeavor, that number now read as
35,899,487. *4 million down, 36 million to go.* It was the calculus that
absorbed her waking hours.

In the year and nine months since her vessel's arrival in the Natonus System, Isadora felt herself becoming further and further di-
vorced from the realities of colonization on the ground. She scheduled
a meeting here, signed a trade deal there, approved a settlement proposal after, and then got to bring tens of thousands or so out of cryo.

Anyone who had been brought out of cryo sleep aboard a colony
ship ferrying 40 million souls from Earth, and who had been

informed by the ship's computer that they were now the ranking political figure aboard, would come to see their job as a kind of numbers game. That, at least, was what Isadora told herself.

Except as of sixty seconds ago, the only number she could focus on was thirty-two.

The emergency report had arrived on her wrister and explained what had happened in terse detail. Several hours ago, on the other side of Natonus' asteroid belt, their New Arcena settlement on Calimor had come under attack. A man wearing a brown enviro-suit had stood up in one of the settlement's canteens with an explosive vest strapped to his chest, shouted "Natonus for the Natonese!" and blew himself up.

The explosion only managed to kill seventeen, but it also blew out the wall behind the bomber, and Calimor's atmosphere was not oxygenated. They were lucky more people hadn't died in the mad rush to the exits. The New Arcena mayor, a jovial and hard-working man named Morris Oxatur, had pulled as many unconscious colonists as possible back into the adjacent pressurized rooms. That was, until he too had collapsed, becoming the thirty-second and final casualty of the attack.

Isadora had met Morris long ago, back during the near-crisis with the Union. His good nature, indomitable work ethic, and enduring cheerfulness had endeared him to her. They'd communicated on the regular, especially since he headed their people's first colony in the entire system. She still had an unanswered message from him about spice quotas on her wrister, she realized with a shiver. The last relic of their talks.

The Natonus Offspring had claimed credit for the bombing within minutes. Isadora felt a sinking feeling in her stomach as she read about them. Their founder had been one of the Union prime minister's top military advisers, a man who'd nearly persuaded the system's government to launch an attack against Isadora's people a year ago. But the plot had failed, the general had been arrested, and the prime minister had assured Isadora that her security services were aggressively searching for the remnants of the Offspring. For the past year, Isadora's days had been mercifully free from worrying about them.

She turned her attention to the wide window panes lining the far wall of her office. It was the beginning of the Obrigan City winter, and the days were all overcast. Isadora was looking across the courtyard at the other embassies when four security guards burst through the door to her office. "Ma'am," one of them said, the strain in his voice conveying his urgency, "we need to get you to a secure location." The others kept eyeing the windows nervously.

"Per established protocol, we're bringing everyone to the basement level," another said. "We have no way of knowing whether the bombing at New Arcena was an isolated incident or the first in a string of attacks. We've issued high-level threat alerts at each one of our settlements throughout the system."

Isadora pushed herself up out of her chair and crossed her office. "I want updates on my daughter," she said.

The five of them exited. "We've already contacted Meredith's security detail," one of the guards said. "Again, per the protocol we've already established, they are monitoring—"

"—I want her taken out of school," Isadora said, trying her best—and failing, she was certain—to keep the growing panic out of her voice. She'd signed off on an emergency protocol six—*seven?*—months ago, never imagining they'd actually have to use it. Any remembrance of the protocol was replaced by a burning ache to have

Meredith by her side, and a certainty than nothing else would suffice.

The five of them arrived at the administrative building's turbolift. One of the guards punched the button for the basement. Two others looked at each other uncomfortably. "Respectfully ma'am, we can't guarantee that travel via aircar is safer than staying at school. If Meredith's location *has* been compromised, it may be safer for her security detail to fortify the school rather than travel out in the open."

Isadora felt cold fear grip her, the kind that nearly impelled her to let out a primal scream. She'd had to leave Meredith in cryo for over half a year after arriving in Natonus, making for an unbearable wait as she'd assembled the trappings of a government and initiated her people's colonial venture.

For the past year, she'd seen her daughter every day. Now, even waiting another few hours for Meredith's school to let out felt intolerable. There were murderous psychopaths out there who were targeting and killing Isadora's people because they weren't native Natonese.

But the guards were making sense. Isadora had an easier time imagining that someone might take out an aircar as opposed to storming a secondary school full of Natonese children.

So she'd let Meredith stay put, even though it shredded her heart. "I can appreciate the logic for Meredith staying at school," Isadora said as the turbolift door opened. "But I still want updates every fifteen minutes. And I want you to work on a plan to provide secure transit for her back to the residence at the end of the school day."

"Yes ma'am," one of the guards said. All four took positions at each corner of the basement. The one she'd spoken to typed her orders into his wrister.

Isadora had seen the basement once, right after she'd first arrived on the planet Obrigan. Their building was an old embassy vacated several years earlier. Her staff had promptly transformed it into an executive building, with each floor assigned to a different department, complete with private residency suites since none of them had any place to live.

The basement had been empty at first, comprising nothing but boxy, concrete rooms. Now, the basement was replete with a circular meeting table, a holographic projection of the Natonus System in the center, and a large holo-screen along the far wall. The holo-vision was playing a report on the New Arcena attack.

Isadora turned her attention back to the turbolift as the other members of her executive cabinet arrived: her ambassador, Katrina Lanzic; her chief of finance, Alexander Mettevin; her attorney general, Gabby Betam; and her head of defense, Riley Tago.

It was the last one she was most eager to talk with. And from her expression, it looked like Riley was keen on speaking with Isadora as well.

Isadora said a polite "hello" and "happy-to-see-you're-safe" to her other three cabinet members before she and Riley stole off to an adjacent room. There were two chairs inside, but no meeting table. The two women sat in the chairs and faced each other.

Riley immediately launched into a discussion about the security situation at their various settlements around the system, although Isadora found it agonizingly difficult to pay attention. There were really two Isadora Satoros, she'd come to believe. There was the Isadora Satoro tasked with overseeing her people's settlement project, and the Isadora Satoro still trying to raise a teenager in the midst of her chaotic life. The two were always locked in a competition for her headspace, and right now the maternal Isadora was winning. It wasn't close.

"Ma'am," one of the security guards from earlier said, peeking into the room. "We just got in touch with Meredith's security detail. They've coordinated with Obrigan City Police to increase patrols around her school. And OCPD has committed to sending over an escort for when it's time to bring Meredith home."

"Thank you," she said, the relief oozing out of her. "Keep me updated."

"Yes ma'am." The guard left her and Riley alone.

Isadora took a deep breath, managed a small smile, and asked Riley if she wouldn't mind starting over, please.

Riley gave her a knowing look and began again. "I've already been drawing up plans to bolster our settlement security. I believe we should institute security screenings at every access point to each of our colonies."

Isadora nodded. Such a thing might've made sense much earlier, especially in hindsight, but until now their threat assessment hadn't suggested there was a need for it. Plus, establishing security checkpoints would be a significant drain on their resources. They'd need to either reassign workers to staff the checkpoints, thus cutting productivity, or bring more personnel out of cryo, who would consume additional resources.

"Such measures would represent a significant drain on resources," Riley continued, as though reading Isadora's thoughts. "Moreover, most of our colonies depend on solar trade for their livelihoods. A system of security screenings will naturally inhibit the flow of space traffic through our ports, which will again lead to a productivity drain."

Her security chief's competence impressed Isadora. The

Preserver computer had initially chosen a different individual—an Earth Defense Forces squad commander named Russ Kama—to serve as her security adviser. But after Russ had nearly pushed Isadora to the brink of a catastrophic war with the Union, Isadora had dismissed him and promoted Riley. She'd seamlessly taken over after Russ disappeared.

Riley had a knack for thinking through all the angles when she gave Isadora policy recommendations. And she could understand the woman's point: implementing a checkpoint system would impose significant costs, both by draining resources and impeding the flow of trade. But thirty-two of her people had just been murdered in their home. The decision was obvious.

"I appreciate the thought you've already given to this," Isadora said. "But I'll sign off on your proposal."

"Thank you ma'am," Riley said, tilting her head slightly. "I'll get to work on an implementation plan and provide frequent updates."

Isadora was about to get up, but she noticed that Riley hadn't budged. "Is there something else?"

Riley looked thoughtful. "Respectfully, ma'am, I worry that a checkpoint system isn't aggressive enough. It's a defensive measure, and combating the Offspring will require us to go on the offensive."

Isadora crossed her fingers over her lap. "What are you suggesting?"

"We have two issues," Riley said. "First, we have no way of knowing where, exactly, the Offspring even are. Or anything about their capabilities. We need to find some way to gain intelligence on their whereabouts and numbers before we can even think about combating them.

"Which leads me to the second issue: although the Union has been graciously taking the lead on gathering information on the Offspring, we can be nearly certain that the government is keeping plenty of intelligence classified. I may be able to work out an intelligence-sharing agreement with the Union, but it would require that we have intelligence of our own to share.

"The solution to both issues is the same: we need our own espionage program. Now more than ever, I believe."

"I can tell you've been thinking about this," Isadora said. "I'll want to review any specific programs or personnel you want to bring out of cryo, but I like the idea. Consider that an official green light," she said.

"Thank you ma'am. The problem is that I've already reviewed the dossiers for our cryo population, and we don't have anyone with professional spying experience. But I have a couple of workaround ideas. I'll run them by you once I have something more concrete."

This time, Riley got up. Isadora followed her defense adviser back into the main room. Her other three cabinet members were talking, and the room had become crowded and hot with dozens of staffers packed inside.

The news anchor on the holo-vision was still reporting on the New Arcena bombing, which meant that there hadn't been any follow-up attacks. Hopefully. Now that she was starting to panic less about Meredith's safety, Isadora could instead focus on her devastation that thirty-two of her people had been murdered. But she was also relieved that more bodies hadn't been added to that count yet.

Sometimes, the only comforts of her job were the cold kind.

As Isadora continued to watch the news report, she realized that her job demanded more than just additional security measures and intelligence operations. She was both a policymaker and a figurehead. Her people needed to see her in public.

That meant traveling to Calimor to eulogize the dead. But that also meant, Isadora realized as her stomach churned, leaving Meredith's side for the first time since she'd brought her daughter out of cryo.

.   .   .

A year ago, Isadora had let her job consume her every waking hour. Ever since Meredith had joined her, however, she'd started taking a few hours out of her day to cook dinner and spend time with her daughter. It was one of the innumerable reasons to be grateful that Meredith was with her now.

OCPD was shuttling Meredith back to their residence. One of the patrol cars was radioing in status updates every minute. *Must be a parent too,* Isadora thought with a grin.

She continued to slice up the sweet potato on her cutting board for the curry she planned to make tonight. A pile of cut-up apples, onions, and carrots lay on the other side of the board, while three shakers of spices cultivated by her people on Calimor—cumin, paprika, cayenne—sat on the other side of the counter. A pot of boiling rice and lentils bubbled gently behind her.

Cooking was one of the small pleasures she could enjoy with Meredith. Her daughter couldn't help Isadora with her job, and even though Isadora was more than willing to help Meredith with her homework, her daughter seemed to be doing fine without assistance.

But today, she wanted to have dinner ready for Meredith when she got back. Especially if Isadora was going to discuss leaving for Calimor. The thought of being parted from her daughter caused Isadora's attention to wander, and the knife slipped through the tip of her finger.

She jerked her hand back and cursed. Already, a stream of blood was trickling down toward her knuckle. She dropped the knife with a clang and ran over to her sink to rinse the cut. Blood splashed into the bottom of the sink, snaking toward the drain.

Isadora was still washing her cut when Meredith walked through the door. "Thanks!" Meredith said, waving to a pair of OCPD officers flanking her.

One look at her daughter's face and everything else seemed to melt away. The attack on New Arcena, Riley's various proposals, her fears about an attempt on Meredith's life—all of it gone.

Her daughter's face was rounder than Isadora's, her hair curlier, her skin tone warmer, and her mouth wider. At several months over sixteen, she was almost the same height as Isadora. "How's it going?" Meredith asked, a simple grin on her face.

Isadora frantically wiped her finger off, leaving a small bloodstain on a dish towel, and ran over to hug her daughter. They stayed locked in an embrace until she felt Meredith stir restlessly. "I'm fine," Meredith said. "I really am."

"I was so worried about you," Isadora said, stroking the back of her daughter's head before releasing her.

"They told me what happened," Meredith said, her face darkening and her brow furrowing in grief. "I feel awful for everyone who was there. It's terrifying to even think about." Isadora could tell how seriously Meredith was taking the news of the attack since she hadn't slipped into Natonese slang yet. *Developed* was the way Natonese teenagers referred to something as cool, Isadora had finally surmised. *Scarce* meant the opposite. Meredith had picked up both within a few months of being enrolled in a Natonese school.

Isadora had wondered how to handle Meredith's education. She was in the unique position of being the only Earthborn teenager not living among their people's outer rim colonies. But Isadora wanted her daughter to feel like the system was her home. Integration was always supposed to be the endgame.

Isadora hadn't worried much about Meredith adjusting, but her daughter had thrown herself into cultural integration with a drive Isadora hadn't expected. Before long, posters of Natonese pop bands were going up in Meredith's room. She was making a handful of friends and going to see Natonese films on the weekend. And her grades hadn't even taken a hit.

Isadora sometimes wondered whether Meredith was just masking an overwhelming feeling of loss for all the friends they'd left behind on Earth, or the handful that'd come with them, but were still in cryo aboard the *Preserver*. Then again, if there was anyone who could process abandonment issues, it was Meredith.

She'd never even known her father, who'd left when she was still two and had never so much as tried to call her. Although Meredith hadn't expressed much curiosity about her long-departed father until her preteen years, she'd seen a therapist back on Earth to work through those feelings. And she'd come out of the process stronger and more resilient than anyone her age had any right to be.

"I know you were probably worried about me," Meredith continued, giving Isadora a knowing look, "but I was safe. I have people looking out for me, and the Union's been searching for the Offspring for months. No way they're still on the core worlds."

Meredith was making a surprising amount of sense, although Isadora wasn't sure whether her daughter was actually presenting a logical position or if it was just the product of her teenage sense of invulnerability. Either way, Meredith seemed to be processing the emotional weight of the bombing far better than Isadora had.

Meredith's face scrunched up. "But...I guess you're gonna have to go, right? To Calimor, I mean. You're gonna have to go be a politician."

Contemplating leaving her daughter made Isadora want to cry, but she was also secretly impressed at how easily Meredith had guessed what had to happen. Hard to tell which emotion was stronger at the moment.

But she knew she couldn't justify taking Meredith out of school for nearly three weeks, including transit time to the system's outer rim. Disrupting her daughter's life felt like letting the Offspring win.

Isadora had already figured out what to do regarding Meredith's safety. The Union prime minister still owed her two personal favors, so Isadora had used one of them to get Tricia Favan to assign members of her own security staff to watch over Meredith in Isadora's absence, complementing the security detail already assigned to her daughter.

"It means I'll be away," Isadora said quietly. "Maybe about three weeks."

Meredith nodded. "That's okay. I know how to take care of myself." Isadora almost detected a hint of reproach in her daughter's tone. Meredith typically wasn't one to argue, and when she was, it was because she disagreed with Isadora's political decisions. Never about curfews or just-one-sip rules when Isadora let her daughter try her wine over dinner.

"I know you do," she said. "It's just—"

"—let's enjoy dinner," Meredith said with a smile. "Worry about the other stuff later."

"Okay," Isadora said, returning the smile. "You're right. Why don't you put your stuff away while I finish up dinner?"

"Will do," Meredith said, heading to her room. Isadora returned to the kitchen, threw the cut-up produce into the boiling pot, and stirred their curry.

Normally, Isadora liked to imagine that there was an invisible barrier protecting their residency suite. She never let herself bring her work stresses and anxieties with her past that imaginary boundary. Not while she could enjoy her precious time with Meredith.

But today, it felt like there was more than work pressures waiting for her outside. She pictured the luminescent eyes of a ferocious predator as it paced outside their residence, stalking them from the shadows. Somewhere in the dark corners of the Natonus System, the Offspring were out there.

And now they had tasted blood.

CHAPTER 2

The entire outer rim of the Natonus System was lit up like a swarm of fireflies. Staring at the holographic projection aboard her survey vessel, the *Exemplar*, Nadia Jibor marveled at the speckles of light across the three planets beyond the asteroid belt—Ikkren, Bitanu, and Calimor—where she'd worked to set up colonies ever since her people had arrived in the system.

There were concentrations of light blips all around red Calimor, a growing number on the Horde-controlled tundra planet of Ikkren, and even a few in the untapped glacial wilderness of Bitanu. Trade vessels connected all three, bearing spices from Calimor, food from Ikkren, water from Bitanu, and other staples arriving from the sunward planets—the ones on the other side of the asteroid belt.

Nadia tilted her coffee tumbler back, letting the warm contents flow into her mouth. She felt lucky in every way: lucky to have the opportunity to lead her people's colonization efforts on the ground, lucky to have found a willing pair of native Natonese to assist and guide her, lucky that their progress was so easily visible and quantifiable.

And lucky for her ship. The *Exemplar* had started feeling like home during the past year. She spent most of her time in space, only heading down the outer planets' gravity wells for a few weeks at a time to survey a settlement site or negotiate a trade relationship.

Her parents, who had come out of cryo a year ago thanks to Isadora's new policy on immediate family, lived at the edge of a massive blue coniferous forest on Ikkren. Her father was working as a hydraulics engineer, while her mother had started a multi-denominational religious gathering. She'd visited their settlement a handful of times, but all three of them understood she belonged in space. Even if their dwelling wasn't quite *home* for her, it warmed her heart knowing her parents had found a place to live and restart their lives.

Maybe she could settle down someday, but only when her work was over. And that was starting to feel like never. They'd even thawed out about a dozen other surveyors to help with the settlement project, but whenever there was something mission-critical, Isadora always dispatched the *Exemplar*. Like with their current mission.

As far as their people had spread across the Natonus System, they still needed more settlements to absorb population growth, cultivate a wider variety of resources, and stimulate further trade. Although they could produce a decent amount of goods in the outer rim, they needed access to the inner planets' varied climates to expand their total yield.

But the settlement charter ban was still in place, prohibiting

Nadia's people from settling Union planets. That left only a single potential planet for further colonization: the jungle world of Enther. Located on the sunward edge of the asteroid belt, the planet was nominally controlled by a military oligarchy known as the Junta.

The problem was that Nadia had made enemies of the Junta during her early surveying days, when she pushed them off Calimor to start her own people's colonization efforts. It didn't help matters when she'd entered a formal alliance with the Horde, which had been skirmishing with Junta recon teams for years.

She hoped that the Junta government's animosity toward her people had cooled over the course of the last year. They'd even started sending small trade shipments to Enther to try to build credibility with the Junta. The colonists could now enjoy a steady supply of fresh Enther fruits.

Asking the Junta to allow her people to set up a colony on Enther would still be a tough sell, but Nadia had a plan. The Junta's main problem was its financial malaise. Intermittent wars with religious rebels for the better part of the last decade had sapped the state treasury. A truce—hell, even just a ceasefire—could give the Enther economy the stimulus it needed to regain altitude. And hopefully, the Junta and the rebels would green light her people settling the planet once they reached a peace agreement.

Nadia didn't find the economics of colonization particularly glamorous, but conflict resolution? That was more to her liking. And she had a reputation that gave her credibility as a peace negotiator. After all, she'd already accomplished the impossible, back when—

—a chirp from her wrister interrupted her thoughts.

Nadia closed the holographic projection of the system's outer rim, taking one last look at the blip representing the *Exemplar* as it glided toward Enther's green orb. She took another long drink of coffee and turned her attention to her wrister.

She figured it was from her parents—*damn it,* Nadia thought, realizing she'd forgotten to respond to their latest message—so she was surprised when instead it was a general dispatch from Isadora's security chief, Riley Tago, titled *RE: New Arcena Bombing.*

Nadia's internal organs all froze up.

The first half of the message described the attack in grisly detail: the Offspring terrorist, the suicide bombing, the deaths of thirty-two of their people. She raced through the list of names, which ended with a chilling *Oxatur, Morris.*

She scanned the rest of the message, detailing additional steps Riley was taking to secure their colonies, but Nadia could hardly pay attention. The man who she'd worked with for the past year and a half—who'd helped guide her journey, who she'd personally recommended for the job—was dead.

She wanted to cry, but she couldn't. She just felt empty. Nadia tried to comprehend a future where Morris wasn't there to greet her when she and her crew called port at New Arcena, where she didn't hear his booming voice shout "Nadia!" as soon as her ship landed, or where she was no longer privy to his support and encouragement.

Nadia was still wrestling with the growing void in her heart when she heard low voices coming from the corridor to her right. Her two crewmates, Boyd Makrum and Derek Hozan, emerged from the port wing of their vessel.

The two men laughed in unison at some joke they must've shared after returning from the *Exemplar*'s rec room. Or at least, that's where Nadia figured they were coming from. Derek was still dripping and his body smelled of chlorine, whereas Boyd's skin glistened with sweat. He had a slight pump in his arm muscles. Their rec room wasn't glamorous, but swimming in a pool sphere or a resistance band workout was better than nothing.

It was an unlikely pairing: a Calimor native from before the mass exodus prior to the *Preserver*'s arrival, and a former Horde raider whose organization had once terrorized the Calimor spice farmers. After almost a year and a half, the two of them had learned how to joke and laugh together. Nadia's delight with their growing friendship still hadn't subsided.

But today, when her mind was still processing the deaths of Morris and all the others, she found herself unable to focus on their conversation. She took another sip of coffee and stared at the lid of her tumbler.

"Are you all right?" Boyd asked, turning to face her with a wide grin spread over his face.

Nadia wrestled with how to break the news to her crewmates. Would it be better to just blurt it out, or ease them into it? "There's been a development," her mouth spoke for her before her mind had settled on a strategy. "It's...it's..."

Back on Earth, she'd worked for a resettlement nonprofit in St. Louis. Back then, she'd barely been able to stand giving refugee status denials to the people she worked to represent. Somehow, she could always find the right words to give good news, but language failed her when she had to give bad news.

Boyd looked at her with dread in his face, while Derek immediately pulled up his wrister. He must've seen a news article on the New Arcena bombing, because he froze in place, his eyes transfixed on the screen. "What happened?" Boyd asked.

Derek, thankfully, took the lead. He grabbed Boyd's shoulder and spun him around to view the article on Derek's device. "They launched an attack on our settlement," Derek said. Boyd didn't seem to need any context to know who *they* were. His eyes went wide as he skimmed the article.

"Holy shit," Boyd breathed, his face aghast. "Morris too?"

Nadia bit her lip and nodded.

"Those bastards," Boyd said, crossing over to the canteen table to give Nadia a hug. The man's embrace was warm, tight, and utterly welcome. "I'm so sorry. We're gonna figure out some way to get back at those assholes. Make them pay for what they did to those colonists."

Considering they were on a diplomatic mission, Boyd's promises of vengeance might've rung hollow. In reality, Nadia drew comfort from the fact that he was trying to help her in any way he could.

Thinking about their mission brought her clarity. There was nothing she could do to bring the Offspring to justice right now. It sounded like Isadora and her cabinet already had a plan in place to bolster their colonies' security, and even if Nadia wanted to abandon her mission to set off after the Offspring, she had no idea where they might be hiding.

No. Continuing the mission as planned was paramount. "The best thing we can do to honor the memories of the fallen," Nadia said, taking a deep breath and releasing the tension in her shoulders, "is to proceed to Enther and carry out the negotiations as planned. They died for the same dream we're working for. The best path forward is going through with the peace summit."

"I completely understand," Boyd said, giving her a sympathetic look. "We're with you."

Nadia looked up and made eye contact with Derek. He'd never

externalized his emotions like Boyd, but he'd furrowed his brow in sorrow ever since reading about the attack. He looked at her and nodded. "Let me get cleaned up, and I'll join you in the cockpit." He turned and headed for his cabin in the ship's starboard wing.

Nadia finished her coffee and set her tumbler next to a wash station on the counter. Its magnetic base latched onto the steel countertop. Then she followed Boyd into the *Exemplar*'s globular cockpit. He took one of the two rear seats while Nadia strapped in at the co-pilot's station.

They were probably still a week and a half out from Enther, Nadia estimated. "Are you okay?" Boyd asked.

"I will be," Nadia said. The summit she'd scheduled between the Junta and the Ashkagi rebel leadership, headed by a longtime resistance fighter named Noah Tasano, would start as soon as they arrived on Enther. It'd be held in neutral territory: the unaffiliated trading hub city of Kal Mekan. She didn't relish the thought of trying to broker peace while still grappling with sorrow.

"If you need to sit this one out, that's okay," Boyd continued. "Derek and I can handle things."

The thought forced a small grin across her face. When she'd first met Boyd, she hadn't imagined he'd stay on with her for this long. He'd spent the decade since his people's evacuation from Calimor flitting from career to career, hobby to hobby. It spoke volumes that he was still on the ship.

But as welcome a companion as he was, Nadia wasn't sure Boyd would make the best mediator. He didn't have the patience or the tact that careful diplomacy required. And if Boyd wasn't exactly cut from the right cloth to lead a negotiation, Derek—with all his quiet broodiness and solemnity—might be even worse. She had to be the one to lead the summit.

After all, she was the one who'd thrown herself—or her vessel, rather—between a Union expeditionary force and New Arcena a year ago, preventing the two sides from coming to blows. She hadn't done it for the fame, but her actions had nevertheless reverberated around the system. Had become mythologized, even.

And now that fame was part of her negotiating strategy. She knew full well that trying to encourage the Junta and the rebels to come to a ceasefire was a fool's errand. Union diplomats had tried and failed for years. But if there was one mediation team that could get the job done, it was her crew. She could only hope that accomplishing the impossible once might bode well for her second attempt.

Derek emerged freshly showered from the corridor behind them. He tilted his head from side to side, cracking his neck, and then settled in at the pilot's station. "Does this change our plans at all?" he asked, glancing at a holographic readout of their approach trajectory.

A discordant tumult thrashed in Nadia's stomach. There was still plenty of grief for the dead, coupled with acute personal anguish at the loss of Morris. Even guilt. Then there were all the nerves she'd expected to feel about the upcoming summit, coupled with not knowing how effective she'd be while wrestling to keep her other emotions on the back burner.

But she couldn't take up Boyd on his offer to cover for her. There was only one way forward.

"No," she said. "We've still gotta make that peace summit." The other two nodded slowly. "Have either of you ever been to Enther?" she asked her companions, hoping a conversation might distract her.

"Once," Boyd said. "It was when I was very young. Back when the planet was still controlled by the old government, the Theocracy. Back then, there were still lots of old temples everywhere. I think the Junta knocked a bunch of them down after coming to power. Used to make for great tourism," he said with a chuckle.

Derek shook his head. "This is my first time on this side of the asteroid belt, in fact," he said.

"Well hey!" Nadia said, excited at the prospect of something to distract her. "That makes this a special moment."

Derek shrugged. "Space always looks the same. Maybe it'll feel more different when we get to Enther."

"Still," Nadia said. "I'm glad we can expand your boundaries." She supposed that, technically, it was also *her* first time seeing the rest of the Natonus System. But it felt like it should matter more for Derek than for her.

Nadia returned her attention to the viewscreen. Somewhere out there, not yet visible to the naked eye, was the green orb of Enther. She tried her best—and failed—to calm the emotional tempest within her as their ship drifted forward. Toward the next best hope for her people's colonization endeavor. And the one Nadia was increasingly certain only she could secure.

CHAPTER 3

A mental health professional comforting a patient wasn't exactly an unusual circumstance for Carson Erlinza. Assuming the patient role was. Even more unusual was the fact that he was shivering in just a pair of briefs, felt like his head was about to explode from cryo sickness, and had just been informed that he'd woken up across the galaxy from Earth in some place called the Natonus System.

"How are you feeling?" a gentle female voice said from his left. He could barely focus on the counselor's face, with a harsh, blinding white haze still devouring his vision. A shiver passed through his body. On cue, a second individual walked up with a thick robe.

Carson accepted the robe gratefully and wrapped it over his torso. "This has got to be one of the worst headaches I've ever had," Carson said, rubbing his temples.

"It usually goes one of two ways," the counselor said sympathetically, nodding. She pressed a handful of buttons on a datapad she was holding. "About half of everyone we've brought out of cryo goes through dry heaves. The other half has terrible headaches for the first twelve hours."

The rest of Carson's body hardly felt much better. His dirty blond hair felt stiff, as though it'd been submerged in chlorine for hours. He ran a hand through his hair and found it difficult for his fingers to navigate. His scalp felt like it had some kind of viscous film layered on top.

The counselor nodded to her assistant, who brought forward a tray with a cup of water and a single pill on it. "This should help with the headaches," the assistant said. Carson slammed the pill down, barely needing the water in his eagerness. In seconds, his head felt better. Or maybe it was just a placebo effect.

"May I ask what you remember before waking up?" the counselor asked. Carson was starting to see better, so he could make out a congenial, professional smile on her face.

He was still having a hard time concentrating, but his memory was returning. "I remember being in transit to an evacuation station just outside of Vancouver," Carson said. "Me and my brother Stacy were on the shuttle."

The counselor nodded and made a note on her datapad. "Very good. We've confirmed that your brother's cryo pod remains functioning nominally."

Carson remembered the shock everyone felt at the arrival of the invading Hegemony fleet back in the Sol System. The mass anguish at the annihilation of Earth's military on Mars. The desperation as everyone who could make it to the evacuation ships rushed to board.

The resignation of family members and loved ones who elected to stay behind.

Carson had been conflicted. It was Stacy who made him change his mind. Stacy had come to the Erlinza family as a seven-year-old war refugee after Carson's parents had been trying to conceive for years, all to no avail. But after the Taiwan Strait War across the Pacific sent thousands of refugees across the ocean, his parents had leapt at the chance to provide a home to one of the countless war orphans. That was how Chen Shuxi had become Stacy Erlinza.

Stomaching the Hegemony's draconian rule over Earth might've been tolerable for Carson—it was for his parents—but for Stacy, it was just reliving the trauma of his past. So Carson had taken Stacy and fled to the *Preserver*.

Carson felt a pang of nausea reverberate in his gut. He keeled over and clutched his midriff. "I'm sorry we've been taking you through the motions so quickly," the counselor said as her assistant rushed over to help steady Carson, "but you're a special case."

A loud beep—Carson couldn't tell if it was *actually* that loud, or if the headache just made any noise feel like it was ripping his skull apart—came from the counselor's wrister. "Ah. The other crew has finished setting up your accommodations. Why don't you take some time—use the bathroom, get a good eight hours of sleep, take a refreshing shower, all that stuff—and we'll continue tomorrow?"

Now that she'd mentioned it, Carson felt like he could use a good piss. And a shower sounded even better. "Thank you," he said, as the counselor's assistant guided him away from the cryo chamber. With every step, the urge to pee got a bit worse. Eventually, it got to where Carson was so distracted he could no longer contemplate what being "a special case" meant.

.   .   .

A good night's sleep and ten minutes in the hot steam of the vapor bath later, it felt like Carson was a new man. He stepped out of the shower stall into the guest cabin and toweled off. Someone had left a pair of clothes for him. He dressed and slapped on a field jacket with a polyester shell to help with the chill of the starship.

Then, he turned his attention to reviewing the datapads they'd left for him describing their people's history in the Natonus System. He was surprised to learn that they'd been here for almost two years, all while he was still in cryo. And his eyes went wide when the primers described the destruction of their sister ship, the *Anointer*, which held all ranking political and military personnel aboard. Along with another fifth of the *Preserver*'s cryo pods suffering catastrophic damage in transit, that meant the refugees had been facing a severe shortage of qualified individuals from the get-go.

The primers then turned to a description of the original four: Isadora Satoro, Nadia Jibor, Vincent Gureh, and the since-disgraced Russ Kama. All of them were brought out of cryo by the *Preserver*'s computer, which had to adjust for the deaths of everyone aboard the *Anointer* and the destroyed pods aboard the *Preserver*.

The primers continued by describing the desperate actions taken by the original crew to secure a foothold in the Natonus System. Carson couldn't help but notice that the reports were mostly silent about what Russ had gotten up to during this period. They then described the role that a radical nativist organization known as the Natonus Offspring played in steering the Union and their people toward conflict.

Carson's eyebrows inched up his forehead as he read about the near-annihilation of their first colony at the hands of the Union. It felt strange hearing the primers move on to talk about their people's warm relations with the government, particularly the sitting prime minister. But everyone else had a full year to get past the mutual animus of their near-war with the Union. Carson, meanwhile, had to forgive and forget in seconds.

Once he'd finished reading about the Calimor crisis, the door to the cabin slid open. The counselor from earlier stepped through. "Are you feeling better?" she asked, the same professional grin on her face.

"Sure am," Carson said. He wasn't just being polite. The headache from yesterday had almost disappeared.

"I hate to rush you. But there are some important people who are very interested in meeting you." Carson nodded and followed her out the door. They passed through a variety of corridors, following signs for the ship's central transit station.

Carson couldn't quite figure out the rush, much less why important people wanted to talk to him. He'd worked as a therapist back in Vancouver. His specialization had been radicalization: specifically, working with violent young men.

An eco-terrorist group calling itself Primordial had become active within the greater Vancouver area in the late 2270s. Primordial maintained that *any* energy consumption, renewable or otherwise, was impure. So they'd started attacking the solar panel fields and wind turbines across the Canadian countryside. As well as the workers who operated them.

Carson had worked with a sizable number of Primordial members, often to great success. He'd even published a couple of papers on his work and advised the UN government on its deradicalization initiatives. He wondered if maybe they'd managed to capture some of those Offspring individuals, and wanted him to see what he could do.

They arrived at the turbolift station, where they took one of the lifts up a half-dozen decks. He'd hardly appreciated just how *big* the *Preserver* was back when he'd been boarding it with Stacy. But with the capacity for 50 million cryo pods, the ship was essentially a city in space.

"After you," the counselor said when they arrived at their destination. Carson emerged in an exterior hallway, with viewscreens all around him showing a tapestry of black with intermittent white speckles. *Must be the habitation deck*, he thought.

Carson and his chaperone arrived at a door at the terminus of the hallway, which swished open and revealed an onyx meeting table within. There were only two individuals inside: a man Carson assumed was from India who looked like he was turning prematurely grey, and a fair-skinned, wiry woman with light brown curls tied into a ponytail. The counselor gestured inside but didn't follow Carson in. The door closed behind him.

The woman had a datapad in front of her, and she barely looked up at Carson as he walked inside. The man placed his hands out in front of him and crossed his fingers. "Carson Erlinza," he said, his voice softer than Carson had imagined. "I am Vincent Gureh. My colleague here is Riley Tago."

"I recognize those names from the primers," Carson said. "It's an honor to meet you."

His work for the UN on deradicalization meant he'd occasionally met with a few political bigwigs. But Vincent and Riley didn't look like the career bureaucrats from Earth. They didn't wear their egos on their shoulders. *None of these people were actually meant for their jobs*, Carson thought, thinking back to the destruction of the

Anointer.

"We understand that you're probably still in the middle of a difficult physical recovery," Riley said, looking up from her datapad. "But what we have to ask you is time-sensitive."

Vincent managed an awkward grin. "We have coffee. Or tea, if you'd prefer."

"I think tea might be better at the moment," Carson said. Even though his headache was mostly gone, thinking about drinking coffee sent a throb between his ears.

Vincent nodded. He stood up, crossed over to a refreshment table on the far side of the room, poured steaming water into a mug, and submerged a tea bag inside. He brought Carson the mug and returned to his seat.

The tea was too hot to drink, and it hadn't steeped fully, but Carson still enjoyed running his thumb up and down the side of the mug. It was just slightly too warm to be comfortable, but the tingling sensation distracted him from the reappearance of his headache.

"We've brought you out of cryo to ask you something difficult," Riley said with a grimace. "But first, there's something you need to know." She described the recent bombing of New Arcena by the Offspring that'd left thirty-two refugees dead.

Carson felt an ache in his heart that matched the ferocity of yesterday's headache. He didn't even know any of the people who'd died in the attack, but it wasn't hard to detect the grief written into both Vincent and Riley's expressions. *They probably signed off on bringing all those people out*, he thought.

As a therapist, he'd worked with plenty of patients who'd bottled up their grief, their anger, or their insecurities until it practically devoured them from the inside out. Carson hoped the two of them were processing their emotions healthily. Or seeking some kind of professional assistance if they needed it.

Riley's hand went to her neck, pulling out a trinket tied to a string beneath her tunic and rubbing it with her thumb. There was a symbol on the front that Carson didn't recognize. He wondered if it could be from some local religion. The Natonus System had apparently been colonized for almost a hundred years, giving them plenty of time to develop their own endogenous belief systems. And many refugees had been out of cryo for long enough that they'd have had time to adopt the spiritual practices of their new hosts.

"We have to do something about the Offspring," Riley said, her voice lowering until it was only a little above a murmur. "Which is why we brought you out."

"I gather you've done a background check on my work with Primordial," Carson said. "I was wondering if you'd captured a handful of Offspring. But I have to warn you, I'm not sure having one of our people counsel Offspring members would make much sense. Just seeing a non-native might be a trigger for them, which would be unproducti—"

"—we didn't thaw you out to play therapist for the Offspring," Riley interjected. Her hand had curled around the trinket and gripped it tightly. "We want you to infiltrate them. As part of our new espionage program."

That shut Carson up.

"I've searched our crew databases from top to bottom," Vincent said. "No one among our 40 million has any kind of espionage experience, much less worked for an intelligence-gathering agency. We have a decent number of police with undercover experience, but they were primarily working with criminal groups back on Earth. Not violent terrorists."

"Undercover work can only succeed when you know how to inte-grate yourself with your targets," Riley pressed. "None of our under-cover police do. We've determined it'd take less time to train someone with your experience how to go undercover than it would to train someone with undercover experience how to deal with violent radi-cals.

"And," she continued, "you fit the profile: male, twenty-eight years old. Your skin tone is lighter than normal for a native Natonese, but you'd still pass. Even among other individuals we considered, you're the best fit for the Offspring demographic. And you have no dependents, either."

Just Stacy, Carson thought. But Stacy was twenty-two years old now, which meant he could take care of himself if something hap-pened to Carson. That's what he assumed Riley had meant.

"So far, you're the most promising candidate for our espionage program," Vincent said. "Of course, there are others we're planning on bringing out as well. But you know how to appeal to the kinds of people who join the Offspring. You can ingratiate yourself with them and provide valuable intelligence on their activities."

If Carson squinted, he could halfway see the logic behind their proposition. Part of therapy was building trust with your patients and relating to their struggles. Carson had developed a knack for provid-ing a space where violent young men—it was *always* men—could feel safe. And then, slowly, come back to their senses. "You want me to undermine them from the inside," he said.

"No," Riley said sharply. "As I said, we don't want you to play ther-apist. We want you to relay back intel on the Offspring so that our security forces can track down and kill as many of them as we can."

Abject horror flooded Carson's veins. He'd taken an oath swearing never to harm his patients. They were asking him to manipulate the Offspring into trusting him, just so he could provide information to his people's military forces, which would in turn lead to the deaths of the same people Carson had manipulated. It felt like a betrayal of everything he stood for.

"I'm sorry, but I don't think I'm the right person for this job," Carson said.

"You're our best candidate. If not you, then who?" Riley said. It looked like she was trying to avoid gritting her teeth. "It doesn't seem like the Union is making much effort to infiltrate the Offspring. All the other candidates we've tapped for the espionage program have some kind of issue: some are too old, some have experience that's hardly relevant at all, some have a significant number of dependents."

Carson frowned. "You're saying I'm expendable, essentially." He noted that they hadn't talked about extracting him when—or if—he completed his assignment. It was an omission easy enough to read through. Now that he'd learned the true nature of the job, going back into cryo sounded better and better.

"We'd pair you with the best trainer we can find," Vincent said. "Of course, we acknowledge that this is a dangerous job. We won't lie to you. But we can use someone with significant undercover experience to teach you how to fulfill your duties and keep yourself safe. Or at least, as safe as reasonably possible."

"If you learn these skills, with your natural, professional affinity for violent radicals, we believe you would be the ideal candidate for the operation. Or at least, as ideal as we can get right now," Riley said.

Carson looked down at the table. It was clean enough that he could see his reflection. He let out a long sigh, feeling the heat of Vincent and Riley's eyes as they glared at him. He'd entered this profession because he believed in helping people. Especially those who everyone thought were past helping.

If he took the job, maybe he'd have opportunities in the field to identify Offspring who might be persuaded to turn. Could anyone else save those who could be saved? Would they even try? But then he considered the danger again, and a shudder passed through him.

Was this really who he was now: someone who was just focused on himself? He thought back to the primers. His people had endured so much already. Individuals who'd never asked to be in this position had accepted what the universe had thrown at them, and done their jobs anyway.

Dammit, he thought. Vincent and Riley had never asked to go back into cryo. Nor had Isadora Satoro or Nadia Jibor. He had a feeling he wasn't destined to become some great hero, but the more he thought about it, the more he felt compelled to do his part.

"Isadora Satoro has put in place new policies that require us to thaw out the immediate family members of anyone we bring out of cryo," Vincent said gently. "If you decide to take the position, we will find a suitable place for your brother Stacy."

Stacy was a filmmaker. The kind of person who probably would be at the back of the queue when it came to vital skill sets needed for colonization. Carson had always protected Stacy, whether it was from schoolyard bullies as a kid, or when Carson had put him in contact with a friend who worked in the cinema industry. It wasn't rational—he knew there was nothing wrong with him and Stacy staying in cryo until things were safer—but he felt tugged by a desire to get his brother out. Otherwise, how could he justify *not* accepting the job after he and Stacy came out of cryo in the future? Stacy would want to help in any way they could.

"We wouldn't even have to give you a fake identity," Vincent said. "I can edit our database, adding or subtracting names as necessary. Even if someone affiliated with the Offspring hacks our vessel's servers, I can make sure they'd find no trace of your existence or your refugee status. You could present yourself as a Natonese native."

Carson figured Vincent was trying to sweeten the deal, but he'd already made up his mind. He'd sworn never to do harm as a therapist, but there was no outcome in their present circumstances that involved zero harm. He had the unique ability, he hoped, to ensure that as little harm as possible was done in their hunt for the Offspring. And giving Stacy the opportunity to start his new life—even if Carson had to be away for a long time, even if he never came back at all—sealed the deal.

"Okay," Carson said. "I'm in."

CHAPTER 4

The Offspring called the New Arcena bombing *first blood*. Everyone except Tanner Keltin. The first salvo of their war with the invading hordes from Earth was when their cryo vessel had showed up, unannounced and uninvited, on the outskirts of his people's home. Killing them wasn't first blood, it was just the first time the Natonese had truly fought back.

And it felt amazing.

All the more so because Tanner had planned it. The other Offspring were bloodthirsty: they wanted body counts, and fast. Tanner was willing to wait, willing to play out the chess game. The New Arcena bombing was a testament to his planning and his vision.

His followers only numbered in the high hundreds, which ruled out any kind of frontal assault on a newar settlement. They needed to hit well above their weight to prosecute their war against the invaders. That meant logistically complicated tactics like suicide bombing or sabotage.

That meant working with the black market—now well entrenched on Calimor, thanks to the newars themselves—to smuggle in Off-spring members to newar settlements. Sometimes, their infiltrators threw out food or spice shipments. Other times, they'd spread rumors and subtly sew chaos.

But that didn't bring recruits, spectacle did. So Tanner had to think bigger, had to keep moving his pieces deeper into enemy territory. He had to recruit someone loyal enough and with nothing left to lose to serve as the bomber. And then had to smuggle explosives into New Arcena via his Syndicate contacts.

None of it was easy, but Tanner had help. Looking up at the vine-infested ceiling of the abandoned Ashkagi temple in the middle of En-ther's vast jungle wilderness, a fleeting feeling of gratitude spread throughout his body. A thankfulness for the advice and counsel of those more experienced.

His new allies: a radical faction of the Ashkagi rebels that'd fought against the Junta for the past decade, but had soured on the rebel leadership. Until recently, the face of the resistance to the Junta had been a former member of the old Theocracy honor guard, Noah Tas-ano. But Noah explicitly rejected the most violent options for fighting back against the Junta, so a breakaway faction had retreated deep into the jungles to start their own war against the government.

Their leader was an impassioned man named Brandon Zahem. He'd started his career as just another freedom fighter, until he real-ized Noah didn't have the fortitude to do what was necessary. Tanner liked seeing himself in Brandon.

Mutual benefit was the foundation of his alliance with the radical Ashkagi. He'd brought hundreds of Offspring from the core worlds to Enther, where they could assist Brandon's forces in carrying out raids or attacks against the Junta, gaining vital field experience while also exponentially increasing the rebels' manpower. And Tanner could learn from Brandon's experience waging a war against stacked odds.

At first, Tanner had found Enther strange and alien, having never left Obrigan's capital city in his life. But the planet had grown on him: its dark, foreboding rainforests, its lush flora, its sense of alluring danger.

The corkscrew-shaped vines slithered downward, approaching Tanner as he reviewed a report on the New Arcena bombing on his datapad. Those vines bit any unaware fingers that drifted too close, and had already sent plenty of Offspring in search of medical care.

There was a certain poetry to a violent jungle wilderness that sheltered Tanner and Brandon's forces, allowing them to plot further violence against their respective enemies. Tanner felt dangerous, even more so than the Enther wilds. According to the reports, the invaders had already brought about 4 million out of cryo. After the New Arcena bombing, that just meant Tanner now haunted 4 million nightmares. Even if they didn't know his name.

He heard footsteps on the decrepit stone behind him. He turned and saw the silhouette of Brandon Zahem appear in the doorway. The man was tall, slightly more so than Tanner, but not as broad-shouldered. He was bald, but sported a permanent layer of thin, greying whiskers across his fair-skinned face. His eyes were grey and piercing.

"Tanner!" Brandon said, drawing his mouth into a grin and spreading his arms in a congratulatory gesture Tanner wasn't sure was genuine. "I understand your operation was successful." His voice was both high-pitched and scratchy. His body moved with the over-confident swagger of someone who'd never been in a fistfight. And who, Tanner suspected, would tap out right after the first punch to the jaw.

Tanner didn't smile. Thirty-two newars were dead, but they could be replaced by the unending herds still aboard their cryo vessel. Probably would be by the end of the week.

"The work isn't over, not until we see the fading lights of the *Preserver*'s engines at the edge of the system," Tanner said, his jaw taut. Even if he couldn't hit the newars directly, he'd strike at them from the shadows, until they were too afraid to bring more out of cryo. Maybe they'd even turn around and leave. Anything else was a failure.

"Of course you'd say that," Brandon nodded approvingly. "You're a doer. You're not someone who talks a big game, only to avoid the hard necessities of actually winning the fight."

The other man had an unmistakable scowl painted across his face, the way he only got when he was talking about Noah Tasano. Brandon could talk about his hatred for the Junta passionately, but it was an academic hate at best. The venom only truly came out when he was talking about the other rebels.

Tanner could sympathize. He'd grown increasingly critical of the Offspring's founder, an old Union military general named Owen Yorteb, whose master plan had involved manipulating the prime minister into launching a military strike against the newars. The plot had failed, and the general had been confined to a cell—at least, until Tanner had planted an Offspring armed with a cyanide pill in the prison's security. The moral was obvious: working through the Union was a non-starter.

Whatever doubts the rest of the Offspring had about his leadership had drowned in the carnage at New Arcena. They wanted bodies, so Tanner slung thirty-two corpses at their feet. Owen hadn't managed to kill so much as a single newar.

Men like Tanner and Brandon would win at any cost. That's why they were both in charge. Still, Tanner had little fondness for the obvious condescension in Brandon's voice every time he addressed him. It was clear he thought of Tanner as a pupil to be instructed. Tanner, by contrast, liked thinking of the New Arcena bombing as his final exam.

Tanner pulled up a file on his wrist terminal. "This is the real victory of the attack," he said, showing Brandon a holographic file showing dozens more—nearly a hundred—from the core worlds pledging loyalty to him and the Offspring, asking for assistance in traveling to Enther.

The spectacle of the New Arcena bombing could placate the bloodlust of his followers, but more importantly, it could help grow their numbers. It was guerrilla calculus: one soldier sacrificed, thirty-two newars dead, nearly a hundred new recruits. A hundred new recruits meant more assistance for Brandon's own rebels, leading to more field experience for his people, who Tanner could then deploy on further suicide attacks that could attract hundreds more.

Tanner figured that the Union's security apparatus was monitoring the Offspring as closely as they could. That was one area where Brandon's assistance had been invaluable. The rebel leader had taught Tanner and his recruiting team how to hide in the dark corners of the net that prying government eyes couldn't reach, and how to attract impressionable potential recruits.

Brandon's eyes widened slightly as he looked at Tanner's

recruiting numbers. "That's impressive work," he said. He only commanded half the forces as Tanner did, though his rebels were far better trained and had contacts across the entire Natonus System.

Tanner leaned back in his chair and placed both hands behind his head. "Are your forces in position for the next stage?"

Brandon nodded. "We have all our eyes and ears on the upcoming summit. And we've been discreetly moving fighters into Kal Mekan for the last few weeks. We won't let Noah Tasano sign away everything we've been fighting for."

"And the newar bitch?" Tanner pressed. Everyone on Enther knew that the invader vessel known as the *Exemplar* was speeding toward the planet to broker peace between Noah's forces and the government. Brandon wanted to disrupt the summit, Tanner wanted the *Exemplar* captured or destroyed. It was the perfect opportunity for further cooperation.

"We'll make sure Nadia Jibor is taken care of," Brandon assured him.

Tanner grinned. Nadia had been responsible for the formation of the New Arcena colony a year ago, plus countless settlements across the outer rim since, blotting out Natonese land like cancerous tumors. Even with the weighty symbolism of the New Arcena bombing, neutralizing the primary newar settlement team would send an even stronger message.

After all, her dumb stunt back on Calimor had foiled Owen Yorteb's plans to destroy New Arcena. Tanner was revolted by all the gushing media profiles about Nadia, her crew, and her work. He wondered what the media would say when he dropped her corpse at their feet.

And from there? Tanner hadn't fully figured out the details. But between the New Arcena bombing and killing Nadia, he hoped the newars might slow their cryo thawing process. Hopefully, down to a trickle. Then Tanner could work on a plan to push the newars back.

The enormity of the task he'd accepted when he claimed leadership of the Offspring weighed down on him. But it felt good to genuinely care about his work. Not like when he was some wage slave at Veltech Colonial Supply, stuck in the stupor of modern living.

"I suppose I should be working on arranging transport for the new recruits," Tanner said. "I'm surprised that you aren't attending evening prayer." He thought he could hear the soft murmurs of Brandon's rebels from back down the hallway, back in the temple's main prayer room.

Brandon winced. Despite leading a hardline religious rebellion against the Junta, Brandon had never shown many signs of being particularly devout. He skipped prayers often, and barely mentioned the Ashkagi gods in casual conversation. Tanner found Brandon's lack of religiosity interesting, to be sure, but not worth acting on.

"I suppose I should return," Brandon said, his voice turning cold.

"Don't let me stop you," Tanner said.

He turned and watched as Brandon headed back for the prayer room. He liked knowing how to push the other man's buttons. Liked knowing that bringing up religion, even subtly, always made Brandon turn cold. As though it was the first time someone had called one of his bluffs.

As for Ashkagiism, Tanner had grown a sense of respect for the religion, even if he wasn't a believer. It was a *Natonese* belief system. By definition, it had to be superior to whatever spiritual nonsense the newars had brought with them.

As the sound of the other man's footsteps ceased, Tanner returned to his wrist terminal. He began looking up possible flight itineraries for his new recruits, planning how to route them through enough way stations to thwart the prying eyes of the Union security forces.

His eyes drooped after planning the first dozen. It was getting late, he thought, looking out the broken window at the far end of the room. A pale beam of moonlight fell onto the floor. Yawning, he placed his datapad back in his backpack and headed for the door.

Sidestepping one of the corkscrew vines as it nearly snapped at him, Tanner headed outside into the jungles. There was a gentle night rain, with the sound of a nearby creek carrying over on a gentle wind. It was humid, but his brown enviro-suit kept him comfortable enough.

The temple was situated atop a short granite cliff, although it was probably just ten feet high. He'd barely seen any rocks during the months he'd spent on Enther, and Brandon had explained that the planet had no real mountain ranges to speak of. The planet was all rainforest, save for the icy expanses at its poles.

Enther only had a single moon, which formed a full circle in the night sky tonight. Tanner looked up at the barren landscape of the moon. Surveyors had tried to find resources there that might save the planet from its long economic malaise, one that'd settled in place ever since the solar price of fruit dropped decades earlier. But the moon was lifeless and resource-scarce.

Growing up in Obrigan City, Tanner was used to many different moons all circling the night sky, each one with different light configurations from all the varied mining operations. When Tanner was young, his parents had told him whenever they went away on business trips that at night, Tanner could imagine himself looking at the same moon as his parents. It was stupid, but it was the kind of stupid that tended to comfort children.

His train of thoughts surprised himself. He'd barely thought about his long-dead parents in years, having spent so much time focused on providing for his younger sister Rebecca—

—Rebecca.

The tear in his heart still ached. She'd be seventeen in a few months. It'd be the second birthday of hers that he'd miss.

The memory of their last few moments together still stung. The dumb argument, the swing he'd taken at her, the give of her cheek as his fist had slammed into it. It'd taken a long time to not hate himself for hitting his sister, so he mostly tried not to think about it.

He saw himself as a failure of a brother. Rebecca deserved better. He hadn't contacted her ever since, mainly in case the Union was keeping tabs on her. But also because she didn't need a reminder of what he'd done to her.

If he couldn't bring himself to ask for forgiveness, ensuring that she had a safe future was all he could do. That was the rationale at the heart of his war against the newars. He couldn't provide for Rebecca in person, but he'd protect her by making sure she'd never have to grow up feeling like an outsider in her own system.

Thinking about his sister brought forth a wave of energy that coursed through Tanner like hot fire. He was no longer tired. He'd work as long as it took to find a way for the new recruits to make it to Enther. He headed back inside the ruined temple, ready to get back to work.

CHAPTER 5

In another lifetime, across the galaxy, Russ Kama's first assignment in the Earth Defense Forces had been stationed on a submarine patrolling the Gulf of Mexico. That was where he'd discovered his discomfort with being underwater. Sailing on an above-water vessel? Fine. Deployed on a starship, separated from the deadly vacuum of space by only a thin layer of metal? Sure, sign him up. But there was something about being surrounded by water that made his skin crawl.

So he wasn't particularly happy when the Syndicate assigned him to a subaqueous station deep in the oceans of the planet Haphis.

To be fair, he wasn't particularly happy with anything about his new job working as a Syndicate enforcer, but he knew it was all he deserved. After his utter failure as Isadora Satoro's head of security, after he'd pushed his people to the brink of annihilation, he couldn't go back to working for her. And nowhere else in the Natonus System would take him.

So he'd signed up with the Syndicate. Which meant long, dusty days on patrol around various Zoledo towns where the sand collected in the beard he'd grown out. It meant lugging around a rifle and looking intimidating, but not actually doing anything. Occasionally, it meant trying to whip Lena Veridor's enforcers into fighting shape, which was a little more to Russ' liking.

He'd leapt at the chance to join an off-world operation. Anything to get out of the oppressive Zoledo heat. He'd never figured that'd involve getting slung into an underwater base. Technically, it was the ruins of an old warship that crashed into the Haphis oceans four decades before the *Preserver* showed up in the system. The Syndicate just installed new infrastructure on top of the ruins.

Every time he walked through one of the glass-lined corridors of the old warship, he got a view of bioluminescent coral polyps that just looked freakish to him. Every so often, they shed organic matter that looked like a jellyfish cap, which only unnerved him all the more. So he spent as much time as possible in the safety of his dorm room, where there were no windows or viewscreens.

The downed ship was the relic of a bygone era, one where the Union wasn't even around yet, where rebels fought a desperate fight against what used to be the reigning government of the Natonus System. The rebels had won, pursuing the remnants of the old regime to Haphis' orbit. It all just felt like an inevitable, endless cycle of war and death to Russ.

No, he reminded himself, there were alternatives. His own lack of imagination was the root of his failure as Isadora's security adviser. Nadia Jibor had realized what he hadn't: that the tensions with the

Union didn't necessarily have to lead to war. Russ still felt a crushing sensation in his ribs when he contemplated how many hundreds would've died if he'd gotten his way back on Calimor.

He took another swig of the whiskey bottle. His assigned bunk unit was in a newly constructed wing of dorms nestled up against the downed warship's still-functional power generator. He'd forced himself to lay off the alcohol the entire time he was working for Isadora, but what was even the fucking point now?

Working as a grunt for a criminal empire was probably one of the worst things Russ could imagine, only marginally better than starving to death from a lack of employment. Or facing Isadora after having failed her. The alcohol helped. It felt like a magic ticket to shortening his days, making sure he never remembered the hours he spent off-duty.

Russ tilted the bottle back, and the cheap whiskey slicked down the plastic neck and wetted his throat. Hardly even burned on the way down. Normally, he'd prefer something with a little more quality, like the bottle of Kentucky bourbon he'd brought with him on the *Preserver*—the one he was saving for a special occasion—but the cheap shit still did the trick.

It took more gulps before he felt the comforting tingle along his temples, but once he did, he lied back down on his bunk unit. He felt calmer, somehow, less irrationally worried that the ocean was going to spill in and drown them all. And he hardly even cared that the other enforcers in the bunk units around him were all snoring obnoxiously.

Then he opened his wrister to check the latest message from Riley.

When he'd gotten her message about the attack on New Arcena, the news crushed him. But since he couldn't share his grief with anyone around him, all he had was trying, and mostly failing, to drown his sorrows at night. Part of him wanted to get back in touch with Isadora, ask if there was anything he could do. But if she wanted his help, she would've reached out. And he knew Riley was more than capable in her new role.

She'd been writing to him ever since Isadora had tapped her as his replacement, confiding in him all her insecurities and self-doubts that she was really qualified to replace him. He always responded the same way: that he'd fucked up massively, that there was no way she could be worse. Besides, she had combat experience and was clearly competent.

The old ritual of Riley unloading her self-doubts and Russ consoling her had disappeared in the bombing's aftermath. Now, she'd leapt into action, running proposals past him—all of them good, he thought—as if she didn't have time to acknowledge her insecurities anymore. Maybe that was good for her.

She'd breathlessly run her new plans for security checkpoints at their people's settlements by him. Technically, her sharing the information was a security breach. One that would've horrified him if he was still working for the refugee government. But she trusted him to wipe the information off his wrister as soon as he finished reading her messages, and Russ never betrayed that trust.

Riley wasn't content playing defense, however, so she'd come up with a plan to use spies to surveil the Offspring. Hopefully, that would produce intelligence that they could then use to take out as many of the bastards as they could.

Russ had been in a minor campaign against guerrilla insurgents back in the EDF, meaning he'd done his reading on how to handle them. He was aware of all the common criticisms that well-intentioned but ultimately stupid people liked to make: that you couldn't kill your way past ideological fanaticism, that aggressive counterterrorism tactics were likelier to help your enemies gain more recruits than actually work, all that kind of crap.

None of it was true. You absolutely *could* kill your way out of an insurgency, and Earth militaries had gotten real good at it, whether through night raids from spec ops teams or just good old airstrikes. The thing was, terrorist cells never attracted the best or the brightest. But once in a while, there was someone genuinely competent at the heart of a violent radical movement. So if you could take out the inner circle, leaving only the dumbasses left who were more likely to blow themselves up than to actually build a working bomb, you could effectively cripple the entire cell. Hopefully without destabilizing too many nation-states along the way.

But that was all reliant on having good intelligence in the first place, so you knew where to point the crosshairs. Hence, spies. And why Russ was so pleased with the moves Riley was making as Isadora's new security adviser. She'd run into a hitch, however, when she realized that they didn't have anyone with actual spying experience frozen aboard the *Preserver*.

That was where Russ had stepped in to help her. He'd recommended bringing a therapist—preferably someone with experience counseling violent radicals—out of cryo and training them as a spy. That was the last message he'd sent her.

Russ, you're a genius, the message from Riley started. *Just finished a trip back to the* Preserver. *Kind of crazy how different everything was...they have almost a hundred crew and medical staff out of cryo now. It's nothing like when you had me pulled out. Not to mention what it must've been like for you.*

Anyway. I found someone who met all the criteria you recommended. Guy named Carson Erlinza, used to do stuff with eco-terrorists back in Vancouver. It took a little bit of convincing, but ultimately Vincent and I got him to agree to our plan. Then we defrosted an undercover cop to help train him and investigate the bombing. I guess it'll probably be a while before we can tell whether or not this plan actually works out.

And I have you to thank for it. I was stumped before you gave me your advice. I seriously don't know how I'd be able to do this job without you. And I don't think it's fair that I'm getting credit for your ideas and input. We should just tell Isadora how you've been helping behind the scenes, and she'll put you back in charge, where you belong.

Russ surprised himself with a faint grin and a bit of mistiness around his eyes. Riley was being damnably humble. She'd been Isadora's head of defense for almost a year and a half, and it seemed like she was on track to be a far better adviser than Russ had ever been. Sure, he helped her out on a few things here or there, but the root of all Riley's ideas came from her. If there was one thing he wished for her, it was to develop a healthier sense of her own competence.

Damn it, he thought, wiping his eyes. He always got too damn sentimental when he drank. He stashed the cheap whiskey back in his footlocker and returned to the closing paragraph of Riley's message.

Now, I'm headed to Calimor. Isadora is going to speak at New Arcena, give a eulogy for everyone that died in the attack, comfort the survivors, all that kind of stuff. The rest of the cabinet is all going with her. It's gonna be a grim trip, Russ. Not looking forward to it. Maybe I'll see if I can bow out of the ceremony and work on setting up those security checkpoints. Sounds like a better and better idea the more I'm thinking about it. I'll let you get going, and I'll get back in touch whenever I make it back to Obrigan.

Assuming Riley would have to stay on Calimor for at least a week, plus another week in transit time back to the capital, Russ figured that meant it'd be a while before he heard from her next. His spirits sank even lower. Hearing from Riley was one of the few things that kept him sane.

The truth was, he missed his old colleagues. Friends. He wasn't sure he could ever face Isadora again after having let her down so thoroughly, but he couldn't deny how much he wished they could bury the hatchet and move on. And he missed Vincent, despite the man's awkwardness and aloofness. He even missed Nadia. *Nadia.* Fuck, working for the Syndicate must really be getting to him.

As he was trying to decide whether owning up to Nadia—telling her she'd been right and he'd been wrong about the conflict with the Union—or just straight up taking a plasma bolt to the gut would be more painful, he was interrupted by loud footsteps just outside the dorm. He quickly erased all traces of Riley's message from his wrister.

The lights snapped on, followed by a chorus of grunts and complaints from the other enforcers. Russ just laid still on his cot, waiting for the door to open. Seconds later, a burly man stormed into their room. His arms were muscular, his legs comically spindly. Sporting a thick moustache and wavy black hair, Ken Susec—Lena Veridor's lieutenant and the head of her enforcer division—was hard to mistake for anyone else.

"All right, people!" Ken shouted, grinning.

Oh, that too. Ken had this habit of grinning the whole time he spoke, and his teeth were absurdly large. Russ recalculated in his head: *apologizing to Nadia, taking a bolt to the gut, or having to*

listen to this clown talk for an hour straight—which is the worst one?
It was almost an impossible question.

"We got orders from the boss," Ken continued. "It's go time in the morning."

Russ didn't know for sure what the plan was, but he had an inkling. The Syndicate ran a huge protection racket for all the private island resorts on Haphis, which attracted the kind of clientele who didn't particularly like Union soldiers breathing down their neck. For the island owners, paying the Syndicate off was more in line with their customers' privacy expectations.

But one of the outlying island resorts had tried renegotiating their deal with the Syndicate. Because the threat of pirate raids had been dropping for the last few decades, they said they'd decided to cut back on paying the Syndicate for protection.

Problem was, Lena Veridor was the last person in the Natonus System you wanted to short. Russ figured they were gonna go have a talk with the island owner, a full array of armed enforcers in tow, and *persuade* them to be rational. It'd be an easy hustle. He'd just have to look intimidating and finger an assault rifle eagerly. Maybe scowl a bit.

It threw Russ for a loop when Ken tossed a ragged uniform and jacket on the ground. "We're gonna be dressing up for this one," he said.

"What are we doing this time?" one of the enforcers to Russ' left said. His name was Daniel, but he went by Drizz—short for Drizzle, a nickname he'd earned for the way he drooled at night after staying up late drinking.

The Syndicate liked its nicknames, Russ had learned. The two others in his squad went by Slip and Tank. Russ had forgotten their real names. He'd been responsible for whipping his squad into shape, at least as much as possible, which meant he'd barely whipped them into any shape at all. Only Slip had some kind of martial arts training in his background, but all three were dim-witted and motivated by money above all else. Which was probably how the Syndicate liked them.

"You all have probably heard about the new deal our island owners are trying to force on us," Ken said, pacing in front of the squad. "Well, we're going to convince them to rethink that."

"Want us to go have a talk with the landlord?" Russ said. He still hadn't figured out what the disguises were for.

Ken walked up to him, grinning with his mouth wide open, and patted Russ on his head. Russ felt nearly every joint in his body cringe. He tried relaxing by imagining how good it'd feel to punch the man in the face.

"This is why you make a great grunt, Kama," Ken said, inches away from Russ' face. "You're simple. Direct. Unimaginative." Russ hadn't earned any kind of nickname yet, which meant everyone just called him "Kama"—a pathetic attempt at making the Syndicate echo a real military. The whole criminal empire was just a bunch of greedy psychopaths playing soldier.

"But here in the Syndicate, we prefer to *show*, not *tell*," Ken continued. "So instead of having a talk with the ownership and *telling* them why renegotiating the deal is a bad idea, we're going to *show* them the danger of skimping on our protection services."

Ken stepped back, giving Russ a welcome reprieve from the man's rancid breath. "They say they don't have to fear pirate raids anymore?" Ken said, his voice rising. "Well...we're gonna give 'em a pirate raid to remember."

CHAPTER 6

Calimor—with its mountainous red dust storms and its fertile green hydroponics bays, with its status as a linchpin in the solar economy and its image as a graveyard of destroyed vessels and decaying bodies from a decade-old war—had always felt ambiguous to Isadora. It was the planet where she'd nearly made the biggest mistake of her leadership, and also the best hope for her people's dreams of colonization.

The last time she'd been on Calimor, she'd decided to take her daughter out of cryo, almost like she was bringing Meredith back to life. Now, she was returning to mourn the dead.

Isadora sat in the mayor's office, the one she'd once commandeered during the near-crisis with the Union. She stared out the window with a frown on her face. Last time she'd taken over the mayor's office, it was only temporary. Everyone had known Morris would re-claim his office after the crisis had passed.

But Morris was dead now. The next occupant would be an entirely different person. There was no going back to normal, no reset button.

Isadora flipped through the saved messages on her wrister. There were a series of messages from Tricia Favan, the first having arrived almost as soon as news of the New Arcena bombing became public. The prime minister had expressed solemn sympathy for the attack and described, in almost frantic detail, the steps the Union govern-ment was taking to ferret out the Offspring.

Ever since their two sides had nearly come to blows, Tricia had seemed desperate to prove that she still had the refugees' best interest at heart. All of this Isadora appreciated, of course, but she hadn't par-ticularly doubted Tricia's intentions. Their personal relationship had, minus a few snarls back during their near-conflict, remained mostly warm. And Isadora didn't blame the Union for the New Arcena bomb-ing. It was a tragic fact of life that some things would always slip through. As far as Isadora knew, the Union security apparatus could've prevented countless attacks.

Isadora closed Tricia's condolence message and reviewed a sec-ond saved message: a communication signed by almost every one of her people's settlement mayors. The document made clear they weren't blaming Isadora for the attack. However, with people's lives at stake, the mayors were no longer comfortable delegating supreme authority to an unelected bureaucrat whose claim to legitimacy was *because the damn computer said so.* And then they'd called for her to make plans for a real election for her position.

She'd received the message three days ago, while she was still on a shuttle burning toward Calimor. Back then, she'd felt a rush of emotions: anxiety, bitterness, a loss of confidence. Now, rereading the message mostly made her feel numb. *None of them were elected either*, Isadora thought suddenly. *How come you only think of the best comebacks after the fact?*

As she stared at the document again, a new meeting request from someone named Sean Nollam popped up. She wondered for only a brief second why that name sounded familiar, until she remembered that Sean had been tapped as Morris' deputy mayor almost half a year ago. Morris had never been confident in his political skills, and as the New Arcena settlement had grown to resemble a real polity instead of just a worksite, he'd asked Isadora to bring someone out of cryo to help him with the political side of his job.

She'd looked through Vincent's database. Unfortunately, because most anyone with actual political experience had been on the *Preserver*'s sister ship—the one destroyed during the evacuation from Earth—those with political experience were few and far between. Isadora had ultimately chosen Sean, a city councilor from Cincinnati, who'd taken office a few years after she had. Which meant he didn't quite have her experience, but hopefully he still knew what he was doing.

She'd never heard from Morris about how Sean was doing in his deputy role, which she took for good news. But with Morris' death, she supposed that Sean was now effectively the new mayor of New Arcena. Although the settlement wasn't actually the most populated one her people had set up, it was their first, and therefore possessed a symbolic weight that other assignments didn't. The mayor of New Arcena would be one of the most important local political leaders in her people's territory. She figured Sean deserved a meeting based on his new role, and she still had half an hour before she was slated to give her eulogy. And meeting him would distract her from ruminating on the other mayors' message. She accepted Sean's meeting request.

She'd returned to her wrister messages for only a few seconds before she heard the door to the mayor's office swish open. Had Sean really been waiting nearby just for her to accept his meeting request? She added that particular data point to her mental assessment of the new mayor.

"Isadora," he said, reaching across the desk to shake her hand. He had slight features, with an ovular face and a hawkish expression. He looked about Nadia's age, although his hair seemed to be prematurely thinning at the top of his head.

She winced at him using her first name. Months earlier, her staff had suggested that she come up with an official title for her position. They'd eventually settled on "chief coordinator" for whatever she was, although somehow Isadora never liked the ring of "Chief Coordinator Satoro." Still, she preferred at the very least being addressed as "ma'am," especially by a colleague who hadn't met her before.

"Sean," she said, a grin on her face that she hoped looked every bit as fake as she intended. She returned the man's handshake and gestured for him to sit. Sean immediately plopped down in the chair facing her, leaned back, and spread his legs outward. "How are you settling into your new job?" she asked, trying to ignore his glaring lack of formality.

"Fine, except for the fact that my office is occupied at the moment," he said.

Isadora narrowed her eyes but kept the fake smile. "You must be wracked with grief, I'd imagine. I'm sure you and Morris were close."

Isadora wasn't just playing political games. It struck her as odd, even concerning, that Sean seemed interested in having this back-

and-forth after a literal terrorist attack had left thirty-two individu-als—*his people*, now—dead.

Grief takes many forms, a voice at the back of her mind said. She supposed she should try to be more forgiving to Sean. Maybe he blamed her for Morris' death, which would be entirely unfair to her and her cabinet, but at the very least explained his behavior.

"Morris did his job well," Sean said, "but I intend to bring about a number of changes."

Isadora arched an eyebrow.

"First, I'm cutting workdays," he said. "Ever since this colony's founding, you've been instituting all-day working hours. Look around you: everyone is exhausted, overworked. All while we subsist on the bare minimum needed to keep us alive."

"Might I remind you that we still have 36 *million* we need to bring out of cryo?" Isadora said. "We can rest after the *Preserver* is empty."

"That's easy for you to say," Sean sneered. "After all, you've been operating unchecked and unchallenged ever since our vessel arrived in this system, thanks to some opaque algorithm from the *Preserver*'s computer that the rest of us are just supposed to trust blindly."

Isadora saw where this was going. Sean was a politician. It was a safe bet that he knew about the document from the other mayors. Maybe he'd even had a hand in convincing them to send it to her. Her own political instincts were telling her that Sean's diatribe was a working draft of an election statement of his own. And if he really was planning on running against her, she could get him to reveal his main lines of attack if she could sit back, feign a hurt expression, and let him do his thing.

"And what've you been doing with all this unchecked power?" Sean asked. "Mandating that every colonist spends all their waking hours producing resources to turn profits that none of us ever actually sees. None of us can choose where to work. We're just commanded from on high."

Sean's bluster didn't faze her much. It was hardly the first time a male politician had used overaggression to try to throw her off balance. Still, she had to concede that her choices had left her people with little agency to plot their own lives. Maybe not enough.

"All this might be tolerable," Sean continued, "if not for the fact that you don't seem to have any qualms about skimming off some of these profits to get the best clothes money can buy in the capital city, while the rest of us are toiling in the dust," he said, eyeing her outfit. "And sending your daughter to the best, most expensive school in the capital, where she's protected by the best security. Assuming the stories are true."

Isadora fantasized about reaching across the desk, pulling Sean up by his collar—she was always superhumanly strong in her fantasies—throwing him on the desk, and strangling him. People saying mean things about her was practically synonymous with politics, but going after Meredith was *too far*. She was no longer in the mood for political games.

"Which brings me to the next thing that is going to change," Sean continued. "I will officially file for candidacy to replace you. I trust you've already received the document from my colleagues?"

On one hand, Isadora felt a certain satisfaction that she'd guessed Sean's game. If he was as transparent at campaigning as he was with his intentions, she figured she'd be able to beat him with relative ease.

But on the other, she couldn't deny a feeling of unease regarding some of his points. After all, she believed in democracy. Holding an election was not unreasonable, especially now that things weren't as desperate as they'd been during their first year in the system. The Offspring threat notwithstanding.

One time, many months earlier, Isadora had thought about holding elections for all major political positions in the refugee government. Especially because it looked like it was going to be a long time— years, hopefully not more than that—before they got everyone out of cryo. But then a dozen other things had demanded her attention, and nobody had ever pressed her on it. Until now.

"I am not an autocrat," she said finally. "I will have my team come up with a plan to hold an election within the next few months," she said.

Sean had the most smug, self-satisfied, rage-inducing grin on his face she'd ever seen before. He'd played his cards decently well, Isadora had to admit: insulting her morals, throwing her off by bringing Meredith into it, then pivoting to make his demand. If she really was going to run against him for her position, maybe she'd do well not to underestimate him.

"I'm glad we could come to a reasonable solution," Sean said. From Sean's perspective, he'd gotten everything he wanted, which must be what he meant by *a reasonable solution.*

"Like I said," Isadora said, her voice regaining some sternness, "I will have my team contact you to work out details. Now, if you'll excuse me, I have a funeral speech to prepare for," she said icily.

He stood up, and neither of them made any effort to shake hands. "Isadora," he said as a form of parting, and departed the office.

Isadora's blood was boiling by this point. She reached deep within a satchel she'd brought with her, pulling out a framed picture of Meredith, the one taken during their camping trip to Mt. Rainier. It was the same one she'd kept on her desk the entire time Meredith had still been frozen in cryo.

Seeing her daughter's face always calmed her, even though it'd only been a week since she'd departed Obrigan. "What've I gotten myself into?" she muttered. But the picture also symbolized the agonizing crucible she'd gone through during her first year in the Natonus System, apart from her daughter. If she'd made it through *that*, she could make it through an election.

Isadora stashed the picture in her satchel and headed out to the conference area where she was going to give her eulogy. In a green room off to the side of the auditorium where thirty-two coffins had been laid out, Isadora saw the rest of her executive staff gathered. Most of her aides were huddled in small circles, conversing in hushed tones.

She immediately spotted Vincent Gureh, and her heart leapt. She figured she'd always have a soft spot for the other three original *Preserver* crew. It saddened her that Nadia couldn't make it to the funeral, but she knew Nadia had her hands full pursuing new settlement opportunities on Enther. And then there was Russ...

Isadora still stood by her decision to dismiss Russ as her security adviser after the last crisis. She didn't know how she could've made any other choice. But she missed his friendship, and a whirlwind of sadness stirred in her body whenever her thoughts drifted to him.

Vincent seemed preoccupied in an intense discussion with a security officer. He nodded toward her with a grim expression, and Isadora gave him a weak wave. She resolved to make time to catch up with him after the eulogy.

She nodded to her other aides and advisers as she passed by, including Alexander Mettevin and Gabby Betam. She paused at the edge of the room, one side of the auditorium visible. The last of her executive cabinet members, Katrina Lanzic, walked over to join her.

"You look like something's bothering you," Katrina said. "I mean, beyond the obvious circumstances." She indicated the coffins in the next room.

Isadora sighed and launched into an explanation of the other mayors' message and her conversation with Sean. After she mentioned that she'd agreed to an election, Katrina's eyes went wide. "It sounds like he must've gotten to you," the other woman said.

"Well," Isadora snapped, before pausing to let the frustration clear out of her head, "I felt that he was making a few good points. I don't want our people thinking of me as some harsh dictator."

"No, but you *aren't* that," Katrina said. "At the same time, you aren't obligated to be a democrat either. You've always been fairly upfront that your job is to bring more individuals out of cryo. Our people aren't entitled to an election for your position."

Isadora snorted. "Well, I did tell Sean I'd go through with it," she said. "I can't really go back on that now."

"No?" Katrina asked. "Why not? You can send some security guards to pick him up and throw his ass back in cryo. It'd send a strong message to whoever you choose to be his replacement, as well as the other settlement leaders. And it isn't like he could do anything to stop you. The colonial defense forces here are loyal to you and Riley."

Isadora found Katrina's suggestion ironic, since Isadora had once considered putting *Katrina* back in cryo when her chief diplomat had proved difficult to work with, initially. But the two women had grown closer since, with bonds forged from a year and a half's worth of mutual respect. Even back then, Isadora had been horrified that she'd even thought about using re-freezing as a punishment.

She was less horrified this second time around. She'd have to work through the implications of that later. But still, she fully intended to ensure that her people's settlement project was as democratic as it could be, and that meant holding an election even if she didn't want to. "Thank you," she said, "but I've already made my decision."

"I knew that's what you were going to say," Katrina said, giving Isadora a knowing look. "Just be careful out there," she said, indicating the crowd gathered in the auditorium. "Thanks to Sean's maneuvering, your eulogy will now be the unofficial launch of your reelection campaign."

Then, a man just offstage signalled that it was time for Isadora to go on. Katrina wished her good luck, and Isadora walked toward the podium slowly, her mind mulling over the political implications of the situation.

She felt pangs of grief for every coffin she passed on her way to the podium. Embers of anger still burned in her gut over Sean's diatribe against her. What should've been a moment of vulnerability and communal healing would now become political theater.

And, dammit, she missed Meredith.

She arrived at the podium and smiled weakly toward the hundreds in the auditorium. She'd do what any good political leader did. *Compartmentalize.*

She glanced off to her right and saw Sean Nollam sitting at the front, a smug grin still on his face. This time, she didn't let it faze her.

"My friends," Isadora said, modulating her voice to be both quiet and powerful, "my fellow Earthborn. We are gathered here today..."

CHAPTER 7

Carson had only been off Earth once, during a family vacation to Mars after his first year of grad school. The stress of his program had marred the whole experience. So descending toward the planet Calimor possessed a certain kind of magic for him. It even helped him forget the desperate stakes of his mission for a moment.

He and his companion—Juliet Lessitor, an ex-undercover cop from Caracas who'd been thawed out to serve as Carson's trainer and ultimately handler—were heading down to the bombsite aboard an auto-piloted shuttle from the *Preserver*. A forensics team had already gone through most of the evidence and written up their findings. But the leadership wanted a detective's eye to find meaning in the forensics report. Hence dispatching Juliet.

Carson knew that the leadership was also working on building a larger espionage program, but he and Juliet were the tip of the spear. As far as he'd heard, Riley was still reviewing dossiers back on the *Preserver*. And when they brought others out of cryo, Carson imagined he wouldn't be in communication with them. He wasn't supposed to contact any other Earthborn refugee unless it was mission-critical. That meant he and Juliet were on their own.

He felt a certain pressure to get to know his companion better, almost like it was their first session of therapy together. "This all still feels unreal," Carson said, hoping to get some kind of reaction out of her.

"You ever manage to get to Mars back home?" Juliet asked, her face pressed into the shuttle window.

"Once, yeah," Carson responded. "How about you?"

"Well, it's just the same shit," Juliet said tiredly. "Red, dusty planet. Mountainous. Nothing new to see." Although Juliet had come out of cryo only hours after Carson, she was still complaining of lingering hibernation sickness and headaches.

She was at least a couple decades older than Carson, he guessed, approaching her fifties. She spoke with a croaky, deep voice and her hair was equal parts dark brown and grey. Carson wondered if age had any effect on how quickly someone could recover from cryosleep.

He turned his attention back to his window, marveling at the vast mountain ranges, canyon systems, and valleys they were flying over. Come to think of it, it *did* look a little Martian. But he wasn't ready to write the experience off as *the same shit*, as Juliet had. As he continued to marvel at the alien landscape, he bit into the chocolate bar he'd been snacking on.

After the refugees had set up a functioning economy, Vincent had told Carson, they could requisition the food and supplies they actually wanted instead of making do with meager rations. So they'd imported tons of chocolate bars from the cocoa plantations on Haphis. The crew had gone through the entire shipment in a few days. Meaning they'd ordered a second shipment, even bigger than the first.

But by the time the second shipment arrived at the *Preserver*, desperate cravings had instead been replaced by bellyaches. So they had what seemed like an unending supply of chocolate bars on their hands, despite the fact that no one wanted them anymore. Carson had asked to take a box with him, and Vincent was all too happy to relinquish some of the unused supply.

Carson had already gone through almost half the box on the flight from the *Preserver*, however, and his stomach was already rebelling against the idea of more chocolate. He could appreciate the trap the *Preserver* crew had laid for themselves.

The shuttle rocked as they passed through a pocket of rough air. Past another mountain ridge, Carson saw the colony of New Arcena come into view. The reds, oranges, and browns of the natural landscape gave way to a mixture of greys and whites. The colony was smaller than he'd imagined.

Their shuttle's auto-pilot swerved until the bow was pointed toward one of the hangar bays closest to the attack. Carson spotted the destroyed section of the colony's exterior, now protected by an energy barrier, as the shuttle situated itself into a docking berth. Metal clamps slid down with a mechanical groan and clasped the sides of the shuttle.

"Well," Juliet said, rubbing her forehead, "might as well get this started."

Carson finished his chocolate bar and followed his partner out of the shuttle, down a narrow catwalk that connected them to the main facility. The corridors seemed deserted, the opposite of what Carson had expected. But a holo-vision along one of the walls showing a funeral ceremony elsewhere suggested a reason for the emptiness.

A woman dressed in an all-black pantsuit, East Asian in her heritage, was speaking solemnly on the holo-vision. Carson immediately recognized her as Isadora Satoro. "Our fearless leader," he said, hoping for at least a chuckle out of Juliet. She only rolled her eyes.

The two proceeded into the cafeteria where the bombing had taken place, with Juliet swiping an ID card into a slot next to the door. The colonial militia, which apparently combined defense and policing duties due to manpower shortages, had closed off the area to the public. Or at least, everyone except for the handful of forensics analysts out of cryo. Everything inside looked almost the same as it would've right after the attack, Carson figured. Another holo-vision overhead continued to stream Isadora's eulogy.

Food trays were scattered everywhere, some on the floor, probably pushed over as colonists had sprinted for the exits. There were drink mugs in disarray, too. One had shattered on the floor. The trays were all conspicuously wiped clean, however. Carson had figured there'd be rotting food still stuck to them. At least there weren't any signs of dried blood or bits of flesh.

He noticed a table at the other end of the canteen with a series of plastic bags on top. One contained all the food scraps that must've been on the trays. The others had pieces of clothing, rubble, or even pieces of the suicide bomber's explosive vest that hadn't been obliterated in the explosion. "Looks like the forensics work is already done," Carson said, indicating the table.

"I'd certainly hope so," Juliet scoffed. "They teach you anything about forensic analysis in therapy school?"

Carson just shook his head. *Therapy school* was a weird way to write off what had been a grueling four-year grind through a psychology PhD program, but he let it slide.

"Me neither," Juliet said, and walked over to investigate the compiled evidence. She picked up a datapad next to one of the plastic evidence bags and started reading.

Carson headed to the other side of the cafeteria, right next to the energy barrier-filled gap left by the bombing. The steel looked like it'd peeled away, with dozens of tiny beams curving out into open Calimor air. He closed his eyes and tried picturing what it must've been like to be there during the bombing. He found his heart filling with equal parts terror and grief.

He was glad the forensics team had already gone through the bombsite. One of his personal rules back in his practice was that he never looked at crime scene pictures. He'd resolved to break that rule if a patient ever asked him to, but no one in his three years running his own practice ever had. Protecting his own mental sanity was important in his line of work. Avoiding grisly scenes of death and bloodshed was part of that.

But putting himself in the shoes of the colonists wasn't his job, Carson reminded himself. He had to put himself in the *bomber*'s shoes, learn how these Offspring thought and acted, so that he could pretend to be one of them.

At first, Carson had felt strangely giddy to investigate the bombsite, like he was a hero in some police procedural drama that he and Stacy liked to watch as kids. But now the real objective of their trip came back into focus: figuring out how Carson could infiltrate the Offspring.

Part of him still thought this whole thing was crazy: how could

Carson ever hope to pass as a member of a group that wanted nothing more than to kill people like him? He'd only ever interacted with a radicalized individual in the safety of his office, never out in the field. And it helped that no one in Primordial ever saw him as a target.

But Carson trusted the leadership that he was the best person for the job, no matter his doubts. He relied on the same techniques he'd once used to help patients calm down, especially after a tough session. Mental recovery wasn't a single big effort, it was a sustained push mixed with lots of progress and backsliding. Carson had always encouraged his patients to think short-term, so as to not let the enormity of the recovery process overwhelm them. For most of them, that was just making it to the end of a session.

So for the moment, that just meant focusing on Carson's short-term goals: figuring out where the bomber might've been coming from, and learning everything they could from the bombsite.

Carson walked over to the breach in the wall, where he figured the bomber would've stood right before he detonated his explosive vest. Carson raised his arms, just like he pictured the bomber doing right when he activated the device. "Natonus for the Natonese," he whispered: the attacker's final words.

What had this unnamed, unknown man's life been like? Carson had read the Union intelligence reports garnered from various interrogations of the imprisoned, and now deceased, ex-leader of the Offspring, Owen Yorteb, where the former general had described his recruiting strategy. He'd focused on alcohol and drug rehab clinics, preying on the perennially unemployed or the recently laid-off.

It was a common story. Social isolation and desperation could always be transmuted into raw hatred by bad people with an agenda. As Carson mimicked the bomber's posture, he wondered at what point the bomber had ceased being a desperate loner and had instead chosen to become a killer. That kind of change was never as sudden as flipping a light switch.

As Carson stood there, he tried to remember anything about the Offspring's probable numbers from the primers. A wave of arrests after Owen Yorteb's capture last year had yielded about a hundred collaborators, but there had to be far more than that. Interesting that there'd only been a single suicide attack so far.

But that was also something he'd expect. The vast majority of people who joined up with a violent radical movement tended to freeze up when their leaders actually put them in danger. It was one of the ways Carson had reached his patients: *Did you ever consider going on a suicide mission? No? Well then, that means some part of you knows that the movement was wrong for you.*

"Are you...pretending to be him?" Juliet asked, her face scrunched up.

Carson shot his eyes open. "Yes. Er, no. Kind of? I'm just trying to get into that mindset."

Juliet snorted, but a brief approving look crossed her face. "That's what you should be doing. Good on you. You're gonna have to tap into your dark side if you want to pass as one of them."

Carson stepped away from the breach and put his hands in his pockets. "I don't know if I have much of a dark side," he said with a grin. He could empathize with the kinds of people who signed up for organizations like the Offspring or Primordial, sure, and that often involved going into dark places. But Carson had always imagined a mental barrier surrounding his old office. After a session with a patient, he never let the experiences follow him home.

"Bullshit. Everyone's got one," Juliet said. "Take our boss," she said, walking from the evidence table over to where the holo-vision was still playing Isadora's eulogy.

"Everything I read about her suggests she's had admirable intentions," Carson said, wondering briefly why he was leaping to the defense of a woman who he'd never met. "And it seems that she's been pretty effective as our lea—"

"—she's a *politician*," Juliet interjected. "And all I'm seeing is an unelected bureaucrat using the murder of thirty-two of her own people to look good in front of the cameras." Juliet shot a look of disgust at the holo-vision and pulled the plug leading into the wall. The screen cut to black.

Carson wanted to argue further, but this was the most Juliet had been willing to talk since the two of them had met. And he wanted to get to know his new colleague. He let her continue.

"Me, I'm an anarchist," Juliet continued. "Politicians, politics...it's all the same."

"I've never gotten the sense that cops and anarchists had much overlap," Carson said.

"It was the cop stuff that *made* me an anarchist," Juliet said, pacing in front of the now-depowered holo-vision and looking at the floor. "See, I was tasked with infiltrating the big pan-American drug cartels back on Earth. And I was real good at it. Managed to bag a bunch of bad guys back in Caracas. But the deeper I got, the more I realized how entrenched they were *everywhere.*

"So I moved around a lot. Most of my fieldwork was in Los Angeles, actually. And the deeper I got, the more I realized just how rotten everything really was. Because the same politicians who were hiring police departments to go after the cartels? You'd better believe they were wrapped up in them as well. But so were their electoral opponents. Usually, the politicians in charge want you to do a good enough job to dig up dirt linking the cartels to their *opponents*, but they don't want you to do too good of a job and dig up dirt on *them*. So I carried around a little post-it note—I know, old-school—with a list of names that were off-limits. And I resolved to only do as good of a job as the people in charge wanted me to.

"So yeah," Juliet concluded, looking back up at Carson. "Dark side. Might as well start getting real familiar with yours."

Carson immediately felt for his colleague. She'd spent decades in the morally murky criminal underworld spanning the Americas, and it was obvious just how much it'd affected her. She was the kind of person who could benefit from professional mental help. Juliet was wrapped in layers of compound trauma that'd made her suspicious of anyone and everyone. But he'd never tell her that. Patients had to take the first step of asking for assistance.

"You ever been in a fight?" Juliet asked, her eyes boring into Carson with an intensity that made the hairs on his arms stand up.

"Once," Carson said. "My brother Stacy was always picked on by his classmates. I was a bit of a protective older brother. So one day, I saw a bunch of people ganging up on him and I...well, I intervened."

That seemed to pique Juliet's interest, and her mouth curled into a grin. "Did that feel good? Teaching the other kids a lesson?"

"No," Carson said forcefully. *Did it*? He'd barely thought about the fifteen-year-old encounter, since it'd been so long ago. Remembering what could've been going on in a young Carson's emotional landscape was impossible. And even if it *had* felt good, Carson was confident those feelings were because he was protecting Stacy.

"I read your file," Juliet pressed. "I saw that you got onto your wrestling team when you were still in school. How soon after the fight to protect your brother was that?"

It'd been so long since Carson had thought about any of this. It was true, he'd joined his high school wrestling team, and yes, it'd been about a half-year after him getting into the fight with Stacy's bullies. Or was it sooner? He was having a hard time getting his personal timeline straight.

But none of that really mattered. What Juliet was implying was obvious: that once he'd gotten a taste of physical combat, he hadn't been able to let it go. Which was ridiculous. He'd spent his entire career *helping* people, dammit. "Look, can we just get back to the job instead of speculating on my motives?" he said, his voice coming out angrier than he'd intended.

Juliet's damn grin still hadn't disappeared from her face. "Fair enough, but I already know where we're heading next."

"Care to enlighten me?" Carson asked. *Still snappy.*

Juliet walked back to the evidence table and picked up the smallest bag, filled with what looked like a layer of dirt. Carson walked closer, squinted his eyes, and realized the bag's contents were actually a large quantity of fine metal shavings.

"Forensics found these shavings everywhere during their analysis: on the bomb itself, in the food, in the human remains."

"And this is important because...?" Carson said. He was no bomb analyst, but he couldn't fathom why metal shavings would be unusual.

"Because the shavings have chemical markers all over them, the kind only found in one major product in the entire system," Juliet said, nodding toward one of the datapads. "Processed steel from the planet Rhavego." Carson was having a hard time keeping all the details about the Natonus System straight, but he thought he remembered something about Rhavego being a mining world rich in iron ore.

"I'm guessing the bomb used in the attack was manufactured on Rhavego," Juliet continued. "And if we want to find the Offspring, then our first step should be to trace the bomber's journey." She placed the bag of metal shavings back on the evidence table. "Which means we're headed to Rhavego."

CHAPTER 8

The emotional tempest raging inside Nadia had found itself in good company as the *Exemplar* descended lower toward the planet Enther's surface. Huge, black clouds boiled across the sky, their groans signaling the onset of a violent storm. The rain came down in sheets thick enough that Nadia might've thought they were flying through a waterfall.

At the vessel's pilot station, Derek was tapping his left foot anxiously. Nadia had always known him to stay about as still as your average statue while he was flying the *Exemplar*. But she supposed a little anxiety made sense, since he'd spent most of his flying career in or around the outer rim planets, meaning this was the first rainfall he'd flown through. He kept his eyes peeled on the canopy in front of them.

Returning her attention to the viewscreen to distract herself from the insistent rocking of the ship's hull, Nadia got a better view of Enther's treeline. The trees themselves were massive, most over a hundred feet tall. Their jade-colored leaves were bigger than anything she'd ever seen back on Earth. Each individual leaf was bigger than the *Exemplar*, meaning that the canopy looked less like bushes and more like a green patchwork quilt. The leaves were bowl-shaped, each one collecting enough rainwater to bathe in.

Slowly, a clearing in the canopy appeared, and the growing image of a city came into view. Kal Mekan: one of the most populated cities on the planet, second only to the capital at Caphila. The Kal Mekan city government, cognizant of its economic vitality as a major trade and shipping hub, had negotiated a considerable amount of sovereignty from the Junta and maintained a careful neutrality between the government and the Ashkagi rebels. Which made it a convenient location for a peace summit.

"Woah," Boyd said, leaning forward in his seat behind Nadia. "That's way bigger than the last time I was here."

With more of Kal Mekan coming into view, Nadia could get a sense of how the city had grown. Although the city center was strictly gridlike, the outlying districts seemed haphazardly built and organized.

The buildings themselves were almost entirely wood-based—*go figure*, Nadia thought wryly—with thatch roofs and walls of logs. However, huge nylon tarps blanketed the entire city, protecting it from the ferocious downpours.

"What do you remember about Kal Mekan?" Nadia asked Boyd as they descended lower. She knew Derek didn't like talking during takeoff or landing.

"Back then, it was just a small town," Boyd explained, chuckling. "My parents brought me here to see the temples, but we stayed here for a few nights. And then we spent the rest of the trip in Kal Jova."

Nadia thought back to the primers she'd read about Enther's history. Kal Jova used to serve a similar function to Kal Mekan, as the planet's preeminent shipping depot. Except it'd been bombed to dust at the outset of the civil war twelve years earlier.

The survivors of Kal Jova's destruction had flocked elsewhere across the planet, although the lion's share had congregated in Kal Mekan. Looking out over the cityscape, Nadia conceded that Kal Mekan looked like a town that'd haphazardly grown into a metropolis.

That was when the grief hit her again, the pangs crisscrossing through her like bullets. If the negotiations between the Junta and the Ashkagi rebels were to go well, Nadia's first call would've been to Morris, telling him the good news. Then she'd have asked him for advice on setting up their first colonies on Enther.

Nadia still couldn't fathom what would make someone want to murder thirty-two of her people. Nadia had always believed that, if you could just sit people down and get them talking, *almost* everyone could be convinced to see reason. That philosophy had stopped a war. Someone with the immeasurable hate of the New Arcena bomber was utterly incomprehensible to Nadia. Almost alien.

Most people aren't like that, she told herself, trying to haul herself up a well of despair. It wasn't worth dwelling on the small minority of people who logic and reason couldn't reach.

Derek tilted the ship's control stick forward, and the *Exemplar* came in for a landing. The Kal Mekan spaceport wasn't particularly large, although it was nearly jam-packed with ships. "I had to remind them we were here for the summit," Derek said. "Otherwise, we would've had to wait in line another half-hour." Looking out the sides of the window, Nadia noticed a handful of ships in holding patterns above the spaceport, each one waiting for an empty berth.

As soon as the metal clamps had locked down their vessel, Derek pulled back from the pilot's terminal and let out an uncharacteristic whoop. It sounded strange coming from a man who rarely broke from his usual low, sonorous murmur. "That storm had me *freaking out*," he said, cocking a wide grin. "I've never flown through anything like that before."

"Seriously?" Boyd asked. "You looked so calm that I was worried you were taking a nap or something."

"I didn't want to scare either of you," Derek shrugged. Now that he'd drawn her attention to his unease around the rain and the storm, Nadia couldn't help but notice how Derek flinched every time the thunder rumbled.

The trio arrived at the vessel's airlock, where Boyd distributed a rainproof poncho to each of them. "The time I visited, I forgot my rain jacket," Boyd said, wincing. "That's probably gotta be the biggest fuck-up you can make if you're vacationing on Enther."

Which they weren't, but Nadia saw the merits of the advice nonetheless. She slipped her torso through the flappy poncho and stuck her head out the neck hole.

The sound of the rain only got more intense as they exited their spacecraft. Nadia marveled at the sound of the downpour, thinking back to the torrential American Midwest rain storms they got every once in a while. There was something comforting about being in a warm building, surrounded by good company, while savage rain fell outside. Assuming the negotiations went well and her Enther settlement proposals got approved, Nadia considered taking a few days afterward to explore Enther with her team.

Also, the temperature! Nadia's hand instinctively flicked to her wrister, where she could regulate her enviro-suit's temperature controls. But Enther, with its pleasant mildness, required no artificial temperature adjustment to be comfortable. Which was a welcome reprieve from the outer rim, where Ikkren was deathly cold, Calimor didn't have a breathable atmosphere, and Bitanu was both deathly cold *and* didn't have a breathable atmosphere.

Before Nadia could get too enraptured by the planet's pleasantness, a squad of well-armed Kal Mekan law enforcement officers filed through a nylon-wrapped tunnel that led into the main conference building. Each was outfitted to the teeth with full tactical gear and plasma assault rifles.

The squad leader walked up and held up her hand. "Nadia Jibor?" she asked in a tense, monotone voice.

"Yes ma'am," Nadia said respectfully.

"Are any of you carrying a weapon?" she asked, eyeing Boyd and Derek from behind the visor of her helmet. All three reported that they weren't. "Any knives, other projectiles, or sharp objects?" the KMPD officer asked again, followed by another round of no's. The interrogation seemed like a moot point, however, since the squad leader led the trio to an x-ray scanning machine. And then all three received rough pat-downs from the other KMPD officers.

Nadia almost let herself get irritated with the stringent security measures, but she supposed that the city had a right to enforce its neutrality in the civil war. This was going to be the first time the rebel leader Noah Tasano and the military chairman of the Junta, Michael Azkon, had met face-to-face in over a decade. Their followers had been killing each other all over the planet in the interim. Nadia figured she'd leave as little to chance as the security forces.

Still, she couldn't help but notice they'd been rougher with Derek than they had with her or Boyd. Did they know he used to be a member of the Horde's raiding forces? Nadia could never tell anything about what planet a Natonese lived on or what faction they were loyal to just by looking at them, but maybe someone born in the system could pick up on subtle differences that she couldn't. She mouthed *I'm sorry* at Derek once KMPD was done with their inspection, but he kept his eyes on his feet.

The officers escorted them to the conference room. The squad leader gestured inside. The room itself felt comfortable, with a mild yellow-white lighting and a large window along the far wall peppered with rain droplets. Every so often, Nadia could make out the muted rumble of thunder that was less unnerving now that she was indoors. All around the other walls were paintings or watercolors of Enther's natural landscapes. *Look at all you're destroying in your war*, Nadia thought they were saying.

Neither Noah nor Michael had entered yet, but a handful of Junta officers in their olive-green uniforms were on the right side of the conference table while several rebels sat on the left. The rebels had no official uniforms, but each wore an Ashkagi trinket around their necks and long, jade armbands that covered almost everything up to the shoulders. The armbands had a maze-like series of spirals on them: Ashkagi symbols, Nadia had read a while ago. All of them were giving the other side frosty glares from across the table.

She, Boyd, and Derek assumed positions at the head of the conference table. They'd only just sat down when KMPD officers escorted the two sides' leadership teams into the meeting room, forcing them to stand up once more.

As General Michael Azkon and his senior officers walked in, everyone on the Junta's side stood up and placed their hands behind their backs. The rebels stayed seated and regarded the general coolly. Nadia had never seen the general before, but he looked like she might've expected. He didn't quite fill out his uniform, and his face was grizzled and scarred, with well over a dozen medals pinned to his chest. *No way he's actually earned all of those*, she thought.

She'd never communicated personally with Michael Azkon after the brief shootout with Junta forces back on Calimor. But Junta diplomats had assured her that they harbored no lingering ill will toward her. She didn't see any reason not to trust them. It'd been almost two years, after all.

Noah Tasano followed, flanked by a woman about his age with dyed pink hair. Nadia remembered from the primers that Noah was pushing forty, but she might've guessed the rebel leader was almost sixty. His eyes were grey and clouded, his warm beige face drawn and forlorn. His hair might've been raven-black at one point, but it'd lost its luster long ago.

From what Nadia had read, she couldn't help but sympathize with Noah and his cause. He'd prohibited his people from attacking civilian targets in their rebellion, and he'd worked hard to redistribute resources from Junta bases he raided to the planet's rural, impoverished villages. And someone fighting for religious freedom—while the Junta sent armed soldiers to patrol the Ashkagi temples—was inherently sympathetic. But she had to remind herself that she was here to strike a compromise. She'd need to keep her sympathies for Noah's cause under wraps.

Noah and his partner—Nadia thought she remembered her to be

Bianca Feidan, an aid worker who'd joined with Noah's cause back in the beginning—sat down directly opposite Michael Azkon. "It's been a long time, general," Noah said. His voice carried neither rage nor warmth.

"It has, *Noah*. Forgive me for not using your title. Or do you even have one? I'm not sure if terrorists have ranks," Michael sneered.

"*Enough*," Nadia said, her voice coming out harsher than she'd intended. "We aren't here to trade jabs. We're here to solve the problem at hand. People have been dying across Enther for a decade. It's time to set aside our differences and think about all those caught in the crossfire."

Noah turned to face Nadia. "My forces would never put innocents in harm's way. I understand that everyone has their own path to walk."

"The hundreds of civilians massacred by your people over the last couple of years would beg to differ," Michael shot at Noah.

"That was Brandon Zahem," Bianca interjected. "You cannot judge us based on the actions of a radical splinter faction."

During the journey to Enther, when Nadia and her crew were all catching up on recent planetary history, Boyd had wondered aloud whether the lines between Noah's rebels and Brandon's radicals were as clear cut as they seemed. But Noah had always been clear about denouncing Brandon and his tactics—terrorism, essentially, in Nadia's view—as far as she could tell.

"Ah yes," Michael said, leaning back into his chair and crossing one leg over the other, "Brandon Zahem. Who gained his logistical competence...where? Oh, that's right, after participating in your rebellion for years. He may have broken off from your own forces, but you trained and shaped him into the man he's become."

Nadia leaned forward in her chair, her fingers pressing into the table to relieve the tension in her body. "I understand there's a lot of bitterness here. But maybe it'd be better to focus on the things that unite us. Both of you have careers dedicated to the improvement of the planet, even if you disagree on your methods."

"I'm not sure the general truly believes in that," Noah said. "Before our temporary alliance so many years ago, he was living off the backs of the villagers where his troops were garrisoned. Like a parasite. And now that he's risen to power, he has failed to bring economic transformation, suppressed religious voices, and closed down popular temples across the planet. So I disagree with your premise that he cares about this planet."

And his people shot at me once, Nadia wanted to say. Junta forces had even killed two of Russ' security staff that went with her to Calimor. She felt a surge of anger as she looked at the defiant egoism written on Michael's face. *Dammit Nadia*, she told herself, *stay neutral.*

"Stirring," Michael countered with a sneer. "But let's look at Noah's history. As an honor guard back in the old Theocracy royal court, he was exiled for dereliction of duty. And then he stirred up the population into a revolt against the last king of the Theocracy based on half-baked conspiracy theories. When my forces jumped in to restore order, Noah instead turned his rebels against *us*. He's been nothing but a force for disorder and bloodshed his entire adult life."

"He's been fighting for the same thing," Bianca interjected again. "It was *you* who betrayed us after the collapse of the Theocracy. You froze the people out of government. Not Noah."

Nadia placed her head in her hands. How was this turning out harder than getting her people and the Union not to kill each other back on Calimor? Plus, the lingering, barely processed emotions regarding the Offspring attack on New Arcena were fraying her nerves. *Like a gnat buzzing around my head, keeping me from focusing.* Then she was horrified that she'd compared the murder of a dear friend and others to an annoying pest.

"This getting to you?" Boyd whispered, almost inaudibly, from her right. "Somehow, I'm getting the feeling this might take a while. I'm gonna head out for a piss. Forgot to go before we landed."

"Good luck," Derek muttered. "I dunno if I saw a single bathroom between the hangar and here." Boyd snorted, pushed himself to his feet, and headed for the exit.

Nadia took her head out of her palm and tried making eye contact with both Noah and Michael. "I understand both of you are frustrated with the other. But surely you didn't come here just to waste everyone's time. You must be here because, on some level, you believe peace is possible." She'd tried to at least smile a bit in her previous statements, but all she could hear in her voice now was raw anger.

Her frustration seemed to soften Noah's face. "We're here as a courtesy to *you*, Nadia," he said. "I don't think any of us expected you to actually broker a ceasefire between us and the Junta. But you've worked miracles before, and we thought we'd give you the benefit of the doubt."

Michael, however, looked almost gleeful. "*We*, on the other hand, have real objectives for being here. It is my understanding that it was you, Nadia, who pushed my own expeditionary force off of Calimor during your mad rush to settle the planet. And then you allied with our longtime enemies, the Ikkren Horde. So we aren't here as a favor to you at all. We're here to let you know that choices have consequences."

On cue, two KMPD officers entered the room. "Kal Mekan may be neutral, but on an individual level, anyone can be bought," Michael said with a grin. "Or properly threatened."

Nadia froze, but Noah leapt into action. He was on his feet and had nearly made it to the first KMPD officer when the alarms blared. Then the power went out, promptly replaced by red emergency lights. An announcer warned that intruders had broken into the conference building, but was cut off before he could relay more information.

And then Nadia heard loud footsteps coming from outside the meeting room. A mob of rag-clad, armed individuals showed up behind the two turncoat KMPD officers and fired their weapons, cutting down both officers immediately.

Nadia only had to take one look at the horrified expression of recognition that crossed Noah's face to know who the intruders were. *Brandon's people.*

CHAPTER 9

Russ' boots kept sinking into the sand as he stared down the island's shoreline. Every few seconds, another wave from the Haphis oceans left a line of white froth across the sand. The mission the Syndicate had given Russ and the other enforcers was chillingly simple: break in to the resort, disguised as a band of marauders, and kill as many of the vacationers as they could. The Syndicate had disrupted all outgoing communications coming out of the resort villa, meaning no one inside could call for help once the attack started.

He'd thought about contacting the resort itself, or, shit, even the Union naval vessels orbiting the planet. But there was nothing he could do. He'd tried arguing with Ken Susec that this was a violent overreaction that might not even work. Ken had just laughed at him.

He'd thought about running, but he knew that'd just end with a shot in the back. And it wouldn't make a difference for the poor assholes who were about to get gunned down. He could hope that the Union might send a scout force to investigate the island due to the comms disruption, but he figured that standard procedure would be to wait at least an hour. No reason to dispatch troops if it was just a common maintenance issue.

Russ knew the Syndicate had operations that they didn't talk about with the common grunts. He'd heard stories, but he knew enough not to pay attention whenever someone was talking about ops like this. He didn't want to know. And he'd never figured he'd actually take part in one.

He turned his face and looked up at the resort, which took up nearly the entirety of the island's surface. Only about a hundred feet separated Russ and his squad—Drizz, Tank, and Slip—from the perimeter wall around the resort villa. Other fireteams' submersible crafts had surfaced at various points along the shoreline. Russ and his squad were the first arrivals from the second wave.

Obviously, Russ wasn't going to shoot any vacationers. He might be working for a criminal empire at the moment, but he was military at heart. That meant you *never* shot at civilians.

But what was the plan, then? Was he just going to stand by and watch as the rest of his squad casually mowed down a bunch of hapless vacationers? What could he even do to stop the raid at this point?

"Hey boss," Tank shouted at him, "you coming?"

"Yeah, sorry," Russ growled, forcing himself to take his attention away from the mesmerizing tidewater and join the other three members of his fireteam. They were already working their way up the beach.

The four of them approached the outer wall of the resort villa. The walls looked like some kind of plastered-over drywall, the kind that looked expensive but was actually dirt cheap. There were security gates stationed at various points along the perimeter, with code-entry terminals placed right next to the gates. Which would be problematic, except for the massive hole one of the previous insertion teams had left in the middle of the perimeter wall.

Russ stepped over the blasted opening, following his team inside. They entered a courtyard area, with a high-rise hotel building off to the left, while there was a large pool with glistening, clear water and a plethora of lounging stations scattered around. At the far end of the courtyard was a VR lounge, a holo-advertisement offering sensory-enhancing drugs inside. *Why come all this way to a beautiful planet just to plug into some virtual reality?* Russ wondered.

His squad made their way across the empty courtyard toward the hotel building. He couldn't help but notice Slip pointing his assault rifle at the back of Tank's head as they walked in a single-file line. *Idiot*, Russ thought. You always pointed your rifle to the sides instead of straight ahead while walking in formation. He was pretty sure he'd drilled that into their thick skulls a million times. Or tried to. *You can bring a moron to water, but you can't make him drink*, Russ thought. At this point, it wasn't even worth bringing up.

Plasma fire had shattered the glass sliding doors at the hotel entrance. Russ stepped inside carefully, the glass shards beneath his boots crunching with every step. Over on the other side of the reception area, there were bloodstains all over the walls. The receptionists' corpses were strewn across the floor, carbon scoring all across their bodies.

Russ knew what it was like to be in a war zone. But this time, the stench of iron and ozone caused a sense of nausea in the pit of his stomach. This wasn't war, this was slaughter. All so the Syndicate could prove a point to the stingy island owners and resume its protection racket.

He stayed in the rear as his team took the staircase up to the fourteenth floor, the one they'd been assigned to sweep. As they moved up the stairwell, they walked past grisly scene after grisly scene. The first pile of bodies they came across was a set of parents and a teenage son. The second was nearly a dozen young women. *Probably a bachelorette party*, Russ thought as he stepped over a leg that'd been shot clean off.

They arrived on the fourteenth floor after another few flights. Drizz pushed the door open. They emerged into a long, narrow hallway. Drizz and Tank took turns firing several rounds of plasma bolts through a couple of doors, but they didn't hear anything from inside.

That was when they heard the scream. Russ snapped to attention, just in time to see a young girl, hardly more than a child, at the far end of the hallway. She sprinted down an adjacent corridor. "Let's get her!" Drizz shouted, and the other three broke into a run.

Russ had pegged his squadmates as stupid, but he'd never imagined they were the kinds of people who could gun down children and shrug it off. Not that it mattered what he thought of them. All that mattered was figuring out what he could do to stop this. *Okay Russ*, he thought to himself as he followed on Slip's heels. *What are you doing here? Think!*

He rounded the corner in time to see the girl, alongside a brother who looked almost the same age, as well as their two dads huddled together at the far end of the adjacent hallway. One of the men was frantically beating every door, asking for someone to let them in. The other crouched on the floor, grabbing his two children and weeping.

Russ' three squadmates all raised their rifles at the family.

What would Nadia do if she was here? Russ wondered, his thoughts suddenly turning, surprisingly, to his former colleague. *Probably ask everyone, very nicely, to calm down, explain rationally why shooting other people is bad, and try to convince everyone to just be friends.* Scratch that. What would *Russ* do, after he applied a little bit of Nadia's moral courage and convictions?

Russ raised his rifle and shot Drizz through the head.

As blood and skull fragments sprayed out onto the wall next to Drizz's now-lifeless body, both Tank and Slip turned around to face him, giving him looks that were equal parts shocked and stupid. Russ decided to go for Tank first, switching his barrel over to the large man. But Slip knocked the rifle out of Russ' hands with an uppercut.

Russ' rifle went flying toward the nearby wall. He cursed under his breath, and kicked Tank in the stomach with as much force as he could muster, sending the man staggering. Then he spun around, grabbed the barrel of Slip's rifle, and pointed it at the wall before he could shoot Russ. Slip pulled the trigger too late. A plasma bolt streaked out and harmlessly ripped through the wall. Then Russ wrestled the rifle free. It dropped to the ground with a loud clang.

Russ tried to land a punch to Slip's temple, but the other man dodged quickly and knocked Russ' hand away. *Damn martial arts training*, Russ thought. Probably the only thing in Slip's life he'd been good at. The other man landed a fierce jab in Russ' gut, sending him back into the wall.

That gave Russ easy access to his rifle. He picked it up, spun it toward Tank, who was recovering from Russ' earlier kick, and shot him through the gut. But Slip closed the distance between them and knocked the weapon out of Russ' hands once more. That gave him the opening he needed.

With Slip's body still in an awkward position, Russ lunged for him. The two tumbled until both of them hit the ground. From there, it was all too easy to pin down Slip's arms. The other man might have an edge on Russ when it came to finesse, but at brute strength, Russ was pretty sure he had the advantage.

Turned out he was right.

Before long, Russ had a leg across Slip's torso. He felt Slip struggle beneath him, but Russ' leg didn't give. With his body pinning down Slip's arms, Russ formed a headlock around Slip's neck. The man began struggling even harder, but there was nothing he could do. Russ snapped his neck, and the last of the squad he'd spent the last few months training was dead. *Never liked any of 'em much anyway,* Russ thought.

Still, he hadn't imagined that all three of them were the kinds of people who could stomach indiscriminate slaughter. Showed how badly he'd misjudged them. Hell, how badly he'd misjudged the Syndicate. Turned out, any action, no matter how horrific, could be bought. Russ felt a rising sense of certainty that he wanted nothing more to do with the Syndicate. But he could figure out where to go from here after helping the vacationers.

Russ looked up to see the horrified family of four still watching him. One of the dads had shielded both of his children's eyes. Russ spat out a mouthful of blood and approached the family slowly. The other dad—the one who was still standing—flinched as Russ got near. And then he keeled over and vomited on the floor.

"Well?" Russ growled. "Get to safety. What are you waiting for?"

"N-none of the doors open," the man said, wiping his mouth. His eyes were darting in every direction. "I think y-your people messed with the controls."

Russ thought back to the reception desk, where other Syndicate fireteams had stormed through before his team arrived. It'd only make sense that they'd input some kind of override command so that the room doors wouldn't open correctly, trapping everyone in the hallways. *Evil assholes*, Russ thought.

"This is a luxury hotel," Russ said. "Think: when you all got here, was there a room near reception where you could store valuables?"

"What about that luggage storage room," the other father spoke up. He took a few breaths to keep himself from hyperventilating. "I think it was down by reception."

"Right," the other father said. "Of course." The shell shock was still apparent in his eyes.

"Okay," Russ said, slinging his rifle over his shoulder. "Come on."

He led the family down the hallway, stepping over the bodies of his three squadmates. "The Syndicate's got people all over the stairwells," Russ explained, gritting his teeth. "We gotta take the elevators."

They approached a pair of elevator doors, and Russ pushed the button to hail one. Moments later, a light flashed with a ding, and Russ aimed his rifle at the lift. No one was inside. Russ ushered the family in, looked over his shoulders to make sure no one was following them, and stepped inside. He then pushed the button to take them down to the ground floor.

Russ was the first one out as soon as the door slid open. He walked slowly through reception, making sure there were no other enforcers in the area. He listened carefully, but all he could hear were the dull thud-pings of plasma fire coming from the floors above them. And screams.

"Come on," Russ hissed, motioning the family over with his arm. The two fathers had switched, so that the one who'd thrown up had his hands over the children's eyes. The other gulped and vomited in his mouth after glimpsing the reception carnage.

While the family made their way to the secure baggage room on the left side of the reception area, Russ went to work at the main desk. He inputted a few commands into the control consoles, overriding the Syndicate sabotage. Russ added new commands, allowing any guest with a keycard to open any room door. That way, even if vacationers were caught outside their room, they could flee into a different one. Hopefully. Russ had no way of knowing whether that'd actually do any good.

Then he headed over to the secure room as the four family members were all getting inside. "I'm gonna reprogram this code so that only I know the combination," Russ explained, tapping several keys on the terminal outside. "I'm gonna make a few rounds, see how many survivors I can round up. Then I'll bring them here. But on the off-chance that something happens to me, you all should be safe here. Don't come out for *anyone*," Russ said. "At least, not until the marines show up."

He programmed the terminal to only respond to a single five-digit code. 70339: his old zip code back on Earth, before he'd joined the military. He hoped the Syndicate thugs would have a hard time guessing that one. "Be safe," Russ said, "and try to stay as silent as possible." Both fathers nodded vigorously. Russ slammed the door shut, and a beeping sound indicated that it was locked.

Russ unslung his rifle and headed back to the elevators. Time to go see how many people he could save.

.   .   .

The answer was forty-seven, not including any he might've saved by messing with the door controls at the reception desk. And it still didn't feel like enough. For every one person he'd brought back down to the secure baggage room, he estimated he saw at least three bodies in his sweep.

Russ understood that death couldn't be avoided during combat. You're gonna lose people, you can't save them all—the problem with the old platitudes was that they fell utterly flat when applied to civilians. Russ' feelings of visceral disgust toward his employers increased every time he crossed another pile of bodies.

He'd been part of this. He'd never shot anyone at the request of the Syndicate, but he'd still been offering his services to them. He'd trained plenty of enforcers, or turned profits that the Syndicate could then use to fund sick operations like this. Russ had done all of that because he'd felt there was nowhere else he could go after what happened on Calimor.

That'd been a disastrous choice. He deserved to see the consequences, he thought, stepping over the shattered glass entrance to the hotel one last time. He checked his wrister. Based on Ken Susec's estimates, Union forces would probably arrive within the next fifteen minutes.

Russ couldn't go back to the Syndicate, not after seeing the kind of people they really were. Plus, he'd taken out another two fireteams of enforcers during his rescue operation. If the Syndicate didn't already know he'd turned on them, they'd find out soon.

He tried forming a plan as he headed down the beach, back to the submersible. He had to get off Haphis, but the main spaceport was on a faraway island. And besides, he had no cash. Which meant he had to get back down to the Syndicate's underwater base, hopefully avoid anyone who'd stayed behind during the raid, recover his belongings, refuel the submersible, and get out before the rest of the enforcers got back.

Russ checked his wrister again. He had about a ten-minute head start. It'd do.

CHAPTER 10

Nadia stayed motionless, but at least Derek reacted quickly. He jumped to his feet and pulled the conference table up until the top was facing the door. Both Junta and rebel leaders backed away.

Realizing what Derek was doing, Nadia grabbed the other pair of legs. She and Derek rushed the door, barricading the entrance before Brandon's forces could fire. They certainly tried, however. Plasma bolts tore through the center of the wooden table, sending splinters in every direction.

As Nadia continued to apply force to the table, keeping it pressed as close to the door as possible, she contemplated her next moves. Even if Michael Azkon's plan to capture her and her team had failed, he clearly had hostile intent. And now that he'd played his hand, Noah and the rest of his rebels had no reason to hold back. Nadia had a sinking feeling she was about to be caught in a three-way crossfire.

Another salvo of plasma fire ripping through the table served as a fitting reminder of which faction presented the most immediate danger.

"Nadia," she heard a male voice grunt from her left. She turned her head to see Noah Tasano inching closer to her. "We need to drop this cover," he said. "Otherwise, we'll be pinned here indefinitely. And I have a feeling more of Brandon's forces will come to reinforce our attackers."

"They have guns," Nadia said.

"I know. I used to be in the royal honor guard. I can take them," Noah said.

Nadia turned to Derek. Her crewmate just shrugged. *If one of us is going to charge two gunmen, unarmed, better that it's not one of us,* Derek seemed to be saying.

"If you're sure," Nadia said. She eased up on her end of the table.

Noah leapt into action. Moving with fluidity and grace, he spun through the air effortlessly as plasma bolts from the two radicals went well wide. Noah landed next to one, yanked the weapon out of his hand, and knocked him out by grabbing his body and hurling him into the nearby wall. Noah took out the next one with a flying kick to the face before she could even get a clear shot at him.

This being Nadia's first experience with a former Enther honor guard, she was duly impressed. The title seemed like less of an honorific and more of a badge of badassery now that she'd seen Noah in action.

With the two radicals taken out, the power dynamics had shifted. They were no longer menaced by enemies, but they still had access to the two radicals' handguns. Noah picked up both. Which meant that now, the leaders of the two factions that'd been warring over Enther for a decade were only a few feet from each other, and only one was armed.

Nadia looked over and saw Michael Azkon tense up. He'd been willing to sit by and do nothing as Noah risked his life to save them all. Now, he was paying the price.

Michael gave a subtle hand cue. He and the rest of his people rushed out into the hallway. They went straight for Noah, who raised one of the handguns but didn't fire. Bianca and the rest of the rebels followed soon after, leaving only Nadia and Derek in the meeting room. The two sides formed lines less than a foot apart. If Noah fired, it'd turn into a brawl. In theory, one of the unarmed Junta officers could tackle him, but Nadia imagined Noah could react faster after what she'd seen. Slowly, she and Derek exited the room.

One of the other rebels picked up the second handgun. "Where are you going?" Noah asked Michael. "We have much more to talk about."

Michael stepped forward until his chest was only inches away from the gun barrel. "My team and I are leaving. The only way for you to make us stay is to shoot me. So...are you going to kill me, my dear old *friend*?" he said with a sneer.

Noah's face betrayed little consideration. "No," he said quietly. "The Ashka would never permit harming an unarmed prisoner." He turned to face his rebels, who stepped back in unison. "It's time for us to leave, and quickly." But then Noah turned to face Nadia and spun the gun around in his hand, offering the grip to her. The rebel with the second weapon offered it to Derek.

The two of them walked forward cautiously to accept the weapons. "Won't you need them?" she asked.

"No," Noah said. "We are more than capable of handling ourselves unarmed," he added. Nadia instantly believed him. "As for the general, he's all yours." Noah fell into step behind Bianca and the other rebels, sprinting toward the other end of the hallway.

Almost as soon as they left, Nadia heard an explosion coming from the other side of the building. She figured KMPD was bogged down with Brandon's radicals. She couldn't blame Noah for wanting to get out as soon as possible.

She and Derek turned toward the line of Junta officers, headed by Michael Azkon. Both raised their weapons at the same time. "So, what'll it be?" Michael asked. "Are you going to fire or what?" he growled.

The Junta had five people to the two of them, and they were only a few feet away. Even if she shot the general, she figured one of his officers could tackle her before she got a second shot off. Plus, if Nadia shot the general in a fit of rage, she could very well destabilize the entire planet. Shooting the general might only bring more chaos and violence to a planet that desperately needed normalcy. And Noah had refused to harm the general. In having to choose between ending a decade-long feud with his political enemy or his ideals, he'd chosen his ideals without question. Noah's brand of personal virtue represented everything Nadia aspired to be.

But she couldn't deny the pull in the back of her mind, the one that wouldn't let her forget that, just minutes ago, Michael was about to have her and Derek either incarcerated or worse. And she was still trying to process the New Arcena bombing. She'd had to suppress all her emotions regarding the attack just to make the summit work. Which, apparently, it didn't. A barrage of plasma fire—this one unnervingly close—reminded her of the stakes.

Nadia half-wanted to scream and punch the wall as hard as she could. The other half just wanted to break down and cry. *What would Russ do if he was here?* The thought seemed to come from the recesses of her mind. *Probably just shoot the general and ask questions later, damn the political consequences or the moral principles.*

She wasn't Russ, however.

"You can go," Nadia mumbled, lowering her arm until the gun was resting harmlessly next to her thigh. "We took Calimor from you, and you tried to have us arrested," she added. "That means we're even. So next time you double-cross us," she said, her voice growing darker, "I might make a different decision."

The general smirked. "I'll keep that in mind." He and the rest of his officers backed away and exited the hallway, leaving Nadia and Derek alone.

Liberated from the crushing responsibility of deciding Michael Azkon's fate and the foray through the darker side of her emotions, Nadia slumped wearily against the nearby wall. She could focus better on her surroundings, and a cacophony of chaos flooded her senses.

The thud-pinging of heavy plasma fire was now coming from all sides, interrupted by loud shouting. Screams. Pleas for help. They had to get out before the situation got worse. Had to get back to the *Exemplar* as fast as—

—*Boyd.*

He still hadn't returned from his trip to the bathroom, Nadia realized, a wave of horror washing over her. He could be caught in a deadly four-way crossfire on the other side of the building. And after the failure of the summit, Michael's betrayal, and the surprise attack from Brandon's faction, Nadia reasoned that she might have to settle for small victories. Something actually achievable. Right now, that meant finding Boyd and getting out safely.

"We need to find Boyd," she said, trying to push away her anguish and her fatigue. She forced herself away from the wall.

"I agree," Derek said. "Although he must be deeper in the complex."

Which meant that the two of them had to journey deeper into dangerous territory. "Good thing Noah gave us these weapons," Nadia said, heading down the left half of the hallway at a light jog.

"An interesting choice," Derek said as they rounded a corner. "Sparing the general, I mean." Almost as soon as he finished speaking, Nadia heard the withering stutter of a plasma repeater cannon a floor above them.

The two rounded another corner and headed for an open door. "You think I should've shot him?" Nadia asked.

"That's what most of my people would've done," Derek said. They arrived at a fourth-floor balcony of a large, multi-story reception area. "Then again, all revenge politics got us was a history of blood feuds and violence," he added.

"Maybe I'll feel better about my decision after we're out of this," Nadia said. She moved to the edge of the balcony and looked down.

The first group she saw were the uniformless Ashkagi radicals, holed up behind several desks on the ground floor. Directly across from them was a squad of KMPD officers clad in blue. On the second-floor balcony, a small group of rebels with jade armbands were exchanging fire with both the radicals on the first floor, as well as a team of Junta soldiers in olive green combat armor on the third floor. Neither Noah nor Michael were with their respective groups.

Both rebel groups also took turns taking shots at each other, while the Junta soldiers also took shots at the radicals. KMPD, meanwhile, mostly focused on the radicals. The plasma bolts were flying in so many directions that Nadia lost track in seconds.

"This is insane!" Nadia said in frustration after dropping quickly to avoid a stray plasma bolt whistling by. The bolt instead struck the room's glass ceiling, sending shards of glass raining down on all the combatants. Followed by actual rain, and a lot of it. The storm outside had settled over Kal Mekan. The rumbling thunder and intermittent flashes of lightning became harder to ignore now that the ceiling was gone. Torrential rain surged downward in sheets. Before long, the balcony was so wet that Nadia had to fight to stay upright.

"I don't see Boyd anywhere!" Nadia said, shouting in a nearly vain effort to avoid being drowned out by the storm.

"There's a door on the other side!" Derek shouted back.

"Okay! Follow me, and let's try to keep our heads down!"

Nadia inched her way along the railing. Every so often, another plasma bolt flew by, sometimes tearing through the balcony. Every time a shot landed unnervingly close to them, Nadia felt her body tense up. For all she knew, she and Derek could be mistaken for any of the various factions. In all the chaos, it'd make sense that the combatants might shoot at the duo on instinct. She wasn't even sure who was firing at them.

As they rounded a corner and prepared to cross the room's longer side, Nadia heard a deep thunk followed by a hissing sound. "Grenade launcher!" Derek said. The hissing got louder, and her companion grabbed her and pulled her back.

A second later, the floor in front of them exploded.

Bits of tile debris flew in every direction, some cutting into Nadia's exposed face. She reeled from the pain and tried to push herself to her feet, but her boots slipped on the wet, rended tiling. She fell down through the gaping hole left by the grenade launcher.

Nadia hit the ground hard. A jabbing sensation came from the outside of her left hip. Before she could roll and try to get up, she attracted the attention of a group of soldiers at the other end of the corridor.

Two of them raised their rifles at her. She panicked before her brain could figure out which particular faction they belonged to. She frantically pushed herself back with her feet.

Derek jumped down after her and sent a volley of plasma bolts at the squad before they could fire at her. Nadia's assailants ducked to avoid Derek's attack and retreated around the corner. As they moved back, a succession of shots from below landed on the railing. Derek cursed as he pulled Nadia to safety.

But their new hiding spot left them more vulnerable to further attacks from below. The wall next to them was riddled with plasma bolt holes. Nadia could just barely keep her torso out of sight. Derek took cover on the other side of the corridor. *So many people they could be shooting at,* Nadia's thoughts raced through her head, *and it feels like everyone is trying to take us out.* She was pretty confident no one in Noah's rebel faction had shot at them, at least.

That was when Nadia heard engines. She thought it was just the storm at first, but the roaring became louder and more distinguishable from thunder. Seconds later, a gunship flew into view outside, just beyond the outer wall of the conference building, and held position.

"Is that more KMPD?" Nadia asked gratefully. If the local security forces rallied, they could hopefully rout the rest of the marauding radicals, and hopefully force both Noah's rebels and Junta forces to back down. Maybe the talks could even continue.

"I don't think so," Derek said sadly.

Nadia inched her eyes above the railing, only to confirm that Derek was right. Three missile salvos shot out from a battery on the gunship's underside. The first collided with the KMPD forces, the second struck the Ashkagi rebels, and the third took out the Junta squad. After three successive, deafening explosions, the entire reception hall fell eerily silent. Not a single person stirred at any of the three impact sites.

The Ashkagi radicals—the only survivors—slowly came out from their hiding spot. One of them made an arm gesture toward a group Nadia couldn't see from her vantage point. Then they began boarding the gunship.

A second squad of Ashkagi radicals emerged from beneath Nadia and Derek's vantage point. There were five of them. Four Ashkagi, plus a captured Boyd Makrum in tow. Nadia's friend and crewmate was bound at the wrists, being forced toward the gunship with a gun barrel planted against his back.

"Boyd!" Nadia called out. Without thinking, Nadia brought her handgun to bear, aimed at the Ashkagi flanking Boyd, and squeezed the trigger. Three shots rang out. Two missed, but the other struck one of Boyd's captors. The man she shot slumped over and collapsed to the floor.

The others responded in force. Three gun barrels flashed at her, forcing Nadia to duck back into cover. Just as she was about to send another volley at Boyd's captors, Derek pulled her arm down. "Nadia," he pleaded, shaking his head, "the gunship."

Nadia wanted to protest—her best friend in the whole system was about to be taken away—but she knew Derek was right. Frantically, the two of them crawled as far away as they could. Which was a good thing, because another missile salvo struck their previous hiding spot mere seconds later. Nadia could feel the heat of the explosion in her toes.

By the time they were as far away as possible, Nadia dared to peek above the railing once more. The last two Ashkagi were loading Boyd onto their vessel, who turned and locked eyes with Nadia. The last thing she saw before the gunship's side door slid shut was a look of terror in Boyd's eyes. Then the gunship's engines fired, and it sped off into the stormy night sky.

Boyd was gone. Nadia slumped against the balcony and finally let out the cry she'd suppressed earlier.

CHAPTER 11

Isadora had been pressing her forehead to the viewscreen pane for the better part of the past half-hour, all while Obrigan grew larger and larger. An election was going to force her to think in ways she hated. After her eulogy on Calimor, she'd directed her staff to covertly take public opinion polls regarding the reception of her speech. Which was disgusting to her, as though the only thing that mattered about a heartfelt goodbye to departed friends was how it made her look. But that was electioneering.

She'd put out feelers, gotten in touch with people in the colonial administrations she knew she could trust. Increasingly, a clear picture had emerged: Sean had been covertly cozying up to the other mayors, building an elaborate patronage system where he promised them high-ranking positions in a future Nollam Administration in return for supporting a challenge to Isadora. This had taken place discreetly over the last few months. *He's been waiting for a crisis like the Offspring attack*, Isadora realized.

That also explained why no one else was running. She'd wondered if other ambitious individuals would come out of the woodwork to challenge her, but none had emerged so far. If all the other probable candidates were already lined up behind Sean, that meant he'd already cleared the field.

Isadora supposed the nuclear option was still on the table. With the local militias loyal to her and Riley, she was pretty sure she could order them to throw the mayors supporting Sean back in cryo. But that'd be a logistical nightmare, and would probably alienate thousands of her people. And even if she didn't like them, she needed competent, experienced executives on the ground with the Offspring on the prowl.

To make matters worse, Isadora had finally received a report from Nadia. She described her efforts to broker a peace between the Junta and the Ashkagi rebels on Enther in terse detail. Isadora had felt an immediate flood of sympathy for her longtime colleague when Nadia described the breakdown of the talks and the capture of her crewmate. Nadia was writing in sentences that were even shorter than usual, and she made a handful of uncharacteristic misspellings or word omissions.

Nadia's report concluded with her plan to go after Boyd. Isadora had only met Boyd a handful of times, but she was infinitely grateful that he'd risked so much to help their people. And they had enough refugees out of cryo that the *Exemplar* wasn't their only survey ship, even if the productivity of Nadia's crew was still unmatched. Isadora responded by giving Nadia the green light to take time off to search for her friend. She worried about Nadia doing battle with radical Ash-kagi rebels, but she knew Nadia could handle herself. She'd always been craftier in a fight than you'd expect.

Isadora leaned back in her chair and sighed. At least she'd get to see Meredith soon. She'd hoped that three weeks wouldn't be any-where near as hard as spending almost a year apart while her daugh-ter had remained in cryo. Which was true, although it was still excru-ciating. It'd be after dinner by the time they landed at the embassy, but she knew Meredith would probably still be up. They could talk and catch up, while all the things weighing her down—the failure of Nadia's Enther campaign, the election, the lingering threat of the Off-spring—could fade into the background.

They'd be landing in just under an hour. Isadora decided that stretching her legs was a better use of her time than pining for Mere-dith. She walked out of her makeshift office into the corridor of the private transport vessel. Although she'd first arrived on Obrigan in a cramped shuttle, they could now spare the funds to commission a more spacious craft than before. Each department—finance, legal, diplomatic, and security—all had separate rooms within the craft.

As she entered the hallway, the first person she saw was one of the new personnel they'd defrosted from the *Preserver*: Gerald Yellick, who she'd tapped to oversee the logistics of coordinating the election. It'd be an enormously difficult job. Their people were spread out over three planets by now, with plenty of remote settlements deep in the backcountry of the outer rim worlds. And he'd have to operate under the same tight budget constraints as the rest of them.

A decent number of the same mayors who'd written the joint doc-ument had themselves volunteered to hold an election for their own positions. And a handful were putting up local issues to a public referendum. Both developments meant that voting would be a long, drawn-out process, with individual ballots for each settlement. Isadora didn't envy Gerald's position.

"Good evening, ma'am," he said. He was a short, aging, frail man with a grey moustache, a bald head, and an utterly monotone voice. He'd been a secondary school principal from Birmingham in the United Kingdom—*how did his students not eat him alive?* Isadora wondered—who had experience setting up polling stations at his school. It wasn't really a great resume point for the task they'd given him, but Isadora had been a city councilor beforehand. A lack of experience was just par for the course at this point.

"Good evening," Isadora said, mustering up the best tired smile she could. "How is everything going?"

Gerald crossed his hands behind his back and stared out the viewscreen. "The situation is...less than ideal," he said. "My staff is currently deliberating how to conduct the actual voting process. Your chief engineer—this Vincent character—assures me he can adequately protect the security of electronic tabulating devices, but I remain, of course, concerned about the real possibility of vote manipulation from nefarious actors. Not to mention these Offspring folk."

Isadora nodded. "I understand. Have you touched base with Riley Tago to provide security personnel to guard polling stations?"

"Yes, we've had a preliminary meeting. Ms. Tago seemed amenable to our needs," Gerald continued.

"Well, it sounds like you've had a good start then," Isadora said. "Is there anything else I can help you with?"

"No," Gerald said, rubbing his lips together as though he were deep in thought. "At some point, more decisions will need to be made, of course. Our people have no common media, so to speak. It could

be difficult to give fair coverage to both you and your opponent's plat-
forms. Not to mention any of the numerous local mayoral races or
referenda. I suppose my department could produce educational e-
pamphlets, but that would require more resources, which, I understand, are in short supply."

It'd also introduce thorny ethical questions. If Isadora was appor-
tioning out funds to her fledgling election commission to create coverage of her and Sean Nollam, it'd be all too easy to provide funding
based on how favorably they reported on her. *Not that I'd ever do
that, of course...right?* Isadora thought.

"Resources *are* tight, yes, but this is important," Isadora said.
"When you've had time to develop a working budget, schedule a meeting with me. I can't promise I will approve everything you might want,
but I will take every proposal seriously."

"That's more than I was hoping you'd say," Gerald said. The two
exchanged partings and Isadora moved further down the hallway.
Although she didn't detest talking to the man, her idea of stretching
her legs didn't exactly involve spending too long chatting with her
new top election official.

She walked further down the corridor, wishing everything weren't
so haphazard with the election. She'd always been too busy to think
about formalizing her people's system of governance. In reality, there
was only an executive branch—with her at the top, operating with virtually unlimited authority—an executive cabinet, and local executives
in the form of mayors. From what she knew, few of their colonies had
anything other than a single official making all the decisions. And until now, none of them had been elected.

There was no oversight from a judiciary, no debate between rep-
resentatives in a legislature. No system of accountability from a

government oversight bureau. No one had seemed to care during their first year in the system, back when *work all day, every day, or else we all starve* were the stakes, or when only a few thousand were out of cryo. But she could understand that a population of 4 million who weren't on the brink of catastrophe might want something more formal and responsive.

Isadora continued her walk, her left hand gently brushing along the bottom of the viewing panels, until she heard the door to her right swish open. "Ma'am!" an excited Alexander Mettevin said, stepping out of the set of cabins reserved for the finance department.

"Hello, Alexander," Isadora said, forcing another smile. The promise of a peaceful walk to stretch her legs was already slipping out of grasp.

"I just got done running projections based on Nadia's report," Alexander said, his tone sobering. Originally, they'd hoped to bring another 10 million out of cryo during the coming year, thanks to the exponential growth of their outer rim colonies. It was an ambitious goal, but the prospect of having almost 15 million out of cryo by the start of 2406 was a hell of a motivator.

"I think we're going to have to round our numbers down a decent chunk," Alexander frowned. "Maybe more like 9 million. Potentially less than that. We'd based our previous estimates on the assumption that Nadia would've found a way to make Enther settlement work."

Which may have been unfair in hindsight, Isadora thought. Everyone had come to regard Nadia as a miracle worker after her heroics last year. Isadora hadn't even questioned her assumption that Nadia could pull off a similar feat on Enther. She wondered for a fleeting moment if she'd been putting too much pressure on her.

"Should I announce our revised projections?" Alexander asked.

"I don't understand the question. Of course?" Isadora said.

"I mean...I'd understand if there are political ramifications to announcing the projections right now," Alexander said.

The election. Optics were now going to play a major part in every decision Isadora made, she realized with a sinking feeling in her stomach. There was an art to releasing unfavorable news: usually during the weekends, when people weren't paying as much attention.

Isadora had never factored in public image before when choosing to release information. That was all going to have to change now. "Let's...let's sit on it for a few days," Isadora sighed, resting her head against the doorframe and closing her eyes. "I'll decide when to release the new projections after we're back planetside."

"That's what I figured, ma'am." Alexander gave her a nod and retreated into the finance department's room.

Isadora moved forward. Next up, she passed by the suite of rooms where her legal team had shacked up, and sure enough, Gabby Betam emerged to talk with her. "Ma'am," Gabby said politely. "I had a quick question I wanted to run by you. It's regarding the legal status of our guest workers."

About half a year ago, Gabby had secured a deal with the Union Ministry of Labor to allow several thousands of refugees to come out of cryo and work temporarily for various corporations in Union space. The vast majority worked in Obrigan City. After their contracts were up, they'd have to return to cryo aboard the *Preserver*.

The program was advantageous in two ways. First, a lot of companies actually renewed their contracts, giving the guest workers something that at least resembled permanence. It was one way of working around the Union's settlement charter ban in the core worlds. Second, every time one of their guest workers left a positive impression on a coworker or an employer, it could shift public opinion further in favor of Isadora's people. They could use that in the long run.

"I've been talking to Gerald about who is and isn't eligible to vote in the upcoming election," Gabby continued. "In particular, the status of our guest workers is a thorny issue. Technically, they're supposed to return to the *Preserver* and go back into cryo at the end of their contracts. And since it might be a while before they come out again— maybe years—giving them a say in the election could be unfair." Isadora could see the logic: why give a say to people who might not have to live with the consequences?

Come to think of it, she'd need to decide how recently someone could've emerged from cryo to be eligible to vote. It didn't make much sense to let someone vote if they'd come out of cryo only days before the election.

"But the majority of our guest workers get their contracts renewed," Gabby said. "So if we don't allow any of them to vote, we'd be disenfranchising thousands. I thought maybe we could selectively give those with renewed contracts the right to vote, but that too could cause resentment from those who were less lucky."

"I think we should either give all guest workers the right to vote, or none," Isadora said. "Anything else would be unfair."

Gabby let out a hollow laugh. "I guess I could conduct opinion surveys among our guest workers to see who they're supporting."

"Yes. Do that." The words came out of Isadora's mouth before she'd even thought the issue through.

Gabby's eyes went wide. "Ma'am, I...I was joking," she stuttered.

Isadora had felt vaguely slimy during her conversations with Gerald and Alexander, but now her skin was palpably crawling. Asking

Gabby to conduct the surveys had been automatic. She hung her head and sighed. "I won't let the opinion surveys affect my decision," she murmured, wondering if that'd turn out to be a lie, "but I'm curious nonetheless."

"I...understood, ma'am." Gabby returned to work, looking over her shoulder to stare at Isadora with a concerned look in her eyes.

Isadora proceeded onward, her stride lengthening in frustration. She passed by a couple of her staff members, avoiding eye contact, until she arrived at the section of the vessel devoted to her defense department. She made straight for Riley's office and plopped down in a chair opposite her security chief.

"Promise me something," Isadora blurted out before Riley could say anything. Riley arched an eyebrow. "No election talk," Isadora said. "No politics. I just want to hear where we are with securing our settlements." There was something comforting about focusing on security matters, Isadora suddenly appreciated. The safety of her people would always take precedence over electoral considerations.

Riley's mouth twitched like she was suppressing a grin. "The perils of democracy getting to you, ma'am?"

"I never thought I'd be nostalgic for our first year in the system," Isadora snorted. Logically, she knew she'd been constantly stressed out and miserable due to her separation from her daughter. She'd always choose the present over the past due to Meredith alone. But some days, she felt that her job lacked the moral clarity or sense of overriding purpose that it used to have.

"I think things will become clearer in time," Riley said, rubbing the religious trinket she wore around her neck.

"I hope so," Isadora sighed. "Anyway. Do you have updates on our security upgrades?"

"I do." Riley put the trinket back beneath her shirt. "We've installed checkpoints at every entrance to our major settlements. Some of the smaller, remote ones still haven't been fortified, but we are making progress. Additionally, I've required our militia forces to undergo new training for how to identify potential attackers and suspicious personnel inside our colonies. Right now, my staff and I are working to upgrade our surveillance capabilities within all our colonies."

Isadora suddenly felt calmer. "So that's it? No complicated, politically weighty decisions you need me to make?"

Riley shook her head and grinned. "No ma'am."

Isadora took a deep breath and tried to relax her shoulders. She took a fleeting, nervous glance at the door to Riley's office. "Do you mind if I stay here for the rest of our descent?" she asked. "I find myself developing a sudden appreciation for the straightforward simplicity of your work."

Riley gave her a knowing look. "Of course, ma'am."

·   ·   ·

"Hey mom!" Meredith grinned at her, using a voice that sounded lighter than she was used to, as though Meredith was suddenly a couple of years younger.

Meredith ran over from the kitchen counter and embraced her. Isadora leaned down and kissed the top of Meredith's head, stroking her hair. "Hi sweetest," she said softly. Something had clearly gotten her daughter worked up, but if it meant an extended hug, Isadora wasn't willing to question it. Not after three weeks of separation.

"I made us dinner!" Meredith said finally, heading back to the kitchen where she had a pot of boiling water on the stove. Her voice was still bright, leaving Isadora wondering if she was excited about something beyond seeing her mother again.

"It's late," Isadora said, collapsing onto their sofa and taking her work shoes off. "I hope you didn't wait for me. And don't you have homework to do?" she asked in mock severity.

"Oh, don't worry about that. I already did it all earlier." Meredith flashed her a bright smile. "I went over to a...a friend's house to work on it."

Meredith brought over a plate of butternut squash-filled ravioli, topped with oregano, rosemary, and brown sugar. While Isadora used her hand to waft the odor toward her nose appreciatively, Meredith sat down in a chair opposite Isadora and nervously crossed and uncrossed her fingers.

"I guess I wanted to talk to you about that," her daughter said, more quietly.

"Your homework?" Isadora asked. She took a bite and immediately winced. *Delicious, but still too hot.*

"No," Meredith laughed. "This, uh, friend. Well, it's just, I kinda met this girl while you were gone."

"Good!" Isadora said, blowing on her ravioli. "Making friends is good."

"Well, it's just...I dunno, she's really great and everything. We've been hanging out almost every day after school. Doing homework. Well, I do my homework, but I don't think she's very diligent about it," Meredith laughed. "And she's just really smart and really nice and quiet but insightful and, uh, *pretty*, in this unique way."

As Meredith went on, her fingers naturally gravitated toward her head, where they took turns curling and uncurling the tips of her hair.

Coupled with the breathless excitement with which she was describing her new acquaintance, it was increasingly clear to Isadora that she was talking about more than just a *friend*.

Which delighted Isadora. Meredith had never shown any signs of desiring a relationship with her classmates back on Earth. Isadora had always thought of Meredith as a dutiful student, maybe even a little too absorbed in her studies. This was a completely new side to Meredith she'd never seen before, and Isadora felt elated. She'd been hoping a change of scenery and attending a school with a bunch of native Natonese might bring Meredith out of her shell.

"So," Isadora asked with a grin, "when do I get to meet her?"

"I was gonna ask about that," Meredith said, laughing. "I was hoping I could invite her to dinner sometime soon."

"Of course," Isadora said. "Anyone special to you is always welcome here. And, remind me of what her name was, again?"

"Oh!" Meredith laughed again. "I forgot to tell you. Her name is Rebecca Keltin."

CHAPTER 12

"Not good enough."

Carson looked up from his bed unit aboard the commercial spaceliner. He and Juliet had departed Calimor for Rhavego, a journey that'd take about a week and a half, from the spaceport outside New Arcena.

Juliet tossed three red handkerchiefs down on the foot of his bed. It was part of his training: he had to hide each of the three handkerchiefs at various points throughout the spaceliner. In a real-world scenario, he might need to leave dead drops at hidden locations for her to pick up. Sending sensitive intelligence over his wrister could be easily intercepted by the Offspring, thereby blowing his cover.

"Antiquated?" Juliet had said when he'd asked why she was using such primitive devices. "You bet it's antiquated. When someone swipes them because you did such a piss-fucking-poor job hiding them, I'd rather not have lost anything that's actually worth shit." Carson could see the logic, but that didn't mean he was getting any better at making a dead drop.

He'd been feeling fairly confident about this most recent practice round. He'd left one hidden beneath a table leg in the ship's canteen, another behind a toilet in one of the bathrooms, and the last one behind a loose grating on the observation deck. After Carson had finished leaving his most recent round of practice drops, he'd let himself be proud of how well he thought he'd hidden them. *Not bad for a therapist*, he'd thought at the time.

Juliet seemed less impressed. She crossed her arms over her chest and regarded him in stony silence. "I thought the plan was for you to be my handler once I'm in the field," Carson said. "So don't we *want* you to be able to find my dead drops?"

"No shit," Juliet said. "The problem is when they're so obvious any dumbfuck with a half-functioning eyeball can spot them."

Carson bristled at his companion's harshness. Back in his old life, his friends had always speculated that he must be an incredibly patient, understanding person due to his profession. And when he walked through the doors of his practice, he absolutely was. But having to always stay composed around his patients had always made him quicker to irritability outside of work.

"You're holding me to an impossible standard," Carson said. "You're trained to look for these kinds of things. Most people aren't. If I did such a bad job, how come no one else found any of the handkerchiefs first?"

He sounded shorter than he was used to. But he was doing some kind of work nearly all day. When he wasn't doing dead drop practice with Juliet, he was scouring the primers for any information he could find on the Offspring. Or he was exercising in their private two-person room. Which meant he had to get creative. He'd scrounged up a makeshift mat and a couple of resistance bands from one of the spaceliner's shops, allowing him to do some strength-building yoga and basic workouts.

After all, he needed to look the part for the Offspring. Almost every violent organization attempted radicalization in three phases: physical self-improvement, activation of latent misogyny, followed by inculcation of actual ideology. Carson wanted to look like he'd been through the first phase already. Problem was, his muscles were still recovering slowly after over a century in cryo. He spent most of his waking hours sore from head to toe.

Juliet regarded him coolly. Carson immediately felt bad, wishing he could go back and speak in a more measured tone. But if he'd offended Juliet, her face didn't betray it. "I wasn't looking very hard," she said at last. "The goal is to hide the handkerchiefs in a way that *only I* can find."

Carson still wasn't sure how Juliet could distinguish between a hiding spot good enough that only she could find it and one that anyone could, but he was weary of arguing. Before Juliet had come in, Carson had been taking a rare break to read a report on his brother Stacy, who'd been brought out of cryo and had boarded a vessel to New Arcena.

As part of the deal he'd struck with the refugee defense department, Carson had sworn off trying to contact Stacy. His brother would be informed that Carson was alive, and given vague indications of what Carson was up to. Anything beyond that could be a security risk. And Stacy was sworn to secrecy.

Every so often, Carson got updates about his brother. Apparently, he'd settled into a new home, and was working on producing a documentary about their people's first two years in the Natonus System. The kind his people's leadership could use to evoke sympathy from Union charity organizations and solicit donations.

Maybe that was why Carson had been even more frustrated with Juliet than usual. As much as he appreciated the news, it made him wistful about what might've been. He fantasized about an alternative reality where he and Stacy were living normal lives out on some frontier town. Where there was no life-or-death struggle against the Offspring. Sometimes, Carson wished he'd just refused Riley Tago's request. Then he could be resting blissfully in cryo, waiting for everything to just blow over.

Juliet must've seen the doubt and weariness in Carson's eyes. Her own expression softened. "Maybe that's enough dead drop practice for now. Let's move on to something else."

Carson almost groaned. "Nothing too extreme," Juliet added hastily. "Part of being a spy is having good passive awareness. When you're behind enemy lines, anything you pick up could be important, even if it's just a side conversation that seems trivial at the time. You'll need to develop the ability to pay attention to anything and everything happening around you. Let's start now."

Carson tried to muster another reserve of energy. He stashed his datapad in the bag beneath his bed unit and sat up. "What do you want me to do?" he asked.

"Another part of being a spy—the biggest part, really—is cultivating a network of informants," Juliet said. "Even if we get you successfully inserted into the Offspring's ranks, they probably won't show a new recruit anything sensitive. So you'll need to form a relationship with someone higher up the chain, get them to trust you, and slowly start leaning on them for information."

Carson liked the sound of that. If there was one way in which his old job had prepared him for his new task, it was getting violent, radical young men to open up. And that sounded more appealing than sneaking around and leaving whatever he could find for his handler to pick up. Which, apparently, he was no good at.

"We're going to practice," Juliet said. "First, I want you to go to a crowded area, and try to just *listen.* See what's worth picking up on, and make a mental note of anything you think is important. Then try to strike up a conversation with somebody and get information from them. We're all headed to the same place, so I'm sure there's plenty we can learn about Rhavego just from listening and talking to people."

"Okay," Carson said. "Sounds better than another round of hiding handkerchiefs, honestly."

"Hmph," Juliet said. "You'd be so lucky. Anyway, I'm going to go do something more interesting with my time, like catching up on some trashy romance novel I had the foresight to pack before boarding the *Preserver.*"

Carson chuckled and exited their compartment. He'd barely been alone since coming out of cryo. After meeting with Riley and Vincent, he'd been whisked off to meet with Juliet, and then they'd mostly been together ever since. The older woman was growing on him, but she could still be a bit much. For the first time since waking up, Carson felt like he could breathe easy. He headed out past the passenger cabins into an observation area.

Massive viewing panes lined both walls, giving a breathtaking view of space. They were passing through the Natonus System's asteroid belt, but you wouldn't know it just from looking out the windows. If Carson squinted, he could see the faint outline of a handful of asteroids well off in the distance, but it was nothing like the hyper-dense rock field he'd pictured in his head.

He took a nearby turbolift up to the deck above him, where more people were congregated. There were a series of cushioned recliners and ottomans next to the viewscreens. A couple dozen passengers were lounging in the area, sipping coffee or tea or their preferred alcohol.

Carson sat down on one of the recliners, debating whether or not to go purchase a drink. The refugee government had agreed to bankroll any expenses he and Juliet incurred, setting up a credit account that only the two of them could access. One that couldn't be traced back to the rest of their people.

He'd read that, for most of his fellow Earthborn, their first year in the Natonus System was marked by severe scarcity. They'd had to budget every expense down to a single naton. Carson felt lucky that he'd been in cryo during that period. Then again, all he'd known was the threat of the Offspring, so maybe there were tradeoffs to only having come out of cryo recently.

As he surveyed the other passengers, Carson noticed a tugging sense of suspicion in his gut every time he looked at someone, as though he was trying to determine whether everyone he saw could be part of the Offspring. His mission had distorted his entire perception of the system.

He hadn't known the desperate, but ultimately triumphant, struggle just to gain a foothold in Natonus. Hadn't experienced the hunger and the rationing that brought people together and forged thick bonds of friendship and community. For Carson, the Natonus System was defined solely by the conflict with the Offspring.

He knew it wasn't rational. The system was home to over 350 million people, and his people's adversaries were nothing more than a drop in the ocean. But the lives and daily struggles of the vast majority of Natonese had a way of fading into the background.

Carson was fairly sure that wasn't a healthy attitude. It was like he was letting his psyche spiral further and further away from the real world. Juliet's words in New Arcena came back to him: *You're gonna have to tap into your dark side*, she'd told him. *Everyone's got one. Might as well start getting real familiar with yours.*

Maybe this practice drill would help Carson reconnect with the real world, the one where there weren't always shadowy forces trying to hurt him and his people. He inched his recliner closer to two adult women who were conversing on a pair of ottoman stools.

They were talking about their children, who were reaching the end of their secondary schooling age, apparently. The two mothers discussed how the universities that had cropped up on Rhavego were not anywhere as prestigious as the ones on major core worlds like Obrigan or Sarsi. They took turns confessing their anxieties over whether their children would get the best education and professional opportunities they could if they stayed on Rhavego.

It was so *normal* that Carson almost teared up.

"Mind if I sit here?" a voice distracted him from eavesdropping. Carson turned to see a middle-aged, balding man with a drink tumbler gesturing to the seat next to him.

"Not at all," Carson said.

The other man plopped down in the seat, took a long drink from his tumbler, and let out a satisfied sigh. Carson caught the unmistakable scent of whiskey.

"Enjoying the view?" Carson asked. Might as well try his hand at starting up that conversation Juliet wanted him to have.

"Sure am," the man said, his voice content and booming. "Feels nice to get out once in a while."

"Travel much?" Carson pressed.

"Not as much as I used to," the man winced, indicating a brace on his left kneecap. "But honestly, Rhavego gets kind of old. But I'm sure you know that."

"This is actually my first time," Carson said, scrambling to invent a backstory to cover his true identity. He and Juliet had already decided the background he'd use for the Offspring: a technician from Obrigan who'd lost his job to a refugee guest worker, and who'd discovered Offspring propaganda on the net shortly after. But he needed a different fake backstory to use for casual intel-gathering like this.

"Oh yeah? Well, I guess you're about to find out," the middle-aged man chuckled. "What were you up to on Calimor?"

"Just some contract work with the refugees," Carson said. "I was working on the capital for a long time. Just had to get a change of pace. So I did some side stuff on Calimor for a while, and now I'm exploring options on Rhavego."

"Well good luck, kid," the man said with a chuckle. "Things aren't exactly great on Rhavego. Almost the entire economy runs on mining. Or at least, it used to. Nowadays, that's all dried up thanks to the machines that are putting a lot of us out of work. Me, I'm a little better off because I managed to save up a lot of my salary from my decades in the mines. But a lot of my old buddies are permanently out of work. Things used to be better until the Union sold off virtually the entire planet to the private mining companies. Tricia Favan promised to reverse that, but that was fourteen years and two election cycles ago.

"It's why I was headed to Calimor, actually. I was looking to see if the newa—sorry, I forget we're not supposed to say that anymore—the *Earthborn refugees* needed any kind of help." Carson appreciated that the man refrained from using the word *newar*, even if he seemed less than sincere. The word had apparently become a slur due to its frequent usage by the Offspring, although it'd originated with the Union military. Carson didn't feel a particularly strong emotional reaction to the word. But then again, he'd never experienced someone hurling it at him with venom. And he'd never been called a racial epithet before either. He felt a rush of sympathy for all the refugees who'd experienced racism back on Earth, only to show up in the Natonus System and get called a *newar*.

"Unfortunately, they're committed to only bringing more of their own people out of cryo," the man continued. "Not hiring outside labor. Not sure how you got that contract gig," he said. Then he sighed. "It's the same old stuff. Everyone's just looking out for their own kind."

Carson narrowed his eyes and then forced them back open. *My people are desperately trying to survive, while native Natonese are trying to murder us, and you're mad we're not giving out free jobs?* Carson then chastised himself for his tribalism. He had to think beyond dividing the whole system into Earthborn and Natonese, *us* and *them*. That was Offspring thinking.

"That's a shame," Carson said instead, desperately hoping his tone of voice didn't give away that he knew far more about the refugees than he was letting on. "If you don't mind, I think I might stretch my legs."

"Suit yourself," the man said, raising his whiskey tumbler. "Cheers." Carson pushed himself to his feet, fighting a wave of soreness in his quads, and headed in search of his next conversation to eavesdrop on or engage in.

.   .   .

By the time Carson returned to the cabin, Juliet was already three-quarters of the way through her novel. She looked up from her bed unit and met Carson's gaze. She took a long inhale from an electric vaping device and hopped off her bed.

"So," she said, "tell me what you found out."

Carson relayed the information garnered from both his conversations and his eavesdropping as best he could. Juliet's eyes narrowed when he described the question of the mines' ownership. "I hope you've got more for me than a politician breaking their promises. That's not intel, that's just the way the fucking world works," she interjected.

Carson paused with his mouth agape. "I mean, there were other things I learned as well..." he said, and continued. Juliet's expression softened as he went along.

"Good," she said after he finished. "So what kind of image of this place are you building in your head?"

"I...I'm not sure," Carson said. "It seems like a common theme is people not sure about the long-term prosperity of the planet. With both the schools and the mining stuff."

"Think bigger," Juliet said. "Start building a *narrative* in your head. What defines Rhavego? Economic insecurity, failing schools, empty political promises, a lack of export diversification..." She took another drag from her vaping device. "Imagine growing up as a young man in those circumstances. Maybe with some technical knowhow, but without any real prospects. Imagine being approached by shady elements, being asked if you could construct a bomb for them. It'd be a big financial windfall. And all you'd have to do was look the other way."

Carson thought he could tell where Juliet was going. "You think we're on the right track, then."

"Well, it's all conjecture at this point, but yes. I do," she nodded. "Not bad work...for an amateur." She dug into her jacket pockets. "Do you feel like you've had a good rest from dead drop practice?"

Carson nodded. He was a little tired, but he felt more rejuvenated. And actually getting a compliment out of Juliet was a shot in the arm.

"Good," she said, and withdrew the three red handkerchiefs from her jacket. "Again."

CHAPTER 13

By his reckoning, Russ had about ten minutes to refuel his submersible and grab his belongings before the rest of the Syndicate enforcers got back to the underwater base. They'd presumably found all the dead bodies he'd shot, noted that he wasn't among them, and figured out he'd betrayed them. But with the comms blackout, the Syndicate forces sent to the island had no way of getting in touch with the base. Still, if he showed up at the base before everyone else, chances were good that someone would attack him on sight.

He guided his craft further down, circling the destroyed husk of a warship where the Syndicate had installed their base, the light beams of his submersible illuminating a half-century's worth of rusted and eroded metal. He approached the wings the Syndicate had added on, newly coated with rust-resistant materials that stood in stark contrast to the warship husk. He lined up the back of his submersible so it could connect with an airlock berth, and he reversed until his craft had latched onto the base's outer walls.

Once his terminal reported a secure, vacuum-sealed contact, he proceeded to the back of the craft and spun open the airlock door. He drew the handgun at his hip, just in case. But he didn't bother with the clunkier rifle the Syndicate had given him. He was pretty sure he was deadlier with just a handgun than a half-trained enforcer with a rifle.

Russ leaned his head out into a hallway in case a plasma bolt went whizzing by. Nothing happened. Keeping a firm grip on his weapon, he advanced into the corridor. He turned to a terminal next to the airlock. Wasn't too hard to get past the Syndicate's encryption, even with his basic hacking training from his time in the EDF. Inputting a few commands, he told the system to fuel his submersible with enough uranium pellets to get him to the main Haphis island chains. Of course, uranium pellets lasted forever, but the Syndicate typically didn't give out more submersible fuel than what was absolutely necessary. Just one of their many ways of keeping control over their employees.

A small tube extended from the base and latched onto Russ' submersible. The terminal quickly reported that he was good to go, and the tube retracted. Russ grinned and headed for the dormitories. So far, he hadn't even heard anyone. But he knew Ken Susec was still down at the base somewhere. There had to be at least a few enforcers skulking around.

Russ arrived at a corridor connecting to the dormitory wing. The corridor was part of the warship, not the new construction, and the way the old metal creaked under his boots made his arm hair stand up. The windows surrounding the corridor showed a dark, oceanic blue, too far down for the Natonus sun to penetrate effectively.

He reached the dormitory wing and rummaged through his foot-locker. He'd always been a light traveler, so there wasn't much to take. He grabbed the rucksack still sitting on his pillow. He made sure to grab the Kentucky bourbon he'd brought from Earth, all the spare cash he had, and a change of clothes. He thought about bringing the cheap whiskey, but he figured he was better than that. Still, he took a parting shot and threw the bottle against the nearby wall. Glass shards and whiskey coated the dormitory floor.

Shouldering his rucksack, he stepped back out into the hallway, surprisingly unaffected by the shot he'd just taken. Maybe that was a bad sign. Or hell, maybe he was just *convincing* himself that it hadn't affected him. Either way, he'd been laying into the bottle pretty heavily during his year with the Syndicate. Maybe cutting ties with the criminal conglomerate was a way to start over in more ways than one.

When Russ got back to the corridor leading into the new wing, he found himself face-to-face with two enforcers. Looks of recognition crossed both of their eyes. And then they rushed him. That was the Syndicate for you: something out of the ordinary? Just kill first and ask questions later.

It made sense why the two enforcers were resorting to knives. Since they were in a glass-enclosed corridor, a single misplaced shot could flood the entire hallway and cut off contact with the rest of the base. He thought back to a fight he'd had on a Syndicate gunship from when he was still working for Isadora, when a misplaced shot had sent the vessel racing for Zoledo's desert surface. Better not to relive *that* moment.

Russ was tempted to just shoot the two enforcers rushing him, but he couldn't guarantee he'd land both shots perfectly. Especially after the whiskey that'd maybe-or-maybe-not affected him.

Knives were dangerous though, maybe more dangerous than a plasma weapon in the hands of an amateur, so Russ leapt into action. He tripped the first enforcer and spun around the second so he was behind her. Russ wrapped his arms around her torso, limiting her arms' range of motion. She swung her knife desperately over her shoulder, nicking Russ' cheek. Maybe the shot of whiskey had gotten to him. He was pretty sure his normal reflexes were faster.

Russ shrugged it off and forced his adversary to the ground. Around the same time, the second enforcer had recovered and was preparing to charge at Russ. His attack was sloppy, and Russ easily sidestepped. As the second enforcer passed by, Russ grabbed the man's knife by the hilt and yanked it out of his hands. Russ swiped the blade along the man's back as he ran by.

Then he returned his attention to the first enforcer. She was recovering, about to swipe upward with her knife, but Russ acted faster. He buried the captured knife into her gut. Her eyes bulged, the color retreated from her skin, and her limp hands dropped the knife.

Russ grabbed her weapon, turned around to see the first enforcer about to rush him once more, and threw the knife at him. The blade lodged through his adversary's neck. He collapsed. Russ shook his head and proceeded down the glass-walled corridor toward the airlock section.

It wasn't far. Even though Russ didn't encounter anyone, his mind was still racing. The encounter with the other two enforcers had delayed him. Although he couldn't see any of the other submersibles returning from the hotel raid yet, he knew they'd probably reach the base soon. Even if Russ left right now, the returning submersibles might pick him up on their short-range scanners.

But they'd face the same fuel constraints he had, he realized with a smirk. He keyed up a list of commands on the airlock terminal. He inputted the refueling command, but left the receptacle category blank instead of specifying a destination.

So when the refueling tube jetted out from the base, it hung suspended in the water with nowhere to go. Countless uranium pellets tumbled out and drifted deeper into the ocean. Russ crossed the airlock and settled back into his submersible's pilot station.

In another few seconds, his ship unlatched from the base, and he was speeding off into the deep ocean. Sure enough, his ship's scanner detected a bunch of submersibles returning from the resort island. He wiped his forehead. Didn't even break a sweat.

But even if he was safe from the Syndicate for the moment, he still didn't have much of a plan. He figured he had to get off Haphis, otherwise it'd be all too easy for undercover Syndicate operatives to take him out. Russ had to make it to a spaceport. He figured the main island—the one in the center of the planet's one and only archipelago— ought to be his best bet for finding transportation off-world.

His veins were still probably choking on all the adrenaline, which he was thankful for. If his fight-or-flight mode had shut off, he knew the bloody images from the hotel raid would start cycling through his head. He was almost certain that'd come after he finally got to safety. He set his submersible on auto-pilot and ran a hand through his unkempt beard. Then he leaned back in his chair, tucked both hands behind his head, and tried to relax. It'd be a few hours until he got to the main island.

.   .   .

The spaceport was closed.

Russ had learned this after parking his submersible behind a few large rock outcroppings on the main island's beachhead. Hundreds of vacationers were lolling in the sun, so Russ had ditched the submersible out of view of the tourists. After changing his clothes and hiding his weapon in the waistband of his pants, he'd headed up the beach.

Which was where he'd immediately encountered Union marines on patrol, at least two deployed on every street. When he'd asked one about the extra security, the marine had told him it was because of reported pirate activity. The entire planet had been placed on martial law for the immediate future, until the vacationers' safety could be assured. Marines were sweeping the outlying island chains for any trace of the pirate raiders.

Russ considered telling the marine about the Syndicate base hidden underwater, but then he'd be taken in for questioning, and Russ didn't imagine he'd fare particularly well under legal scrutiny. His resume after arriving in the Natonus System only had two bullet points: head of security for Isadora's refugee government, and common thug for the Syndicate. The Union military probably wasn't particularly likely to look at either of those professions with much magnanimity.

Russ thanked the marine for the info and headed to a central pavilion, where he found an unoccupied bench with a view of the shoreline. He was surprised that there were still so many people out along the beaches, with the news of the Syndicate attack—*ahem, "pirate raid"*—public. But denial was a hell of a drug, and he could imagine being so deluded to think that having a handful of troops nearby meant you were perfectly safe.

Then again, he'd been living in denial since Isadora had fired him.

Denial about the Syndicate's true nature, denial about how much he'd come to rely on the bottle to get him through the day. He knew the rest of the refugees deserved better than him, but after that hotel raid, he wasn't about to sit on his hands and do nothing while the Offspring were on the prowl. What he *was* going to do was still very much up in the air, however.

He saw a young couple walk by, a fruity drink in both of their hands. Russ instantly craved alcohol. With all the sugar plantations planetside, he figured Haphis ought to make some mean rum. *No*, he told himself. He wasn't in the clear till he was off-planet, and he had to keep his wits about him if he wanted to get off Haphis safely.

Maybe a snack might help with the alcohol cravings. Pressing his palms into his knees, Russ stood up and searched for the nearest food cart. The closest one was an ice cream stand. Russ' stomach didn't react with much excitement to the prospect of ice cream—he hadn't ingested any calories outside of whiskey in almost twelve hours—preferring something greasy and savory. But Haphis' economy ran on four sectors: sugar, cocoa, coffee, and tourism. The planet wasn't for those who didn't want either caffeine or sugar-induced jitters.

He'd reluctantly lined up to get an ice cream cone when Russ noticed someone working his way through the crowds right toward him. It could be nothing, but he'd learned to trust his sixth sense for danger. It'd only let him down once.

Turning his head, he saw another man striding toward Russ from the other direction. Neither wore military uniforms, so there was only one logical conclusion: they were Syndicate agents. The timing even made sense, since by now the rest of the enforcers would've arrived at the base, pieced together what'd happened, and let everyone else know that Russ had betrayed them. And between the imposition of martial law, Russ depriving their submersibles of fuel, and the lifting of the comms blackout, he figured activating field operatives to hunt him down made sense.

He'd never been privy to the full inner workings of the criminal empire, but everyone knew that the Syndicate employed a sizable number of assassins that could be called on in a moment's notice to take out anyone who had crossed the Syndicate. Which, as of a few hours ago, meant him.

Russ quickly evaluated his options as the two men closed in on him. He could alert the authorities, but that would probably mean outing himself as someone affiliated with the Syndicate as well, which would be a bad move. He could fight back. Assuming they were planning on knifing him—which they probably were, so as to not create a scene—he could stand a chance. But he had a feeling these two were better trained than the enforcers he'd taken out earlier. That meant his best option was probably running.

Or at least walking briskly. With all the marines around, causing a scene was bad news. He stepped out of line and headed for the island's interior, taking long enough strides to get him there quickly while stopping short of breaking out into a jog. Both his two pursuers sped up their own pace to match his and shifted course to follow him. Which confirmed they were after him.

Russ entered a busy shopping district, with small boutique shops, restaurants, and even a few repair shops or health clinics. He spotted a couple of Union patrols at various street intersections, but the crowds were too thick for them to get a good view of everyone.

Russ' pursuers must've been thinking the same thing, because he spotted both of them speeding up. They were both jogging lightly. Russ muscled his way past an older couple, an indignant "Watch where you're going!" coming from behind him, and broke out into a jog of his own. He leapt over a thick shrub lining a restaurant patio, hoping the dense plants might help escape from his pursuers' view momentarily.

He found himself face-to-face with two couples dining together at a four-person table. A quick glance at their meal fare indicated unremarkable ingredients. Probably imported from all over the system.

One of the diners stood up indignantly, puffing out his chest as he moved to confront Russ. "Just what do you think you're doing?" the man half-screamed. In another situation, it'd almost be comical: some snobby vacationer whose forehead only came to Russ' nose, who was probably paying at least thirty natons or something absurd like that for a disappointing lunch, trying to intimidate him. But with two assassins on his tail, he was just impatient.

"Get the fuck out of my way," Russ grunted.

He ran down an aisle between tables, drawing scornful looks, a "Who is this guy?" and a "Get out of here!" A waiter waved frantically at him and told him to stop.

Ignoring all of them, Russ hopped over the railing on the other side of the patio, finding himself in an alleyway mercifully free from Union patrols. He broke out into a sprint. He'd almost made it to the other side when he heard footsteps behind him. Sure enough, it was his two pursuers. *Determined fuckers*, he thought.

He exited the alleyway, finding himself in view of a large shipping dock. Several dozen boats had docked along a shoreline harbor, with workers unloading large crates from each one. The majority were being brought toward the island, whereas others were simply being placed on different ships. The sudden, overpowering aroma of coffee was an onslaught on his nostrils.

Russ wasn't sure whether this was the best place to lose his pursuers, but there weren't any soldiers around. If he got into a good position, maybe he could use his handgun. He sprinted down toward the docks.

Only once he arrived, dodging a worker carrying three boxes, did Russ dare to check on the status of the two assassins. Both seemed to realize that Russ had more opportunities to use his weapon without the Union troops breathing down their necks. They circled the docks carefully.

Russ worked his way down the dock, keeping his eye on the Syndicate assassins while making sure not to run into any workers. He finally found refuge behind a group of boxes stacked up. Ducking behind the crates, he was about to slip his handgun out of his waistband when a voice interrupted his concentration: "You in some kind of trouble, son?"

Russ turned his head to see an elderly man looking down on him, his hands placed along his waistline. "Nothing I can't handle," Russ said, gritting his teeth.

"Be my guest," the man said, "but I get a feeling if you shoot those two Syndicate assassins, the Union is gonna have something to say about it."

Russ had questions. Namely: how did this elderly man know his pursuers were Syndicate operatives? But he mostly ignored them, saying, "I'm not sure I have a better choice."

The elderly man nodded, a thoughtful expression on his face. "Can you pick a coffee bean, son?"

"Doesn't seem that hard," Russ said.

"Then why don't you come back to my island with me. It's peak growing season, and I could use an extra pair of hands. And if you're in trouble here, there's not much you can do about it other than running away," the man said.

Russ took another glance at the two assassins. They'd made it to the docks, and he thought he saw a knife in one of their hands. The man was right: even if Russ shot them, he'd have a hard time concealing the bodies before the marines showed up to investigate. All his options were bad.

"Fine," Russ said, and took his hand off the grip of his weapon.

"Good," the elderly man grinned. "I was about to ship out. Luckily for us, planetary trade isn't covered by the lockdown," he said. "Hop in."

Russ complied. Almost as soon as he was aboard the older man's shipping craft, they took off from the island. Leaving the two assassins on the docks, watching them go. Russ stood at the edge of the boat and watched the watery distance between him and his pursuers grow.

Although not as fast as his growing certainty that they wouldn't stop pursuing him.

CHAPTER 14

The Enther jungles were enthralling. Or at least, they might've been if Nadia hadn't been missing Boyd something fierce while still sulking over her failure at the peace summit. Under Brandon's leadership, Ashkagi radicals were storming towns and settlements across the planet, and Nadia was pretty sure she'd already burned whatever goodwill she had with the Junta, which meant she had few places to find safe harbor.

She and Derek had followed Noah and the other rebels back to their territory. She was mostly sure they hadn't taken shots at either of them during the all-out brawl back in Kal Mekan, and if the radicals had taken Boyd, Nadia hoped the rebels might at least point her in the right direction. She didn't know what kind of information or assistance the rebels could provide, but she wasn't aware of any other leads.

It was a relatively short ride aboard the *Exemplar*. Their destination appeared to be a small encampment about fifty miles outside of Kal Mekan. As Derek circled their craft around the encampment, waiting in a queue behind several rebel vessels to land in a jungle clearing, Nadia placed her cheek in her palm and watched the canopy brush against their hull.

The storm had subsided, but the rainfall was still steady. From what she knew of Enther, even heavy rain probably didn't count as a *storm*. She wondered where Boyd was right now, whether he was bound and couldn't watch the rainfall behind a mask or a hood or whatever, or whether he was even still—

No. She couldn't think in those terms. Wouldn't even let herself. Boyd had to be alive.

Derek finished bringing the *Exemplar* down to the forest clearing in silence. The two of them hadn't so much as exchanged a word during the flight from Kal Mekan, and Nadia was secretly grateful. She knew she still had plenty of talking ahead of her—she'd need to convince Noah to help them figure out where Brandon's forces might be hiding Boyd—but all she really wanted to do was curl up on her bunk and shut herself off from the world.

They touched down on a flat patch of underbrush, and the engines stuttered for only a second before cutting out. "Do you want me to go with you?" Derek asked solemnly. Nadia turned to look at Derek's face for the first time during the flight. His eyes had lost most of their luster, as though he'd fully retreated inside himself. His shoulders slumped. *So this is what grieving Derek looks like*, she thought.

She appreciated the thoughtfulness behind the question, although she couldn't decide whether his company would help or just distract her. "Can you make sure we're ready to leave quickly?" she asked. "I want to set out after Boyd as soon as we get a sense of where he might be." She wasn't ready to even think about a Plan B if Noah couldn't give them any useful information.

Derek nodded. "I'll make sure we're good to go."

While Derek looked at a diagnostic report on his terminal, Nadia headed down to the airlock. She crossed the airlock and brushed a wet strand of hair behind her ear. The rain came down steadily, an insistent pitter-patter coming from the hull of the *Exemplar*.

She trudged through the grassy field, her boots slogging through the mud with each step. Muck spewed up with every footfall, creating a brown splatter on the legs of her suit. She passed rows of other rebel vessels that'd landed in the clearing. Most of their occupants had already departed.

Nadia followed a series of water-logged footprints down to a large, bowl-shaped clearing. All around the perimeter were tents, huts, and collapsible shelters. At the center was a large, jagged piece of spacecraft hull plating. It was about five stories tall, and wedged into the ground. The metal slat appeared to be a mix of titanium and steel alloys, although Nadia figured it was covered with special anti-rust coating to protect it from the rainfall.

"This is the Left Foil," a voice said from her right. Turning, she saw Bianca Feidan approaching her. The older woman stood next to Nadia and crossed her arms, keeping her eyes fixed on the piece of hull.

"It's considered a pilgrimage site for all Ashkagi," Bianca explained. Sure enough, all the other rebels took positions kneeling down in concentric circles around the Left Foil. Noah himself was near the inner ring, surrounded by a number of individuals wearing cleric robes.

"It kind of looks like—" Nadia began.

"—a big piece of debris?" Bianca asked with a wry grin. "It's okay, it's not offensive. One of our good friends said the same thing the first time we brought him here."

"I guess I'm a little lost," Nadia said. Although she was trying to breathe deeply, she felt a tangible sense of anxiety twisting around in her stomach. She wanted to talk to Noah, figure out where to go next, and head out after Boyd *now*. But if the slat of starship hull in front of them was one of the most holy sites for the Ashkagi in all of Natonus, Nadia supposed she could stand to show a little reverence. Still, she wondered how long the prayer session would last.

"The Left Foil is a remnant of the cryo vessels that ferried our ancestors to the Natonus System," Bianca explained. "Our own *Preserver*, if you will."

Nadia had been born on Earth in 2257, well over half a century after the original wave of settlers left for Natonus in 2191. But she knew that plenty of gargantuan cryo vessels had left Earth between the 2150s and her time, each one headed to a different part of the galaxy.

Bianca must've noticed that Nadia kept tapping her foot incessantly. "Don't worry. This is just a short prayer for those we lost back in Kal Mekan. You'll be able to talk to Noah in a few minutes."

"There's so much I don't understand about Ashkagiism," Nadia said, trying to be polite, but mostly grateful that it'd be a brief prayer session.

"Ashkagi theology maintains that the craft bearing our ancestors wouldn't have successfully made it to this system without divine intervention," Bianca said. "Their gods, the Ashka, shielded the craft from mechanical malfunction, allowing our ancestors to arrive safely. So the physical crafts themselves became important symbols to the early Ashkagi. Manifestations of divine grace, in other words.

"And think about it: most cryo vessels are designed to be broken down upon arrival into prefab shelters, smaller transport ships, or other infrastructure. Early colonial society featured bits and pieces of the old cryo vessels *everywhere*. From an Ashkagi perspective, you would've been seeing divine grace all around you, all the time."

Nadia was well aware of the cryo vessels' secondary functions. The only reason they couldn't break down the *Preserver* was because the ship still housed 36 million cryo pods aboard. And it made her settlement efforts all the slower, since she either had to scout previously occupied locations, like New Arcena, or Isadora's finance minister had to negotiate a contract for a bulk shipment of colonial supplies.

Still, she saw the logic behind the Ashkagi faith. If you believed that the Ashka's benevolence was embedded in the cryo vessels, having constant visual exposure to their components would've had to have been a profound religious experience for the early colonists.

"I'm having a hard time telling your own thoughts on the matter," Nadia said. "You talk about Ashkagiism as though you aren't a believer."

Bianca paused. "I wasn't born as one. But then I worked for an aid organization here on Enther, back before the rise of the Junta. That was when I met and fell in love with Noah. The strength of his convictions can be...convincing. But to be honest, I'm not always sure what I believe."

Nadia could empathize. Her parents had grown up Muslim, and had always maintained their faith, but they never really urged her to follow in their footsteps. And even though Islam had become at least somewhat popular across most of Earth by the twenty-third century, she rarely met any other Muslims in rural western Kansas. She didn't know how she'd answer if someone asked her about her beliefs. But she had a sense her own response might mirror Bianca's.

As Nadia continued to look around, she noticed a number of pale lavender flowers among the rebels. They were connected by a system of vines. The flower petals bloomed and closed in a gentle rhythm, almost as if they were breathing. "Those flowers are all connected," Bianca explained, following Nadia's gaze. "During meditation, Ashkagi are taught to sync their breathing to the opening and closing of the flower petals."

"Are they native to Enther?" Nadia asked.

"Yes. Ashkagiism developed on Obrigan, originally, but there was a mass migration of Ashkagi from the capital to Enther after the Union's founding in the early 2360s. These flowers are relatively common, at least in the undeveloped parts of the planet. So the earliest settlers saw the flowers as indicators that they were following the right divine paths, especially when it was so easy to integrate them into their rituals."

Nadia watched the closest meditators to her, entranced, as their chests rose and fell alongside the flower petals. It was easy to lose track of time. But time was something Boyd didn't have, and just thinking about her captured friend made it impossible for her to enjoy the moment. *How soon is this going to be over, exactly?* she almost asked Bianca.

She didn't have to wait much longer. In another five minutes, the gathered rebels slowly rose to their feet and congregated in small conversation groups. Noah met with a few of the clerics before joining her and Bianca at the edge of the clearing.

Noah and Bianca clasped hands, quiet looks of love and acceptance passing between them. Then the rebel leader turned to face Nadia while Bianca stole off. "I appreciate your patience," Noah said gravely.

Nadia wished she could empathize with Noah's position more fully, but what she really wanted was guidance of her own. "Back at the summit, you mentioned you didn't think the peace negotiations would work," she said, hoping to elicit a conversation that would end, ultimately, in a better sense of direction.

"No," Noah said, shaking his head. "Here in our resistance movement, we haven't had any illusions about Michael Azkon for a long time. But I believe I mentioned that we had faith in *you*."

"Because of what happened on Calimor a year ago?" Nadia asked. It now seemed like such a simpler time, she realized bitterly, even if she knew she'd been terrified back then.

"In part, yes," Noah said, a thoughtful expression on his face. "But it's *more* than that. It's what your people represent. I saw you talking with Bianca...I assume she filled you in on the doctrines of our faith?"

"I got a summary," Nadia said.

"We believe in the divine foundation behind our ancestors' migration to the Natonus System. Since then, we've only had a single wave of followers. Your people, Nadia, are quite literally heralds of the gods. So when I said we had *faith* in you, I meant that in more ways than one."

Nadia was taken aback. A year ago, she might've been flattered to learn of her people's place in Ashkagi doctrine. But after a terrorist attack on her first settlement, Morris Oxatur dead, the utter collapse of the peace process she'd chaired, and the capture of Boyd, she wasn't sure she wanted to be considered a *herald* or anything else.

She didn't feel like a manifestation of the divine. Just a scared young woman who wanted her best friend back.

"I appreciate that," Nadia said gratefully, bowing her head. But she saw her opening, and she intended to take it. "If your people revere mine so highly, then I'd appreciate whatever help you can offer to recover my friend. He was captured by Brandon's forces back in Kal Mekan."

Noah's face fell. "If I knew where Brandon Zahem was hiding, I'd march on his hideout alongside you. But I don't, and I fear my path leads in another direction. Have you seen the news reports?"

Nadia shook her head.

"While some of Brandon's people assaulted Kal Mekan, his followers carried out simultaneous attacks all over the planet. They burned entire villages supporting the Junta, massacred civilians...the death toll is nearly at a thousand, and I fear it could climb higher.

"What is so disquieting is Brandon's numbers. Years ago, when he splintered off from our resistance, he only had a couple hundred followers. He's probably grown his ranks since then, but to carry out an attack of that magnitude? He must have well over a thousand fighters backing him. I have no idea where he got those numbers.

"But my people must respond. If we don't denounce him, the populace will rally behind the Junta. Our gods would never condone terrorism, much less killing civilians. We must make our own case that both the radicals and the Junta are wrong for this planet. But I fear Brandon's attacks may have made our job all the more difficult. All this is to say: I'm sorry, Nadia, but I'm afraid we have too much on our hands. We cannot go chase after Brandon Zahem right now."

If Nadia was being perfectly logical, she might've understood Noah's feeling of being squeezed from both sides. She might've even agreed that he had no choice but to lick his wounds and contain the damage from Brandon's attacks.

But Nadia didn't feel like being logical at the moment. "If you really think my people are heralds of the Ashka," she said, her voice coming out harsher than she'd intended, "I'm baffled why you won't offer even the bare minimum of assistance to our cause."

Noah's face lost its warmth, and his eyes turned stony. Nadia regretted her sharpness almost immediately. Just another personal failing of hers in the last few hours.

"I believe I was clear that there is nothing I can do," Noah said, frowning. Nadia could see the personal disappointment in the man's face. At the start of the day, he'd risked much out of his conviction in her. She'd let him down in more ways than one.

"I'm sorry," Nadia said, fixing her eyes on her toes. The bottom of her feet had almost sunk into a layer of mud. "That wasn't fair of me to say."

Noah sighed. "I understand that you are hurting. And, look...maybe there *is* something I can do for you. A name: Saul Worska. Not much to go on, I know. But it is a path to tread."

"Saul Worska?" Nadia asked.

"He used to be part of our rebellion, until he became disillusioned with what he perceived as a lack of progress. So he disappeared to join Brandon's radicals. However, just a few weeks ago, he sent me a cryptic message indicating he was having doubts. You can find him on the planet Rhavego, in the mining town of Kurskyn."

"Rhavego?" Nadia hadn't anticipated going off-world in search of Boyd.

"In hindsight, I suppose Saul's message foreshadowed the growing scale of Brandon's operations. He gave no details regarding the nature of his work on Rhavego, only that he was having severe moral qualms about it. But that's all I have. I considered dispatching some of my people to investigate, but they'd be gone for weeks. And I need everyone I can get right now."

"That's..." Nadia caught herself. She was about to say *a start*, but she was still regretting snapping at Noah earlier. She could say *a lot*, but that wasn't being truthful. "That's something" was what she settled on.

"It's a trailhead," Noah said. "I believe our paths are taking the two of us in very different directions. But I feel we may see each other again, someday. Goodbye for now, Nadia. And trust in the path before you."

Noah left to go talk with another group of rebels, leaving Nadia cold, wet, and alone. But no longer directionless.

CHAPTER 15

If Isadora remained as anxious about all her meetings as she'd been during her first year, she would've keeled over by now. Still, once in a while, a meeting came around that she truly dreaded. Her first election strategy meeting was filling that niche nicely today. So she'd scheduled an impromptu one-on-one with Tricia Favan to avoid thinking about that. The two women were sitting on a pair of lush, cushioned recliners in Tricia's office.

Isadora had met with Tricia personally in the prime minister's office a handful of times, although she'd gotten the feeling that Tricia preferred meeting in other locations. Still, Isadora liked the atmosphere of Tricia's office. The lighting was dim, with only a gentle dark yellow emanating from a pair of lamp units on Tricia's desk. There was a rock garden over in the other corner of the room, where the soothing sound of trickling water had helped calm the nerves Isadora felt the first time she'd been here. The wood used for the furniture was rich and dark, and a window gave a magnificent view of a grass-covered balcony outside the office. It was a sunny, early winter day on Obrigan, and brilliant sunlight cast beams across the floor.

"So," Isadora said, taking a drink of her morning coffee, "let's talk about our leaking problem." Based on the outreach she'd been doing, she'd discovered that Sean Nollam had been putting out information accusing Isadora of having mismanaged the crisis with the Union that'd nearly ended with New Arcena's destruction. The primers were mostly false, but had just enough nuggets of truth to be problematic.

And considering the specificity of the intel, Isadora's staff had traced the source of the information to some disgruntled, unknown worker in the Union's security apparatus. She'd explained the situation to Tricia when setting up their meeting.

Tricia winced. "We're pushing further on surveillance every day," she said. "When it comes to possible ties to the Offspring, I couldn't give two shits about civil liberties or whatever else my lawyers are complaining about. But the thing is, this is exactly their concern: if I expand the scope of the ISB's snooping on government employees, that's a fairly serious breach of privacy."

"I don't suppose it'd make a difference if I asked really nicely?" Isadora said, flashing a grin. "It's fairly easy to justify, after all: you want to help our people with the Offspring problem. Do you really think Sean Nollam will do a better job than I would? Assisting me is, in a roundabout way, effective counterterrorism."

"Ouch," Tricia said. "Playing hardball, huh?"

Ever since the incident on Calimor a year ago, the dynamics between Isadora and Tricia had changed. During the refugees' first year in Natonus, mutual suspicion defined every conversation Isadora had with the Union prime minister. But even then, the two women had a natural affinity. The kind that both seemed to recognize might make them friends in another life, one where they weren't the preeminent authorities for two different polities.

The suspicion had mostly evaporated after the cathartic near-disaster on Calimor, allowing their friendship to really blossom. Their meetings became more informal, and they'd been meeting without accompanying aides more frequently. But Tricia seemed unable to move past the Calimor incident, as though it was a weight hanging around her neck.

And it made Isadora feel somewhat guilty for trying to exploit that vulnerability. She looked down and stared into her coffee mug. "I'm sorry. That was an impossible ask. I shouldn't have even set up this meeting."

"Look, I think your opponent is a lousy opportunist," Tricia said. "This is just a *big* damn ask. Let me find some other way I can pull some strings to help you. I'll find something, don't worry."

"You're right," Isadora said. "Honestly, it feels like I've put myself into a bind."

The prime minister took a drink, an amused look flashing across her eyes as they hovered above the rim of her own coffee mug. "Remind me again why you ever agreed to an election?"

"Because I felt obligated to provide a more democratic political framework for my people," Isadora said. "With the threat of the Offspring, the stakes are too high for them to feel comfortable trusting an unelected bureaucrat to manage them from on high."

"Sounds rehearsed," Tricia said, the amusement not yet gone from her face.

Isadora looked out the window and was nearly blinded from the harsh winter sun glare on one of the nearby corporate skyscrapers. As she'd started growing closer with Tricia, she'd come to appreciate their chats. It was hard to find anyone else in the entire system who could empathize with her difficulties as fully as the Union prime minister.

"We all came from Earth, which was run by the elected United Nations," Isadora said. "Technically, the secretary-general—the best counterpart for my position—served ten years, and I'll have only served for two if I lose reelection. But seeing as I was never elected in the first place, I didn't think it'd be fair to hold office for a full decade." She took another look out the window, wondering if it'd take a full ten years to empty the *Preserver*. She had a sinking feeling that it'd take at least that long.

When she returned to meet Tricia's gaze, the other woman had a bewildered expression. "The UN got teeth? My memory of old-Earth political history is...spotty, but I remember everyone thinking they were a wet noodle."

"You all left for Natonus at the end of the twenty-second century," Isadora said. "My people left at the end of the twenty-third. Turns out, people ended up *really* liking delegating more authority to a transnational body when the oceans were swallowing some of the coastal cities back on Earth."

"Of course," Tricia said, rolling her eyes. "Instead of a bunch of different incompetent bureaucracies trying to fix something, let's see if we can consolidate everything into one *big* incompetent bureaucracy, so we can pretend we're trying."

"I'm having my legal department establish an electoral system for most major positions in our political structure," Isadora continued, ignoring Tricia's comment. She'd been worried about dumping too much on Gabby Betam's plate while she was still busy litigating the settlement charter ban in the Union courts, but Gerald Yellick had been helping her write formal election codes in his own free time. They'd eventually settled on allowing anyone over the age of sixteen to vote, but the registration cutoff was in a few weeks. That meant anyone brought out of cryo three months before the election would be ineligible to vote.

"Whoever wins, me or Sean Nollam, will get a full decade," Isadora continued. "Over the next five years, we're trying to get each new colony to develop a plan for local elections, but we're giving them a lot of leeway in how they're doing that."

"Makes sense," Tricia said. "Even I don't tell the planetary governments in Union space how to run their own shows." She took a long drink of coffee.

From what Isadora had read about how the Union operated, it reminded her of the various regional trading blocs back on Earth: the African Union, the Pacific Partnership, the European Union. For the refugees, however, loosely copying the UN structure made sense. It was at least familiar and universal for a multinational population.

But right now, all Isadora had was an executive branch, whereas the Secretariat had only been a sixth of the total governing bodies at the UN. Which made her government look a lot more like a bureaucratic oligarchy than she was comfortable with.

"Well, I think you're a lot more generous than I was," Tricia continued. "Technically, I first got this office through appointment. And you better bet I served the whole five damn years until I went up for reelection."

"Maybe my generosity will mean you'll have to be dealing with someone else for the next ten years," Isadora said with a grin.

Tricia almost spat out the remnants of her coffee. "I had my staff do research on that asshat. How the fuck is anyone even considering voting for him?"

"He's promising them everything," Isadora sighed. "More time off from work, more money, and no interruptions in the settlement project. I highly doubt he'll be anything more than a minor nuisance. I'd just rather not put in the effort when there are so many more important things I could be doing with my time."

"Ah, so, he's making *impossible* promises," Tricia said. Then she shrugged. "It's frustrating how often those kinds of things work, isn't it?"

"I'm half-considering just calling off the election. I have a meeting with my new campaign adviser that I *really* don't want to go to."

"And I *really* don't want to spend ten years having to work with Sean Nollam," Tricia said, her brows furrowing in mock sternness. "So you better go win this thing. Which means you better get out of my office and go meet with your campaign adviser. Now shoo."

.   .   .

After her venting session with Tricia, Isadora felt better about the meeting she'd been dreading. After a short ride back from the Government-General, she headed to a conference room in her people's embassy.

Sean Nollam had been making the rounds across the outer rim in the last few weeks, giving stump speech after stump speech criticizing her. All while the Offspring issue was draining Isadora's energy reserves—in hindsight, that was probably part of Sean's strategy—and she hadn't made so much as a single campaign-related appearance.

If Isadora wanted to bolster her chances at winning, she needed a good team. And she and Sean had a common pool of talent in the form of everyone still frozen aboard the *Preserver.* So she'd prioritized finding someone with the most campaign experience in cryo, and requisitioned them before Sean got a chance to take his pick. Eventually, Isadora had settled on an individual with experience running internal polls for the National Action Party back in Mexico.

As Isadora headed for the conference room, she passed by a holovision, where a recording of one of Sean's campaign speeches was playing. He was going through his usual stump speech: reduced working hours, larger individual stipends, more refugees coming out of cryo, and a more democratic system of governance. He was excited and upbeat on the campaign trail. The audience erupted as he hammered home each part of his agenda.

Did the math add up? Hardly. Alexander Mettevin had already crunched the numbers, and a combination of decreased productivity and increased incomes—already implausible—made it impossible to bring anyone else out of cryo. But the problem with making *my opponent's math doesn't add up* your campaign slogan was that it generally meant you were losing.

Isadora entered the meeting room and greeted her new campaign chief: a young woman named Valencia Peizan, who had light brown skin, a thick head of curly hair, and a mouth that seemed fixed in a cocky smile. "It's so good to finally meet you, ma'am!" Valencia said in a bright but somewhat deep voice.

Isadora immediately appreciated Valencia's enthusiasm. At least one of them was having fun.

Valencia was nursing a cup of coffee. Catching a whiff of the drink made Isadora crave another cup for herself, the buzz of her coffee from her meeting with Tricia already wearing off. Walking over to a refreshment table on the edge of the room, Isadora refilled her mug. She briefly remembered thinking she should cut back on caffeine during her first few months after arriving in the Natonus System. *Those were the days*, she thought, stifling a chuckle and returning to her seat.

"Let me get straight to the point," Valencia said, withdrawing a datapad from her satchel. "I collected plenty of polling data on the flight from the *Preserver*. Not much else to do while you're scrunched up in a shuttle that takes weeks to cross from one end of the system to the other."

Isadora marveled at the young woman's ability to jump right into the middle of her new job. If she had any lingering doubts or traumas from the shock of awakening in a new solar system, she displayed none of them. *Youth*, Isadora thought wistfully. She took a drink of coffee and her eyes felt less heavy for a merciful few moments.

"The data I collected was both good and bad," Valencia continued. "Which one do you want first?" she asked.

"Oh, how about the bad," Isadora said, gesturing with her hand.

"You got it," Valencia said. "Well, the bad news is that it seems there's a big generation gap in terms of which candidate everyone is considering. And I don't mean age, I mean when they came out of cryo. Anyone who got defrosted during our first year in the system is totally in your corner. But those brought out during the second year are seriously considering Sean Nollam," Valencia explained.

Isadora figured that made sense. She'd won accolades for how she'd managed the Calimor crisis, but she didn't have as many big triumphant moments during their second year in the system. Plus, she couldn't be as visible and personable as she used to be when she only had a few thousand constituents, not millions. And with all the promises Sean was making, she figured it made sense that the new-comers might be open to voting for him. They hadn't really seen her in action yet, and the Offspring threat was so recent that it hadn't given her adequate time to demonstrate her competence.

"The problem," Valencia continued, "is that roughly three-fourths of everyone who will be eligible to vote in the election came out of cryo during our second year. Which means that Sean has a much higher base of potential support than you. Preliminary head-to-head polling puts you ahead, 54% to 33%, with 13% undecided. That's not a bad place to start, but I can guarantee you will lose support as the election ramps up based on the generation gap alone. So unfortunately, 54% is *not* a great place to be right now."

Isadora felt a jarring stomach drop. She hadn't even seriously considered the possibility that Sean could *win. A minor nuisance,* she'd called him back in Tricia's office. But the prospect of actually losing her position brought up a curious mix of emotions.

When Isadora had been apart from her daughter, still learning the ropes, she would've jumped at the opportunity to turn the reins over to someone else. Maybe if Sean had approached her about an election during her first few months in the system, she might've just conceded outright.

But over time, she'd settled into her office. It was a political phe-nomenon Isadora knew well: the deeper into your tenure you got, the more defensive you were against anyone trying to take your job away from you.

And she'd leapt at the chance to formalize an election with Sean as her opponent, rather than one of the other mayors dissatisfied with her performance: hypothetical opponents who would, presumably, bring a degree of political competence that Sean wouldn't. Was she so out of touch with her own people that she'd badly underestimated Sean's appeal? She thought back to the adoring crowds from the holo-vision.

"And what is the good news?" she asked, quieter than she was before.

"The good news is that your opponent is playing himself into a corner," Valencia said. "He's running on issues. You, on the other hand, are presumably going to run on experience. You've already been through all the harrowing situations, the hard decisions. And with the threat of these Offspring assholes bearing down on us, who would our people rather trust: someone who's gotten them this far, or an untested colony leader?"

Isadora furrowed her brow. "The good news is that I can play on our people's fears?"

"Well...yeah," Valencia said, as though she didn't understand Isadora's objection. "Picture this: a black-and-white holo-ad, with a picture of Sean Nollam's face looking stupid, ominous music in the background, and some deep, gruff male voice telling you that Sean Nollam doesn't have the right experience to keep you safe," she said. "It'll *work*."

Isadora didn't necessarily like the idea of scaring people into voting for her, but she couldn't deny Valencia's electoral acumen. Fear-mongering was an age-old political tactic for a reason.

"But what's really good about our set-up is that he can't take your experience, but you *can* take his issues," Valencia continued. "See, we're not bound by political parties or ideology. There's literally nothing stopping you from passing all the major reforms he wants to pass.

Or at least, a more mathematically feasible version thereof."

"You mean, co-opt his entire agenda?" Isadora asked.

Valencia nodded. "Just pretend it was your idea in the first place."

"What would I say?" Isadora asked.

Valencia shrugged, a bewildered look on her face. "I dunno...just lie or something? You're a politician."

Isadora felt deflated. She'd lied plenty of times in her career before, but she'd been hoping that she could leave the squalid side of politics back in her old life.

She found herself longing for the clear moral lines of her people's security initiatives—her people were good, the Offspring were evil. She'd just have to get used to feeling dirty. She thanked Valencia for her time, finished her coffee, and left the meeting room, promising to give Valencia's suggestions some thought.

But she'd already decided. Stealing all of Sean's issues was a good strategy, and it'd handicap his main source of appeal to voters. And then, with any luck, she'd be able to put this whole thing behind her.

CHAPTER 16

By the time Carson made his way to the observation deck, the spaceliner was already arriving in Kurskyn's spaceport. As the biggest mining town on the planet, Kurskyn was a natural place to start in their search for clues about the New Arcena bomber. A pity he hadn't thought to come to the observation deck earlier, he rued. He might've liked to see the view of their descent into the planet.

Still, the spaceport had plenty of striking views of its own. Several dozen hangar bays were embedded in a cliff face, forming a grid of light that stood in stark contrast to the blackness of space—Rhavego had no natural atmosphere—and the deep brown hue of the carbon rock that formed the entirety of the planet's surface. Carson could see veins of iron, or nickel, or platinum spread throughout the cliff face.

The Kurskyn settlement itself stood on top of the cliff face, protected by a large transparent dome structure. The hangar bays were the only part of the colony exposed to the outside, each one protected by a vacuum-sealed sliding door.

Somewhere deep inside the colony might be the bomb maker who'd built the device that'd killed thirty-two of Carson and Juliet's fellow people. Juliet wanted to start the search almost immediately, seeing if they could scrounge up any info about local Offspring connections. Carson supposed he should be focusing on the mission, but truthfully, he just wanted to rest. He'd hoped a luxurious weeklong flight to Rhavego would be the perfect time to get his head on straight before the mission began in earnest. A never-ending series of espionage drills with Juliet had quickly dispelled such notions.

Still, he was getting "less utterly atrocious" at dead drops, to quote Juliet's exact words. He'd performed better at eliciting information out of people, but hey, he figured that was the easier part considering his old career. He hoped he'd have met more of her standards once it was time for him to infiltrate the Offspring. For now, they were still following the clues.

His companion walked up and joined him at the viewing pane. "Enjoying the view?" she asked.

Carson had learned by now that Juliet didn't really care. She'd probably just fire back some snarky remark. Carson shrugged and headed to the ship's exit. They were approaching one of the hangar bays, and he figured they'd be docking in another minute or two. The hangar's door slid open, and a red emergency light flashed from within, indicating that the bay was now depressurized.

"Chatty today, huh?" Juliet said, following him to the exit.

"I'm just tired," Carson said.

"Oh. Well, gotta learn how to work through that," Juliet said.

They lined up behind a group of passengers preparing to disembark. The sounds of conversation all around them let Carson get away with mumbling a response Juliet couldn't hear.

He heard a loud hiss fill the chamber as the spaceliner finally came to a rest. A docking clamp latched down on top of the hull. A large exit door slid open, revealing an extendable tube connected to the rest of the colony. Carson and Juliet waited for the bulk of the crowds to flood the tube before heading out themselves.

The colony's air recycling systems hadn't been able to clear the air of the industrial stench from all the mining activity going on deeper in the planet's crust. Carson coughed twice. Juliet didn't seem particularly bothered.

By the time they got into the colony proper, a large security apparatus came into view. There were screening gates all around, thumb scanning stations where you had to leave your thumbprint—presumably so security services could identify you later, if necessary—and rifle-carrying guards on patrol everywhere.

"Think security would be this tight if it hadn't been for the Offspring bombing?" Juliet asked as they got in line for one of the gates.

"I just hope we have something like this back at New Arcena," Carson said. He was still worried about Stacy, although he'd been following news on his wrister about the security upgrades the leadership was trying to implement in their settlements. Hopefully, having something like this to protect New Arcena would keep Stacy safe.

A Union soldier waved them through, and the scanner cleared both Carson and Juliet. Then they had to leave their thumbprints on a nearby machine. As Carson placed his finger on the scanner, he saw a terminal light up, declaring his name and his made-up status as a resident of Obrigan. He and Juliet headed for the exit.

The actual colony was not what he expected. The walls looked like they were crumbling, with large sheets of plastic peeling off. There were stains everywhere: dirt, soot, probably the remnants of some food or drink. Or the regurgitation thereof. The fluorescent bulbs overhead flickered intermittently.

"Nice place," Juliet scoffed from behind him. "Come on. Let's ditch the crowds."

Carson was grateful for that. He didn't consider himself a claustrophobic person, but the narrowness of the corridors, the sensation of walking and breathing in a massive underground complex, and the crowds of disembarking spaceliner passengers got a bit of panic out of Carson.

They ducked into an adjacent corridor, this one lined with restaurants, drinking dens, and cafes. Each with a real hole-in-the-wall type of feeling to them. Juliet headed briskly for a small cafe, mostly deserted. It was the middle of the night, local time—not that anyone could tell, given the lack of a sky—so Carson figured not many people were looking for their caffeine fix right now.

They sat at a run-down table, with a deep cut having nearly taken off one of the corners. No one came to greet them, so Juliet cleared her throat. A server emerged from a back room. "Two coffees," Juliet said to the server. Even if Carson preferred tea, he was tired enough that he didn't mind that Juliet had mixed up his usual order. "And make sure they're in clean mugs," she added.

The server gave her an empty stare and then got to work on their drinks.

"I'm guessing that means we aren't gonna crash just yet," Carson asked, his voice heavy.

"You need to learn how to push through the weariness," Juliet said, frowning. "When you're undercover, there *won't* be any breaks. You'll be spending every waking moment keeping your cover up around our adversaries."

Just thinking about that made Carson place his forehead in his palm. The server brought over a pair of steaming coffee mugs. Carson's mug had a chipped top, so he made a mental note to drink from the other side. "If you want cream and sugar, they're over there," the server said, indicating a table behind them. Then he retreated into the back room.

Carson rubbed his thumb on the chip in his mug and tried to let the rising steam wake him up. "They all say Isadora Satoro slept three hours a day during the entire first year of her tenure," Juliet said. "If the sociopath can do it, you can too."

"Sociopath?" Carson asked, perking up. He finally took a sip of his drink and winced immediately. Calling it "coffee" was generous.

"She's a *politician*. That's practically the same thing." Juliet took a sip of her coffee and gagged. "Shit, I coulda made better coffee with a few drops of black food coloring and a dissolved caffeine pill."

Well. At least he and Juliet could finally agree on something.

Carson walked to the other table and retrieved the sugar. Maybe if he could drown out the rancid taste of the drink with enough sugar, he could manage to drink it.

"As I was saying," Juliet said, "it's natural for politicians to see everyone else as just a number on a datasheet. Comes with the territory. But Isadora? She takes that to a whole other level. Most politicians have to at least pretend to see other people as human. All she has to do is look at some database, and then she gets to choose everyone who lives under her rule.

"Hell, that's probably how she picked us. Somewhere, she's got a list of names, each one with relevant skills and experience. 40 million cryo pods' worth of real people are just *resumes* to her. So she sees 'Carson Erlinza - therapist; worked with violent radicals' and 'Juliet Lessitor - undercover cop,' and that's how we get this shitty detail."

Carson had never thought about it like that, but it sounded coldly impersonal the way Juliet told it. Still, he wasn't sure there was any way to make a massive enterprise like getting 40 million people out of cryo any less impersonal. "Does that mean you're gonna vote against her in that election they're holding?" he asked, taking a sip of his coffee. It was a little sweet now, but he didn't mind.

Juliet just shrugged. "A smart person once said if voting changed anything, it'd be illegal."

Carson had never worked with a dyed-in-the-wool anarchist before, but dealing with people who had stubborn political views was part and parcel of the deradicalization process. Arguing was never the right thing to do. You had to ask them genuine, good-faith questions, let them sit with the logical contradictions themselves. But his goal wasn't to change Juliet's mind, so he didn't bother responding.

Still, he remained skeptical of her take on the system's political situation. Most people, even politicians, were usually trying their best. Some jobs were just harder than others. That was why he preferred therapy to politics: doing good was always easier and simpler on a microscopic level than on a grand scale.

"Speaking of politics," Juliet said, "I think it's time to get to work. We know we're looking for a bomb maker. I have a couple ideas of where to start our search, but I want to see how your investigative instincts are coming along. What would *you* do?"

Carson paused with his mug halfway to his mouth. Juliet was career law enforcement. Why was she asking him to do the work she was good at? "You need to learn how to make these kinds of judgment calls," Juliet added, anticipating his objection. "So tell me: if you were in charge of the investigation, where would you start?"

Carson wasn't as tired after a few sips of coffee—"*coffee*," he thought—but he still didn't feel up to figuring out how to do Juliet's job.

So he went back to basics. Unfortunately, he hadn't spent much time with his patients back in Vancouver talking about their recruitment experiences. And the ones who he'd talked to had been recruited online. His experience wasn't exactly leading him in the right direction at the moment.

But the Offspring clearly had contacts on Rhavego, which implied that there were at least sympathizers here, if not full supporters. He knew radical organizations relied on dog whistling and online referrals, so maybe it'd be the same in person. If he posed as a potential recruit and used the right language, someone might take notice. And then word-of-mouth might get the organization's attention.

"I should find someone to talk to, and start casually hinting that I'm interested in the Offspring. Without using the actual name, of course," Carson said.

Juliet's face betrayed no sense of what she thought of his plan. "Well, have at it then," she said, shooing him away with a wave of her hand.

Carson downed the rest of his drink and left the cafe. One of the nearby establishments was a mostly empty dive bar, but there were still enough people in there to strike up a conversation. He entered, waved down a server who looked only slightly more enthused than the cafe worker, and ordered a beer.

She brought him the drink almost immediately, and he paid her a handful of natons. The glass was too full, with foam sloshing around at the top and dripping down the sides. Carson took a drink and stood at a small circular table at the edge of the bar. The beer was almost as flavorless as the coffee, and even though he could tell it wasn't particularly high in alcohol, it'd been long enough since he'd eaten that he immediately felt a pleasant lightness in his head.

At the other end of a room, a man and a woman were playing some kind of electronic console game. He looked sloppy drunk already, placing his arm on the wall to steady himself. The woman, who was busy playing the game, seemed unimpressed.

At the counter were two burly men who struck Carson as miner types. They were huddled over identical drink orders: a beer and a shot of glowing purple liquor. The patrons had an aura of resignation, as though they were unhappy with their lot in life, but not desperate enough to actually do something about it.

Carson wished he could do something to help these people. From what he'd seen so far, the planet felt soulless to him, as though it'd gone through its glory days while Carson and the rest of his people were still lumbering toward the Natonus System in the *Preserver*. And everyone's body language suggested they knew that too.

But that wasn't why he was here. He shook himself awake, took another long drink of beer, and pressed on. He joined the two miners at the bar counter.

He couldn't hear what they'd been talking about, but both stopped talking and stared at him after he sat down. "Can we help you?" the one farther from him said.

"I'm looking for someone," Carson mumbled.

"Lotta people here," the one closer to him said.

"Someone who can *help*," Carson said. "Some *newar* guest worker took my job back on Obrigan," he sneered, drawing from the back-story he and Juliet had crafted. Now that he knew *newar* was a kind of dog whistle, he hoped he could use the term to subtly indicate who he was looking for, while still being discreet. "I'm fed up with it. So I want to do something about it," he added.

"You talking about the Offspring?" the second miner said. *Shit*, Carson thought. He turned his head, worrying that the bar staff or the other patrons might've heard them. But no one reacted. "Those people are all trouble," the second miner continued. "We don't want newars or Offspring here."

The first one slapped his companion's forearm. "Neither of you are supposed to say that anymore. It's offensive." He belched loudly in the middle of "offensive."

"Well *sorry*," the second one chuckled, rolling his eyes. "But like I was saying: we don't want Offspring here. Take your problems somewhere else."

"We're all Natonese," Carson hissed. "We're the same, you and I. The *newars* are the ones who don't belong."

"We aren't the same at all," the first miner said. "You look like some core-world rich kid who's throwing a tantrum first time something goes wrong in your life. Leave us out of it. And leave our whole settlement out of it, while you're at it."

Carson wrinkled his nose and left without saying goodbye in his disappointment. He departed without finishing his beer and headed back to rejoin Juliet in the cafe across the corridor.

He slammed his palm down on the table. "Didn't work," he said, pouting.

"You thought it was gonna be easy like that?" Juliet said. "It was a lazy attempt."

"Then why did you let me try?" Carson asked, not even bothering to hide the frustration in his voice.

"Because I thought it'd be a good *learning* experience," Juliet said. "You can't cut corners in this line of work. Better to learn that now—*really* learn it—than when you're in the field and the stakes are higher."

Carson sighed. "Then what should we do?"

"*Think,*" Juliet said. "This is a mining planet. And they're down on their luck, lacking the resources they used to have access to. What's an essential supply for mining?"

"I dunno. Proper clothing? Protective masks?"

"Goddammit, Carson! Think about *why we're here.* We're looking for a fucking bomb maker."

Carson placed his fingers on his temples, like maybe that could help him think better. "Blasting equipment?" he said at last.

"Yes. *Thank you.* Imagine this: desperate miners, threatened by job losses and suffering lower returns on their shipments, who can't afford to buy the kinds of explosives they need to do their jobs in the first place.

"And imagine some young man living here. No prospects, no hope for a better future, but he knows a thing or two about explosives. He gets some experience making blasting devices for the miners, cheaper than the stuff they'd import from the core worlds. Then, a group calling itself the Offspring gets in touch with him, offers more money than he's ever seen in his life, and his eyes go wide. That's our guy right there." Juliet's eyes seemed to sparkle the further along she got in her explanation.

There were times Carson worried that Juliet didn't have her head fully in the game, especially when she went on her long political rants.

But the way her eyes twinkled as she went along let Carson know that, deep down, Juliet wanted them to succeed. The prospect of solving a case was too intriguing for her, anarchist beliefs or otherwise.

Her hypothesis made sense to Carson, and he was impressed at how seamlessly she'd built her narrative based on everything they'd learned so far: the desperation, economic downturn, the threat of automation, declining prospects for young people. He had no idea how she'd been able to do that so quickly and effortlessly.

"I don't even know what I'm doing here," Carson said, slamming his forehead into his forearm. "I don't belong here. I'm not cut out for this. I wish I'd never accepted the leadership's offer. I wish I'd just told them to throw me back in cryo."

Carson felt embarrassed almost immediately, like he was a little kid again, throwing a fit. But the sleep deprivation and the hunger were getting to him, and the coffee and the beer had made him both more energetic and uncharacteristically forthright, respectively.

He felt like he just wasn't good enough. Nothing he'd done so far had been up to Juliet's standards. The closest he'd gotten was gathering information from other passengers back on the spaceliner—*big whoop,* he thought, *I had a few damn conversations*—but everything else had made him feel like a failure.

Stricken by embarrassment, Carson finally forced himself to look up. He wished he hadn't. Juliet just looked unimpressed. "Are you done?" she asked.

Carson nodded solemnly.

Instead of telling him to get back to work, as he'd expected, Juliet ran a hand through her hair. He thought her face softened a bit, but maybe it was just his imagination. "Look...it's late," she said. "I get it. How about we go find some cheap, run-down motel where we can shack up for the night, and get back to it tomorrow morning?"

A tide of gratitude surged inside of Carson, drowning out all the shame and frustration. "Yes, please," he said immediately. They stood up in unison, Juliet finished her coffee, and they departed the cafe.

CHAPTER 17

The work was hot, and it took most of the day, but Russ was starting to kind-of-maybe-not-mind picking coffee beans. His days started before the Natonus sun even rose, so he got to watch the shades of pink and orange reflected by the surface of the Haphis oceans, all from his tractor's cabin as he drove through rows of coffee plants.

He spent middays by himself, eating a sandwich he'd packed, trying to ignore the sweat drenching his brow and beard, and enjoying the view. The island where he was working was essentially a small mountain that rose several hundred feet out of the oceans. Unlike the resort isles he'd already been to, the plantation island was covered with dense, low-lying green foliage. Mostly shrubs. Given he was the only living person employed by the plantation owner, Russ liked being alone as he looked out over the green-and-blue expanse of the island and the shoreline.

Afternoons, he and the old man—he'd learned his name was Hector Grako—each went to work at the processing mill adjacent to Hector's farmhouse. Russ would operate a husking machine, removing the day's yield of coffee beans from the ruby-red cherries they came in. Hector, meanwhile, operated a grinder where he de-skinned the beans after Russ husked them. Then, the two of them would sort out the beans based on quality.

Russ was proud that his yields were always higher-quality than those brought back by the automated harvesters. Hector had commented on Russ' diligence one day, telling him that, thanks to Russ, he'd signed a new deal to export more coffee beans to the high-income planets of Obrigan and Sarsi. "Meanwhile, we ship all the bad beans to places like Rhavego," Hector had explained to him with a chuckle at the start of the job. Once they'd filled enough bags, they'd take them down to a shipping dock on the north side of the island where space transport vessels sometimes touched down. Hector always handled those transactions.

They spent the evenings on Hector's porch, where the two men sat on rocking chairs and watched the sun go down. Hector would make some kind of drink. Usually lemonade, but recently Russ had asked Hector to make him some sweet iced tea instead. It reminded Russ of his childhood, sitting out in a lawn chair in the late Louisiana fall at a campfire outside their trailer, wearing Pa's too-large camo jacket and drinking sugary iced tea as he'd watched the dying embers of the fire.

Russ liked keeping his days busy with physical toil. That meant he slept deeper. Meant that the nightmares of all those civilians gunned down by the Syndicate didn't bother him as much. But every time he turned in early or didn't work hard enough to deplete his energy in full, the nightmares returned and he woke up in cold sweats.

It was a shitty time in his life to cut back on alcohol. The bottle had always been his way of forgetting. Sure made him think less, at least. But every time he remembered the carnage back at the resort, a wave of self-loathing followed the misery. He wasn't the one pulling the trigger on all those civilians, but he'd worked with the same people who *had*.

At least Hector was nice enough not to burden Russ with conversation in the evenings. The two men would just sit in silence, maybe commenting about how pretty the sunset was, sometimes talking about the quality of the day's harvest, and nurse their drinks. He appreciated that Hector didn't ask him questions about his past.

It'd been three weeks, and Russ was surprised the Syndicate hadn't shown up yet. They'd still be hunting Russ, and their assassins had seen Russ leave with a coffee planter back on the main resort island. But the planet wasn't at a loss for small coffee-growing islands, and he knew the Syndicate presence on Haphis wasn't as widespread as on Zoledo. But he knew they'd find him someday.

"They're gonna come for you eventually," Russ said one night after taking a long drink of iced tea.

"I know," Hector said, letting out a ponderous sigh. "I don't keep that old rifle you might've seen back in the shed for nothing."

"You think you're gonna take on a squad of enforcers all by yourself?" Russ asked.

"What, and here I thought you might help me out." Hector chuckled. "You look like someone who can handle himself in a firefight."

Russ frowned. "Honestly, I think I might be more of a danger to you if I stay. I'm the one they're after."

"I don't expect them to be too kind toward me either way," Hector said. "And besides, if I had to pick the best way to go, going down guns blazing against my old employers might be damn near number one."

Russ raised an eyebrow at that. He'd had a sneaking suspicion that Hector used to be Syndicate, or had at least done business with them—otherwise, how had he been able to identify Russ' pursuers back at the main island as Syndicate assassins? But Hector didn't elaborate, so Russ left it at that. He sank into his rocking chair and watched the last vestiges of sun rays disappear beneath the horizon. Hector's automated fluorescent light unit snapped on.

Ten minutes passed, and Russ assumed they'd come into a tacit agreement to go back to their usual silence. But it seemed that their brief exchange had gotten a rise out of Hector. "You haven't asked me why I did what I did," the old man said.

Fine, Russ thought, *I'll play your game.* "Why did you do what you did?" he asked.

"Because I was in your position once. Or at least, I have a hunch I was."

You used to be the security adviser for the Earthborn refugee government, before you were fired in disgrace and had to work with the Syndicate because no one else would take you? Russ wanted to ask. He stayed silent and let Hector continue instead.

"Long time ago, I grew up in some dead-end town on Obrigan. Not Obrigan City, mind you: one of the old farming towns way outside the city. I was part of a big family. Mom and dad were always in and out of jail. Drugs were everywhere. It was the kind of place the big criminal gangs really cleaned up with their recruiting drives.

"They got me and all my siblings. Except one brother, who was lucky enough to land some gig on a deep-space salvage job. One day, he came back for all of us. Got us all out before it was too late. But then we got old, and we all scattered.

"Somehow, I ended up here. Used to hire seasonal labor during the warm months, then I invested in the automated harvesters that everyone else uses. That's why I still had a handful of manual harvesters sitting in the shed, waiting for someone like you to show up.

"Back then, they weren't called the Syndicate—this was before the big consolidation where the Syndicate started up and forced everyone else out of the black market—but it's the same principle. I know the kinds of people they employ. I know how they carry themselves. And I know who they prey on."

Hector turned to look at Russ. His stare gave Russ a feeling that he'd guessed far more about Russ' background than he felt comfortable with.

"I don't know the specifics, but I know enough about you," Hector said. "Desperate people always turn to the criminal underground. They always get chewed up and spat back out. And then the Syndicate send their henchmen after them. Rinse and repeat."

"Sounds like you have me all figured out," Russ said, averting Hector's stare. He swirled his glass. About half the ice had melted, so he took a long drink of slightly tea-flavored cold water.

"I was hoping you'd fill me in on the specifics," Hector said. "After all, I just bared my soul for you to see." The old man laughed.

"What's it to you?" Russ asked. "I just work for you." Not that he was even getting a salary. According to the terms they'd negotiated, Russ' free room and board was the entirety of his payment.

"Well, I figure you'll be off soon, and it gets lonely here. Especially now that the damn robots do everything," Hector said.

Russ sighed, staring out over the thin patch of ground still illuminated by the porch light. He'd come to trust Hector, although he didn't feel like telling him everything. Especially not his status as a refugee. Hector hadn't really talked much politics with him, but what if Hector was an Offspring sympathizer?

"I...used to run with some people," Russ said finally. "Good people. Not like these Syndicate types. People you could trust, people who always had your back."

"Uh huh," Hector said, nodding along. "Did they die or something?"

Russ shook his head and looked at the wooden floor beams between his feet. "I let them down. I failed them. They...were trusting me to do a job. And I thought I was doing the job really well, but it turns out I wasn't."

It was the best way to paraphrase that Nadia ended up doing a better job keeping their people safe and secure than he did. Or at least, the best way he could come up with on the spot. Not a day went by where he didn't think about Isadora's final admonishment: *You were brought out of cryo to be my security adviser, and yet, your actions have done little but make us less secure in this system.*

"So they let you go?"

"No. I was...demoted. But I couldn't bear to face them again after failing them so badly. So I left."

"Just like that?" His tone of voice suggested that Hector was genuinely aghast.

"They deserved better than me."

"So you joined the Syndicate to punish yourself?"

Russ opened his mouth to respond that, no, of course not, it was just a matter of practicality. But wasn't that effectively what he'd done? He could've taken another job in Isadora's government, albeit lower-ranking than chief security adviser. He still remembered Isadora calling after him as he'd turned to leave the underground bunker beneath New Arcena, her voice echoing in the tunnels. What would she have offered if he'd turned around instead of ignoring her? Maybe joining the Syndicate really *was* an act of self-flagellation.

"I don't know," Russ shrugged. "Honestly, I don't know a lot of things. I used to be real sure of myself. That's what got me in trouble in the first place."

Hector nodded, digesting the information. The two sat in silence for some time, before the old man spoke up again. "If your people are still out there, and they're as good as you say, they'll take you back. Might do you a lot of good to get out of the black market world. Trust me." The old man's voice turned softer and kindlier than Russ had heard so far.

The thought of facing Isadora again, or even Nadia or Vincent or Riley, just felt like too much. "They're better off without me," Russ muttered.

Hector frowned but accepted that, and they returned to sitting in silence. "Well," the old man said eventually, "it's getting late, and we're getting a shipping vessel tomorrow. Might try to turn in early, get a good night's sleep."

Russ stayed out on the porch for half an hour after Hector went to bed, listening to the gentle splashes of the ocean way down on the shoreline, and the wind rumbling through the foliage.

·   ·   ·

The next day, Russ was reading an update from Riley on her new security procedures during his lunch break when he heard the shot ring out. It was coming up the mountain, from Hector's farmhouse. Russ immediately sprinted in that direction. He drew his handgun from his holster as soon as he got to the farmhouse, crouching low below a window. He figured the low foliage would make for a perfect hiding spot for a team of Syndicate enforcers. Better to not take any chances.

Russ pushed the window open and hopped over into Hector's dwelling. His boots crunched over shattered glass, a trail that led him into the study on the other side of the house. That was where he found Hector gripping his plasma rifle, crouched low right next to a shot-out window.

Russ ducked immediately, and a shot flew in through the window and struck the wall where Russ had been standing just seconds before. Plaster crumbled off onto the floor. Russ' mind played back the screams of the hotel residents every time another shot flew by. "Syndicate sharpshooter team," Hector explained.

"Any idea what their position is?" Russ whispered, crawling forward to join him.

"Hell if I know," Hector said. He edged the barrel of his rifle out of the window, peering through the scope, and pulled the trigger. Then he got back down into cover and another shot flew through the window in response. "Damn! Dunno if I got anyone," the old man said.

"I'll circle around back," Russ said, "you cover me. We'll catch them in a pincer."

Hector shook his head emphatically. "No. *No.* This isn't your fight." Then he tilted his head toward the north side of the island. "There's a shipping vessel coming in today. Head down to the dock.

Hopefully, you won't run into any Syndicate on the way."

"I thought you said you wanted me to help you fight," Russ growled.

"Can't you tell that was a damn joke?" Hector said. "And besides, I'm old. I've lived a good life, and like I said last night, giving my old bosses the middle finger on the way out is a good way to go. You go find those people you used to work with. They'll take you back. Don't spend your whole life wallowing in bitterness."

Russ gritted his teeth in response. He wasn't just going to leave a man behind on the firing line. He'd seen so much death in the last few weeks that one more casualty felt like too much.

"Go!" Hector shouted, drawing more fire from outside the window. "Run! Or I swear I'll shoot you myself!"

Russ didn't want to leave Hector, but images of Isadora and Riley and Vincent and even Nadia flashed through his head. He resolved to link back up with them someday. Apologize. It's what Hector wanted for him, and with the clarity of battle dawning on him, it was all Russ could think about. So he grabbed his rucksack from an adjacent room and ran. "Thank you," Hector called to him as Russ ran. "Thank you."

He raced through the shrubs, not daring to look back every time he heard another shot ring out. He didn't slow his pace until the shipping dock was in view. By then, the sounds of shots ringing out had gotten too quiet to hear if you weren't paying attention. Russ came to a halt and regarded the situation from behind a tree.

Sure enough, a supply shuttle had landed on the helipad. A crew of two was working on loading coffee bags into crates, and then loading those crates into the back of the shuttle. Russ figured a transport vessel was in orbit, and that the shuttle would head back up soon.

It only took a few seconds to come up with a plan. He worked his way around the perimeter, avoiding attention from the two workers. Eventually, Russ made his way to the crates stacked up near the rear of the supply shuttle. Waiting for the two crew to start talking, Russ made his move.

He tiptoed over to one of the crates, took one of the bags of coffee out, and gently placed it back on the ground. Then he slipped inside and pulled the lid back down. He took a small laser cutter out of his utility belt and began working on a series of holes in the crate's side to provide breathability.

It wouldn't be comfortable, but stowing away in a coffee crate was the best way to get off Haphis without drawing Syndicate attention. And he could open the lid to get out, stretch his legs, and steal supplies from the transport vessel once they were underway. Once he'd figured out the crew's routines.

He hoped that they were heading to a planet nearby, so he wouldn't be cramped up for weeks. He looked at the shipping manifest pasted to the underside of the lid. He was in luck.

Apparently, they were heading to a settlement called Kurskyn on the planet Rhavego.

CHAPTER 18

B oyd's absence from the *Exemplar* was starting to feel oppressive. Normally, they structured their days to include plenty of overlap: Nadia's first half of her days overlapped with Boyd's second half, and then Derek woke up once Boyd was done and Nadia had completed the first half of her day. The three of them would share a meal in the canteen, and then Boyd would go to bed.

Now, she and Derek worked opposite shifts. Nadia spent most of her days alone and in silence, other than a couple hours of overlap with Derek. But Derek's way of dealing with Boyd's absence usually involved reading alone in his room, which took away even the little socialization she was used to.

Nadia's newfound solitude wasn't too difficult to deal with. They'd be getting to Rhavego in just a few days, at which point she and Derek would have to go back to the same schedule. What *was* harder to deal with was picking up Boyd's slack.

If they ever got Boyd back—*when we get him back*, Nadia forced herself to think—she'd have to do a better job appreciating all the things he did to make the ship run smoothly. His background as a colonial mechanic and then an architect made him much better than either her or Derek at making sure the ship's systems were all working at peak efficiency. She still hadn't figured out how Boyd had worked his magic with the water recycling systems. Now, shower times were down to about three minutes.

Passing by a vent, Nadia caught a sudden whiff of a musky stench. She bent down and pulled the air filter out from a slot underneath the vent. Sure enough, it was coated with grime. "Dammit, Derek," Nadia muttered.

Both she and Derek had been having to cover some of the slack generated by Boyd's absence. Often, that meant double the work. First, reading all the archaic manuals and looking at ship maintenance how-to vids on the net just to figure out what the hell to do in the first place. Second, actually doing the damn jobs on top of their normal duties.

Nadia had tried to be patient with Derek, assigning him disproportionately less of Boyd's job duties. She'd even given him the simpler tasks, like cleaning the air filters. Apparently, he couldn't even remember that.

A frustrated Nadia stormed toward the canteen. Along the way, she passed through the vessel's mural hallway. A little less than a year ago, after founding a new settlement on Calimor, the children brought out of cryo to live in the settlement had asked to paint a mural inside the *Exemplar* to express their thanks. Nadia and her crew couldn't say no. Ever since, they'd had a colorful painting of about a dozen smiling stick figures—including Nadia, Boyd, and Derek—decorating the canteen corridor.

Inside the canteen, Derek was finishing his dinner. If he kept to his normal schedule, he'd head to his room in another few minutes. "Look," Nadia said, dropping the dirty air filter on the table, "I've been really patient. When you had a hard time figuring out the engine calibrations, I took that one. Same thing with the missile scrambler maintenance. But seriously? *Cleaning the air filter*? What exactly is so hard about this job?" Her voice rose far higher in pitch than she'd intended.

Derek put his fork down, leaving a few bites of potato and textured protein mash uneaten in his bowl. "I'm sorry," the man said, avoiding eye contact. "I just forgot."

"I know it's been hard, but it's been *days* since Boyd was...taken," Nadia said.

"I have no excuse," Derek said, his countenance fixed in a drooping position.

"Dammit," Nadia muttered, wiping her brow with her forearm. She wished Derek would at least fight back or something. It was hard to stay angry at him when he was being so mopey. "Just...try to do better, okay?" she asked finally.

Derek nodded. He took his food bowl over to their composter, scraped the remnants of his dinner in, and placed his bowl and fork into the washing unit. Nadia caught a glance of the DH written on the side of the bowl. Another colony they'd founded a few months ago had made engraved porcelain dinnerware for the whole crew, using a local kaolinite deposit near their settlement. Derek left for the ship's dormitory wing in silence.

Nadia sighed and headed for the cockpit. She hadn't been sleeping well ever since she'd learned about the New Arcena bombing, and the breakdown of the Enther peace talks and Boyd's capture had only exacerbated that. She'd nearly doubled her time spent in the *Exemplar*'s pool sphere, but the exercise didn't seem to relieve her stress like it normally did.

Plus, she'd never been good at dealing with the sting of failure. Looking back, it felt like everything had just gone so well during their first year in the Natonus System. Which was ridiculous—at the time, Nadia had always felt like she was on the brink of catastrophic failure—but the ways her mind had processed the events of the first year had made her feel almost indestructible. The past few weeks had brought her crashing back down to reality.

And now she'd sunk so low that she'd taken it out on Derek, who'd been a true and loyal companion ever since they'd met. He'd risked his life countless times for their mission, and saved Nadia's life countless more. Sure, maybe he could stand to learn a bit of diligence when it came to shipboard chores, but was that really such a sin?

Once she got to the cockpit, she settled into the co-pilot's chair and checked her messages. The computer had logged a new transmission since the last time she'd checked. The sender was listed as Jibor, Leila. *Mom*. Nadia grinned and opened the message.

The message began with a meandering explanation of how Leila and Nadia's father Rashad had been working hard on setting up a regular interfaith community gathering. At first, the other colonists had done private congregations, but religious diversity in the colony was so high that single-faith gatherings might only attract a handful of individuals. So Leila had been pressing to do a wider communal get-together. When he wasn't helping Nadia's mother with community outreach, Rashad had been upgrading the automated irrigation systems with newer, high-quality materials they'd imported a month ago.

Then, Nadia's mother closed with a gentle request that Nadia let her know she was safe. Leila had read the news reports coming out of Enther, she explained in her message, and was worried about Nadia's safety. Although she knew that nothing bad was going to happen to her.

Nadia felt her eyes water. Nothing like the comfort of a mother's unconditional love to get her through dark times. She immediately typed a response, telling her mother how horribly the peace summit had crashed and burned, followed by Boyd's capture, although Nadia left out exactly how many people had been shooting at her. No need to scare her poor mother. She then described the visit to the Left Foil, and finally, their desperate voyage to Rhavego.

Nadia felt calmer—even something as simple as making sure her inbox was clear helped slow down her racing mind—and realized that Derek deserved an apology. Sure, he could do a better job keeping up with his share of Boyd's chores, but Nadia had been unduly harsh with him. She pushed herself out of her chair and headed for the dormitory wing. On the way, she passed by a couple of pictures taken of her, Boyd, and Derek they'd printed out to decorate the starboard wing. Most were group photos at sites they'd surveyed for future settlement.

When she got to Derek's cabin, she saw the distinctive soft-yellow reading light that was always on before he went to bed. She rapped her knuckles on the door lightly.

Derek was sprawled out on his bed, reading a dusty old book with an intense look in his eyes. Unlike Boyd, who had a meticulously arranged room, or Nadia, with her soaring inspirational posters and her mother's cross-stitch, Derek's room was almost painfully minimalistic. He had a desk that was completely barren, a clothes drawer—equally empty, at least from the outside—and only a single bedsheet. The only life in his room came from a bookshelf he'd installed over his cot, with well over a dozen decrepit texts he'd brought with him from Ikkren.

Derek looked up and closed his book. "Come in," he said softly.

Nadia walked over to his desk and pulled out the ottoman beneath. She sat down and crossed her legs, shifting from side to side uncomfortably. Apologies had never come naturally.

Derek must've seen the awkwardness in her expression, because he held out the book. "Do you want to see what I've been reading?"

"Sure," Nadia said immediately, leaping at the chance to postpone the apology.

"It's a book of Ikkren poetry," Derek said.

After feeling the graininess of the brown synthetic leather cover, Nadia was almost afraid to touch the brittle pages. A couple felt like they were about to rip out. Carefully, Nadia peeled the spine open to the page Derek had been reading, catching a whiff of that perfect old-book smell.

"The first time settlers arrived on Ikkren, in 2383—I was only two at the time—we barely had anything at all for the first few years," Derek explained. "Everyone spent their entire lives in tents, huddled for warmth, while we desperately tried to import more colonial supplies and chop down the forests to construct settlements."

Nadia hardly dared to breathe. Derek talking about his past was so rare she could count the times it'd happened on one hand.

"I have no real memory of any of this, of course," Derek continued.

"But the stories all say that reading poetry by firelight became a common practice during the early years. We didn't have access to the solar net at that point, and communication with the core planets was spotty. So the early settlers would take turns writing and reciting poetry over campfires until the middle of the night. Luckily, they'd brought plenty of empty physical books with them."

Nadia figured that explained why the book she was holding, as well as the others on Derek's bookshelf, looked so much older than just two decades. It might've been printed in the earliest days of Natonese settlement. A vivid scene swirled into view in her head. Nadia had spent many nights huddling in a tent in the middle of the frozen Ikkren wilderness, so she didn't find it hard to imagine the tents flapping in the fierce night wind, a dozen hardy settlers all sitting on logs around a roaring campfire.

It was a comforting mental image. One that helped dispel the surging anxiety and frustration that was ravaging her. She loved the contrast between the rugged toughness that life on the frontier required and the artistry of poetry readings.

She looked down at the page Derek had been reading. It was a simple, unstructured three-line poem:

Icy expanses bathed in moonlight and flickering fire
Tearing winds that hew the soul asunder
An empire's ambitions frustrated.

"From the very beginning, our people's discontent with the Union took center stage in the colonization efforts," Derek continued. "Most Ikkren settlers came from rural Obrigan, where we supported the Union rebels against the old regime. But the Union government never seemed to do much to repay their debt to us."

An empire's ambitions frustrated. Nadia had often felt that the Union ought to be considered an empire. What else would you call an expansionist political power with an overwhelming military superiority over its rivals? She couldn't help but admire the dogged optimism of thinking that a few backwater settlements could halt the Union's expansion.

But those tent encampments eventually grew into real colonies, united under the Horde defense umbrella, which had gone toe-to-toe with that same expansionist empire's military machine and come out bruised but unbeaten. And for the rest of Tricia Favan's tenure, Union expansion had ended at the Natonese asteroid belt. *An empire's ambitions frustrated indeed*, Nadia thought.

"What do you think about all that?" Nadia asked gently, still calmer than she'd been when she entered.

Derek looked at the wall, lost in concentration. "Hating the Union was more common among the first generation: the ones who were already well into adulthood during colonization. Growing up, I always saw myself as part of a bigger system. I was just as much Natonese as an Ikkrener.

"But that was all very hypothetical back then. As a teenager, all I wanted was to go to university, thinking that was my ticket off-world. But then the university closed, and the only way anyone my age was getting off Ikkren was signing up for an expedition party. I did that for almost a decade until we met back on Calimor."

"So this is both of our first time coming to the core worlds, to Union space," Nadia realized.

Derek nodded solemnly. "I already noticed it on Enther. The way that people look at me when they learn who I am. It's hard thinking

I'm Natonese just like them when all they do is give me dark looks. Sometimes I...I've been missing home. For the first time in my life."

Nadia didn't really understand how Derek would've been identifiable as an Ikkrener, other than *maybe* his long-ish hair. But she figured the media focus on her and her crew in the aftermath of the near-conflict with the Union might've brought Derek and his background into the public limelight as well.

"Do you miss Earth, ever?" Derek asked, a forlorn drawl to his voice.

It was a strange question, one that Nadia was surprised she hadn't really considered, even two years after arriving in Natonus. She'd always just been so busy, always throwing herself into her work, that she'd never paused to take a breath and consider whether she was homesick.

"I...I miss my parents' farm," she said at last, trying to assess her feelings on the fly. "I miss the closest neighbor being out of visual range. I miss walking to her house, barefoot on unpaved dirt roads."

She missed her work to an extent—the resettlement nonprofit had always been fulfilling, morally uncomplicated—but her new job as Isadora's settlement adviser was just an extension of her old career.

Her mind jumped back to the task at hand. Derek still deserved an apology. "Look..." she said, staring at her feet.

"I know what you're going to say," Derek interjected. "And you don't need to. We've all been under so much stress ever since we heard about New Arcena. Plus, I understand missing Boyd. He...has become a better friend than I would've thought possible. Just like you."

"And *you*," Nadia said, standing up to leave. She passed Derek back his book of poems and headed to the door, pausing before she exited. "I understand missing home," she said. "But just know that this ship will *always* be your home too."

Derek nodded in appreciation. "Thank you. And goodnight." The two exchanged grins and Nadia closed the door shut. And then she went back to her shipboard duties. She was still upset and frustrated, but some of the burden hanging on her shoulders had finally lifted.

CHAPTER 19

Tanner was nearly giddy with excitement at the sound of the approaching gunships. Brandon Zahem was finally returning to their joint hideout in the Enther jungles alongside the rest of his fighters, supposedly with several captives in tow. Tanner hoped that Nadia Jibor was among them. She'd die by his hand within the hour.

The aircraft arrived at the helipads outside of their wilderness refuge. Their engines stuttered before coming to a rest. Tanner watched from the edge of the nearby forests, his arms crossed over his chest, as Brandon's fighters jumped out of the gunships. Almost a dozen blindfolded captives were in tow. Tanner scanned the field of captives with hawkish eyes, trying to figure out which one was the newar settlement leader.

Even partially hidden behind the blindfolds, however, none of the prisoners matched Nadia Jibor's profile. Tanner's mouth flinched for a moment. He went storming after Brandon.

The radical Ashkagi leader hopped out of one of the gunships, shouting orders at his underlings as they continued to unload more prisoners, ordnance, and wounded comrades from their aircraft. His chest inflated far more than was necessary as he shouted his commands.

Tanner walked straight for Brandon, placed his hands on the other man's shoulders, and hissed, "Where is Nadia?" He stood as tall as he could, towering over the stout figure of the Ashkagi leader.

Brandon shrugged Tanner's hands off violently, but his troops nearby didn't respond. Even when confronted, Brandon didn't inspire enough loyalty to get his followers to intervene: a useful data point to keep in mind. "We looked for her, but we couldn't find her," he said, averting his eyes.

Tanner searched the man's eyes, trying to determine whether Brandon was telling the truth. On one hand, the man could be right: it was no doubt chaotic in Kal Mekan, and finding one individual in all the mess would've been difficult, not to mention dangerous. On the other, Brandon hardly had any incentive to try. The fight against the invaders wasn't his fight.

Something about the way the other man avoided Tanner's gaze suggested it was the latter.

Tanner regretted not pushing harder to send some of his own people on the Kal Mekan raid. But most Offspring forces were deployed across the planet, helping bolster the Ashkagi radicals. And Brandon had handpicked his people for the Kal Mekan attack, due to its vital nature to the plan. Tanner, meanwhile, had been stuck guarding the hideout.

Brandon turned to his people. "Come on! Let's get these people processed!" he shouted. Several Ashkagi took the blindfolded prisoners to a stairwell leading to the hideout sublevel.

Then the man turned to Tanner once again. "Even if we couldn't get Nadia for you, we were able to capture a member of her survey team: Boyd Makrum."

Tanner tried to recall any details about Nadia's crew. He knew she headed a survey team of three, and that the other two were native Natonese. He followed the other man into the hideout while Brandon relayed orders to two of his subordinates. The four of them moved down a series of stone hallways.

"The only reason your attacks succeeded elsewhere on the planet was because of Offspring fire support," Tanner hissed, cutting through the chattering of Brandon's two subordinates.

Brandon turned, let out a frustrated sigh, and waved away his two followers. They headed down an adjacent corridor. Brandon rested a hand on the wall to steady himself, his forehead buried in the other hand.

He looked tired, probably more so than Tanner had ever seen him in their yearlong working relationship. His forces' coordinated attacks on Junta towns and villages had dominated the planetary news coverage. Almost overnight, Brandon Zahem had become the most notorious resistance member on the entire planet, eclipsing even Noah Tasano.

Tanner knew Brandon had been planning the attacks for a long time. Still, there was a difference between being philosophically prepared for a big moment and actually going through with it. Tanner had been there.

But the Offspring were the key puzzle piece at the heart of

Brandon's plans. Their numbers nearly doubled Brandon's forces. If Tanner hadn't allowed Brandon to command his own people, Brandon's attacks would've been toothless and easily repelled by government security forces.

"The only reason *your* attack on New Arcena was successful was because of the training my people gave yours," Brandon said, narrowing his eyes. "Cooperation is a two-way street."

Tanner opened his mouth to respond, but he realized he didn't have a good retort. In some ways, he and Brandon were in opposite positions: Brandon was looking to start a mass uprising, despite having a small number of well-trained followers, whereas Tanner was trying to carry out technically demanding operations with a cohort of untested recruits.

"Now if you'll excuse me," Brandon said, brushing past Tanner, "I have more work to do."

Tanner scowled at his back and then headed for his room. He stormed past the doorway and desperately searched the top of his desk for anything he could throw at the wall. Coming up empty, he slammed his palm into the stone instead. Wet moss collected between his fingers.

He ripped his chair back from the desk and plopped down immediately. His entire plan had been to follow up the attack on New Arcena with a live cast execution of Nadia Jibor. It'd be the perfect spectacle, especially while the bulk of his forces were out helping Brandon. Somehow, he didn't think killing a Natonese native like Boyd for all the net to see would have the same effect.

Beyond that, there were larger issues looming. For the foreseeable future, more and more Offspring members were going to be tied down fighting under Brandon's banner. Leasing his forces to Brandon had been a necessary evil to secure the training they needed, but it limited Tanner's options in the short term.

And while he'd never completely trusted his counterpart, it was increasingly hard to shake the feeling that Brandon had played him. Maybe he'd even purposely neglected to bring in Nadia, since he knew that delaying Tanner's plans would keep Offspring forces in limbo. That would then funnel more manpower into Brandon's own operations.

Tanner's eyes narrowed, fixating on a small patch of wood in the middle of his desk. Perhaps it was time to start rethinking their partnership.

But it'd be best to leave such considerations for another time. For now, the vast majority of Offspring personnel were off to the far reaches of the planet. Brandon maintained a sizable majority of the manpower at the hideout. Trying anything right now would be suicidal.

Tanner's thoughts turned to the one asset he had: Boyd Makrum. Tanner's mind started running through a series of possibilities. Maybe he could interrogate Boyd and learn something that'd bring him closer to capturing Nadia herself. Maybe he could even convince the man that subservience to an invader—a *female* invader, no less— was unbecoming.

What if Tanner could convince Boyd to see the error in his ways? What if he could get Boyd to publicly denounce Nadia, the newar settlement effort more broadly, and state support for the Offspring in a live cast net video? Tanner felt his arms shaking in excitement at the prospect. It was no public execution, but it was *something*. And it'd keep the Offspring in the public limelight after the carnage at New Arcena.

Most of Tanner's recruitment experience had been with individuals already sympathetic to the Offspring cause. He'd never handled a conversion case like Boyd before. Unfortunately, many of his most experienced recruiters were out in the field, which meant he'd need to see what he could do on his own.

Putting aside his growing frustration and suspicion with Brandon, Tanner leapt back to his feet and headed for a stairwell opposite his dorm, taking him to the sublevel. With each step, Tanner's boots left another slick, muddy footprint.

Normally, taking prisoners wasn't part of the radical Ashkagi's MO, so the sublevel had only recently been converted into a cell block. Months earlier, the Ashkagi had used the area to practice marksmanship with new Offspring recruits. As Tanner headed for the far end of the sublevel, he passed by what used to be a shooting range. A plasma-proof holographic target was lying in the middle of the floor.

Tanner headed down another few hallways and finally arrived at the cell block. He nodded to the two Ashkagi on guard outside, who directed him to the rearmost jail. The block had been a practice fire zone, where Offspring and Ashkagi used to assemble into two teams to work on squad tactics. The twisting walls and maze-like corridors made it easy to lose track of where you were.

Tanner followed the meandering path until he arrived at the last cell. He pushed past a haphazardly constructed wooden gate and found himself face-to-face with a blindfolded Boyd Makrum.

The man was not what Tanner had expected. When he pictured the kind of person who'd give up a good career to play second fiddle to a newar woman, it was someone so desperately plagued by insecurities that they were blind to their own weakness. He imagined Boyd as a hunched-over, self-loathing loser, not unlike the man Tanner used to be when he was just some corporate wage slave working for Veltech.

Boyd looked nothing like Tanner had imagined. He was tall, broad-shouldered, with light brown skin and a buzz cut. He seemed muscular enough, kept his back straight, and sported a well-defined jawline. He didn't seem like the kind of person consumed by self-hatred.

That could only mean one thing: that the delusion went far deeper than even Tanner could've imagined. It was like Boyd was so deep in a forest—appropriate, given their location—that he'd lost all sense of direction. Boyd was so disoriented that up was down and down was up.

It was Tanner's responsibility to help guide the man back to the light. Just looking at the prisoner immediately dashed any hopes of quickly producing some kind of denunciation vid. Tanner would have to spend a long time working on Boyd. But he hoped that, given long enough, he could show Boyd the error of his old ways.

He walked up to the other man and gently eased the blindfold off his face. "Where am I?" Boyd asked immediately, his eyes darting frantically from one end of the cell to the other. If Boyd was trying to keep the panic out of his voice, he was doing so poorly.

"You're in the middle of the Enther jungles. Far away from any town, city, or village," Tanner said.

"Where are my friends?" Boyd asked. "Are they safe? What happened back at Kal Mekan? Are you part of Brandon Zahem's radicals? Can I at least get my wrister back?"

Tanner grinned and stopped himself from rolling his eyes. *We'll play twenty questions first*, he thought. *Then the conversion work begins.* Tanner let Boyd's usage of the word *wrister* slide, even though it was a newar bastardization. And Boyd calling Nadia his *friend* made him cringe. "The newar you traveled with has left En-ther," Tanner said.

The other man narrowed his eyes. "That's a dirty slur. Has been for the last year. Maybe you aren't aware of it if you haven't been on the core worlds recently."

Tanner frowned. "It's a combination of *new* and *arrival*. It's purely descriptive: that's what they are."

"Maybe it *used* to be purely descriptive," Boyd said, shrugging. "But now it's been tarred by association with the Offspring. And Na-dia's probably my best friend, so I *don't want to hear it*."

"I think we should move on," Tanner said, trying to keep the frus-tration out of his voice. *This is going to take a* long *time,* he thought. "My name is Tanner Keltin. You probably haven't heard of me, but I prefer it that way. And I'm not affiliated with Brandon's Ashkagi rad-icals at all, although my organization has partnered with them for some time. I am Offspring."

Boyd's head shot up and his eyes widened. "Murderer," he said. "You butchered innocent people at New Arcena."

"No one at New Arcena was innocent," Tanner said. "Do you know what people call it when millions of outsiders show up at the edge of our system, ignore our laws, set up colonies, and expand throughout the outer rim? That is an *invasion*. But because the Union is headed by some weak-kneed coward in the form of Tricia Favan, we're calling it a *refugee migration* instead.

"So what my people did—what I commanded them to do—on New Arcena wasn't murder. It was self-defense. The media lapdogs are calling it *terrorism* because they're just as blind as the Union govern-ment."

"You're not just part of the Offspring," Boyd said. "You're their leader."

"Correct," Tanner said. "Ever since Owen Yorteb was captured, I've taken his place. But when the invaders arrived, almost two years ago, I was just like you: blind to the threat they posed, unaware of the fragility of Natonese society. That's how I know I can help you."

It felt damn good to reveal his control of the Offspring to someone on the outside. Tanner mostly didn't crave the notoriety that came with being in the public limelight, but no one outside of his immediate circle knew who he was. Even Rebecca didn't know he was affiliated with the Offspring. Deep down, Tanner believed every man had primal fantasies about being recognized as dangerous.

"I don't want your help," Boyd sneered. "I want to get out of here, off this planet, and go see my crew. But I'm guessing you're gonna torture me for information, right? Try to get me to give up intel on my friends?"

Tanner shook his head vigorously. "Of course not. You're one of *us*, Boyd. You're Natonese by birth. That means you belong here. The problem is, you've been flying with Nadia for so long you don't even question it. She's been giving you orders, bossing you around, all while using you for your labor. Tell me: what are you getting out of all this?"

"I…" Boyd said, looking at the floor, "I got to see my homeworld for the first time in a decade. And after spending years always staying on the move, never committing to anything, I finally found a place that felt like home."

Stupid sentimental bullshit, Tanner thought. At least Boyd wasn't refusing to talk to him. He could tell the man was fearful, and fear turned some people highly talkative. Tanner pegged Boyd as one of those types. "I mean, materially," Tanner said. "What is Nadia providing for you?"

"You mean, besides free room and board on the *Exemplar*?"

"Yes. I understand that flying on Nadia's ship gives you a sense of purpose. Or at least, you think it does. But how is serving her in *your* best interests? Is she helping set you up for your future? Giving you career opportunities?"

"It...it doesn't work like that," Boyd said. His voice had gotten quieter.

That seemed like a promising start, at least. The doubt creeping into Boyd's voice was apparent. Now for the first push. "You are a strong person, Boyd," Tanner said gently. "You aren't meant to be a slave for some woman who wasn't even born here. Join me. Join *us*. Together, we will save this system before it is overrun by the enemy."

Boyd muttered something. Tanner was fairly confident it sounded like "could I get some water, at least?" but he couldn't be sure. And if he was right, that already felt like a breakthrough. Providing comfort to your prisoner was the first step in forming a real connection.

He leaned in closer to Boyd, just to make sure. "What was that?" Tanner asked. Boyd muttered something again, still mostly inaudible, so Tanner leaned even closer. The two men's noses were only inches apart.

Which was when Boyd's head snapped up, and the man spat straight at Tanner's face.

A wad of saliva landed square on the bridge of Tanner's nose and began dripping toward the floor. "I'll never join you," Boyd said fiercely. "You're just some killer."

Tanner stood back up, wiped his face with the mesh fabric around the elbow of his suit, and turned to leave. "Then you can rot in this cell until you see reason," Tanner snarled. He stormed out, slammed the wooden gate shut, and left Boyd behind in the dark, damp cell.

CHAPTER 20

The flurry of correspondence every time Isadora opened her wrister had only gotten longer after agreeing to an election with Sean Nollam. She was used to the status updates on the settlement project, but that was now accompanied by polling data, news clips from a couple of independent refugee-focused media organizations that'd sprung up to cover the race, and strategy recommendations from Valencia Peizan.

Today, sitting on a bench outside of a large convention room in downtown Obrigan City, she hardly had the attention to focus on her inbox. She was about to hold a virtual town hall—an idea pitched to her by Valencia a few days earlier—where she'd be live cast to thousands of wrister projectors across the Natonese outer rim. Meanwhile, she'd be standing in an empty auditorium they'd rented out for a half-hour, surrounded by holographic projections from thousands of potential supporters.

She was no stranger to constituent meetings, although she was pretty sure the largest one she'd held as city councilor in Seattle was only attended by about a dozen people. And they'd mostly just complained about property taxes. It was *always* property taxes.

Isadora had always been most comfortable in small groups. She'd never been one to give huge, thundering speeches before large crowds. Somehow, even tax-related whining was making her nostalgic. She'd crossed her right leg over her left, and her right foot bobbed rapidly.

At least she had something to look forward to when it was over. After over two months, Meredith had finally agreed to bring Rebecca Keltin over for dinner. Isadora found herself surprisingly nervous about that. Since this was Meredith's first girlfriend, Isadora had never been in this position before. It was kind of like a first date, where you wanted a stranger's approval, but without any romantic subtext. Isadora just wanted Rebecca to like her, and to not get in the way of her daughter's budding relationship. Maybe check to make sure Rebecca wasn't some deranged psychopath, but Isadora had always trusted Meredith's judgment of her peers.

She took a deep breath. *Just one more hour, and then you can go home and get started on cooking*, Isadora thought, closing her eyes. *Just make it through. You can do it.*

She checked her wrister. Still had ten minutes left. She went through the torrential flood of messages to pass the time.

The first was an update on a near-scare from a remote colony in the Bitanu wilderness. Apparently, a man had smuggled a firearm past their new security screening services and was planning a shooting rampage. They'd only averted the carnage when a concerned bystander pointed out the would-be gunman's suspicious packages to colonial security forces. A team had then apprehended the gunman, who confessed his affiliation with the Offspring but killed himself via cyanide capsule before security personnel could conduct an investigation.

It was a pity they were still so in the dark with the Offspring. The little they'd gleaned from Owen Yorteb before his death indicated the Offspring had been a fairly small, streamlined operation. But the spying Tricia Favan had done on Isadora's behalf suggested that the Offspring's ranks had grown considerably. Still, they had no idea if they were dealing with a decentralized set of individual cells, or if someone had replaced the rogue Union general at the top of the Offspring hierarchy.

There was a follow-up note from Riley, explaining that she was reviewing the lapse in security that'd allowed an Offspring to smuggle a firearm through. She'd enhance screening procedures as soon as the review was completed. Still, the problem was that there were always going to be weak points in any security system.

Isadora flipped through a number of other messages, composed herself, and headed into the auditorium. It was a little early, but she could get comfortable in the space before the town hall officially started.

She had good reason to be confident. On Valencia's suggestion, Isadora had pulled the rug out from under Sean's issues-focused campaign. Alexander Mettevin had been working furiously to restructure their entire economy, providing small cash stipends for settlers on top of bare necessities and vital resources. Additionally, workdays had been cut to ten hours, not twelve.

That'd slow down the rate at which they were bringing people out of cryo, but such was the price of electoral politics. They'd thought they might be able to bring an additional 9 million out of cryo by year's end. Now, that number was hovering closer to 7 million.

The elected Consultative Committee was still a way's off, but Isadora had at least gone on record with the promise. She'd left Sean's campaign scrambling, trying to find some way to regain the momentum. All while Valencia had been flooding the airwaves with campaign ads describing Isadora's experience, how she'd navigated the complicated situation with the Union and avoided a calamitous war. The ads always ended with ominous music played over footage from right after the New Arcena bombing, and a reminder that only Isadora had the experience to keep everyone safe. In recent weeks, Sean had settled on a new line of attack: that Isadora was a phony, a flip-flopper, who couldn't be trusted since she'd stolen his platform. She had a feeling her ads were better.

It was time. Isadora stepped into the auditorium, which was completely empty.

A single chuckle escaped her mouth as she surveyed the unoccupied seats all around her. The room was silent, other than the faint echoes of her laugh and her footfalls. It felt funny that they'd rented the entire room, and she'd be the only one physically there.

She regulated her breaths and mentally rehearsed her talking points as projections started filling up the seats. From her perspective, it looked like a holographic constituent was sitting in each seat. From theirs, she'd appear as an ordinary wrister projection.

Since almost everyone was casting in from the outer rim planets, that meant there'd be a decent amount of time lag. To solve those issues, they'd employed a text chat synced to her wrister that'd send her messages submitted ahead of time. Participants could boost each other's questions either by simply clicking that they approved, or replying with a related question. Isadora would then respond in real time, which would be cast back with a time delay of a few hours. Unideal, but such were the logistical frustrations of conducting solar-wide politics.

Within another minute, she was surrounded by shimmering photons of light. She waved and smiled pleasantly as more and more projections flickered to life around her. *Don't show too much teeth*, she thought, remembering the advice Valencia had given her. *Back straight. Show warmth, but not weakness. All poise and grace.* The advice she'd gotten as a chief executive was always very different from the kind she'd gotten during her run for city councilor. Back then, everything was about relatability.

"Welcome," she said, once the projections stabilized. "Thank you all for taking the time out of your busy days to discuss some of the most important issues facing us today." She launched into her stump speech, briefly describing her experience, her trustworthiness, and her future plans.

Her wrister beeped with the first pre-recorded question. The message was flagged as security-related. Isadora hoped for a softball. "Our first question," she said to the audience, summarizing as she read, "is on the New Arcena attacks. The poster is asking what steps my administration is taking to ensure those attacks are never repeated."

A softball indeed. "Thank you for your question," Isadora continued graciously. She folded her hands over each other and placed them at her waist. "No other issue is more important to me and my team than the security and safety of all our people. My heart, like all of yours, I'm sure, still aches for everyone we lost at New Arcena," she said, her voice turning graver. "I am proud to say that, under my direction, we have upgraded screening and surveillance procedures at all our settlements.

"Just earlier, our new training protocols proved their effectiveness. Our security forces at one of our Bitanu colonies apprehended a suspected Offspring affiliate," she said. Better to jump out ahead of the issue and highlight the success of the training protocols, rather than the failure of the screening procedures. It was a bit of a misrepresentation, but it was one she figured she could get away with.

Isadora looked at her wrister for a follow-up question. There was a heavily approved reply, also flagged as security-related. *How can you seriously say you'll keep us safe*, the message read, *when you've been lying about the role you played in the New Arcena attack?*

Isadora had no idea what the poster was on about, so she kept reading.

The report your government released blamed a local Syndicate cell on Calimor for smuggling the New Arcena bomber and his explosives in, the message continued. *But YOU were the one who let the Syndicate set up shop on Calimor in the first place! So my question is: how can we trust you to keep us safe when you were partially responsible for the attack?*

Isadora felt her blood go cold. The poster wasn't totally wrong. She had, after all, directed Russ Kama to establish a relationship with the Syndicate last year. The price of securing weapons was helping the Syndicate set up a presence on Calimor. And Riley's report on the bombing implied the Syndicate was responsible for smuggling the bomber's explosives into New Arcena.

But Isadora hadn't personally negotiated the deal with the

Syndicate. And she'd kept the details of the deal strictly classified. The only three people who knew the full story were herself, Russ, and Riley. But plenty of other staffers could've pieced the puzzle together. It wouldn't have even been particularly hard to figure out.

Isadora's entire body felt like it was reeling from a punch as she tried to figure out how to respond. She never got a chance.

The chat on her wrister was suddenly flooded with accusations of Isadora being a liar. Dozens of projections stood up in the back rows, shouting "How dare you!" at the top of their lungs. With the time delay, it had to have been staged. There was no other explanation.

That pointed to Sean. Valencia had prepped her for all the awkward questions they'd expected related to Isadora's "phoniness." But, she guessed, he'd organized a campaign to sabotage the town hall and flood the text chat with a pivot to a different issue: one accusing her of a conspiracy. Sean's attack ads had all been feints.

Isadora could hardly speak over the jeers. Much less did she even want to. She figured anything she said would just be shooting herself in the foot. "I'm getting an urgent message from my staff," she lied, trying to at least feign concern on her face. "I'm sorry, but I'm going to have to cut this town hall meeting short."

She pressed a button on her wrister. Thousands of projected constituents fizzled and disappeared instantly. Frustrated and anxious, Isadora turned and left the auditorium.

Fuck.

.   .   .

Isadora felt utterly miserable, balled up on the couch in her residence, reading poll numbers on her wrister. Checking on polling updates was its own kind of addiction, even though the numbers didn't really change that much day-by-day. The averages suggested she was at 52% to 41% for Sean Nollam, with 7% undecided. She still had a decent lead, but she'd lost support, and all the undecideds seemed to be breaking for Sean.

And the polls hadn't captured her disastrous performance at the town hall earlier. She should've seen it coming. Anyone could register, which meant Sean could easily get all his die-hard supporters to sign up. She was sure that was what'd happened.

She heard a bubbling hiss from the kitchen and realized her pot of pasta had boiled over. Cursing, she closed the polling data on her wrister and ran over to the stove. She stirred the pasta and lowered the heat, and in another few seconds the water level went back down. Politics aside, at least she'd always have cooking. She wondered vaguely if it was problematic that her one stress-relieving activity was something necessary for survival, but she didn't feel like thinking through the implications of that right now.

Then she turned her attention to the vegetables she was sauteing next to the pot. Once everything was under control, she brought her wrister back up. *I'm doing pasta with tomatoes, green onions, peppers, and peas*, she wrote to her daughter, who was on her way back from school with Rebecca. *Do you think Rebecca will like that?*

...yes mom, I think she likes pasta, Meredith responded moments later.

Isadora frowned. *Well, can you ask her? And what kind of drinks does she like?* she typed. The town hall had left her anxious, with an irrational fear growing inside her that Rebecca wouldn't like her.

...I asked her, and she said pasta was fine. She drinks water was Meredith's response.

Okay, okay, I get it. I'll see you two soon.

Isadora went back to finishing up dinner. Once everything was done, she poured the sauteed vegetables on the pasta, and plated it with a drizzle of olive oil, rosemary, and oregano on top.

As Isadora put three plates on the dining table, making sure the napkins were all arranged perfectly, she suddenly began to fret about her appearance. She hadn't changed out of the blazer she'd worn to the town hall, making her look overdressed for the occasion. She nearly sprinted into her bedroom and tore through her closet, eventually finding a cardigan to swap for the blazer.

She couldn't pretend she wasn't the political leader of the Earthborn, but she wanted her position to play as small of a role in the evening's conversation as possible. For once, she didn't want to be Isadora Satoro, chief coordinator for the refugees. She wanted to just be *Mom*.

She heard the door open almost as soon as she'd hung her blazer back up. She smoothed her blouse out, composed herself, and headed out to meet Rebecca.

The girl was not exactly what Isadora had expected. She had light brown skin, with a ridge of freckles over her nose. She wore her hair straight, its color matched by the black nail polish she'd chosen for her fingers. Rebecca's dress and boots kept up the all-black theme. Meredith, on the other hand, was wearing a floral dress, had curled her hair, worn sandals, and painted each nail a different color.

"It's a pleasure to meet you," Isadora said warmly, extending her hand to Rebecca. Meredith watched with an awkward grin as Isadora shook Rebecca's hand. "You can just call me Isadora," she said with a wink.

"Good to meet you, Isadora," Rebecca said, her voice quiet. She enunciated each word with care.

"Come, sit!" Isadora said, gesturing to the table. The two girls shuffled over and took seats together, facing Isadora's lone chair. She went back to the refrigeration unit and retrieved a pitcher of water.

"So," Rebecca said as Isadora filled her glass, "I hear you're running in an election?"

Isadora winced but smiled. "Well, yes, although I don't think we need to bring up politics while—"

"—I think your opponent's a *dick*," Rebecca interjected.

Meredith laughed nervously, her eyes immediately darting to Isadora's face to see how her mother would respond to such language.

Isadora just cocked a wry grin. "I happen to have a similar assessment."

The three of them began working at their plates. "Tell me about yourself. I know you live with your aunt and uncle," Isadora said. Meredith had told her all about the tragic death of Rebecca's parents in an aircar crash almost eight years ago: a topic she was naturally planning on avoiding. "But do you have any siblings?" Isadora asked.

She looked away, pausing with her fork halfway to her mouth.

"No," Rebecca said finally. She had a habit of not making eye contact when she spoke, although it seemed more noticeable now than earlier. "Just me."

Isadora nodded, chewing on a tomato. "What about school? Any favorite subjects?"

"I dunno," Rebecca shrugged. "They're all kinda easy," she said with a smirk.

"Rebecca's *really* good at math," Meredith interjected. "I mean, I thought I was good at it, but I guess the century in cryo made me a little rusty. Rebecca's practically the only reason I'm passing at the moment."

Isadora knew her daughter was being modest, but the way Meredith's face lit up every time she talked about Rebecca produced a surge of joy in Isadora's chest. She found herself liking Rebecca: her attitude, her slight overestimation of her academic abilities that, most likely, would come back to bite her one day. Isadora could understand why Meredith was drawn to her.

And she was surprised at how relaxed she was feeling. Maybe she really could just leave everything else outside—the election, the threat of the Offspring, the everyday logistical issues of colonial development—and just be a mother meeting her daughter's first girlfriend. For the first time since arriving in Natonus, Isadora felt like her old self.

And if Sean Nollam wins this thing, she thought with a sudden twinge of anxiety, *I suppose that's all I'll be.*

CHAPTER 21

The motel Carson and Juliet were staying in was just as run-down as Carson had suspected it'd be. The carpet was ripped up in all the corners, plaster was peeling off the walls, and there was a giant wet circle in the ceiling. He half-expected a cockroach to scurry out from under his bed, before he remembered, thankfully, that the vermin hadn't followed humanity off Earth.

Juliet must've realized that she'd been pushing him too hard. She'd given him a few days to himself while she went around, trying to follow a couple of leads with the Kurskyn miners. She still maintained that their best bet was to investigate who was making their blasting equipment.

Still, Carson wasn't idle. In the mornings, Juliet had asked him to head to a shooting range at a nearby gymnasium—an odd combination, although he'd since learned that a lot of buildings were multifunctional, given the physical space limitations underground—so he could practice his marksmanship. "Never know when you'll need to fire a gun in this line of work," she'd told him, "and it's better to be a fuck-up at it now than when it counts."

Juliet would join him in the afternoons, and they'd practice sparring in the gym. Carson at least had a background in hand-to-hand combat thanks to his wrestling days, but it was good to work out the cobwebs.

When he was in his room, he spent most of the time watching the early episodes of the documentary series Stacy had been working on. Each episode was under twenty minutes long, and featured plenty of interviews with all generations of colonists, interspersed with soaring vistas of the Calimor landscape.

He always liked watching the vids Stacy produced. It made him feel more connected to his people, like what he was doing actually mattered. The more he saw the actual faces of people whose lives were threatened by the Offspring, the greater his sense of conviction grew. Apparently, Stacy had gotten hired to produce a couple of campaign videos for Isadora Satoro, so each episode ended with a disclaimer that the documentary was not trying to advocate for a specific candidate.

He checked his wrister and realized he was late for his scheduled target practice. Cursing, he closed the vid file he was watching, grabbed a naton credit chit in case he needed to buy anything while he was out, and left the motel.

The longer Carson had stayed in the mining town, the more he'd grown to appreciate the vertical structure of the settlement. The majority of the colony was underground, embedded in the Rhavego planetary crust. The deepest levels were the mining tunnels. Most workers lived in the lower underground levels, corralled into tiny, overcrowded, and run-down apartment units. The handful of families with money got to live in the dome-covered aboveground settlement, where the university was also located. The domed surface was where all the artificial parks, ponds, and lakes were located.

That all explained why the motel was squeezed in between two other hotel blocks. The cost of developing new real estate was expensive, since the colonial government had to invest in digging new tunnels beneath the crust to accommodate the developments. That meant everything was as small as they could get away with.

Carson squeezed through the crowds and headed for the gym. He was never quite sure where everyone else was going, since so many were chronically unemployed, subsisting off whatever they'd saved from the heyday of the planet's mining boom. But with over a million and half Natonese calling Kurskyn home, he supposed it made sense that everywhere was crowded.

He arrived at the gym and swiped his pass underneath a scanning unit at the door. The attendant hardly even looked at him. He figured he could probably just walk in if he wanted to, and no one would be any wiser.

Carson entered the gun range, checked out a standard-issue plasma handgun, and headed over to one of the lanes. He was the only one there. He put a pair of noise-cancelling headphones over his ears, even though the report of plasma weapons was nowhere near as loud as traditional slug-throwers. One time, he'd taken Stacy to a shooting range back outside Vancouver—they'd both hated it, Stacy more so— and all he could remember was how painfully *loud* it'd been.

The gentle thud-ping of plasma weapons was a welcome relief.

Plus, plasma weapons were lighter and recoiled less than slug-throwers. Carson didn't consider himself a *great* shot or anything—Juliet definitely didn't—but he felt he was improving, even over a matter of days. He was better about using his inhales to line his shots and his exhales to fire. There was almost a meditative quality to it, the kind that made it hard to remember he was handling a deadly weapon.

He pressed a few buttons. A holographic projector at the end of the range emitted a vaguely humanoid projection. Carson brought the plasma handgun to bear, lining up the sights in front of his right eye, and pulled the trigger. He hit the second innermost ring. The image displayed a red splotch where his shot had landed.

At first, Juliet had insisted on being with him, since he was "probably gonna be an idiot and shoot himself in the leg," in her words. But after only a few days, she trusted him enough to let him practice on his own. *Progress*, he thought, taking another couple shots. He was able to consistently hit the second innermost ring, with a handful in the center, and a single shot landing in the second outermost ring.

After a good half-hour of practice, and with a computer-generated accuracy score of 71%, he turned in the handgun and went to the gym's sparring area, where he always met Juliet for hand-to-hand drills.

Today, she was waiting for him. She hadn't changed into her workout clothes yet, and she was wearing a ridiculous, cheap-looking wig.

"Got a lead," Juliet said, barely even giving Carson time to wonder whether the plan had changed. "It's time sensitive. So go change, and I'll explain on the way."

Carson nodded and headed to the closest bathroom, where he switched from his gym clothes to the jumpsuit he normally wore.

After changing, he followed Juliet outside. They took a winding path down several corridors, each one seemingly more crowded and in greater disrepair than the last one. It was like they were going from the just-a-little-seedy part of Kurskyn to the super-fucking-seedy part. "No use sparring, anyway. You always kick my ass," Juliet muttered.

Which was true. Hand-to-hand combat was one of the few skills where Carson naturally excelled, and often beat Juliet soundly. It felt good, like it was a way to take out his lingering frustration over her harsh methods. She'd even called him out on his aggression once—"See? I told you everyone's got a dark side"—so he'd been more restrained ever since. It was like there was a constant struggle for his soul, between the kind of person Juliet thought Carson needed to be to become an effective spy, and the kind of person he felt he truly was.

"I finally had a breakthrough with a few of the contacts I've made. I met a handful of out-of-work miners," Juliet explained, "and they confirmed my suspicions. Most crews are buying blasting equipment from someone besides their normal supplier. I think he's some off-worlder. But even though these people didn't know who he was, my contacts said the supplier took a couple of classes at the university. Apparently, he has a close friend who frequents a mech fighting den in this part of the colony."

"Mech fighting?" Carson asked.

Juliet shrugged. "Apparently, it's a big deal here. The automated drones that've put so many miners out of work aren't exactly intelligent. A couple of entrepreneurs set up cage matches between repurposed mechs where the locals can bet on the winner. And you've got a large population who absolutely *hates* the drones—read, people who'd like nothing more than to watch two mechs beat the shit out of each other—so it became profitable real quick."

Now that Juliet had drawn Carson's attention to the phenomenon, he started seeing signs of betting everywhere. There were crowds of huddled Kurskyn denizens, with hand-drawn grids on the walls or the floor, where they took turns placing bets.

He knew plenty of his colleagues in grad school went on to help gambling addicts after graduation. It was sad to Carson that desperate people found ways to splurge on gambling while struggling to make ends meet, but hearing his colleagues' stories had made it clear that it was a normal phenomenon.

Even still, it hurt Carson to wade through a sea of human misery and desperation. He'd always known it was impossible to help everyone, but now he felt like he couldn't even help *anyone*. He kept his eyes straight ahead or slightly pointed upward, avoiding eye contact with the huddled masses on all sides.

The closer they got to the fighting arena, the louder a bass-and-synth medley got. When Juliet opened the door, the music turned deafening. The arena was packed, with various aromas—alcohol, hops, sweat, and unwashed bodies—all assaulting Carson's nostrils. The lighting was pitch-black, but a frantic strobe light gave Carson a headache almost instantly.

He hated it.

At the center of the arena were two mechs taking turns hitting each other. Every time one landed a particularly potent punch, sending pieces of the other mech's plating flying off toward the arena floor, the crowd roared in delight. It was almost funny to Carson: the two mechs pummeling each other almost reminded him of a certain set of fighting robots that every kid on Earth probably got as a holiday present. Seeing a childhood toy turned into a brutal release of catharsis for a desperate population was disorienting.

Carson and Juliet pushed their way through throngs of spectators, eventually finding an unoccupied bench on the upper levels. A staff member offered them a canister of glowing, neon green pills as they passed by. Both declined.

"Free drugs," Juliet said, having to practically shout in Carson's ear so he could hear her, "another way of making sure the customers keep coming back. And I bet they rake in more than enough profits from gambling to cover the cost of the drugs," she said.

If Carson had more time to think about it, he might've gotten disgusted with the fighting ring's predatory practices. As it stood, Juliet didn't let him reflect on it. She pulled up her wrister, displayed a holographic profile of a young male, and tapped a few buttons. "This is our target," Juliet shouted in his ear.

Carson pulled up his own device, and Juliet uploaded the profile onto his wrister. "He's somewhere in this shithole." She then dispatched another file to his wrister. "Here's your profile: a young, independently wealthy, wannabe mining tycoon who's trying to score some cheap blasting equipment for a big lead you just got. That way, you can strike up a conversation and figure out who our guy is," Juliet said.

"Got it," Carson said, studying the file. "Are you coming with?" he asked her.

"I already tried talking to him. He said I spooked him. Like I was an undercover cop or something. Ironic, huh? Anyway, that's why I hauled you along." *Guess that explains the wig*, Carson thought.

He began working his way through the spectators, trying to ignore the yelling every time he interrupted someone's view of the fighting ring. He looked down at the first file Juliet had sent him, which included a profile picture of the person of interest. As he was busy studying the picture and looking one way to see if he spotted the face anywhere in the crowds, he felt a sweaty body crash into him. Followed by a wave of foamy beer.

Carson's head spun around, where a man carrying two sloshing pints began shouting at him. Mostly unintelligibly, given his presumed level of intoxication and coupled with the noise interference of the arena. Carson mumbled an apology that didn't appear to satisfy the man even slightly, and pushed his way past a few audience members before the man could make a scene. He tried to ignore the fact that his jumpsuit was soaked, sticky, and smelled like hops.

As Carson arrived halfway around the arena from Juliet, he heard a loud crashing sound. In the ring, one of the mechs had landed a powerful hit on the other one's head. The wounded mech's ocular unit had detached, swinging around wildly and hanging by only a single wire. The crowd erupted in cheers.

Carson looked back down at the profile picture for only a minute. He heard a loud belch from his left, and a wave of hot air assaulted his cheek. Carson ducked and held his breath, trying desperately not to inhale the stench, and looked through the crowd.

When a beam from the strobe light landed on one row of people, Carson spotted the man from the profile pic. He started pushing his way toward him. When Carson was close enough, he waved, trying to attract his contact's attention. The young man seemed only partially focused on the fight, turning to face him almost immediately. "Can I help you?" he asked. The two retreated to the back of the audience stands so they could hear each other speak.

"I'm looking for someone, and I was told you know how to put me in contact with him," Carson said. He'd been improving at using cover stories in recent weeks, crediting his therapy background. He'd never completely misrepresented himself, but all therapists had to sometimes act in ways different from their real personas to build rapport with a patient.

"I got a lead on an untapped cobalt deposit on the other side of the planet," Carson said. He tried to project swagger and unearned self-confidence: the character traits he naturally associated with the kind of person who'd try to make it big on a risky business proposition. "Me and some buddies are trying to get there before the big corps stake a claim," he continued. "Thing is, we're looking for blasting equipment, and importing's too expensive. That's when someone dropped your name."

The young man nodded. "Yeah, I know a guy. Problem is, things are getting real dicey with all the extra security around. I think the government's getting all spooked ever since New Arcena and those Enther attacks. So my contact's trying to lie low for now."

Carson cocked a grin he thought would look ridiculous, but would be in-character for his persona. "I know how these things work. How much are you looking for?"

The man shook his head. "It's not a money issue, it's a *security* issue. No money's worth getting my name on some Union watchlist or whatever."

"I know some guys who work for the ISB," Carson blurted. It was an utterly implausible lie, but things weren't going well, and he was trying his best to improvise. "I can make them look the other way."

"Yeah? Seriously? I'm glad you heard about that cobalt deposit or whatever, but you don't sound like the type with *those* kinds of connections. Sorry."

Carson rubbed his lips together, trying to figure out his next move.

"Look," the other man said, sighing and placing his forehead in his palm, "you seem like you're on the level. I can give you my guy's name, but it might be a few weeks. Just gotta wait for all the paranoia to die down," the other man said.

"By that time, everyone's gonna know about the cobalt deposit," Carson pressed.

The young man just shrugged. "I'm sorry. Can't help you. If you give me your contact information, I'll put you in touch with the guy I know in about a month or so."

"Don't bother," Carson muttered, and left without saying good-bye. Given the time crunch he and Juliet were working under, waiting a month—potentially more, he suspected—didn't make sense. He headed back to Juliet, taking a winding path through the crowds so the man he'd talked to couldn't see where he was going. Meanwhile, it looked like one of the mechs was finally wrapping up the fight. It was continuously stomping its foot onto the other's mainframe, sending sparks, wires, and shards of metal plating everywhere.

"You get anything?" Juliet asked immediately once he returned.

Carson shook his head in disappointment. "Our contact said the heavy security presence was making our potential bomb maker keep quiet."

Juliet just shrugged. "Did you keep him talking, at least?"

"Yeah. I don't see how—"

"—then that's all we need. I installed a hacking program on your wrister when I uploaded the contact profile. Got it from Vincent Gureh back on the *Preserver* actually, before they shipped us to Calimor. He said it was some big secret, next-gen spying technology. Got all cagey when I asked which Earth corporations had been developing it, whatever the fuck that means. If you were talking to the person of interest for long enough, it'd automatically trawl through their recent communications."

Maybe before the last few weeks, Carson would've objected to feeling used. But by this point, he was starting to learn that was just Juliet's style. Sure enough, he checked his wrister and found a series of messages sent and received by their contact. As Carson scanned the list, he saw a single name appearing frequently: Saul Worska.

"I bet that's our guy," Juliet said. "What do you say we go try to find this Saul character before we get trampled?"

Sure enough, the arena workers were cleaning up the destroyed mech, and people were flocking to the exits. Carson couldn't object. He just wanted to get out of this place. Away from the naked greed, the despair cloaked in substance abuse and violent catharsis, and especially the feeling of being nothing more than a glorified errand runner for Juliet. "Let's go," he muttered.

CHAPTER 22

The trip from Haphis to Rhavego had to be one of the worst weeks of Russ' life. When he wasn't stuck in the coffee crate, his legs constantly cramping and aching, he was desperately skulking around the supply ship, waiting for when the crew went to sleep or was preoccupied in the cockpit, to steal food, water, or relieve himself. He'd almost gotten caught in the bathroom once, so he'd snuck into the shower unit and pretended to be one of the crew members while another was brushing their teeth. A sudden cramp had almost made him grunt and give himself away.

Getting to Rhavego, finally, was a shot of sweet relief. As soon as Russ heard the engines finally cut out, he pushed himself out of the coffee crate, opened the loading ramp, and headed out into the facility.

The loading dock was massive, enough to accommodate probably six supply ships the size of the one from Haphis. They must've arrived during a slow day, however, since they were the only ones there. There were still hundreds of crates piled up at various points throughout the bay, each one marked with a different commodity. Russ hurried over to a nearby pile and hid behind a crate before the crew could catch sight of him.

He still had to be careful. He figured these boxes were piled up for a reason, which meant there was probably some extensive security screening procedures on the other side of the loading dock that'd produced the backup. He thought back to when he'd gone through a security station to board a commercial spaceliner back when he was still working for Isadora—*better times*, he thought—and security there was about as airtight as a chewed-up warship after a space battle. Honestly, that might've been generous.

But Rhavego wasn't the belt. It was Union territory, which meant that actual trained, professional troops would be handling screening. He had no illusions about being able to just walk through without ID and with a firearm stashed in his waistband.

Fortunately, he'd already spotted a ventilation shaft on the ceiling of the loading dock. Which would've been impossible to reach, had it not been for all the crates. A career in the security business made it easy to spot all the ways to get through a screening system. Even the best ones still had holes.

But that meant a precarious climb. Russ reached for the top of the crate he was hiding behind and pushed himself up. His feet flailed around below him, trying to help propel him upward. Luckily, he'd stayed in pretty good physical shape even during his tenure at the Syndicate. Unluckily, he'd gotten piss-poor sleep for the past week, and the cramps were killing him.

When he managed to push himself on top of the crate, his right calf erupted into white-hot pain. He keeled over, clutching his calf and wincing. Back in his early twenties, Russ might've gotten right back up after a cramp like that. Now, it kept him twitching for another good minute. *To be young again*, he thought wistfully, eventually pushing himself back to his feet. He drew circles with his ankles, stretching out his leg muscles, and continued the climb.

He made his way up another few crates when his legs started seizing up again. His ankle rolled from under him, and he slammed down hard on the top of the crate, his torso nearly sliding off the edge. He estimated he was at least twenty feet off the ground. At least the supply crew hadn't heard him.

Grunting, Russ pushed himself to his feet once more, sat down with his back leaning against one of the stacked crates, and performed a couple of other leg stretches. He looked up at the ventilation shaft grate. It was just two more crates' worth of climbing. Right now, that felt like one of the hardest ten-foot stretches in his life.

Russ clenched his jaw and climbed onto the next crate. *One more.* He cracked his knuckles and pushed himself on top of the final one. And then he found himself face-to-face with the grating. He pulled out a tool from his utility belt, unscrewed the bolts, and carefully lowered the grating down.

His reward for an ache-inducing climb up thirty feet of stacked crates: a crawl through a narrow ventilation shaft. The muscles in his back burning, Russ grabbed the shaft and pulled himself inside.

The smell was awful. He liked to think of himself as a connoisseur of various types of shitholes, and the industrial ones were always the worst. He thought back to a museum he'd visited with his parents when he was very young, which displayed vehicles from a bygone era. A young Russ had been fascinated with a twentieth-century diesel truck, although when he'd gotten a whiff of the fumes from the truck's exhaust pipe, he'd gagged for what felt like an hour afterward.

That was what the ventilation shaft smelled like. Except he didn't have the luxury of coughing in his sleeve and walking away. He had to figure out something to actually do here.

Now was as good a time as any to start thinking about what the hell his plan was, he thought as he crawled past the Union's security screening checkpoint. He needed a source of income, and he wasn't sure how many people would be inclined to hire someone without ID. If that was even legal.

He finally made it to a supply closet, pushed his way out of the shaft, and headed into the main settlement's corridors. A quick glance around suggested that Rhavego was a "core world" in the same way that Haphis and Zoledo were. The Union maintained a security presence, but it didn't appear the government allocated many of its resources here.

The walls were dilapidated, with plaster filings clumped up in heaps on the floor no one had bothered to clean up. There was practically a rainbow of stains every few feet. Russ' hand accidentally brushed against one such spot as he exited the supply closet. His fingers came into contact with a sticky film, causing a quick recoil.

The pedestrians seemed numb to it all. Russ strolled aimlessly through the corridors, getting lost in the sea of blank faces. The same qualities of the Kurskyn settlement that horrified him must've just become daily little miseries for the colonists.

He was surprised that there were so many people walking around, given that his wrister told him it was the middle of the Rhavego workday. He knew the planet's economy mostly ran on mining, and that more and more miners had been losing their jobs in recent years. But the middle of the workday looked like a weekend at a crowded shopping center. The problem was more severe than he'd realized.

But that gave him an idea. Wherever there was chronic unemployment, there were people who tried to profit off of it. Specifically, employment agencies that preyed on desperate people, securing temporary jobs with shit pay, all while taking a cut from the new hire's salary. He figured those kinds of parasites could make a killing in a settlement like Kurskyn.

He wasn't wrong. Rounding a corner, he saw a flashing neon sign advertising some hole-in-the-wall employment agency. This one looked way too sketchy to be Union-affiliated, which increased the likelihood that they'd set him up with a gig where his future employer was inclined to look the other way if he didn't have ID. He hoped. Most of the letter lights on the sign had been busted, so it actually read EM YME G CY.

Russ walked in and was immediately surprised that there weren't more people inside. Maybe the chronically unemployed had stopped bothering. That assumption fit with everything else he'd seen of Rhavego so far.

A tired, elderly woman sat behind a reception desk. "Looking for work?" she asked in a voice that was only barely distinguishable from a monotone.

"That's why I'm here," Russ said. A cramp shot up his right leg, causing him to stumble. The receptionist didn't seem to notice. Or care.

"Name?" the woman asked, pulling up a form on her terminal.

"Russ Kama." No sense lying about that.

"Previous employer?"

"I...did a private security gig on Haphis," he said. Probably not smart to reveal his connections with the Syndicate. Nor his affiliation with the refugees.

"Reason for leaving?"

"Falling out with my employer." Russ winced. That was putting it lightly.

"What kind of skills would you say you have?"

Russ thought about claiming veteran status. Economic bleakness aside, ex-military implied certain skill sets that others just didn't have. But he hadn't been part of the Union military, which is what the employment agency worker would probably assume.

"I dunno. Been in the security business for a while," Russ said with a shrug.

"That's all I need. I should let you know that the average job search in Kurskyn takes about one and a half years, although that's been increasing recently. If you leave Kurskyn for whatever reason, it is your responsibility to inform us if you want to be taken off the job search. If we connect you with an employer and you decline, you'll owe us a cancellation fee equal to the first three months' salary of whatever job you declined. Once we connect you with a job, you will be asked to provide documentation regarding your legal status to work in Union space." The woman's eyes got droopier the longer she went on. Russ wondered how many times she'd given the exact same spiel.

That last point gave him pause, however. Russ didn't have the legal status required to work in Union territory by any means. But he hoped that the kinds of businesses that were hiring in a colony like Kurskyn would be more likely to turn a blind eye to requirements like

that. It wasn't a good sign that even the sketchy, unofficial employment agencies were asking for ID, but he supposed it could've just
been a formality.

He inputted his wrister frequency in a nearby terminal. "Do you
need anything else?" Russ asked.

The woman shook her head, and her eyes returned to her terminal.

Russ headed back out into the corridor. He hoped that he'd be
able to find work in a shorter amount of time than one and a half
years, but it sounded like Kurskyn wasn't the most promising place
for employment. He had a decent amount of cash saved up from his
work for the Syndicate, and he'd always lived frugally, but he didn't
think he could cover a year and a half off.

That meant his funds would be better put to use getting off
Rhavego. He decided to head to the spaceport and try to figure out a
flight plan to get somewhere he could find a paying job. He thought
briefly about booking passage to link up with his people—Hector's dying wish—but he wasn't ready for that. Not yet.

As he made his way through the crowds and the loiterers, he noticed someone shadowing him. A man in a black and white suit was
following him from the other end of the corridor. Just to make sure,
Russ took a couple of unnecessary turns before working his way back
toward the spaceport.

Yep. He was being followed.

It had to be the Syndicate. Who else would recognize him? Plus,
he thought back to his conversation with Hector Grako on Haphis:
the Syndicate was always present in the shitholes of the Natonus System, trying to clean up among the desperate and the destitute.
Kurskyn checked all those boxes.

Still, there were Union troops on patrol. He was pretty sure Syndicate goons weren't dumb enough to try something out in the open like this. They were probably just following him to get intel on his whereabouts. In a way, he was flattered. Lena Veridor must've *really* wanted him dead.

But the situation worsened once he got to the spaceport. He immediately noticed two men making their way straight for him from opposite ends of the room. It was crowded enough, and the Union marines were far enough away, that it'd be easy to shank him if they got in close.

Russ turned around and headed down a different corridor. He thought he'd lost at least one of his pursuers, but he soon caught sight of him when he rounded a corner. The third pursuer was at the other end.

Russ cursed and sped up down another hallway. Sure enough, another Syndicate agent was waiting for him. The three of them were encircling Russ, preparing for the kill.

He had to get out of here, and fast. He broke into a run down another corridor, pushing his way past throngs of people. Russ was surprised more people didn't seem to mind.

As he rounded another corner, he fell into step behind a large group of people in dirty, smeared work suits. Each had a large utility belt with a variety of mining tools. They were walking toward a freight elevator in the middle of the hallway, presumably heading down for the mines.

Which would be the perfect place to shake his pursuers. He followed the miners into the freight elevator and frantically pressed the close button on the lift's control terminal. "You take a wrong turn?" one of the miners closest to him said.

"Just some people I need to get away from," Russ said.

Two of the Syndicate agents appeared in view. They broke out into a jog, heading straight for the turbolift. "Stop!" they shouted. Russ jammed his finger into the button even faster.

Just as the first Syndicate agent approached the turbolift threshold, the transparent door slid closed. Russ locked eyes with his pursuer and flashed a grin as the elevator began its descent. The agent just watched him, giving him a dark look.

"Hope you all don't mind," Russ said, turning to face the miners.

A couple looked spooked from the near-encounter with the Syndicate agents, but most didn't pay him any attention.

The lift descended for a good couple of minutes until they came to a halt, and the door slid open again. Russ let all the miners out first for good measure. Might as well be polite.

They'd arrived at a large transit station, with trolley tracks leading off to various worksites within the underground system. A tram arrived moments later. Most of the miners filed into the vehicle.

Russ still hadn't figured out exactly what to do. Any Syndicate personnel in Kurskyn would've been activated by now. Taking the turbolift back up would be suicide.

He'd survived, but he'd also cornered himself. Syndicate goons would be watching every elevator in the lower levels. Hell, they might even send people down to get him.

But as long as the miners didn't seem to care that he was in their workspace, Russ figured he was okay. The mining tunnels seemed vast, and he could lose pursuers in the dark, twisting rock corridors with ease.

Best to stay put, he decided. Hopefully, some opportunity would present itself soon.

CHAPTER 23

The part of Nadia's mind that could still enjoy dramatic vistas was captivated by their descent into the settlement of Kurskyn. The Rhavego planetscape stretched on for miles, with no atmosphere to reduce visibility. It was like the *Exemplar* was plunging toward an ocean of rock.

The surface had the occasional off-color splotches, but mostly it was a pleasant shade of brown. The fissures and impurities and craters that'd seemed miniscule earlier looked massive now. There were craters that looked larger than the size of a colony. She could probably fit a dozen New Arcenas in one of the bowl-shaped depressions, she figured.

What Nadia had assumed were hairline fissures were in fact incredibly deep crevasses that seemed to cut through the planet like deep gashes, the depths invisible from space. Rhavego didn't have the mountains that dominated Calimor's wilderness, but it had its fair share of rock spires and outcroppings. For all the trouble it seemed to throw at Nadia, the Natonus System sure had some damn beautiful views.

But that was only part of her mind. The other part was still worried about Boyd, blaming herself for her naivety—for having the presumption to think she could actually end the civil war on Enther—and fearful about her people's safety in the face of the Offspring attacks. Apparently, some psycho had almost shot up a colony she'd founded on Bitanu.

As she continued to watch the Rhavego surface grow closer and closer, it was hard to avoid feeling a sense of loss. She'd sailed over the landscapes of Calimor, Bitanu, or Ikkren with nothing but innocent joy in her heart. Her first foray into the core worlds should've felt less empty.

"What do you think?" she asked Derek, hoping to distract herself with conversation. She'd been making a special effort to be extra nice to her remaining crewmate since she'd lashed out at him almost a week ago.

"I'd imagined it'd be...more settled than this," Derek said. "With the stories the older generation told us of the core worlds, I'd assumed they'd be dripping with cities as far as the eye can see. But the next closest settlement to Kurskyn isn't even visible from here. Still," Derek continued, "the lightshow feels...different."

He must've been referring to the blanket of yellow light pollution coming from Kurskyn, visible even from when they were further away. Having spent many days gently orbiting Ikkren, Nadia had always been mesmerized by the way the entire planet looked dark at night. No urban sprawl, no cities-that-never-slept, no around-the-clock electricity grids.

"I'm getting a request to input our ship's transponder codes," Derek said, half in surprise. It was a perfectly normal procedure for an arriving spacecraft, but having spent the last two years on the Natonese frontier, Nadia had gotten used to being able to land whenever and wherever she damn well pleased. It was just another hiccup of returning to civilization.

"We're being directed to one of the hangar bays on the eastern cliffside of the settlement," Derek said, angling the ship to veer to their right. As he did, one of the giant crevasses came into view. The fissure marked the rightmost edge of Kurskyn. A huge grid of hangar bays were embedded into the cliff face.

A swarm of spacecraft hovered just beyond the hangar bays in holding patterns. "Looks like the Union moved us to the front of the queue," Derek said. "I'm guessing they must've recognized us." The last time Nadia had interacted with anyone from the Union directly, she'd been pleading with them not to turn New Arcena into a radioactive heap. Hard to tell whether that made them more or less likely to like her, but given the way the last month had gone, she was afraid it was the latter.

Derek guided their vessel to one of the leftmost hangar bays. A door slid shut behind them, and their vessel came to rest on the ground. The *Exemplar*'s landing gear shot out and pressed down on the bay floor. "Looks like they're advising us to keep our weapons on the ship," Derek said.

Nadia felt a curious anxiety as she passed by the weapons footlocker near the airlock. She'd never felt the need to constantly carry a weapon before, but with images of the Enther civil war and the

Offspring attack on New Arcena constantly flashing through her brain, she had to admit it might feel better to have a gun strapped to her hip.

She shook her head as she followed Derek down the landing ramp. That was a Russ thought, not a Nadia thought. She could handle being unarmed for the hopefully short amount of time it'd take to find Noah Tasano's contact in Kurskyn. After all, it seemed like Union military presence was high. What could be the danger?

Sure enough, a squad of marines were ready to meet her and Derek at the far end of the hangar. The bay was small enough that the *Exemplar* was the only ship that could even fit. The squad leader walked up to meet them.

"Nadia Jibor?" the commander asked.

"Yes ma'am," Nadia said. She looked at the marine's face to try to discern how she felt about the *Exemplar* touching down in Kurskyn. She mostly just looked suspicious. Nadia could live with that. The label of *troublemaker* seemed fairly appropriate.

"I'm going to need to ask you a few questions," the soldier continued. "First, what is your business on Rhavego?"

Nadia's first instinct was to tell the truth. They were looking for Noah's contact, Saul Worska, who could hopefully point them in the right direction to find where Brandon Zahem's radical faction was hiding. Where Boyd was being kept prisoner.

But she immediately reconsidered. With security this heavy, did Nadia want to tell the truth that they were searching for someone at least tangentially affiliated with a terrorist organization? Nadia wasn't sure what kind of legal power the soldiers had, but she could imagine them delaying her or even asking her to leave.

"We're looking for someone," Nadia said. Lying had never come naturally to her, but she knew to couch the lie in a decent amount of truth. At least, that was the kind of thing you tended to read and hear about lying. "We're working on settlement rights on Enther," she continued. "We received a tip that someone here has ins with both the Junta government and Noah Tasano's rebels. We were hoping to meet and get advice on restarting the peace talks."

The soldier narrowed her eyes. "What kind of affiliation with the Ashkagi rebels?"

Nadia froze, wondering how well the Union understood the distinctions between Noah's rebels and the radical faction headed by Brandon. "Our contact was discreetly smuggling medical supplies—no military ordnance, I can assure you—to the rebels for the last few years," she explained, hoping the lie was non-threatening enough to satisfy the marine.

"We'd be very interested in talking to this individual as well," the soldier said. "If we let you into Kurskyn, we'd like you to surrender your contact into Union custody as your exit ticket."

Nadia had no idea how she felt about surrendering Saul to the Union. It might make trying to get information out of him harder, assuming she told him about the deal. But for now, agreeing to the soldier's terms was her only path forward. "Okay," she said.

The soldier tapped away at her wrister before continuing. "How long do you expect your search to take?"

Nadia exchanged glances with Derek, and her crewmate shrugged. Really, they just had to find someone and have a conversation. That could take anywhere from a few hours to a few weeks, depending on how hard it'd be to find Saul Worska. And how talkative he'd be when they found him.

"I'm...not sure, honestly," Nadia said.

The soldier stared at her. "I'll clear you through, but if your search ends up taking longer than a few weeks, then we'll need to have another talk. And remember that we have a strict no-toleration policy for carrying weapons or other contraband. If our security forces or soldiers catch you with either, we'll impound your vessel and place you under arrest immediately."

The trooper made another few notes on her wrister, and then waved the two of them to the hangar exit. Nadia had already been struggling against a rising tide of anxiety—who knew how long they had to find Boyd before something bad happened to him—and the soldier's timeframe didn't help with that. But at least she was inside the settlement.

Now came the hard part. Finding a single individual in a settlement as big as Kurskyn was like looking for a single drop in an ocean. A net search on Saul they'd done back during their approach hadn't yielded any meaningful information, and it didn't seem that Noah had known Saul well enough to provide any additional information that might help them find him. That meant they'd need to ask around, or try to find someone willing to broker information that could lead them in the right direction. Nadia and Derek exchanged determined glances. Finding Boyd would make it all worth it.

.   .   .

It'd almost been a week, and Nadia still didn't feel any closer to finding Saul Worska than when they'd arrived. The impending Union deadline and the frustration that any delay placed Boyd's life in more danger made Nadia's head throb, which made it harder to concentrate.

She and Derek had found a place to stay at a relatively cheap inn—going through a security checkpoint every day if they stayed on the *Exemplar* seemed like a waste of precious time—and they split up during the day to pursue various leads. Which really meant hitting up places people gathered, like bars or cafes or shopping centers, and asking around.

The answers were always the same: no, they'd never heard of Saul Worska, and could you please stop bothering them?

Dejection was starting to feel normal to Nadia, so each time she got a no from someone, it got easier to tolerate. After the past month, the days of heady success—touching down at a wilderness site, completing a successful survey, then recommending a colony to Isadora for approval—felt like a distant era.

She'd also gotten the feeling that at least a few people here knew who she was from the newsfeeds. Most people she walked by didn't acknowledge her, but every once in a while, she'd hear someone mutter "newar" while passing by. Hearing the slur directed at her was just another reminder about how the core worlds were less inviting than the frontier.

At least they'd shacked up in a decent part of the settlement. There were a variety of small shops and restaurants outside their inn, some of which surprised Nadia with their offerings. There was one place that was offering gyros, complete with tzatziki sauce, except with standard Ikkren fare: carrots, turnips, and wheat protein shaved off a vertical rotisserie.

She'd never seen, much less heard of, the Natonus System offering gyros before. Some days, she'd sit at a table inside the gyro restaurant for lunch and read up on the latest Natonese culinary trends on her wrister. Apparently, chefs from one end of Natonus to the other were starting to incorporate Earth cuisines into their own fare. Another restaurant on the block featured sushi wraps, mostly with fresh vegetables from Sarsi. Other restaurants in the settlement advertised tacos, pizza, ramen, even hamburgers, all with some kind of Natonese twist.

Derek walked up as Nadia was finishing her gyro. "I think I might've found something," he murmured before she could say hello. She wiped the corner of her mouth with her napkin, gesturing for him to go on. "I talked to someone who was recently let go from one of the local banks. He kept a partial client database on his device, so he thinks he can help us locate Saul, who has an account with his old employer."

Nadia finally finished the bite in her mouth. "That sounds amazing," she said, her heart leaping a bit—was this the first break she'd gotten since arriving on Enther?—but her head cautioning her. "But is it legal?" she asked.

"That's the catch," Derek said. "It's not strictly legal in two senses. First, him keeping client info is illegal. Second, us asking for it is also illegal."

Nadia deliberated for only a second. She was sure the Union was keeping tabs on her, but she was just so damn *tired* of everything, and she owed it to Boyd. "I don't see an issue," she said. "Let's talk to him."

Derek waved at a man hovering by the entrance to the gyro restaurant. The man looked over both his shoulders and entered. Nadia was surprised the ex-banker wanted to meet in a public place like the restaurant, but there weren't many patrons inside, and private conversations distracted the ones that were. Plus, Union troops didn't seem to patrol this part of the colony as much.

The man walked up and sat across from them. "I understand you're looking for someone," he muttered.

"We are," Nadia said, dropping her voice to match the man's volume. "Saul Worska."

"Not so fast. Payment first," the ex-banker said.

Nadia felt a sudden fear: what if this was a set-up? Some kind of test devised by Union security? What if there was a team waiting nearby to take her into custody as soon as she handed over the cash?

She considered the two outcomes. If the man was who she thought he was, he might provide a key piece of the puzzle that'd lead to Boyd. If he was undercover security, she'd message Isadora and ask her to pull some strings to get her and Derek out of custody. Nadia couldn't imagine Isadora particularly *appreciating* that, but with a chance to get a lead on Boyd's whereabouts on the line, the choice was clear.

"Okay," Nadia said. "Name your price." The man quoted her several hundred natons—an exorbitant price, given that the labor was just doing a quick search on his wrister—but she didn't care enough to haggle. She'd saved enough of her stipends to cover even an inflated cost. She authorized a financial transfer from her wrister.

The ex-banker nodded and began perusing a file on his own device. *Guess that means he's not Union security*, Nadia thought. After a couple minutes, he looked up. "I found your guy," the man said. "Looks like he opened his account about nine months ago. Most of his deposits are coming from one of the mining corporations, plus a couple of undisclosed deposits on the side. And it looks like he withdrew cash to pay one semester's worth of tuition at Kurskyn University."

"This means he's working the mines?" Nadia pressed. The other two details seemed superfluous to her.

"It seems so," the ex-banker said. "Now, is there anything else I can help you with?" Nadia shook her head vigorously.

After the ex-banker departed, Nadia and Derek headed for the closest freight elevator that'd take them down to the mines. The turbolift took a few minutes to get them all the way to the ground, but Nadia kept her mind occupied by viewing the patches of metals embedded in the rock as they descended. Every few seconds, they passed by a chalky red-orange iron deposit or the golden luster of a platinum deposit. The deeper they got, the more the view resembled a mosaic of different colored minerals.

When the doors opened, Nadia and Derek emerged into what looked like a transit hub. Twelve tracks converged at a central station, each one leading off into its own dark tunnel.

A squat, round-faced man emerged from the hub station. "Take a wrong turn?" he asked. Nadia assumed he was the foreman on duty.

"We're looking for someone," Nadia said. "One of your employees. Saul Worska."

"Saul? He's not an employee. More like a—wait, who are you? You with the government?"

Both Nadia and Derek shook their heads vigorously. "He knows some people back on Enther we need to get in touch with," Nadia said.

The foreman still had a suspicious look on his face. "Y'know, Saul's been pretty popular today. Two other people wanted to talk to him just a half-hour ago. Said they were from the university."

Nadia and Derek exchanged a glance that meant neither of them wanted to deal with the foreman's bullshit. "Look," Nadia said. "Let's cut the crap. I know how the world works. How much do you want for info on Saul? I promise we're not going to hurt him. We're unarmed.

I just want to ask him a few questions."

She figured the foreman didn't have much reason to care about Saul, given that he apparently wasn't a full employee, but she hoped her assurances would give him confidence that he wasn't putting Saul in danger by giving his info away. And a bribe probably didn't hurt, either.

"How much is he worth to you?" the foreman asked, stroking his chin.

Nadia struggled to think of anything she'd rather do less than haggle with the foreman. "A hundred natons," she blurted out, knowing the amount was absurdly high, but not caring.

The man's eyes lit up. Nadia hoped it was a high enough amount to dissuade him from even trying to bargain upward. "Okay," he said, "deal."

The foreman smiled appreciatively at his wrister after Nadia wired over the funds. "Saul's currently taking equipment down to the south site," he said. "You can take the tram. No one's working there right now, so you won't get in anyone's way."

Nadia thanked him, and she and Derek boarded the tram. The vehicle raced off through the dark tunnels. "Well," she said, letting out a relieved sigh. "Maybe for once, it looks like things might just work ou—"

She was cut off as the entire mine rumbled. The rock ceiling shook violently, and then broke apart entirely. Huge chunks of rock tumbled down onto the tracks right in front of them. And then crashed into the nose of the tram.

CHAPTER 24

The mines were even bigger than Carson had imagined in his head. When he and Juliet reached the entrance to the mining tunnels well below Kurskyn, he'd imagined maybe a small workstation and two or three shafts. In reality, the hub station was large enough to look like a small office building, almost filling up the entire rock cavern, with a dozen shafts all around. As they arrived, a tram full of miners was shuttling off down one of the tracks. The tram disappeared behind a face of sheer rock.

"Come on," Juliet said, powering toward the hub station with long strides. Carson followed her, trying to keep up with her frantic pace. The closer they were getting to Saul Worska, the more urgent all of Juliet's movements had become.

Juliet banged on the door to the hub station. A man with a round

face and a short stature emerged. His eyes darted back and forth between the two of them. "Can I help you?" he said. "Is everyone back
up in the settlement gonna come down to bother us today?"

"You have other visitors?" Juliet asked.

"One other, yeah. I think he was fleeing from some trouble,
though. What are you two doing here? I can't keep taking in strays all
day."

"Relax," Juliet said, although Carson wondered if anyone could
relax after hearing the strain in her voice. "We're just looking for
someone. Saul Worska."

"What do you know about Saul?" the foreman asked, crossing his
arms over his chest.

"We're with the Registrar's Office at KU," Juliet said, producing a
fake ID she'd gotten forged earlier. The man they'd bought the fake
credentials from let them know, helpfully, that no one who worked at
Kurskyn University called it by its full name.

The foreman's eyes narrowed. "Are you university snobs here to
extort more money—sorry, *tuition*—out of Saul? Because I'm not telling you shit."

"No. The opposite, actually. Thanks to a clerical error, we need to
reimburse Saul for some of his tuition payments from last semester.
It appears we overcharged him," Juliet lied. "We were just gonna
credit his account, but there's some kind of extra security there, so we
have to do it wrist terminal-to-wrist terminal."

The foreman raised his eyebrows. "Honestly, this is the first time
I've ever heard of you KU types trying to give money back to the community."

Juliet shrugged. "First time for everything."

The suspicion left the foreman's eyes. "Fair enough," he said with a chuckle. "Right now, Saul is setting up equipment for the day at the south site. I think he should be there by himself. If you take a tram now, you should be able to catch him before my people go to work."

Juliet thanked him, and the two of them walked over to an empty tram on their right. The door slid open, and Carson took a seat in the center. With a soft hum, their car took off down the tracks into the darkness of the mine shaft. Juliet paced near the front.

"Are you doing all right?" Carson asked.

"It's just been a while since I've done this," Juliet sighed. "I feel like I'm about to piss my pants like it's my first sting again."

Carson liked hearing stories about Juliet's past, even if they were few and far between. She seemed to enjoy talking about other things: ranting about politics, complaining that Carson wasn't doing good enough, making snide remarks about how much of a shithole Rhavego was. But every time she let some little detail slip about her old life, it made her seem more human. Like there was a real person underneath the dejected, angry facade. Someone who had the same anxieties and insecurities that plagued everyone else. Maybe it was just the dim lighting of the mining tunnels, but Carson thought the lines creasing Juliet's face looked softer.

"But what if this Saul Worska lead turns out to be a dead end?" he asked gently. "I know you think he fits the bill, but isn't it possible he's not our guy?"

"Oh, it's possible, I suppose," Juliet said, looking out one of the tram's windows at the barely visible rock formations. "But I doubt it. I've been in the business for so long that I just get these *hunches*, you know? Our guy might not be able to tell us everything we want to know, but I'd bet he can at least give us a few answers."

Carson accepted that and turned his attention to the tunnels. As much as he hoped that they were on their way toward getting answers about the New Arcena bombing, he couldn't help but feel a sense of dread rising in his chest. If Saul could point them toward the Offspring, that meant they'd soon enter the second phase of their assignment: active infiltration.

He didn't feel ready. Sure, he'd been practicing all the various skills Juliet thought he'd need in the field. But how could the drills prepare him for spending all day around a bunch of murderous radicals who wanted Carson and everyone else like him dead? How could he be ready for that? How could *anyone* be ready for that? But then he thought back to Juliet's mention of her first sting. It sounded like she'd gone through all the same jitters, and here she was.

The door slid open before such thoughts could marinate in Carson's mind. They stepped out into a small station at the end of the tunnel, which widened into a large cavern. Carson glanced over and saw dozens of mechs like the two back in the fighting ring, all lying dormant in charging stations. As he followed Juliet into the cavern, he noticed various heavy machinery devices piled up just beyond the mouth of the tunnel.

The cavern was decently large, about the size of your average grain silo you'd see off the highway back on Earth. It was well lit by a half-dozen overhead lamp units embedded in the rocky ceiling. A central bridge spanned the chamber, a spiral path leading downward along the outer edge of the cavern. As Carson and Juliet crossed the bridge, he noticed a lone man down at the very bottom of the chamber.

"Saul Worska?" Juliet called down. Her voice reverberated off of every wall around them.

The man turned and looked up at the two of them. "What's it to you?" he called up.

"We need to ask you some questions," Juliet said.

A pause. "You with the Union?" came Saul's response.

"No."

Another pause. "Okay," Saul said eventually. "I'll talk. For a bit."

Juliet headed over to the spiral ledge that led to the bottom of the cavern, beckoning Carson to follow her. "Let me do the talking," she whispered to him as they descended.

They reached the bottom, giving Carson a better view of Saul. The man was short and scrawny, with eyes that seemed to constantly shift from one end of the cavern to the other, not bothering to linger on a single spot. It looked like he was working on setting up a blasting device against one of the walls. "Are you the two people Noah sent?" Saul asked suddenly as they walked toward him.

"Noah?" Juliet asked. "Who the fuck is that?"

"Nevermind," Saul said, shaking his head in frustration. "You know what, why did I even bother? If Noah didn't send you, I don't have anything I want to say to you." He turned back around and tried setting up more equipment. His hands were too shaky to be even remotely steady enough to properly set the equipment, however.

"You know, I've seen a lot of people like you," Juliet said. She rolled her tongue from one end of her mouth to the other and narrowed her eyes. "People in way over their heads. You probably fell in with some bad people, people who got you with the usual grandeur that ropes in all the dreamy kids. And now you're in deep, deeper than you ever wanted to go. You're looking for a way out. Well, *we* are your way out."

Saul had stopped messing with the equipment entirely. Carson felt a faint shiver, as though his body was saying *this is what Juliet looks like in her element.*

"You don't know anything about me," Saul said with a whimper.

"Yep," Juliet said, a cocky smile on her face that didn't strike Carson as even a little overconfident. "That's usually the first thing they all say. Because they never believe me at first, even if they want to. I get it: sounds too good to be true. A way out? No, not for you. *Definitely* not. But what if...no, can't let yourself get your hopes up. But you're sure as hell wishing that what I'm saying is true."

Saul said nothing, which was the same thing as saying everything.

"So how about this," Juliet said, "My friend and I have the skills, the connections, and the resources that can get you off planet. Away from the people you're working for. All you need to do is give us a little bit of information, and then we can start figuring out how to make this all go away. In a few months, it'll just seem like a bad dream."

Carson thought he could hear a quick sob coming from Saul. The man's shoulders slumped. "I never meant for it to get out of hand like this," he said quietly. "I just thought what Noah was doing was too slow. I wanted to make things change."

Again with this "Noah" individual, Carson thought, wishing he knew who Saul was talking about. If Saul was affiliated with the Offspring, was this Noah the leader of some kind of "moderate" nativist movement? An anti-refugee politician?

"They sent me out here and told me I had to start making explosives. You wanna know what they threatened to do to me if I refused?" Saul asked.

Please say no, Carson thought. "We get the picture," Juliet said. *Whew.*

"I couldn't refuse. I was weak." Saul slammed his palm into the face of rock in front of him. "I never asked what they were planning to do with them. I didn't want to know."

"We know some people who got hurt by those bombs," Juliet said, her voice turning solemn. "We're not blaming you. We know you weren't the one who gave the orders. But after New Arcena—"

"—wait, New Arcena?" Saul interrupted. He turned around with a bewildered expression on his face. "You think I work for the *Offspring*?"

Juliet paused with her mouth open. "Sorry...who *are* you working for, exactly?"

"Brandon Zahem," Saul said. Carson and Juliet exchanged equally confused looks. "Enther-based radical Ashkagi leader?" he offered. Both Juliet and Carson shook their heads.

"You know what, it doesn't matter," Saul said. "You have to listen to me. There's not enough time to get off Rhavego. We have to get to safety. Brandon's looking to make waves. He saw what the Offspring did with New Arcena, and he wants to do the same thing: attract recruits, notoriety, all that. So his people have set up explosive devices all over Kurskyn, right under the Union's nose. I never wanted it to get this far. I just wanted my homeworld to be free again."

A pang of fear ricocheted through Carson's stomach. Were there really bombs placed all throughout the colony? Had he and Juliet been sitting on a massive powder keg the entire time they'd been here?

If Juliet was concerned, she didn't show it. "We have good evidence that one of your bombs was used in the New Arcena attack. That's what we're here about. We need to know how the Offspring got ahold of it."

"I swear, I don't know anything about the Offspring," Saul said, raising his palms. "All I know is—"

A series of successive booms cut Saul off. Each one was louder than the last. It sounded like they were coming from far above, but they were getting closer.

Saul was right, Carson realized. The Ashkagi terrorists he was working for must've placed bombs all around Kurskyn. It'd be a spectacle of death and destruction far beyond what the Offspring had wrought at New Arcena.

Just as the horrific realization of what was going on dawned on Carson, the entire cavern ceiling shook. With an awful ripping sound, huge chunks of the ceiling came barreling down on them.

Saul just froze, cursing and staring up at the rocks coming down on them. But Juliet leapt into action, grabbing Carson's forearm and sprinting toward the spiral ledge. As a large boulder came tumbling down toward them, Juliet shoved Carson to the ground and shielded him with her body. Carson's hands shot to his face as the rock collapsed on them. And then everything went black.

.   .   .

When he woke up, Carson assumed he'd only been out for a few minutes. He could remember where he was and why he was here, which meant he probably hadn't gotten serious brain damage from the impact.

Looking up, he breathed a sigh of relief when the cavern roof was still mostly intact. It wasn't a complete cave-in. He felt a sharp pain from his ribcage and a throbbing sensation in his head as he tried to sit up, but he managed to look over where Saul had been standing. Rocks blanketed the entire area. The man had to have been crushed.

"Thanks for pulling me out of there," Carson grunted. If Juliet hadn't acted so quickly, both of them would be dead right now.

Juliet didn't respond.

Carson looked down, where Juliet's head was resting on his lower torso. A line of blood circled her brow. "Juliet?" Carson whispered. If she hadn't woken up yet, she could be in a more serious condition. He had to get them out of here. Fast.

"Juliet?" he said more loudly, pushing himself out from under her and the pile of rocks on top of her body. As he moved, Juliet's body slid limply toward the ground. Carson placed his hands under her armpits to pull her out of the rubble. She felt cold. One of Carson's hands moved shakily to her neck. Nothing.

"...Juliet?" he whimpered. "Please no. Please don't go." Tears began stinging his eyes. "I can't do this without you." He rested his back on the wall behind him in utter defeat. "I have no idea what I'm doing. I'm not ready for this. I'm no spy, I'm just some therapist playing pretend. Please come back to me. I *need* you."

Carson hadn't been killed by the rockfall, but it felt like he'd been buried nonetheless. He was at the bottom of a deep mine shaft, with no idea how to proceed on a mission that was probably impossible. No one knew where he was. The only person who cared about him in the entire Natonus System was his brother, who was on the other side of the system.

And Juliet was dead.

Carson lowered his forehead to his knees and let the tears come. He'd never seen anyone die before, much less sacrifice their own life for his. What had he done to deserve that? What could he do to repay that kind of action? Every time he took a breath for the rest of his life, he'd owe it to Juliet. The weight of her sacrifice felt far heavier than the impact of the rockfall.

All he could do to honor her sacrifice was to proceed with the mission. But he had no idea what the fuck to do. He wasn't sure he even had the strength to get up.

That was when he heard the footsteps.

Carson wiped his eyes on the fabric of his pants and looked to his left. At the edge of the bridge—the part that hadn't collapsed—a man appeared from the other end. He was tall, wiry, and had short reddish-brown hair with a scraggly beard the same color. He had a gun drawn.

Carson panicked. The Union was careful about screening everyone for firearms before they could enter Kurskyn. That meant this man could be dangerous.

But as soon as he saw Carson, he lowered his handgun and holstered it. He ran over and pulled Carson to his feet. "You're gonna be okay," he said in a gruff, deep voice. He held his fingers up in front of Carson's eyes and moved them from side to side. "Doesn't look like you have any kind of brain damage." The other man then took a quick look at Juliet before returning his attention to Carson. "I'm sorry about your companion," he said with a grim look. "Who are you?"

"Carson Erlinza," he blurted out without thinking.

Shit, he immediately thought. He should've lied. He was supposed to be staying low, not telling anyone anything they didn't need to know. But with his spirits sunk so low, with Juliet dead, and with the whole damn system feeling like a cold, uncaring place, Carson wanted at least one person to know who he was. Even if he might be dangerous.

Besides, his real name wasn't connected to the *Preserver*'s database anymore. The only people who associated the name Carson

Erlinza with an Earthborn refugee from Vancouver were the higher ups in the refugee government. For his actual infiltration of the Offspring, the plan was for him to use his real name.

A look of recognition crossed the new arrival's face. "Holy shit," he muttered. He extended a hand toward Carson, who regarded it with skepticism. "Name's Russ Kama."

CHAPTER 25

Carson Erlinza. Carson *fucking* Erlinza.

Over a month ago, Riley had confided in Russ that she had no idea who to pull out of cryo for the infiltration mission she had in mind. Russ had recommended someone with experience working with radicalized individuals, even if they didn't have espionage training. Her response had been to pull out a therapist from the *Preserver*'s cryo storage who'd built a career counseling violent radicals back on Earth. And that was Carson.

What were the fucking odds?

All of Russ' other worries—what'd caused the sudden rockfall in the mining tunnels, whether he could evade the Syndicate goons chasing him, what should he do with his life assuming he even made it out of Kurskyn alive—all faded away. He was a soldier again. And

Carson was a mission-critical asset to his people's war effort against the Offspring.

Russ had to get Carson to safety. Get him back on track to infiltrating the Offspring. Everything else was secondary.

But if the man in front of him was Carson Erlinza, that meant the dead woman partially buried underneath the fallen rocks was Juliet Lessitor, the ex-undercover cop Riley had tapped to oversee Carson's training and serve as his handler in the field.

Carson, to his credit, seemed to be keeping it together. Mostly. Russ could tell he'd been crying, but he kept his square face stoic. He surveyed Russ from behind his grey eyes. Probably wondering if he could trust Russ.

Which was absolutely the right call. The kid had enough sense to not just go spilling everything to Russ immediately, minus the whole using-his-real-name thing. Then again, Russ figured he ought to be thankful as fuck that he'd dropped his name. Juliet had to have done something right, if she'd gotten a rookie to mostly respect operational security.

"Look, I know you have a lot of questions," Russ said. "I'm not sure how much you know about me, but I was Isadora Satoro's security adviser for most of our first year in the Natonus System. Until I fucked up. Made a bad call. I had to leave after that."

"I thought your name sounded familiar," Carson said finally.

"You're probably wondering if you can trust me. Thing is, I know exactly everything I did wrong. And despite it all, I've never stopped caring about keeping every single one of our people safe. I know who you are because I've maintained contact with Riley Tago."

At the mention of Riley's name, a look of recognition crossed Carson's eyes. Would've been an obvious tell if Carson was actually undercover, but he figured he could iron that out later, once they were safe. For the moment, he hoped dropping Riley's name might elicit enough trust in him so they could at least work together to get out of Kurskyn.

"You don't have to trust my judgment," Russ continued. "Hell, I'm not even expecting you to trust me. All I'm asking is for you to let me help get you out of here. So you can get back on track with your mission."

Carson turned his gaze to his dead partner, then looked back at Russ. "I dunno if you're blaming yourself over Juliet's death, but if you are, I can promise that's bullshit," Russ said. "There was *nothing* you could've done, son. But the best way to honor her is to forge ahead with the mission." Russ hesitated for a moment, then laid a comforting hand on Carson's shoulder.

Carson returned his gaze to Juliet's body. "Are we just gonna...leave her there?" he asked quietly, trying to keep his voice from shaking.

Russ grimaced. "There's nothing we can do. All that matters is getting you out of here. It's what she'd say if she was still alive."

"Okay," Carson said weakly. "Let's go."

"All right," Russ said, gesturing for Carson to follow him out of the cavern. The bridge spanning the chamber would be the fastest way back to the turbolifts that'd take them up to the main settlement, except that it'd collapsed in the rockfall. And the partial collapse of the ceiling had done a number on the other side of the chamber. The entire tunnel leading to the tram station was hidden behind piles of boulders. Because of course it was.

Russ kept his ears primed to listen for the sound of any more explosions from above. Another massive rockfall, and he was worried the entire mines might collapse, which would make saving Carson a moot point. But nothing came.

They headed back out into the corridor where Russ had been wandering around before he heard the bombs go off. It was funny: just ten minutes earlier, all Russ' thoughts had been preoccupied by how to evade his Syndicate pursuers. All of that seemed secondary now. He wondered briefly if the enforcers might've followed him down to the mines, but they probably had bigger problems to worry about now. Assuming they hadn't gotten crushed.

Still, the problems were roughly similar. He still had to get out of Kurskyn, probably off Rhavego, and neither he nor Carson, presumably, had a ship. That meant they had to get back up to the main settlement. Who knew what condition the colony would be in, however. He'd heard at least five bombs go off, but he couldn't see many other options besides heading back up.

Russ activated the light beam function on his wrister as the two men moved down the tunnel. They hadn't run into any signs of rockfall in this part of the tunnels, but Russ half-expected the ceiling to shift every time he looked up. "So how'd you end up here?" he asked Carson. The mines repeated his line back to him.

"We were following a lead based on the bomb the attacker used at New Arcena," Carson said. "We were in the middle of questioning the person who manufactured the device when the bombs went off."

"So wait, the Offspring are down here, too?" Russ asked, rapidly expanding his mental tracker of potential nearby hostiles. If those nativist assholes were here, and considering that Carson didn't have a sidearm, they'd need to rethink their whole formation.

Carson shook his head. "He said he was working for some Ashkagi radical group. But before we could ask him anything else, the ceiling came down."

Whew. Russ found it comforting that, at least based on what they knew at the moment, he didn't have to worry about Offspring on top of Syndicate assassins, violent Ashkagi fanatics, and the threat of more bombs going off.

They rounded a corner, and Carson pulled Russ back. "Careful," the other man said. "Looks uneven." Russ' eyes darted to the ground, where he noticed an impurity in the rock where he was about to step. *Too much time thinking about hostiles, and you weren't even watching where you were walking,* he chided himself.

And it was more than a little impressive that Carson still had the capacity for situational awareness, despite what he'd just been through.

Russ heard Carson lose his footing and stumble a bit—which was weird, since they were past the uneven patch of ground. When Russ turned around, Carson was leaning against the wall, wincing, with one hand clutching his midriff. "You okay?" Russ asked.

"My ribs haven't been feeling good ever since the rockfall," Carson said, fighting to keep the strain out of his voice.

"Let me see," Russ said, bringing his wrister to bear on Carson's midriff. Carson pulled his shirt up, and Russ' light beam illuminated a patch of severe discoloration along the left side of his ribcage. "Discoloration's good," Russ said. "Plus, you've been able to walk. That means it's probably bruised, not fractured." He rummaged through a bare-bones first aid kit he kept on the back of his utility belt.

"My head hurts like hell, too," Carson said.

Russ frowned. "Not sure if I can help you there. But I think I can get this rib bruise all patched up, at least till we can get you some real medical attention." He took an adhesive bandage out of his medkit and began wrapping Carson's midriff.

Carson winced as Russ jerked the bandage tighter. "I know it hurts," Russ said. "Just gotta grin and bear it." After Russ finished wrapping up the other man's torso as tightly as possible, he gave him a painkiller from his medkit. Carson swallowed the pill gratefully.

Russ was starting to genuinely admire his new companion. Sure, folks like Russ or Isadora hadn't been anywhere near qualified for their jobs, but at least he had prior military experience, and Isadora had prior political experience. Carson didn't even have that luxury. And instead of collapsing under the weight of his responsibilities and all the hardships he'd faced so far, he was keeping his head low and moving forward. He didn't come from a military background, and yet, he was soldiering on.

Even if he knew he was walking into what might be a death trap. For an espionage expert, a mission like infiltrating the Offspring would be dangerous. For Carson, it might be suicidal. And yet, Russ hadn't heard him so much as whine.

"Ready to go?" Russ asked after Carson handed back the pill bottle.

"Sure am," Carson said. Russ found the other man's capacity for endurance equal parts commendable and heartbreaking.

They approached a T-intersection, the right path blocked off by rockfall. "Guess that makes the choice pretty easy," Russ muttered, leading Carson down the left path. They arrived at a deep chasm in the tunnels. Russ estimated that the pit was at least fifty feet deep. Even accounting for the somewhat weaker pull of Rhavego's gravity well, the fall would almost certainly be deadly. Especially since Carson was already injured. The chasm was about a dozen feet across, meaning that jumping probably wouldn't work.

The enviro-suit Russ wore was equipped with propulsion thrusters that could speed him across the pit. But if he held Carson as he jetted across, the added weight would probably make the propulsion thrusters ineffective. And then they'd both be dead.

Russ also had a grappling device on his utility belt, but again, it was only designed to support a single person's weight. The more he thought about the problem, however, it was clear what they had to do: they had two one-man methods for crossing the chasm, and two people they had to get across.

The suit was the more convenient option. The grappling device could latch onto the other side of the chasm, but as soon as the user jumped off their side, it'd send them smashing into the far wall of the pit. Russ wasn't about to subject an injured, mission-critical individual to that. He began releasing the latches on his enviro-suit.

"What are you doing?" Carson asked.

"Have you used a propulsion suit before?" Russ asked.

"Once, yeah," Carson said, a wistful look in his eyes. "Stacy and I were mountaineering on Mount Waddington, and we used jetsuits for our descent."

Russ had no idea who Stacy was, but it didn't particularly matter right now. He finished taking his suit off and passed it over to Carson. "Here. This is how you're getting across," Russ said. The other man was shorter than Russ, and slightly less muscular, but he figured the suit would fit him just fine.

"What are you going to do?" Carson asked while latching the suit onto his body.

"I've got a grappling hook attached to a retractable rope," Russ said, patting the device on his utility belt.

A look of concern flashed across Carson's eyes. "But that won't—"

"—I'll be fine," Russ said. "The most important thing is getting you across safely."

Carson gave him a skeptical look.

"Okay," Russ sighed. "Guess it makes sense to have a backup plan." He withdrew his handgun from his holster and handed it to Carson. "If I don't make it, you take this and head back up to the main settlement. Shoot anyone who gives you trouble." He noted that Carson instinctively checked the weapon's safety before securing it in his waistband.

"The Union's gonna have everything on lockdown," Russ continued. "But I know how these things work. There's gonna be all kinds of enterprising criminals looking to smuggle people off-world as fast as possible." Russ pulled up his wrister, synced up to Carson's device, and wired the entirety of his Syndicate savings to the other man. Carson's eyes went wide. "It's not a fortune, but it's enough. You do whatever it takes to get off Rhavego as fast as possible. But don't trust anyone. Once you're safe, contact Riley Tago. She'll know what to do."

Carson still looked concerned, but he nodded and finished donning the enviro-suit. Once he was ready, he walked back a few paces and broke into a run, heading straight for the chasm. Right as Carson's first foot reached the ledge, he activated the suit's thrusters and sailed effortlessly over the pit.

All right, Russ thought, *easy part's down.* He pulled the grappling hook out of his device and pressed a button that'd allow him to pull out as much slack as he needed. He pulled a couple armfuls of wire-thin rope out until he was confident he had enough length to span the pit.

He tossed the grappling hook onto the far side of the chasm and asked Carson to make sure the hook was embedded deep in the rock.

"Okay," Carson shouted back. "I got it pretty firmly wedged into a fissure. You're good to go."

Russ threaded the rope back into his device until it was taut. *Well,* he thought, *here goes nothing.* He pressed the button, and the rope began to retract automatically. Pulling him right into the chasm, into thin air.

His body hurtled for the far wall, a single drop of nervous sweat flying off his forehead. He slammed into the rock. The force of impact spread across his torso, pelvis, and upper thighs. *That one's gonna hurt in the morning,* he thought.

The rope continued to retract, pulling Russ up with it. Looked like the plan was going to work. That was, until he saw that the rope had gotten caught around a jagged rock outcropping. As the rope continued to slide over the rock, the friction sent rope fibers shearing clean off. Russ cursed and grabbed frantically for any part of the cliff he could find.

Just as his hand settled on a handlebar-shaped piece of rock, the rope snapped in two. Russ' legs went wide, with all his weight now on his left hand, and frantically searched for any place to rest. He finally found a decent toehold with his left foot.

He heard Carson curse from above. "Are you okay?" the other man shouted. For the first time, Russ thought Carson sounded genuinely panicked.

He looked up, trying to spot a series of handholds he could use to climb to the top. It was only about another five feet to the ledge…he could do that, right? Somehow, the ability to maintain calm even under enemy fire wasn't quite preparing him to maintain calm while dangling unroped almost fifty feet off the ground.

"I'm okay," Russ said, gritting his teeth. "I can climb out."

Carson's face appeared over the edge. "Here," the other man said, offering his hand. "If you jump, I can catch you."

"You're hurt," Russ protested.

"That pill and the bandage are making me feel a lot better," Carson said. "And it looks too dangerous to climb."

Russ had to admit, climbing would be risky. The handhold he was grabbing was the last well-defined feature on the wall between him and the ledge, and he'd never been much of a climber. A fall would be almost certain death.

"If you're sure," Russ said, mentally preparing for a desperate leap.

"I'm sure. I'm bracing myself against the ground. And I can use the suit once you make contact."

"Okay," Russ said. "Gimme a countdown, at least." As Carson counted down from three, Russ bent and unbent his left leg nervously. When Carson finished his countdown, Russ transferred all his weight to his left foot and shot himself upward. His right hand went high, frantically stretching as far as his fingers would go.

It didn't look like he was going to make it. As Russ felt himself slow down, his hand short of Carson's, his mind went still. *So this is how I go*, he thought.

His hand brushed Carson's. The other man reached down further and grasped Russ' wrist tightly. Then came the hum of the suit's propulsion thrusters, and Russ felt himself shoot up and out of the pit. Before he could contemplate the sudden reversal of his fortune, he landed hard on the tunnel's rocky floor.

The two men slowly pushed themselves to their feet. Carson began unbuckling the suit, then handed it back to Russ. As he was putting his suit back on, he couldn't help but let out an impressed laugh.

"You know what? You're okay," he said to Carson. "I think you're gonna be just—"

Just fine, Russ was about to say, except he was distracted by a pair of light beams coming from an adjacent tunnel. Carson instinctively drew Russ' handgun, but Russ grabbed the barrel and took the weapon back. "Get behind me," he told Carson. The two men moved to the side of the tunnel. Most likely, it was just a pair of disoriented miners. But taking chances had a way of biting you in the ass later.

Two figures rounded the corner, both in enviro-suits. They froze when they saw the gun pointed at them. When Russ saw that neither was armed, he lowered his weapon. "Sorry," he said, "just can't be too careful."

The individual in front, a woman, lowered her wrister. The lack of glare from her illumination device gave Russ the chance to finally see her face. It was angular, with brown skin and a thick head of black curls worn parted to the side. Like a ghost from the past, reminding Russ of the depths of his failure as Isadora's security adviser.

For the first time in as long as he could remember, Russ' voice failed him. "N-Nadia?" he finally stammered out.

CHAPTER 26

Russ Kama. Russ *fucking* Kama.

The last time Nadia had seen him was aboard the *Preserver*, back when the only ones awake were her, Isadora, Russ, Vincent, and a handful of support staff. Before Nadia had embarked for Calimor, before she helped start a network of colonies dotting the entire frontier, before tensions with the Union nearly spilled into open hostilities.

The latter was a development fueled by Russ' constant whisperings in Isadora's ear. All his incessant *what-ifs* and worst-case scenarios had pushed Isadora away from cooperation and open dialogue with the Union. It was a mistake that'd nearly culminated in the outbreak of war—and in Nadia's death. By Russ' order, no less.

Not a day went by when she wasn't thankful that cooler heads had prevailed, but that didn't change the fact that the man facing her had been willing to have her and her crew killed. Had been willing to risk the deaths of nearly their entire population rather than hash out a compromise with the Union.

She hadn't sympathized with Russ after Isadora demoted him. She felt no sympathy for him now. He might've grown out a scraggly beard since, but everything else about him was the same: his wiry frame, his cropped reddish-brown hair, his suspicious eyes. Russ was still just a paranoid, would-be murderer.

"What are you doing here?" she hissed. Her voice sounded harsher than she'd ever heard it come out before, and she still felt she was being too nice. She looked over at Derek, who also would've been one of Russ' victims at New Arcena, expecting to see him mirror her own anger. To her surprise, she found Derek's face expressionless. *Guess you had to know the guy*, Nadia thought.

"Look," Russ said, interrupting her thoughts, "it's a long story. But that's not important. Carson is what's important."

Russ gestured behind him to his companion. Carson was a hair shorter than Russ, sporting a trim figure and a square face with wavy, dirty blond hair along with a pair of grey eyes. He waved awkwardly at her. If Nadia was supposed to recognize him, she didn't.

"Isadora tapped him to infiltrate the Offspring," Russ explained. "He's our first spy."

All that was news to Nadia. She exchanged glances with Derek, who just shrugged. Isadora had grown their government structure to encompass a variety of departments during the past two years, and Nadia supposed there was little reason for the settlement division to know what was going on with their espionage division.

And despite all his faults, Russ had always been trustworthy.

Especially about anything related to the safety and security of their people. Nadia had no reason not to trust that Carson was exactly who Russ said he was. Which meant that if Nadia could help Carson out, she would. They were working on the same team.

But first, Boyd. "We're looking for someone named Saul Worska," Nadia said. Carson's head shot up. "Our colleague Boyd has been captured by a radical faction of Ashkagi rebels on Enther, and we're hoping that Saul can point us in the right direction. We were on our way to meet him when the tunnels collapsed on our tram. After we find him, we'll help *Carson* get on his way," Nadia explained, taking care to emphasize that Russ was excluded.

"Don't bother," Carson said. "Saul's dead."

Nadia almost had to steady herself against the cavern wall. After everything that'd happened, she felt she'd earned this lead working out. But it was another dead end, and the universe had somehow thrown Russ Kama in her path instead of pushing her closer to finding Boyd. She looked at Derek, who had a concerned expression on his face and one hand cupped over his mouth. Probably the most worried she'd seen him, honestly.

"How did you hear about Saul?" Carson asked, his brow furrowed. "Unless...did someone named Noah direct you to him?"

"Yes, actually," Nadia said, cocking her head. "How did you—"

"—he mentioned Noah had sent people to contact him. We were also tracking Saul. We thought he might've constructed the explosive device used on New Arcena," Carson explained. "He told us that he was working for your radical faction. Which, in turn, implies that they're working in concert with the Offspring."

All the puzzle pieces that'd been floating around in Nadia's brain suddenly locked in place. After the series of terrorist attacks across

Enther, Noah had expressed disbelief that Brandon Zahem could amass such a large following. What if Brandon's numbers were artificially inflated due to a partnership with the Offspring?

It didn't get her any closer to Boyd, but it gave her a new lead to follow. And if Carson was tracking the Offspring, that meant their goals aligned. "Okay," Nadia said. "Let's refocus: getting back to the *Exemplar* and getting off Rhavego. That'll give us a safe place to figure out where we go next."

There was a part of Nadia—smaller than it used to be, she realized—that wanted to run around and try to save as many miners as possible. But she figured rescue teams would be on their way, and she trusted that they were qualified professionals who didn't need any help. Or maybe she was just numb from all the death and destruction that'd been following her around.

"The way we came from dead-ends," Russ said, tilting his head toward the tunnel behind him and Carson. "What about you?"

"Same with this direction," Derek said, indicating the tunnel to their left.

"Sounds like we have one option then. Let's go," Nadia said quickly, before Russ had time to take charge. She wasn't about to let him get away with steamrolling over the rest of them like he had back in the beginning.

They headed down the tunnels. There were plenty of piles of fallen carbonaceous rock lining the path, with whole chunks missing from the ceiling. Support beams had bent but not broken, even if the light fixtures had all shattered. Still, the light beams embedded in their suits provided enough illumination to navigate the dark tunnels. Nadia and Russ led the way, with Derek and Carson bringing up the rear.

"I'm surprised we haven't run into more miners," Carson said.

"Sounds like the Ashkagi set off a lot of bombs. The cave-in might've killed a lot of miners," Russ said.

Joyful as always, Nadia thought, her face naturally contracting into a sneer. She figured it was better to keep her thoughts to herself, however, given that Russ was both a loose cannon and, unfortunately, the only one of them with a weapon. Maybe he'd at least be useful in helping them get off the planet.

The four of them arrived at another transit station. There was a single tram in its berth, with the words NEW WING marked on top. "We should take the turbolift back up to Kurskyn and get to the hangar as fast as possible," Nadia said.

"Hang on," Russ countered. "I've been thinking: we have no idea what the security situation back in Kurskyn looks like. We've got Ashkagi terrorists running around, I know for a fact that the Syndicate has a decent presence up there, and the Union security forces are gonna be detaining anyone and everyone they can. Letting the asset into all that chaos is a major security risk," he said, nodding toward Carson.

Already referring to a living human being as an "asset," Nadia thought. "It's the most direct path to the ship," she said instead. "Any detours risk more things going wrong."

To her surprise, Russ didn't bark some angry retort back. Instead, he lowered his head and stared at his feet for a few seconds. "Look, Carson's had it real rough," Russ muttered, soft enough so that only Nadia could hear. "He came here with a partner who was training him. She died during the rockfall."

Nadia's thoughts returned to Carson's description of his encounter with Saul Worska. He'd been saying *we* the whole time, she realized with horror. She hadn't even thought to read into those implications. She looked back at Carson, whose calm disposition suddenly looked a lot more forced.

"I'm just trying to keep him away from more death and destruction," Russ continued. "Do I think the security situation is problematic in the settlement? You bet. But on top of that, it's also worth preserving whatever's left of Carson's sanity. I think the new wing is the right call for both reasons."

Nadia swallowed deep enough to force down her pride, and then turned to Derek and Carson. "All right. We'll try to figure out another way to get to the *Exemplar*."

Derek walked over to a map next to the transit hub. "Back during our descent, I remember that the colony was built into one side of a large chasm. It looks like this new wing is on the other side," he said, indicating the tram that'd caught Nadia's attention earlier. "That means the bombs going off likely wouldn't have damaged it."

"Then let's head there," she said.

The four of them boarded the tram, and Derek pushed a button that shot them through a glass-enclosed tube across the chasm. As the tram spat them out beyond the cliff face, they turned to view Kurskyn. "Holy shit," Carson said, wide-eyed. It looked like the explosions had blown a huge chunk out of the cliffside settlement. The dome on top looked undamaged, at least. It was too far away for them to tell, but Nadia thought she could see a few fires burning inside the hollowed-out hole. Maybe Russ had been right to avoid the colony.

About halfway across the chasm, an awful metal screech nearly split Nadia's eardrum. The tram came to a halt.

"Shit," Russ said. "Explosions must've knocked out the power at the recharging station. I bet this thing was running on fumes, and we just expended everything that was left."

Derek walked over to the controls. "If I can access the engines, it should be easy enough to jumpstart them. Wouldn't be a big charge, but I bet it'd be enough to get us to the other side."

All four of them walked to the back of the tram and started trying to access the engines. "Damn," Derek said, looking at an inaccessible metal panel. "Looks like the engines can only be accessed from the exterior. I suppose the design makes sense under normal conditions."

"We could use our suits to hover just outside," Nadia said, but she was far from confident that'd work. The thrusters on their enviro-suits were made for jetting across short distances, not hovering in place. Especially not while performing a maintenance operation.

"I could try," Carson said. "But I don't have a suit."

"If you're as important as Russ says you are, I don't think that'd be the best idea," Derek said.

Nadia drew in a breath and was about to volunteer, when Russ beat her to the punch. "I'm the one going," he said, using a definitive tone that immediately cut off debate. He activated his suit's helmet function and handed his handgun over to Carson. "Same drill as before," Nadia heard him mutter. "You know what to do if I don't make it back."

Carson just nodded.

"All right folks," Russ said, grabbing the rail next to the tram exit. "I'm gonna override the lock and force the door open. Everyone hold your breath until you repressurize the cabin."

Nadia inhaled. Russ pried the door open, activated a gentle thrust on his suit, and stepped outside. Nadia and Derek rushed to seal the door behind him before they lost too much oxygen. Russ, meanwhile, bobbed along the window.

Nadia looked over and caught Derek watching Russ move to the posterior section of the vehicle. "Kind of poetic, really," Derek said. "After threatening to blow up our ship, now he's putting everything on the line to keep us safe."

Nadia made sure he wasn't looking before rolling her eyes. She was having a hard time deciding whether she was more mad at Russ, or at Derek for *not* being mad at Russ. Seconds later, the engines hummed to life, and the vehicle began moving again. Nadia heard Russ frantically grab the exterior railing to keep up with the vehicle.

They passed beyond the cliff face on the other side of the chasm. The tram decelerated until it came to a halt, at which point Russ jumped down and ushered the other three outside. Nadia, Derek, and Carson exited into another transit station, this one also devoid of human workers. A single mech walked by, its legs moving in mechanical angles as it headed toward an undeveloped hole in the rock to the right. The mech ignored them.

"Here," Russ said, heading to a turbolift on the far side of the station. The sign was marked GARAGE - SURFACE ACCESS.

"What are you thinking we'll find up there?" Nadia asked.

"I dunno," Russ growled. "But it beats wandering around in the dark for another hour or two." The others followed him inside.

The turbolift took a few minutes to open again, but once it did, they'd arrived in a large vehicle bay. There were tool stations nearby, with all kinds of surveying and prospecting equipment. On the far side, lined up in front of a large airlock door, was a six-wheeled rover. No one was in sight. Nadia couldn't decide if that was because the new wing was still too underdeveloped to require a permanent staff, or because the miners had retreated to safe rooms once the bombs went off.

"I can drive that thing," Derek said, indicating the rover. "We can cross the chasm and use grappling devices to lower ourselves down to the hangar bay with the *Exemplar*."

Nadia turned to Russ, half-expecting him to argue. Instead, he just shrugged. "Sounds like a good plan. But Carson doesn't have an enviro-suit, much less a grappling device. Might want to see what we can scrounge up in here."

Nadia headed over to a locker on the other side of the garage. Sure enough, there were a set of yellow-and-black enviro-suits inside, each one equipped with propulsion thrusters. She pulled out one of the suits and passed it to Carson. Derek, meanwhile, had been scouring a nearby desk and recovered a standard utility belt.

"What? No lecture about how *stealing is wrong*?" Russ asked, his voice genuinely baffled. Carson immediately started fitting the suit over his clothes.

Nadia shrugged. "After the month I've had? *Fuck* that."

Once Carson was ready, the four of them hopped into the rover. Derek took the driver's station, while Nadia sat in the passenger seat. Carson and Russ sat in the back. "Looks like the controls are frozen," Derek said, opening a panel beneath the steering wheel. He pulled a couple of wires out and cut through them with a pair of pliers on his utility belt. "Fairly easy workaround, though," he said, then started the engines.

Using the driver controls, Derek depressurized the garage and opened the airlock door. The rover shot out of the garage quickly. It only took seconds for Derek to accelerate the rover to its maximum speed. They raced along the edge of the chasm.

The drive provided an even better view of their surroundings. The damage to Kurskyn looked worse from their new vantage point than it had earlier. It was hard to get a sense of how big the settlement was, since most of it was subterranean, but the hole in the cliff looked sizable. Nadia just hoped the death toll was as low as could realistically be expected.

"I'm checking the news feeds," Russ said, looking at his wrister. "Already over six hundred deaths between the explosions in the main settlement and the collapse of some of the mining tunnels. Looks like it's just starting to hit Union media networks right now. So that death count is gonna go up." Russ grimaced.

They approached the far side of the chasm, where Derek angled their rover to the left and rounded the bend in the rock. Then, they took off down the other side, back toward Kurskyn.

In another few minutes, they were just outside the dome covering the colony's upper levels. They fastened their helmets, exited the rover, and headed over to the edge. Each of them embedded their grappling hooks in various rock features, and they rappelled down to the hangar bay. Russ crawled his way over to the airlock door's outer controls, where he must've inputted a hack. The airlock door slid open.

Once Nadia was near the bottom of the bay, she pressed a button on her device, halting her descent. Then, she swung her body back and forth until she had the momentum to jump past the hangar threshold. Once inside, she retracted the rope and headed toward the *Exemplar*.

Derek and Carson made it first, leaving Nadia and Russ on either side of the landing ramp. "Look..." Russ said, avoiding eye contact.

Letting him on her ship was the last thing Nadia wanted to do. After all, he'd been willing to destroy it and kill two of its current inhabitants just a year earlier. But leaving him here with all the chaos in Kurskyn seemed cruel. Nadia wouldn't let herself stoop to his level. And, she thought grudgingly, he *had* put himself in a lot of danger to get them out safely. Although that might've just been because of his concern for Carson. For "the asset."

"Get in," she said icily. Russ just nodded and headed up the landing ramp without looking at her. Nadia followed him.

"Looks like the port authority has a lockdown in place!" Derek shouted from the cockpit as soon as Nadia raised the landing ramp.

"Radio them our situation and explain that we're leaving," she shouted back. "And maybe activate the missile scrambler for good measure." She didn't think the Union would actually shoot her down, but being around Russ again had spiked her paranoia. Seconds later, the ship's engines fired. Nadia felt the vessel go airborne, execute an about-face, and rise toward orbit. No missiles chased them.

Before Nadia did anything else, she wanted to get in touch with Isadora. She deserved to know about the links between Brandon Zahem's faction and the Offspring. And maybe Isadora would have more clarity in terms of what to do with Russ.

As soon as she got to her dorm room, Nadia opened her private terminal and started a new message to Isadora. *We just got off Rhavego,* Nadia began the message, *and you'll never guess who we ran into.*

CHAPTER 27

What'd seemed likely to be a quiet end to Isadora's workday got complicated when she reviewed the latest polling data. This set had surveyed a representative pool of refugee guest workers on Obrigan, and her numbers were much lower than Sean Nollam's. 38% to 59%, 3% undecided, to be specific. The 3-4 point margin of error wasn't even comforting at that point.

Sean had been investing heavily into targeted advertising at the guest worker population, saying that he'd renegotiate their contracts to make them permanent. How? Through a mix of unreasonable promises—threatening Union corporations with higher tariffs, which Alexander Mettevin assured Isadora absolutely wouldn't work—and false hope. Two things that tended to play frustratingly well in politics.

Isadora looked over at her desk terminal. On it was a fully drafted message to Gabby Betam, authorizing her to release a legal opinion that guest workers were ineligible for voting rights, based on their non-permanent status. Seeing as Gabby ran their people's judicial operations, it'd pass for law. Sean Nollam would probably challenge the ruling, and it'd then go to Gerald Yellick's election commission—the one that reported to Isadora. It wouldn't be hard to twist enough arms to make Gabby's opinion become settled law.

Isadora's finger hovered over the SEND button. This felt like a bigger step than anything else she'd done to secure an advantage in the campaign. But it looked like a tight race, one where Sean's sizable margins among even a small slice of the electorate could be decisive. If she believed she was the right person for the job, and that keeping her position was her priority, there was only one decision available. She pressed the button. Hopefully, it'd be the last gut-wrenching decision she'd have to make for the rest of the—

—that was when Isadora's wrister blew up.

First came a report from Riley, relaying information she'd received from the Union intelligence agency. Isadora blinked several times, trying to switch from electioneering to security. Riley's message was terse, describing an attack in the biggest Union mining colony on the planet Rhavego. A series of explosions in Kurskyn had led to widespread cave-ins throughout the mining tunnels beneath the colony. Death toll estimates had climbed to over a thousand. Early intelligence reports from Union agents on site suggested it was a terrorist attack.

All the devastating images Isadora remembered from the New Arcena bombing rushed through her head. And Riley's brief report made it sound like the Kurskyn bombing was even more destructive.

As much as Isadora grieved for the innocent lives lost, she was at least thankful that no refugees were on Rhavego. She wondered if the Offspring could be responsible, but that fact alone made it unlikely.

Her wrister beeped once more. The new message was from Nadia: *We just got off Rhavego*, the message began. Isadora hadn't even realized Nadia had been on the planet. All she knew was that her settlement expert was looking for her captured crewmate. Isadora might've had an entirely different reaction to the news of the bombings had she known Nadia was in the midst of everything.

Luckily, Nadia had already preempted Isadora's worries. She returned to the message. *And*, Nadia continued, *you'll never guess who we ran into.*

.   .   .

The next hour of Isadora's life was a blur. It ended with her walking through one of the most intense security screening procedures she'd ever been through in order to enter the Union Government-General. She'd been here before, of course, but never granted the highest levels of security clearance.

Union soldiers were all around her, all of them equally stoic and expressionless. Isadora wondered whether any of them had been part of the detachment of troops that'd nearly attacked New Arcena last year. Either way, she was sure they'd at least *heard* about the incident. *And now look where I am*, Isadora thought as she walked past the final screening gate.

Isadora had called Riley to her office immediately after receiving Nadia's report. Riley had read it all with a detached, professional expression on her face: the attack, the partial collapse of the mining tunnels, the linkages between a radical resistance faction on Enther and the Offspring, the death of Juliet Lessitor and the confluence of Nadia and Carson Erlinza. Only when the report shifted to a discussion of Russ Kama's role had Riley's jaw quivered momentarily.

The two women had a lively debate over whether to pass along the report to the Union prime minister. Nadia had provided a key piece of intel regarding the probable whereabouts of their foremost adversary. Isadora knew that the Union intelligence bureau had two separate divisions working on the Offspring and the Ashkagi radicals, but they'd never pooled their information before. Comparing notes might lead to a valuable breakthrough.

Initially, Riley had urged caution in sending such a valuable piece of intelligence to the Union, although Isadora had made a compelling argument to the contrary. Sure, they'd always have to keep secrets, even from allies. But their first half-year in the Natonus System had more than demonstrated the pitfalls of keeping *too* much to themselves.

So Isadora had dispatched Nadia's report personally to Tricia Favan. And now, an hour later, she was walking into the halls of the Union Government-General, with a personal invitation to not just Tricia's office, but to the situation room in the basement.

It was an unprecedented move. The only people allowed down there were Tricia, the highest-ranking military officials in the entire damn system, and a smattering of intelligence officials. Inviting someone like Isadora into the situation room was a breach of decades of precedent.

The halls of the Government-General were lined with ornate, fluted white columns of imposing heights. Small patches of standard starship hull plating were woven into the walls. As Isadora was enjoying the scenery, Tricia herself rounded the corner. "I'm glad you came," the prime minister said brusquely. "This is the best part of my job."

"My heart grieves for all the lives lost on Rhavego," Isadora blurted out. If anything, she was surprised by how calm Tricia looked. Didn't she know that over a thousand of her people had just died? Then again, she'd *never* known Tricia to ease up on her sardonic nature, crisis or no. This was probably just the other woman's way of coping with calamity.

"The way I see it, politics isn't really about wishing bad things hadn't happened," Tricia said with a shrug. "It's about finding the right ass to kick after they do." She turned abruptly and headed down a winding staircase. Isadora followed her until they arrived at a heavy, secure door. All the while, she wondered why Tricia had invited her. Sure, it seemed like Isadora had provided a missing piece of the intelligence puzzle, but she'd already passed along Nadia's report. Knowing Tricia, she probably had some kind of ulterior motive in mind.

Tricia slid a keycard into a slot underneath a terminal to the right. The door lumbered open, and the prime minister stepped inside without so much as a second thought. Isadora hesitated for only a second before following her inside. A cursory glance inside the room showed the deployments of the vast Union navy via a central holographic projector. Fifteen chairs were arrayed around the projector, with a few armed marines stationed at various points in the room's corners.

A dozen pairs of eyes all shot her way as Isadora stepped into the room. Tricia pulled a chair out next to her, beckoning Isadora to sit. Isadora sat down, crossing her legs and placing her hands on her lap. The officers all wore uniforms colored mustard yellow, with a litany of medals indicating each one's storied career. Isadora searched for friendly faces and found none. The best she'd get here was indifference.

Tricia pulled a cigarette out of her breast pocket and moved her hand over to her right, almost as if on instinct, before retracting her hand and lighting the end herself. "You smoke?" Isadora asked.

Tricia shrugged. "Only in here." Then she turned her attention to the assembled security officials and officers around them. "Everyone be nice to Isadora," Tricia said. "I know all of you advised me not to invite her, but you got outvoted, one to twelve." Her mouth curled into a grin. Isadora wasn't sure if Tricia was deliberately ribbing her, but knowing no one else even wanted Isadora in the room was hardly comforting. "Anyway, this concerns her people as much as it does ours."

One of the generals closest to Isadora, a broad-shouldered woman with cropped blonde hair, cleared her throat. "We have surveillance footage of one of the radical Ashkagi camps," she said.

"Thank you, General Jedden. Now throw it up there so we can all see," Tricia said, pointing to the central projector. The general tapped away at her terminal. The holographic image of the Natonus System was replaced with footage of a hidden encampment deep in what looked like a jungle planet. Isadora noted a handful of armed guards patrolling the perimeter.

"Welcome to the Enther wilderness," Tricia explained. "That intel you passed along was the missing puzzle piece. See, we'd already been tracking a transport of radicalized Offspring recruits heading for the outer rim. Once I realized the Offspring were in cahoots with the fuckers who killed my people, I directed everyone—and by *everyone*, I mean every asshole I could find—to track the transport's probable trajectory.

"That got us here. And sure enough, the Ashkagi radicals are shacked up there too. Along with your bad guys." Tricia indicated a cluster of guards who were sporting brown Offspring enviro-suits. Isadora's eyes went wide. They'd been searching for the Offspring for the better part of the last two months, and *here they were*. At least some of them. There was no way of knowing if this was their primary hideout, or just one faction's base of operations.

"Anyway," Tricia continued, "the Sixth Fleet is on patrol near that region of space. But even at a decent burn, it'd take them two days to get there. I'm interested in action *now*. I mobilized a fleet of un-manned drones to fly from our base in the asteroid belt to Enther. That's how we're getting this footage. Anyone object to me blowing these assholes straight to hell?" Tricia asked.

Isadora then realized why she'd been invited. This wasn't an in-telligence sharing session. This was a military operation, conducted against a common foe. Or rather, against two foes who happened to be allied. Tricia was offering to kill off at least a good chunk of the people who'd butchered the New Arcena colonists.

"Given our assessment of Michael Azkon," an intelligence liaison spoke up, referring to the chairman of the Enther Junta, "he'd regard a drone strike on his planet as a serious breach of sovereignty. We don't know how he'd react."

Tricia looked at the ceiling like she was genuinely considering the objection. She puffed out a large cloud of smoke. "Yeah, don't care. I only tolerated these Ashkagi terrorists as long as they stayed out of Union space. But now they've murdered *Union citizens*. Sovereignty can shove it.

"But you've got skin in the game," Tricia continued, looking at Isa-dora. "What do you say?" Everyone else suddenly turned to face her.

Isadora looked back at the surveillance footage, focusing her attention on the Offspring circling the perimeter. From this perspective, it was so easy to just think of them as pests, not human adversaries. A missile strike would feel more like swatting a bug that'd crept into your house than warfare.

This was a good thing...right? But Isadora couldn't shake a sense of unease, compounded by the fact that a dozen of the most powerful people in the system were all staring at her. She could feel the sweat pooling at the edge of her hairline.

If she could work past this weird feeling of guilt—guilt of approving the deaths of dozens or hundreds with a wave of her hand from a comfortable, air-conditioned room on the other side of the Natonus System—she had to admit that, logically, a strike on the Offspring/Ashkagi camp was in her people's best interests. Who knew whether the strike would wipe out the Offspring's leadership structure, but it'd put them on the back foot for the first time since the New Arcena bombing.

Then why did she feel so uncomfortable, still?

"Okay," Isadora said weakly. "I have no objections."

"Good! You have a go order," Tricia said, giving a hand signal toward an officer to her left.

The finality of it left Isadora feeling nauseous. As the others began conversing among themselves, she passed the time by turning inward. She'd always envisioned her role as someone who helped people. Someone who provided for them, who kept them safe. As though her new job was just an extension of her old position as city councilor back on Earth.

But she'd have to become more than that. Her job wasn't just bringing her people out of cryo, it was also removing anyone who sought to do them harm. The drone strike on the Offspring camp was only the beginning. If they could successfully insert Carson Erlinza into the Offspring's ranks, that opened the door for more military action. Which meant more occasions watching people die from hundreds of millions of miles away.

Isadora liked being able to retreat from her work in the evenings and look her daughter in the eye over dinner, comfortable that Meredith would see someone of integrity and principle looking back at her. It'd been harder to imagine that recently, especially with all the ways she'd been tampering with the election process. And now this.

No, Isadora told herself. She had to be stronger than this. She'd bear any discomfort on behalf of her people.

And then, about a half-hour later, it happened.

Isadora was surprised by how fast it was. She was in the middle of a long exhale when the projection screen lit up in a white plume, engulfing the jungle camp. Many people's lives had just ended in less time than it took for Isadora to blink. Did she really feel safer now than she had a few minutes ago? Did it make her a horrible person if the answer was *yes*? The nausea worsened, sinking deeper into her stomach. She excused herself from the situation room.

Isadora ascended the staircase outside quickly, desperately looking around the halls of the Government-General for some kind of balcony or outdoor corridor. Any means of getting a breath of fresh air. She eventually spied a balcony on her right. The sun had set quickly, and a crisp breeze made her hands grasp the edge of her blazer for warmth.

She looked out over the skyscrapers as they lit up the night sky, neon light beams arcing across the air. Then she stepped toward the edge of the balcony and nearly threw up over the side.

"I was like this my first time," a raspy voice said from behind her.

Isadora turned and saw Tricia standing near the entrance to the balcony, leaning against the wall with her arms crossing her chest. "Back when we almost went to war, all I remember is the *nausea*," Isadora said. "I'm not built for this kind of thing."

"No one is. But it's what the job demands," Tricia said. "Someone trying to kill your people? You're practically obligated to go out and kill them first." Tricia walked forward and leaned on the balcony next to Isadora. "And if you don't have the stomach to do it, someone else *will*." Someone like Sean Nollam, Tricia didn't need to add.

"You know why I *really* invited you to the situation room?" the prime minister asked, her voice growing quieter. Isadora shook her head. "Here," Tricia said, pulling up her wrister and opening a file of photos of the two of them, sitting at the head of the table.

"I told you I'd find a way to help you. You can use these pictures for your reelection campaign," Tricia said. "You'll come out of this looking good. Turns out, blowing a bunch of motherfuckers up makes you look like a leader. Truth is, I *like* dealing with you. Much more so than that limp-dick asshole who's challenging you. So make sure you kick his ass."

Isadora looked at the pictures and almost didn't recognize herself. Her face seemed more drawn, her eyes more sunken, her hair greyer than she remembered. But despite the emotional tumult she'd been going through, she looked poised. Dignified. The kind of leader who projected calm and safety.

"Thank you," Isadora muttered.

"Look, if it makes you feel better, I was gonna order the strike no matter what you said. Only reason I asked you there was for the photo op." The two women stood in silence as the wind hissed by them.

"How about I call you an aircar," Tricia continued. "You've had a long day. Go back and spend tonight with your daughter. It'll cheer you up. Besides, I'm about to have to answer a bunch of really annoying questions from the media." Tricia retreated inside.

Seeing Meredith usually *did* cheer Isadora up. But she wasn't just afraid Meredith would look into her eyes and see someone who lacked integrity. The prime minister's assurances notwithstanding, she feared her daughter would look at her and see only the eyes of a killer staring back.

CHAPTER 28

Sometimes, on the days when Tanner's room inside the hideout was feeling oppressive, he left the encampment and wandered out into the nearby jungles to do some solitary thinking. It was usually a calming moment. Not so today.

He was still fuming at the plan Brandon Zahem had discussed with him several weeks ago: a plot to detonate a series of explosive devices on the planet Rhavego, ostensibly to protest the Union's trade relations with the Junta. He'd told Tanner that it'd work out just as well as the Offspring's attack on New Arcena.

Tanner had begged to differ. Killing newars was one thing, pissing the Union off was another. But Brandon hadn't even entertained a debate about it. The man's mind was made up, and all Tanner could do was fume in the jungles.

So much for a calming walk.

That was when a whistling sound tore through the night air, followed by a deafening explosion and a giant white plume back from the hideout, now about a half-mile away from Tanner. Going out to clear his head might've just saved his life.

It took him a second to realize what'd happened. At first, he wondered if someone had mishandled the explosives they kept back in the camp. But their devices generally didn't have the blast radius that Tanner had just observed. And that didn't explain the whistling sound.

No. They'd been attacked. And he was almost certain it was Brandon's fault.

Tanner took off through the jungles, dozens of low-hanging wet leaves and underbrush sliding against his brown suit. When he muscled his way past a thicket, he saw that his initial suspicions were correct. The top of the camp had nearly caved in, with the surrounding landscape having cratered out from the impact of a projectile. He was sure an airborne missile was responsible.

Tanner wondered if it could've been the Junta, although it was too easy to rule that out. The Enther government hardly had an impressive navy, and state-of-the-art war drones were out of reach for their budget. Plus, it didn't make sense why the Junta would've waited till now to launch a strike.

It had to be the Union. Being right so often was a curse sometimes.

As Tanner drew closer, the costs of Brandon's error became easier to see. Bodies had been literally blown apart in the drone strike, with a mangled mess of limbs scattered throughout the blast site. He walked over to a dead Offspring whose torso was severed from his legs, which were lying a few feet away.

Violence and death had never made Tanner flinch. The first time he'd seen someone die was his old coworker back at Veltech, whose brave self-immolation and righteous political screed had started Tanner down this path. The second was the Offspring's assassination of a Union Parliament member.

In both cases, he'd felt no surge of emotions in his gut, no visceral disgust. Just calm detachment. The stream of consciousness in his head surveyed the immediate area with nothing but clinical coldness: *six bodies, all in various states of dismemberment. No survivors.* But there'd almost certainly be survivors inside, and cold detachment wouldn't comfort his traumatized disciples. He'd need to project calm. Empathy. Leadership.

Tanner walked inside the encampment. Two Offspring survivors huddled in the corner, shivering from fear, their faces stained with dirt and ash and blood. The two embraced each other for comfort. "You'll be okay," Tanner said, offering his hand to them. "It will all be okay. They're attacking us because we're powerful, and because we're *right*. They're afraid of our truth and our might." Gentleness didn't come easily for him, but he tried to soften his voice as much as he could. It was only through performative empathy that Tanner could refocus his followers on their true goals.

Four fearful eyes looked up at him, as though they wanted to believe him but were still immobilized. "You are both still alive for a reason," Tanner continued. "And you are both heroes. The people who attacked us are the ones who've sold us out to the invaders."

One of them reached his shaking hand up. Tanner pulled the man to his feet with a firm grasp. "In time, the pain of this moment will fade, brother. Only victory awaits."

Tanner pulled the other one up. "Go into the jungles to clear your heads," he said. "But don't stay out for too long. We must be ready to leave this site soon. More attacks may be coming." The two nodded and departed for the surrounding wilderness, stepping over the carnage outside.

He then walked through the camp and surveyed the damage. The upper floor had nearly been decimated, with most of the roof collapsed. Broken, jagged stones were lying everywhere, often trapping some hapless individual below. The initial blast had probably only killed a portion of the ultimate victims. The collapse of the encampment would account for many more.

He wandered into a nearby room and found two of his people crouched over a third, who was lying crushed beneath a large piece of rubble. The man's eyes were glazed over. An idea crept into Tanner's skull. The attack on the hideout was a setback, to be sure, but it was his job to find whatever opportunities he could. "There's nothing more you can do for him," he said, trying to keep his voice gentle and moderate, as before. "But there is something you can do for *us*, if you can stomach it."

The two surviving Offspring looked up at him.

"The Union has now massacred its own people on behalf of the newars," he said. Technically, that was only a half-truth—more likely, Brandon's forces had been the target, and the Offspring had just been caught in the crossfire—but Tanner knew that media narratives could be manipulated.

"Take footage of every one of our brothers who perished. Flood the net with those images. Show the Natonese public every severed arm and every bloody leg. Show them how the Union regards its own people. The violence it is willing to inflict under the malign influence of the invaders. Make them reckon with it."

The two exchanged glances, clearly uncomfortable with Tanner's orders. "Everyone who perished died as heroes," Tanner said, clenching his jaw. "This is the best way to mourn them. To serve the cause that claimed their lives."

That seemed to work. The two nodded in agreement, pulled out their wrist terminals, and began to record footage of the damage inflicted on the camp. They lingered on the dead man lying in the middle of the room.

A grim smile crossed Tanner's face, and then he left them to it. He walked back through the ruined hideout, ignoring the death and destruction all around him. After a while, the corpses and the rubble blended together.

He headed for the basement, hoping his prize captive Boyd Makrum had been unharmed by the strike. The man had been frustratingly tough to break so far, but there was even less of a chance to convert him if he was dead. Luckily, it didn't seem that the lower levels had suffered much damage. The walls were mostly intact, and Tanner passed by a good number of Offspring and Ashkagi who were still alive.

"You're okay," Tanner said, walking up to a group of Offspring guarding one of the cells. "Many of our brethren on the first floor and standing guard outside have lost their lives, but this is the price that we must sometimes pay in our crusade. Go upstairs and help your brothers pack supplies and belongings. We will need to leave this place soon."

As the Offspring filed out, Tanner walked to the back of the basement level, took a right, and entered the cell area. He passed by a handful of cells with prisoners inside he didn't care about. Finally, he reached Boyd's cell. Luckily, a wide-eyed but very much alive Boyd was curled up in the corner of his cell. "What was that?" the man asked almost as soon as Tanner caught sight of him.

"Union drone strike, most likely," Tanner said. "Does it make you feel better to know that your government is willing to kill you to protect outsiders like Nadia?" Tanner didn't feel it was necessary to mention Brandon's operation on Rhavego. It'd just dilute the point he was trying to make.

Boyd stared back at him. "I'm sure you gave them a reason," he said quietly.

"Reason? Do you want me to take you to all the bodies lying crushed under the rubble? Will the eyes of a dozen dead men give you the proper *reason* for this brutality?" It was hard to avoid righteous anger seeping into his voice, but Tanner mostly kept it cool. He was trying to awaken Boyd, not indulge in moralizing.

"That's all bullshit considering what you pulled on New Arcena," Boyd said.

"Attacking the newars is an act of self-defense," Tanner countered. "People are *meant* to defend their own tribes. It's practically the whole point. I would *never* do something like this to my fellow Natonese people. But it looks like the prime minister cares more about a handful of people from across the galaxy than those she's sworn to protect. There is no comparing this heinous attack to our actions in New Arcena."

"So violence is justified based on where someone was born?" Boyd asked.

"*Yes*. That is practically the foundation of a society," Tanner pressed.

"Whatever. You're just a psycho," Boyd said, wrapping his arms around his knees and curling his torso forward. Tanner suppressed a grin. He was glad the prisoner had survived the attack. Tanner enjoyed getting under his skin.

"We'll be leaving soon," Tanner said. "Make sure you're ready to go."

"Just let me pack my things," Boyd sneered at him, gesturing toward the empty cell.

Tanner ignored his comment and headed back upstairs. The two Offspring he'd assigned to video the carnage passed by, taking footage of a ruined wall with three dead Offspring lying beneath.

The booming sound of approaching engines muted all other activity in the camp. At first, Tanner feared it might be a Union or Junta attack. But more likely, it was Brandon Zahem, returning to survey the damage. Tanner headed outside, where he glimpsed one of Brandon's gunships descending through the canopy.

The gunship swerved in midair until it came to rest in a small clearing just outside the hideout. Tanner strode forward, impelled by raw fury. He almost wanted to pull his gun out and shoot Brandon in the head.

The man had miscalculated horribly, thinking the same tactics that'd spurred the Offspring's recruiting drive could boost his own numbers. But Tanner would never target a Union settlement. When he'd pointed that out to Brandon, he'd just shrugged that off, claiming that an attack on Union space could drive a wedge between the Union and the Junta that he could then play to their advantage.

Here's your hard-won "advantage," Tanner thought, glancing back at the carnage. He returned his gaze to the gunship, where Brandon and a small escort of his followers had emerged. Tanner leaned back against a nearby tree.

Brandon's face looked pale, his hands trembling as he walked forward and saw the extent of the destruction. "I can't believe it," the man said breathlessly. "I never thought the Union would actually go through with something like this."

It took all of Tanner's might not to narrow his eyes. Honestly, nothing could be more satisfying than socking the other man in the jaw right now. Brandon had always struck Tanner as the kind of man who'd go down after a single, solid punch to the face.

"How many died?" Brandon asked, turning to face Tanner, as though he couldn't even bear to look at the dead lying nearby.

"Does it matter?" Tanner asked. "This place is compromised. We need to move our people to safety. And we should assume that the Union is conducting surveillance on us, so we need to be careful in how we plan our movements."

If Brandon was doing any thinking, it didn't show on his face. He was still just staring at the blast site, his mouth open like a fucking moron.

"Think!" Tanner hissed. "You know this planet better than I do. And my people's lives depend on you finding a proper hiding spot."

"Ruhae," Brandon said at last. "It was an old royal retreat, back when the planet was still under control of the old Theocracy. Most of the retreat is underground. Should be perfect for avoiding airborne surveillance."

"Good. Work on a plan to transfer our people safely and discreetly to this Ruhae, *now*. Otherwise, we could be vulnerable to a follow-up attack."

Brandon seemed so deflated that he hardly reacted when Tanner gave him an order. *Soft in the face of violence*, Tanner thought. He'd been spearheading an armed insurrection for years, and yet he still froze up at the sight of actual bloodshed. Brandon was weaker than he realized.

"Okay," Brandon said, avoiding eye contact. His shoulders slumped in submission. Tanner held all the power now. Brandon and his escort headed toward the camp.

Tanner stayed rooted to the spot, his back still leaning against the tree. But he turned his gaze skyward, where the planet's night sky suddenly looked more threatening. The Union had the capability to observe and destroy them from unseen heights, something that made them far more dangerous than the newars or even the Junta.

That changed the game. Tanner had been imagining the contest between the Offspring and the invaders as a chess match, where both sides had their fair share of strengths and weaknesses and were, in a final analysis, relatively evenly matched. But thanks to Brandon's short-sightedness, the Union was getting involved. He felt less like a chess player and more like an insect in the path of a marauding giant.

And there was only one proper move in a game where the deck was stacked against you: flip the table.

Tanner had to rethink his entire strategy. Brandon Zahem had proven useful so far, helping train the Offspring in the skills necessary to carry out anti-newar operations across the system. And if he could move them to safety at the royal retreat he mentioned, he could prove useful still.

But after that? Tanner's partnership with the Ashkagi radicals suddenly seemed less advantageous. And he was unwilling to play out a losing game. If the Union was going to mobilize its formidable surveillance network against the Offspring, he needed utter chaos. A smokescreen that could blanket the entire outer rim, warding the Union's watchful eyes away and giving his people the space to operate.

But how could he introduce such a massive amount of chaos? He didn't have an answer to that yet, but he had some ideas.

CHAPTER 29

Everything felt like a blur, Carson reflected as he stared into a tea-filled tumbler set on the central table in the *Exemplar*'s canteen. Only yesterday morning, he'd been tracking Saul Worska with Juliet. Now, both of them were dead, and he'd been whisked off Rhavego by Russ and Nadia. They'd been holding orbit over the planet for the last six hours. The escape from the mining tunnels, the drive across Rhavego's rocky surface, and blasting off in the *Exemplar* felt like a strange dream.

And yet, here he was. The entire time, he hadn't allowed himself to think about Juliet, because he knew he'd just break down. His body told him he was tired, but his mind knew that sleeping would only bring about the inevitable nightmares all centered on Juliet's limp, unmoving body. She'd died to save him, and he hadn't even had the decency to give her a proper burial.

He was a shell, filled only by a grim determination to continue on his mission. Even if it killed him. Following Russ and Nadia out of the mining tunnels had mostly been an exercise in going on autopilot.

He looked across the table at Derek Hozan, Nadia's remaining teammate, who hadn't so much as said a word after piloting the *Exemplar* into orbit. He nursed a coffee while reading some old, dusty book he'd brought from his room.

Derek must've caught Carson looking at him, because he looked up and made eye contact. "Everything okay?" Derek asked.

No. Absolutely nothing is okay. I'm miserable and hopeless, Carson thought. "Yeah," he said.

"All right then," Derek said, accepting Carson's answer and returning his attention to his book. "Let me know if you need help finding anything on our ship."

Carson had already found the vessel's med bay in the *Exemplar*'s port wing, nestled between the work offices and the ship's rec room. Carson almost thought about getting a workout in, but it looked like all they had were resistance bands and a pool sphere. He missed the punching bag from the gym he'd frequented back in Kurskyn.

And besides, his side was still aching from the falling rocks. He'd replaced his bandages, which had gotten sweaty and soggy from the hike across the mining tunnels, and had taken another painkiller.

Russ walked in from the left and leaned against the wall. "Had to get something for the knee," he said with a wince. "Real twenty-fifth century solution: an ice pack," he added with a grin, giving Carson a wink. The man crumpled up a plastic bag and pressed it against his knee.

Carson hadn't been able to figure Russ out. The primers he'd read back on the *Preserver* portrayed Russ as an unhinged renegade: getting into bed with the black market, assuming an aggressive posture toward the Union that'd almost destroyed their people, that kind of thing.

Nothing like the man before Carson now. Russ was clearly cynical and prone to worst-case scenario thinking—a catastrophizer, not unlike a number of Carson's old patients—but he seemed to have lost the edge the primers said he had. Carson had a hard time seeing the Russ in front of him as a warmonger.

"How're you and Nadia holding up?" Russ asked Derek.

Derek put down his book for a moment, a thoughtful expression on his face. Although Carson had only known him for a few hours, he was already getting the sense that the man was rarely spontaneous in his speech. He usually paused before he said anything, a contemplative look on his face.

"The truth is, both of us are missing Boyd," Derek said. "Nadia...hasn't been in the best place ever since he got kidnapped. I think she blames herself for what happened."

"That's rough," Russ said. "Look, what happened last year—"

"—don't worry about it," Derek said. "It's water under the bridge to me. I understand you were just doing what you thought was best. So were we."

Carson remembered from the primers that Russ had ordered the New Arcena defense militia to destroy the *Exemplar*. He hadn't put the pieces together fully—he'd been too focused on just making it off Rhavego alive and processing the emotional devastation of Juliet's sacrifice—but that meant Russ had almost killed Nadia and her crew. Carson had detected some resentment from Nadia toward Russ back in the mining tunnels, but they'd kept things mostly professional.

A slow, horrified realization dawned on him. If Nadia was still mad at Russ and had suppressed those emotions back on Rhavego, coupled with the unresolved search for Boyd, she could be on the verge of an emotional explosion. Right now, the only person around who'd directly tried to harm Boyd was Russ. It'd be too easy to project everything onto him.

On cue, Nadia entered briskly from the starboard wing of the ship. She leaned against the wall and crossed her arms over her chest, her eyes fixed on Russ, glowering. "I finished sending Isadora a more detailed report on our operation," Nadia said.

Russ seemed to perk up at the mention of Isadora's name. "How is...how is she doing, with everything?"

"Just fine," Nadia said through gritted teeth. "No thanks to you."

Russ cast his eyes downward. "Look, I don't think that's very fai—"

" —hell, I'd probably even say she's better than ever, now that she doesn't have some warmonger perched over her shoulder. And she brought her daughter out of cryo. Hard to tell which one was better for her, mentally. Pretty competitive, don't you think?"

"Because you've always given good advice?" Russ shot back. "Tell me: how has your whole *actually-everybody-is-nice-and-why-can't-we-all-just-get-along* approach been working with the Offspring? Have they responded well to *reason*?"

"I've probably made a bad decision here and there," Nadia said. "But at least I owned up to it and got better, instead of whimpering away. I didn't abandon our people when my back was against the wall."

Nadia, Carson remembered, had received a glowing portrayal in the primers. She was the idealistic heart behind the refugees' struggle, a perfect complement to Isadora's calm, steady hand. That description seemed almost as inaccurate as Russ'.

Nadia struck Carson as someone who was just barely succeeding at reining in a deep-rooted rage. She seemed consumed by anger, her face giving everyone and everything a dark look ever since he'd seen her, except for a few fleeting moments of sympathy—after she'd learned about Juliet, for example.

"Your problem is your ego," Russ said, his voice sharpening. "You convinced yourself that you were some big shot after that stunt you pulled on Calimor last year. Only problem is, you didn't do *shit*. Isadora was the one who saved us, by passing along the information I provided to Tricia. All you did was wave your arms around dramatically while the adults in the room actually solved the problem."

"From where I'm standing, it sounds like I did a hell of a lot more than the one who got us into that mess in the first place!" Nadia said.

Carson looked across the table at Derek, who'd pulled the book up so it covered his face almost entirely. He looked down helplessly at his tumbler, wishing he had some way to retreat from the argument. Then again, he supposed he could do better than mere conflict avoidance. If he could get Nadia and Russ to refocus their attention on how they'd just overcome a challenging situation through cooperation, that might cool down their tempers.

"What matters is that we're all safe," Carson said. "And we were able to put aside our differences back on—" He gave up when he could barely hear his own voice over the sound of Russ and Nadia hurling insults at each other.

Scratch that. Time to try something else. Carson pushed himself up and walked over to the kitchen. He placed his empty tumbler in the dishwasher and scoured the food cabinets for anything he could make.

Cooking and baking had gotten him through the most stressful parts of his grad program—along with energetic sessions with the punching bag, of course—and there was something comfortable about falling back on old habits. His hand explored the pantry and lingered on an unopened box of waffle mix pods. He glanced over at the counter, and sure enough, they had a waffle iron that looked brand new.

Seemed close enough to comfort food—*no Canadian maple syrup*, he rued—and it'd be easy enough to make. Carson opened the box, withdrew one of the pods, and slotted it into a receptacle at the top of the iron. Then he connected a tube at the back of the device to a water spigot. The machine activated with a hiss. Water coursed through the tube, wisps of steam slipping off the surface.

While working on the waffles, he'd almost been able to tune out the raging argument between Nadia and Russ. Which was, in turn, keeping him from thinking too much about Juliet. Distractions on distractions on distractions.

By the time the waffle iron beeped, Carson was pretty sure none of the other three had even noticed what he was doing. He cleared his throat. "Anyone want a waffle?" Carson asked.

Nadia and Russ went silent, both their mouths agape as they turned to face him. From behind the cover of his book, Derek raised his hand. Carson peeled the waffle off the iron and threw it across the room. The waffle sailed perfectly into Derek's outstretched hand, which retracted back behind the cover of the book.

"Well...shit, if you're offering, sure, I'll take a waffle," Russ said.

"Coming right up," Carson said. He put the used mixture pod in a trash receptacle and placed another one in the open compartment.

"See? If you'd managed to blow up our ship, Carson wouldn't have been able to make you a waffle with our iron. Funny how that all works out," Nadia said, flaring her nostrils.

"Would you cut all this bullshit out?" Russ snapped. "I get it: I made a bad call. If I could go back and undo everything I did, you know what? I'd fucking *do it*. But I can't, and I've spent most of the last year drinking myself to sleep over how bad I fucked everything up. You're not telling me anything I haven't already told myself. You think a man can't change, Nadia?"

Silence, merciful silence.

Nadia looked at her feet, Russ did too, and Derek dared to peek his eyes up over the cover of his book. Carson sighed deeply, appreciating the sudden tranquility, when the waffle iron beeped again. He pulled out the waffle, tossed it to Russ, and then prepared a third mixture pod.

The silence that'd descended on the canteen had somehow shifted from merciful to awkward. Nadia and Russ still weren't even making eye contact. "So," Carson said, "how about that election coming up?"

"Sean Nollam is scum," Russ said. "And Isadora is a goddamn hero."

"Isadora is the best of us. It's not a hard choice at all," Nadia said. "I sent in my absentee ballot right before we landed on Rhavego."

"Ah, shit. I need to get around to doing that," Russ said.

"Not eligible," Derek chimed in.

And that's how you do it, Carson thought. He had a professional lifetime of practice burying his own emotional turmoil in order to bring peace and harmony to his surroundings. Good to see those skills were still sharp.

He pulled up his wrister, hoping a quick survey of the news headlines would keep him occupied until Nadia's waffle was ready. The first headline made his eyes go wide: *Union drone strike targets radical Ashkagi faction, Offspring.* According to the first few paragraphs of the article, the intel leading to the strike had been provided by none other than Isadora Satoro. Presumably, thanks to the report Nadia had sent her earlier. That meant they knew where at least some of the Offspring were.

At last, Carson thought he could see light at the end of the tunnel. Finding the Offspring had always been his and Juliet's goal. And if the Offspring could be found, that meant they could be infiltrated.

The mental gears in Carson's head turned, so much so that he hardly heard the beep from the waffle iron. "Nadia," he said, "you mentioned you were looking for your other crewmate. The one who was captured by the Ashkagi radicals, right?"

"Yes," Nadia said. "I don't see how that—"

"—you might want to check your wristers," Carson interjected.

All three of their heads immediately bowed down to read from their wrist devices. One by one, all of their eyes widened. "That was a gutsy move," Russ said. "Glad Isadora and the prime minister made the right call on that one."

"I don't see how this gets us any closer to Boyd," Nadia said. "And I, uh, I think my waffle might be ready..."

"Right. Sorry." Carson flipped open the lid, scraped off the burnt edges into the composter, and threw the waffle over to Nadia. "This means that the Union—and by extension, our boss—can track the Offspring. I want to find the Offspring in order to infiltrate them. You want to find the Ashkagi who are holding your friend, and we know they're working with the Offspring. Our goals are aligned."

Nadia's brow furrowed, and she looked at the ceiling.

When Carson turned to Russ, he saw that the other man's face had softened. "If we fly to Enther for your insertion, that means you'll be behind enemy lines in as little as two weeks," he said. "Think carefully. This is a big step, the most dangerous part of your whole assignment. And you'd be truly on your own. Are you really ready for this?"

Carson knew all that. But present company aside, he'd been feeling alone ever since the rockfall crushed Juliet. There was no room left inside him to worry or to doubt himself, even if he knew, logically, that his odds of success were slim. He had to forge ahead. Just a little bit longer. "No," Carson answered honestly, "but I don't think waiting around for another month or two is going to make me feel any better."

Russ closed his eyes and nodded. "Good answer."

Nadia had finished her contemplation and shifted her gaze toward Carson. The anger and edge in her eyes had dissipated. "You don't have to do this if you don't want to. You don't owe your life to anyone," she said.

"I know," he said, although that wasn't entirely true. He owed his life to Stacy, to Juliet, and to all the others who'd put their hopes in him to do the job. He didn't think he was the best person to infiltrate the Offspring, but if they did, then he owed it to them to try. "I've made up my mind," he continued. "This is what I want."

Russ ran a hand through his scraggly beard. "I still have contacts back in the New Arcena militia, back from when..." his voice trailed off. "Anyway, I can get in touch with them. See if I can get them to send a detachment to rendezvous with us over Enther. I could lead a raid on their outpost, while Nadia goes after Boyd and Carson slips behind their lines. It'd look like a single assault, but it'd actually be a three-pronged operation, with me leading the distraction team."

"If we can figure out where they might be holding Boyd, I can plot a course for Enther," Derek said, finally showing signs of life. "We could get there in a week and a half."

Nadia hesitated, shooting Russ a dark look. One by one, the other three turned to look at her. "It makes sense," she said finally. "And I guess it'd be good to have someone around who knows how to plan a military operation," she muttered.

Carson waited until the other three had all left—Derek to plot a course for Enther, Nadia to get in touch with Isadora, Russ to contact Riley and their militia forces on Calimor—to head to his dorm. The adrenaline surge had finally ended, it seemed, and his eyes drooped. He'd need his energy if he was going to be among the enemy in a few weeks.

Maybe the nightmares wouldn't be so bad, he thought as he entered his room. After all, everything he'd just suggested, and everything he was about to do, would be in Juliet's honor. All he could do was hope that her memory would be satisfied with that and allow him a restful sleep.

CHAPTER 30

Isadora seemed to fall back on her worst habits when Meredith wasn't around: constantly checking election polls between her and Sean, or spending all night reading updates from her advisers instead of taking the time to unwind. Her lead had almost evaporated, 49% to 47%, ever since her disastrous virtual town hall. Under Valencia's advice, they'd flooded the net with the image of Isadora in Tricia's situation room during the Enther strike. Maybe that'd move the needle a bit, but Isadora wasn't holding her breath.

As the situation had grown more dire, her cabinet officials had diverted some of their working hours toward making appeals to the electorate. Isadora hadn't asked them to do so, but it secretly delighted her to watch Riley, Alexander, Gabby, and Katrina all defending her. Katrina had been especially vociferous in her defense of

Isadora. Her go-to pitch: "you don't know what it's like to be in the chair when the hard decisions get made. Neither do I. There's only one of us who has been there, making the hard calls, from day one. And that's Isadora Satoro." Isadora wondered what she might've thought about Katrina sticking her neck out for her this time last year.

Her front door shook from a heavy knock, and Isadora put her wrister away. As a distraction effort, she'd invited Tricia Favan over. After-hours, informal meetings had become an irregular ritual for the two women. The Union's security services had swept the entire embassy so many times that they knew it was safe. Isadora was pretty sure Tricia labeled their meetings "strategic diplomatic outreach" in her schedule.

"Come in!" Isadora called. Tricia entered almost immediately after, clutching a bottle of red wine in her hand.

"When's the last time you had a good drink?" Tricia said, wearing a lopsided grin.

"Before I woke Meredith up, probably." Isadora walked over to the kitchen to grab a pair of glasses. Tricia sat down at the dining room table.

The vast majority of the time, political realities defined Isadora and Tricia's relationship. Even though the refugees and the Union's relationship was far warmer than it used to be, they still kept things professional during their work-related meetings. Extracurricular get-togethers like this only had one rule: no business. They were just two women, enjoying some well-needed relaxation off the clock.

"What's Meredith up to?" Tricia asked as Isadora brought the wine glasses over.

"Camping trip with her class, up in the mountains to the east of the city," Isadora said. "Under the watchful eyes of her personal detail, naturally." She set one of the glasses down on the table, and Tricia poured about double the amount that Isadora wanted.

Isadora placed the other glass in front of Tricia, but the other woman moved the glass aside and set the rest of the bottle in front of her. Isadora suppressed a chuckle, clinked her glass to Tricia's bottle, and they took an inaugural sip.

"I've been to those mountains a couple of times," Tricia nodded. "Actually, it was where my ex-husband proposed to me. Haven't really gone back since." She took a long swig of wine.

Tricia had talked to Isadora a few times previously about her ill-fated marriage. It was easy for her to empathize, even though she hadn't gotten so far as a proposal with Meredith's father.

"What ever happened with the dad?" Tricia asked, as though she'd read her thoughts.

Isadora's mind felt like it was doing somersaults. Meredith's father, a man whose commitment to both her and their daughter Isadora had sorely misjudged, had departed their lives when Meredith was still two. Isadora had spent the next two years pleading with him to come back, convinced that he could still turn himself around. She'd wised up around the time Meredith turned four. Some people never change. Leaving Isadora was something she'd learned to forgive, but abandoning Meredith and depriving her of a second parent? That made him irredeemable.

"Honestly...it's been so long since I've even thought about him," Isadora said. The last time she'd consciously thought about Meredith's father was early in her tenure, before she'd brought Meredith out of cryo. She'd checked the *Preserver* crew roster to see if her old partner was among them. He wasn't.

That meant he'd either been killed during the Hegemony invasion of the Sol System, or died of old age under the heel of his new overlords long ago, all while Isadora had been slumbering in cryo aboard the *Preserver*. And now she stood at the apex of the refugees' political hierarchy. Sometimes, fate delivered the most satisfying revenge possible.

"I don't think he was a particularly good person," Isadora said eventually. "It took me a long time to develop good judgment of character. *Too* long, probably." Even during her first year, she'd still struggled with this. She might've avoided the near-conflict with the Union if she'd pushed back against Russ' war preparations sooner.

And now I'm working with him again, Isadora thought. Indirectly, of course, since Russ was flying with Nadia, but fate was steering them toward a reunion. She figured he'd earned a personal apology for scapegoating him after the Calimor crisis. Maybe she'd get the chance sooner rather than later.

"So few people are," Tricia mused. "Good people, I mean." The prime minister took another long drink of wine.

"Sometimes, I'm worried I'm not much of a good person anymore," Isadora muttered.

Tricia arched an eyebrow. "I mean, that's bullshit, and I'll tell you as much, but what makes you say that?"

Isadora sighed and listed off all the ways she'd been giving herself an unfair advantage in her election campaign. Tricia nodded along as she went. "You have to learn that everyone uses dirty tricks in politics. Every single politician you've ever known has put their thumb on the scale at some point in their career. The more morally scrupulous ones do it less often, but they still do it.

"The thing is, politics is about *governing*, about gaining and wielding power to improve people's lives. Or it should be, at least. It doesn't really matter what you have to do to gain power in the first place. Hell, it's probably better to pull out all the stops in order to beat one of the power-hungry assholes." Then she shrugged. "But I'm not an ethicist or anything. Just someone who's too old for those moral scruples about electioneering.

"What *really* matters is what you do after you win. Victory alone can't be enough. And here I go rambling." Tricia chuckled, taking another drink. "Maybe I've been in the game too long, and I'm just some tipsy motherfucker way past her prime."

Isadora saw a flash of doubt cross the prime minister's eyes like a flickering flame. She'd never imagined she'd get to see this side of Tricia—her doubts, her insecurities, her introspection—during their first meeting so long ago. Tricia had seemed like everything Isadora wasn't: confident and powerful, so much so that she barely had to flaunt her power. It was just assumed, just *there*.

But there was still a living, breathing woman underneath it all. Isadora had gotten to meet that woman, gotten to see her slip out from behind the mask Tricia wore in public.

"That isn't true," she pressed, taking a drink. "You've been a good counselor to me. And a good ear, on nights like these."

"I'll drink to that," Tricia said, raising her bottle. Although from the looks of it, she seemed willing to drink to just about anything. "I'm real glad we didn't end up killing each other last year."

"Killing each other? I'm pretty sure you were the only one in a position to do any killing."

"Hmph," Tricia said, wrinkling her nose. "Details. And as I remember, I'm the only one who actually ended up getting shot at during that whole ordeal."

The two women sat in a comfortable silence, taking deep breaths and nursing their wine. "I've been getting back into figurine-carving recently," Tricia said, her voice hushed and her eyes fixed on a point in the middle of the table. "The other day, I just started making ones of all my old squadmates. I didn't even know what I was doing. It was like I was on autopilot.

"There was Damian, Emilia, and Reid," Tricia said, as though the names were always at the forefront of her memory, waiting to be recalled. "We flew starfighters for the anti-Union rebels almost two decades ago. Damian and Emilia were killed in the final days of the fighting, Reid...after that. He couldn't live with the deal I signed to restore the Union Parliament during the coup, so he took our warship and went pirate. I ended up having to send the fleets after him a couple of years later."

She turned her head and looked out Isadora's window at all the skyscrapers that'd gone dim, minus a few intermittent yellow specks from someone working late. "I've never had a Meredith, or even a Nadia or a Vincent," Tricia whispered.

Isadora saw the grief written in the prime minister's creases. The way Meredith's father had treated her left scars, of course, but she'd always have her daughter. And she had loyal colleagues who she trusted completely. All Tricia had was a litany of ghosts: an ex-husband, three dead squadmates, and even an old trusted admiral who'd been killed by the traitorous Owen Yorteb during the Calimor incident.

The only close confidant Tricia still had was...Isadora. The realization ricocheted through her stomach, suddenly putting their informal meetings in a new light. "That's why you've been so aggressive in going after the Offspring," Isadora breathed.

They'd assassinated a Union Parliament member, and they were affiliated with Brandon's forces, who *had* killed plenty of Union citizens, but Isadora had never fully understood why Tricia had been so relentless in pursuing the Offspring. She'd turned draconian surveillance measures against most of her own people, and had passed new laws barring anyone suspected of Offspring affiliation—even for something as innocuous as sharing content from an Offspring-affiliated dark net organization—from employment eligibility.

"I just caught one of the bastards in my own administration," Tricia said, perking up. "Emil Gurtrin, or something like that. He was sending out disgusting political cartoons sourced from the Offspring's propaganda arm. He was out of a job in a heartbeat once I found out."

Isadora appreciated the sentiment, but she'd never *asked* Tricia to do any of that. But she realized that Tricia was still hollowed out by the guilt of having nearly been manipulated into war by Owen Yorteb. She was doing anything—everything—to prove to Isadora how horrible she still felt.

"Tricia," Isadora said warmly, "you know I don't blame you for what happened?"

Tricia just stared back at her.

"I was just as suspicious of you as you were of me. If our positions had been reversed, the same thing would've happened. And I don't blame you for the Offspring. Or for the attacks they've carried out, or tried to carry out. I know whose side you're on."

Tricia still didn't say anything, but she nodded her head slightly. The prime minister still hadn't made eye contact with her.

Isadora pondered how to proceed. She hadn't *just* invited Tricia over for a casual chat. She'd recently received a detailed report from Nadia Jibor outlining a plan for a three-pronged attack on the

Offspring's base of operations. Nadia would seek out her captured crewmate, while Carson Erlinza would infiltrate the Offspring's ranks and Russ would create a distraction. Isadora had gone over the plan with Riley, who'd approved sending a New Arcena special operations detachment to rendezvous with the *Exemplar* over Enther.

But critical to the plan was knowing where to strike. Tricia had identified the previous Offspring/Ashkagi radical hideout after tracking a vessel filled with Offspring recruits. But Tricia's most recent plan was to send a warship to intercept the transport. It was a heavy-handed tactic, just like the spying and the drone strikes. Isadora knew Tricia meant well, but she was in charge of a vastly superior military and security apparatus. Dealing with the Offspring required a scalpel, not a hammer. Which was exactly what Isadora and Riley had been preparing for.

"I don't need you to prove to me how guilty you feel by taking a hard line with the Offspring," Isadora pressed. "What I need is an *ally* in the fight against them."

Tricia's reply was immediate: "Of course. Whatever you need."

"The transport of recruits heading to Enther," Isadora said. "I want you to let it proceed unimpeded." Seeing the confusion in the prime minister's face, Isadora continued immediately. "I have a team ready to insert an espionage agent into the Offspring's ranks. But we need an arriving vessel of recruits to serve as a likely cover for his infiltration. And I won't know where to send my team unless we know where the recruits are heading."

If Riley was here, she might've been horrified that Isadora had just revealed the full extent of their fledgling espionage operation to Tricia. But Isadora was tired of playing games with the Union. She trusted Tricia enough to lay all her cards on the table face-up. Mutual suspicion hadn't ever brought them anything good before.

Tricia drank in Isadora's words, her eyes moving up and down as though pondering the idea. "I thought our one rule during times like these was no business," Tricia said.

"I'm talking about *you* though. About our relationship outside of work," Isadora said with a grin. "I think it'd do you good to take a step back and let my people handle ourselves. All we need is a little bit of assistance from you. Track the vessel for us, but let it proceed to its destination. And," she pressed, "you promised me three favors last year. I'm pretty sure I still have one left."

Tricia finished the rest of the wine bottle, and a deep laugh escaped her throat. "You're getting good at this, Isadora. You're a natural politician."

"I'm looking out for a friend's mental well-being," Isadora said. "And I *also* just happen to be getting what I want along the way."

Tricia finally looked her in the eyes and grinned. "Well played. I'll let the transport proceed to its destination. And look...I'm really glad you asked me over. I needed this."

"Me too," Isadora said. Part of her wanted to send a dispatch to Nadia immediately, giving her official authorization for her planned operation. But the *Exemplar* was already heading to Enther. She didn't need to know right away.

For now, Isadora would sit back and enjoy her fleeting time left with Tricia. As friends, improbably.

CHAPTER 31

Russ wiped away the condensation that'd gathered on the mirror in his cabin's bathroom aboard the *Exemplar*. Finally, the face staring back at him looked recognizable. He'd always kept his hair short and cropped, even during his year with the Syndicate, but he'd let his beard grow wild and scraggly. Now, he'd finally cut it back down to size: a few thin hairs circling his mouth, no sideburns.

Everything had happened so fast in the last few days. They'd gotten approval from Isadora to conduct their planned raid on the Offspring camp housing Boyd Makrum. And with intelligence provided from the Union government, they finally had their target: an abandoned subterranean retreat named Ruhae in the planet's southern hemisphere.

The only problem was, it'd still be almost two weeks until they got to Enther. Rhavego and Enther's orbital cycles put them at opposite ends of the Natonus sun, unfortunately.

It was easy to get antsy before an operation, even more so when it was still weeks away. Russ had been spending a lot of time in the *Exemplar*'s rec room, but swimming in circles and using resistance bands had a way of getting real boring, real fast.

So he'd done some target practice with Carson. Kid knew how to shoot. When Russ had told him that being a good shot would only be useful if things went wrong in the field, Carson had pointed out that it'd be a way to stand out in the cripplingly insecure, hyper-macho world of the Offspring. Which was a damn good point, Russ figured.

He'd spent most of his days running drills with Carson, but he practically didn't need to. The other man clearly knew a thing or two about dead drops, his physical conditioning was good, and he was at least decent at keeping up a cover story under scrutiny. Juliet Lessitor must've been a goddamn miracle-worker to get a shrink trained to be a proper spy, although it took Carson aback when Russ pointed that out. *Guess Juliet must've been a real hardass*, he thought.

Although the jury was out until they got him behind enemy lines, Russ was optimistic about Carson. He'd come to like the guy, and not just because he was the only one really willing to talk to him aboard the ship, with Derek mostly keeping to himself and Nadia avoiding him.

At least there was always stuff to do aboard a spaceship. The crewmate of Nadia's who'd been taken captive was their mechanic, apparently, because everything seemed to have fallen into disrepair. Russ didn't have much beyond a basic level of maintenance skills, and even he could do a better job than Nadia and Derek had been doing for the past month.

He wiped his face dry and threw on a tunic he'd sent through his cabin's cleaning bin the night before. Then he headed out to the ship's engine section in the vessel's rear. He was going to go to bed soon, but he liked doing a final circuit before getting some shuteye. Helped relax his mind.

It was easy to flush out the engines while they were coasting. The *Exemplar* was still gliding across the Natonus System, relying on the speed provided from its initial burn. He flipped a couple of switches, causing automated cleaning systems to spray water around the thrusters.

Then he walked over to a readout station and queued up a diagnostic report. While the ship began going through a series of checks, Russ played a message on his wrister he'd gotten earlier.

Riley's voice filled the engine room. "I just finished getting in touch with Will Figgin," a projection of her head said, referring to the captain of the New Arcena militia. "He approved sending a squad of operators to rendezvous with you at Enther. I figure you'll go in with them, guns blazing." The projection flashed a wistful grin. "I almost wish I were going in with you. But thanks to you, I'm here working this shitty desk job."

Russ chuckled and looked over the diagnostic report, knowing Riley didn't really mean that. The engines were operating at around 78% efficiency. A couple connectors needed recalibration. Russ walked over to a large panel on the left side of the room, removed it, and began tightening some of the tube connectors.

"I just want you to be careful," the recording of Riley continued. "We don't have a lot of intel on the Offspring's strength at Ruhae. We can't get proper eyes on the site, since most of the facility is underground. Probably why the bastards picked it. Plus, we know they're allied with the extremists, so you might run into a lot more resistance than you're bargaining for."

Russ liked that Riley avoided using the word *Ashkagi*. She never talked about her faith in their correspondence, but she still wore an Ashkagi trinket around her neck. He wished he'd been more accepting of her decision to pursue Ashkagiism back when they were actually working together. He worried that all his snarky comments and his suspicion had turned her off from confiding in him. He'd have to let her know that his thinking had changed—that it was okay to talk to him about her faith, that he didn't associate her beliefs with batshit radicals like Brandon Zahem—next time he sent her a message.

"But I'm optimistic about the Enther raid," Riley continued. "I'm working on a plan with Isadora to contain and destroy the Offspring. She's going to launch a diplomatic offensive with the Junta soon," the recording continued. Russ couldn't help but hear Riley's screaming lack of enthusiasm for dealing with the Junta, which made sense, since their bread-and-butter politics was religious suppression.

"If we can coordinate a partnership between the Union and the Junta, funneling whatever intelligence we glean from your raid and from Carson, we might be able to limit the Offspring's operations to Enther. And from there, it shouldn't be too hard to hunt down the stragglers."

Russ returned to the diagnostic station. The engines were now operating at 92% efficiency after his tinkering. He'd take it. "I think this is gonna work," Riley said. "And hopefully soon enough, we'll finally be able to turn the page on this whole Offspring thing and get back to bringing more of our people out of cryo. Those are the stakes. But I know you're gonna get it done." The projection fizzled, and the recording ended.

Russ had already listened to it three times.

His communications with Riley had never ceased, even after he'd gone to work for the Syndicate. But her most recent one felt different. She wasn't providing updates to a distant third party—he was very much included in her plans. Vital to them, even. He was at least on the outskirts of the inner circle again. It was a jolt to the system, like he was *Russ* again, not some imposter just going through the motions in his skin.

He left the engine room to go unwind with a juice or something in the canteen before heading to bed. Say what you would about Nadia, at least she had the good graces to keep her fridge stocked with cold drinks. Priorities.

Russ contemplated the plan Riley had proposed as he walked, realizing how much of it was based on *cooperation*. They were reliant on a symbiotic intelligence-sharing relationship Isadora had cultivated with the Union, and they needed to get the Junta on their side in order to finish completing their encirclement of the enemy. Suspicion only got you so far in the security business. Sometimes, kicking ass required having a couple of friends backing you up.

He was surprised to see Nadia in the canteen. Derek and Carson were nowhere in sight. "You still up?" she asked him, averting her eyes. Russ was pretty sure they hadn't made eye contact since their spat after departing Rhavego.

"Just checking to make sure the engines were running smoothly," he grunted. He opened the fridge and grabbed a juice pouch.

He was about to turn to head back to his cabin when Nadia stopped him. "I'm sorry," she blurted out. "About everything I said. Most of that was cruel and unfair."

Russ lingered at the hallway heading to the dormitories. He

rubbed his thumb over the juice pouch, measuring how to respond. "I get it," he said at last. "And I...I think you were being reasonable. I made a lot of real bad calls back in my old job. As much as we don't really see eye-to-eye, I get the feeling we agree on how bad I fucked up. And I'm betting both of us spent the better part of the last year being mad at me."

Nadia's mouth twitched like she was suppressing a laugh. Then she looked up at him for the first time. "The thing is, after the past few months, I'm starting to wonder whether I ever really had it right. Wanna throw me a beer?"

"Sure thing." Russ reached back into the fridge and tossed Nadia a pouch. She opened it immediately. And then she launched into a long explanation of what she'd been up to for the past few months: the failed peace summit she'd tried to convene on Enther, letting Michael Azkon go free even after he'd double-crossed her, how Boyd had been captured, and how she'd lashed out at Derek.

"Sometimes, I can't help but wonder if I'm just a fucking moron," she said. "That thing you said back during our argument? That I didn't actually do anything special on Calimor, that it was all Isadora passing along the Syndicate intel to Tricia? I've been thinking the exact same thing."

"I said that in anger," Russ said. "Obviously, you saved a lot of good people's lives back on Calimor. And I would've gotten them killed if you hadn't intervened."

"But then why didn't the same thing work on Enther?" Nadia asked, exasperated. As though she wasn't so much asking him, but the universe.

"Because even if you're right that people can see reason most of the time, you're gonna run into some real assholes once in a while.

They'll take advantage of your good nature and turn it against you. But honestly...I've come around to thinking that's only a fraction of people. It's better not to assume everyone's like that. More often than not, your way works."

"Well, the times it doesn't fucking blow," Nadia said with a hollow laugh. She took a long drink from her beer.

Of all the places Russ would've predicted he'd end up after his stint with the Syndicate, trying to convince *Nadia Jibor* to hold on to her bubbly, idealistic nature probably would've been last on his list. "That's where folks like me come in," Russ said. "I'm good at dealing with that fraction of people."

"Like the Offspring. Or the Ashkagi radicals."

"Yeah. I'm not sure anyone's gonna be convincing them of anything."

Nadia shook her head. "And it'd be dumb to even try."

They sat—or stood, in Russ' case—in silence for another few moments. "Well, I spilled my guts about what I've been up to," Nadia said at last. "What about you? Where'd you go after...?" Her voice trailed off. Better to leave some things unspoken.

"Believe it or not, I started working with the Syndicate," Russ said. "Kept up with it for over a year. But eventually, I got asked to do something I wasn't comfortable doing, so I opted out. And the Syndicate doesn't really take *no* for an answer, so they sent hitmen to chase me all over Haphis. I escaped by boarding a supply vessel to Rhavego, which is how I ended up in those mining tunnels."

"Is that *Russ Kama* taking a moral stand?" Nadia asked with a twinkle in her eyes. Her mouth curled in amusement.

"Don't push your luck, now," Russ said in mock anger, extending the hand holding his juice pouch and pointing an accusatory finger at

Nadia.

The two nursed their drinks and traded anecdotes from the last year. Nadia shared an event where she, Boyd, and Derek had nearly gotten trapped in an unexpectedly ferocious snowstorm while surveying the Bitanu wilderness, while Russ talked about a time when he had to break up a barroom brawl at the Syndicate headquarters.

"Say," Russ said after another silence had settled on the pair, "where'd you learn to shoot? I've been doing drills with Carson—shrink's damn good, by the way—and I noticed your accuracy logs are practically military grade."

"Thanks," Nadia said, wearing a smug grin. "Back home in Kansas, when I was growing up, an elderly woman lived down the road from us named Arloa. And by 'down the road,' I mean almost a half-mile away from my parents' farmstead."

"Naturally," Russ nodded. "Although I don't remember ever learning where you were from." Had he seriously never asked Nadia where she grew up? Somehow, he'd never pictured her as a farm girl. "Was *we're not in Kansas anymore* the first thing you thought when you came out of cryo?"

Nadia shot him an icy glare. "Y'know, I've made it almost two years without anyone making that joke. Two. Years. And here you had to ruin that streak."

Russ shut his mouth, but his snicker was still audible.

"Anyway," Nadia continued, "on days when I'd get back from school and my parents hadn't come home from work, I'd walk to Arloa's farm. She made great iced tea that we'd drink from her porch." Russ' mind immediately shot back to the coffee grower he'd met on Haphis. He'd been doing the same thing only a few weeks earlier.

"She was always nice and accepting. But one day, she asked me about that thing my mom wore around her head. I know, I know, it was the twenty-third century and all, but it was also *very rural Kansas*. Anyway, I taught her what a hijab was, and she taught me how to shoot. She was always very respectful about it, and even asked me a lot of questions about my parents' faith. And I got pretty damn good, if you don't mind me saying so."

Russ shrugged. "The accuracy reports don't lie. Mostly, I'm just shocked to be hearing about your childhood. It wasn't at all what I'd pictured."

Nadia finished the beer left in her pouch. "What about you?"

"I grew up in a trailer park in the middle of nowhere, Louisiana. My parents were both career military, just like all my grandparents. And my great-grandparents. And so on."

"See, that's almost *exactly* what I'd pictured," Nadia chuckled. Russ finished his juice. "How about you grab us a round?" she continued, gesturing toward the fridge.

Russ winced, thinking about his efforts to lay off the alcohol ever since leaving the Syndicate. "I guess *one* drink wouldn't hurt. But I've got something better."

He retreated to his cabin. Opened up a secure footlocker resting under his cot, which contained the rucksack he'd hauled all across Haphis. Withdrew the heaviest of its contents: the one he'd been saving for a special occasion. He figured burying the hatchet with Nadia ought to qualify.

"It's a bottle of Kentucky bourbon," Russ said as soon as he got back to the canteen. "One of the few things I brought from home. So you could say it's aged pretty damn well."

"Kentucky bourbon?" Nadia asked, cocking her head.

Russ poured a small amount in two tumblers he pulled from one of the cabinets next to the fridge. "Hell yeah. Best kind you could get Stateside," he said wistfully. "After the Hegemony did their number on Earth, I doubt places like Kansas or Louisiana or Kentucky even exist anymore. Or if they do, they're nothing like they used to be. So this is practically the last bottle in the whole damn universe."

"I'm...honored," Nadia said. Her voice had grown quiet.

"We're gonna go kick the Offspring's ass straight to hell," Russ said, placing one of the two tumblers in front of Nadia and sitting down across from her. "And afterward, we're gonna need people like you to pick up the pieces. Remind everyone that life doesn't have to be one fucking inevitable, endless cycle of war and death."

"But in the meantime, we'll go in guns blazing," Nadia said fiercely.

"Exactly."

"Exactly."

They raised their tumblers at the same time. The clink echoed all throughout the silence of the *Exemplar*.

CHAPTER 32

If there was a way to get through the election with Isadora still in office, it ran through a debate stage her staff had hastily constructed in a rented auditorium space in Obrigan City.

It stood to reason that Isadora and Sean Nollam should have a chance to go head-to-head in a live debate, but even deciding where to hold the event had produced plenty of discord. Sean had insisted that they hold the debate on Calimor, considering it was the site of their people's first colony in the Natonus System, and no one besides guest workers lived on the core worlds. Isadora had countered that Obrigan was the site of their executive building. Since they were competing to run their people's government, why not hold the debate as close as possible to their future workspace?

With both sides crafting compelling arguments, the decision came down to the fledgling election commission headed by Gerald Yellick, who decided it should come down to a randomized computer selection. But since Isadora was Gerald's boss, it was all too easy to ensure that the random selection went the way she wanted it to.

After all, having to travel all the way to Obrigan—over a two-week round trip—effectively kept Sean off the campaign trail for an extended period of time. Isadora wasn't about to let herself get handicapped like that. Not while she was busy working on plans to encircle the Offspring. If anything, keeping her from traveling to the outer rim and pulling her away from her work was a security issue.

She sat cross-legged on a stool in a waiting room next to the debate stage. An aide was applying make-up to her face to ensure she glowed spectacularly in all the holo-reels. Valencia Peizan stood next to her, scrutinizing the aide's job. "Flatten out the hair more," Valencia said. "We don't want her to look like she just spent twelve hours on the job after getting a few hours' sleep."

"The problem is, I *did* just work for twelve hours after getting a few hours' sleep," Isadora said.

"Right, but you're not supposed to *look* like that," Valencia said. Her knuckles were on her chin, with her index finger pointing up and resting on her upper lip. "But not too straight either. This is a debate, not a cheap dinner."

Isadora shot her a look.

"Let's rehearse your talking points," Valencia said.

"Really?" Isadora asked. "We've done that a dozen times in the past few days." They'd even been doing a handful of mock debates, with Valencia playing the part of Sean. She'd proved astoundingly competent at the role, just *nailing* the man's pompous air and the way his posture looked like an overly inflated doll.

"And besides," Isadora continued, "I think our late-breaking good news ought to count for something." Just a few hours ago, Isadora's team had announced a major breakthrough. Thanks to almost a year's worth of legal efforts, Gabby Betam had won a partial victory in the Union courts: the settlement charter referenda banning refugee colonization on core worlds could be overturned by a simple majority vote by any planet. And Katrina Lanzic had been directing the bulk of her diplomatic outreach to the planetary government of Sarsi, which had always been relatively sympathetic to their people.

Both efforts had simultaneously paid off. Sarsi had immediately held a planetary vote, clearing the way for refugee settlement. Although humid, with endless stretches of swampland, the planet was far more habitable than anything in the outer rim, and offered far greater resource yield potential.

Isadora just hoped it'd be enough to dent Sean's momentum. Valencia was refusing to tell her the latest poll numbers—"Just go on stage, you'll be fine," she'd told her earlier—which she figured was a bad sign. If the poll numbers were good, Valencia would give them to her as a confidence boost. If they were bad, she'd give her some empty platitude about how Isadora didn't really need to see them. Which was exactly what she'd done.

"All right, let's wrap this up," Valencia said, checking the time on her wrister. She gave the aide a hurry-up gesture.

"Thank you for your help," Isadora said graciously. The aide grinned at her and left the two women alone.

They walked up to the edge of the debate stage. "Okay," Valencia said, taking a deep breath. Between the two of them, Isadora wasn't sure who needed to relax more. "You've got this. Remember: you win on policy. You win by playing on people's fears. You win on experience. Just keep hammering those points home, and shrug off anything Sean Nollam says. He's just gonna try to throw you off."

"Thank you," Isadora said, trying to avoid a mocking roll of her eyes. *Maybe Valencia thinks the advice will stick better if she tells me ten times*, she thought.

"Hey," Valencia said, catching Isadora's exasperation, "if you lose, no way Sean's keeping me around. I bet he'll throw me back in cryo. At least," she said with a shrug, "that's what I'd do."

Isadora shook her head, grinned, and walked onstage. Immediately as she passed into view of the crowds—once again joining via holo-projection, as in the disastrous town hall she'd conducted a few weeks ago—her face turned serene and professional.

The audience clapped. *Already getting off to a better start than that damn town hall*, she thought as she crossed the stage to shake Sean Nollam's hand. She flashed her opponent a thin smile and narrowed her eyes: her best fuck-you look.

Sean wore a sloppy grin on his face, the kind she planned to wipe right off his mouth in the course of the next couple of hours. He'd proven to be an effective communicator on the campaign trail when he didn't have her around to trade jabs with him. But the debate was an opportunity to finally counter his lies and empty promises. They shook hands and retreated to opposite sides of the debate stage.

"Good evening—or morning or afternoon, depending on what planet you're on," Gerald Yellick said from a desk facing the two of them, "and welcome to the official debate for chief coordinator. By virtue of incumbency, the first opening statement will go to Chief Coordinator Satoro. Afterward, Mayor Nollam will have the chance for a rebuttal, and Chief Coordinator Satoro will get a short time to respond."

Chief Coordinator Satoro was such a mouthful, Isadora thought. She'd gained an appreciation for why Tricia Favan preferred to go by just "Tricia."

"I'm not going to mince words," Isadora said, launching into her opening statement. As best she could, she tried looking into the primary recording device just behind Gerald. "We are under a grave threat from the Offspring. Already, my government has taken steps to mitigate the Offspring threat, upgrading our security infrastructure at every single one of our colonies."

She had to keep her people safe, which meant she had to win. Scaring them a little was essential to that. But then she had to switch to hope. "But we cannot let fear of the Offspring deter us from our original mission," she continued. "We are in this system to make new lives, and to get everyone still on the *Preserver* out of cryo. We will not cower in fear from the Offspring. Our colonization efforts must proceed unimpeded.

"The challenges that face us are immense. And they require a steady hand at the helm. That is where I've been through every crisis we've faced so far in this system. I am asking for your vote to stay at the helm, and I assure all of you that I will see us through this crisis as well."

"We now turn to Mayor Nollam for a response," Gerald said. Time to see what Sean had in his pocket.

"That all sounds well and good," Sean said, "but my opponent is lying about significant parts of the story. It is true she has been at the helm during our many crises—both before and after many of us came out of cryo—but she is neglecting to mention how badly she's mismanaged them. Including our conflict with the Offspring.

"We need someone with the foresight to anticipate future

problems, so we're not playing catch-up every time something goes wrong. And we need a leader with the judgment to not make the inevitable crises *worse*. Which, I'm sorry to say, my opponent has done in almost every case."

"Chief Coordinator Satoro?" Gerald prompted her, turning back to face her. "How do you respond?"

"My opponent's claims are all very hypothetical," she said, exaggerating a raise of one of her eyebrows in amused disbelief. "He claims he'd be adept at responding to a crisis, despite having never actually done so. He has no record to lean on, no list of accomplishments. He is asking you to trust his judgment on blind faith, without anything to show for it."

"Isa—Chief Coordinator Satoro nearly got hundreds of people killed after mismanaging our relationship with the Union," Sean blasted out before Gerald had a chance to say anything. *Was he seriously about to call me "Isadora?"* she wondered. She resolved not to let his petty little power games get under her skin.

Gerald raised his index finger to try to cut Sean off, but the mayor kept talking. "The Calimor crisis a year ago didn't just *happen*. It was created—through my opponent's incompetence," Sean said. Isadora raised her hand to respond, but Gerald allowed Sean to continue.

"And take the New Arcena bombing. An investigation suggested that the only reason the Offspring were able to smuggle in explosives was due to their black market contacts in the Syndicate. The same criminal organization my opponent invited to Calimor in the first place!" Sean leaned comically far over his podium, and his arms were wildly gesticulate as he spoke. He jabbed his finger at Isadora every time he leveled an accusation.

"Chief Coordinator Satoro," Gerald finally got in, "did you or did you not play a role in allowing the Syndicate to set up a presence on Calimor?"

Isadora kept her back straight and her hands out of sight. "Allow me to set the record straight," she said, frowning. "The Syndicate is only on Calimor thanks to a rogue adviser named Russ Kama, who I've since ejected from my cabinet. At no point has my administration *ever* negotiated with the black market."

It was a practiced lie. She'd personally approved the deal Russ struck with the Syndicate. It was the same thing the angry protesters at the town hall had accused her of, allowing her to craft a better response. She felt guilty about throwing Russ under the bus, but with Russ now working alongside Nadia, she imagined she'd get the chance to offer him a personal apology soon enough.

She supposed it could cause a media fuss if anyone found out that she'd approved Nadia and Russ' proposed joint operation, thereby bringing her ex-security adviser back into the fold. But she and Riley had kept everything about the mission classified. Hopefully that'd allow her to keep publicly blaming Russ for everything just a while longer. Just till the end of the election campaign.

"My opponent's case has so few legs to stand on that he relies on baseless conspiracy theories to attack me," Isadora continued. "He is papering over his thin record by peddling in utter nonsense." It felt dirty, lying and blaming everything on Russ, but Tricia's words during their informal chat still echoed in Isadora's head: *it doesn't really matter what you have to do to gain power in the first place. Hell, it's probably better to pull out all the stops in order to beat one of the power-hungry assholes. What* really *matters is what you do after you win.* She just had to get through the debate. Win, hopefully. Then things would change.

"Mayor Nollam," Gerald said, "how can we trust someone without Chief Coordinator Satoro's level of experience to do the job?"

"Let us not forget that my opponent and I possessed the same level of experience when we first arrived in the Natonus System," Sean said. "We were both city councilors. The only reason she is holding her office is because the *Preserver*'s computer happened to zero in on her. But our resumes until then were practically identical. And I would add that my record since arrival only appears thin because I was brought out to replace Morris Oxatur. Who is dead because of my opponent's negligence."

Gerald turned to Isadora, silently prompting her to respond.

Isadora's fingers gripped the sides of her podium fiercely. She saw her knuckles go white. But then she looked out at the sea of holo-projections, all of them silently judging her, waiting for her to make a small misstep. Sean could get away with unhinged ranting. She couldn't.

She felt her face go hot under the audience's scrutiny. Relaxing her grip on her podium, she took a deep breath. "Morris' death was a tragedy," she said solemnly. "I had the honor of making his acquaintance during our brief time together." She turned to face Sean for the first time during the debate so far, glowering at him. "And it is offensive for my opponent to use his death as a political prop for his own egotistic ambitions."

She'd kept her voice deathly cold, but it was still the sharpest language she'd used against Sean to date. "Why don't we move on," she said, giving Gerald a look.

Sean was playing the debate well, she thought. The more he could turn it into a cage match between the two of them, the more he could distract their people from her qualifications, and his utter lack thereof. She needed to control the message better.

"Mayor Nollam," Gerald said, spinning in his seat to face Sean. "Recently, our government has announced plans to begin a full-scale colonization effort on Sarsi, in light of the planetary government's overturning of the charter ban. What are your plans for further colonization, and how are they superior to Chief Coordinator Satoro's?"

Sean nodded, mulling over the question. "My opponent has only brought out, what...5 million people from cryo? Out of 40 million? I'm not a mathematician, but that sounds pretty low to me. I'd reconsider our relationship with the Junta and negotiate for more settlement options on Enther. I'd threaten to cut off our duty-free import deal with the Horde unless they agree to allow more colonization of Ikkren. And I'd use our spice shipments from Calimor to the core worlds as a bargaining chip with the Union. As chief coordinator, I'd threaten to hold up spice shipments unless the Union Parliament agrees to reconsider the settlement charter ban in full."

"Chief Coordinator Satoro, why are your diplomatic initiatives better than Mayor Nollam's proposals?" Gerald asked.

Isadora allowed herself a grin. "My opponent appears to not understand the value of diplomacy. Just the other week, a Horde expedition party discovered and destroyed an Offspring supply depot in the Calimor wilderness. And our operations against the Offspring have been greatly aided by the Union's intelligence services. Alienating our allies will leave us alone with the threat of our enemy hanging over us.

"As for Enther, I acknowledge that there have been setbacks," she said, thinking back to the failure of Nadia's peace summit. "But I've coordinated with the Union military to destabilize our enemies' operations on Enther. And I promise you this: if I am reelected, my first trip will be to Enther, where I will secure settlement rights for our people."

Isadora had no idea if she'd actually be able to accomplish that. But she'd already told plenty of lies for most of the debate. Why not add impossible promises on top of that?

She glanced over to Sean as he started on his response. He still spread his torso out over the podium, but he was no longer waving his arms around as frantically. So far, he'd been approaching the debate like a boxer, while Isadora was playing the part of a fencer. She had a good feeling that her approach was working. All she had to do was keep up the momentum.

But then she thought about how Valencia hadn't given her the latest poll numbers before she walked onstage. Even assuming a best-case scenario, the race was probably close to tied. Which meant she was fighting for her political life.

She felt her face go hot again from the strain and the anxiety. Her hand fumbled for the water bottle inside her podium and took a sip. Sean wrapped up his response, meaning it was her time again.

Better get to it, then, she thought. The only way out was through. She cleared her throat and launched into her next talking point.

CHAPTER 33

The Enther night looked as dark and stormy as ever, Tanner thought as he looked out the shuttle's window. He was en route to the planetary capital, a city called Caphila, located in the middle of the lush equatorial region.

Well. According to what he'd told Brandon Zahem before departing their new headquarters at Ruhae, he was "going to check up on his people in the field." A smirk crossed his face. The Ashkagi leader had been thrown off ever since the Union drone strike. It'd been all too easy to lie straight to his face.

Tanner looked at the two armored marines facing him, each with green combat armor: the unmistakable uniform of the Junta military. In reality, Tanner was on his way to meet with Michael Azkon. He'd never communicated with the head chairman of the Junta before, but the general was receptive when Tanner had reached out to him.

Especially after Tanner promised him Brandon's head.

Michael Azkon had asked Tanner to assassinate Brandon personally, but Tanner had refused. It was like the general was expecting him to be an amateur at negotiating. Everyone knew you had to hold off on what your adversary wanted until you made headway on getting what *you* wanted. Tanner wasn't an idiot.

The Junta general had then acquiesced to a private meeting between the two of them. A lesser man might've been scared, especially with armed Junta soldiers on all sides. But for the Junta, killing Tanner would be unproductive. He had nothing to fear as long as he held all the cards.

The shuttle passed a large patch of forest growth, with the giant leaves giving way to city lights that shone through the black night. Tanner had only ever lived in the subsuming urbanity of Obrigan City, or the jungle ruins that'd been his people's hideouts for the past year. Caphila resembled neither.

The Enther capital was larger than any other city on the planet, but it still looked small to Tanner. The city was surrounded by large stone walls and battlements on all sides, which felt oddly anachronistic. Tanner thought he'd read something about how the first Ashkagi settlers had thought walls could keep out Enther's fast-growing flora, but the snapping vines now covered most of them. The actual dwellings looked more modern, with processed steel and plastics on most buildings. Unlike the impoverished towns he'd seen, there seemed little need to rely on wood or thatch for housing.

As the shuttle got closer, drawing a wide loop around Caphila with its engine trails, Tanner saw large holographic billboards projecting Junta propaganda. Stern-faced soldiers or officers commanded residents to stay indoors after hours, report any suspicious activity to the authorities, and comply with all official pronouncements.

Tanner smirked. The Junta hadn't been able to close out its ongoing civil war with both Noah and Brandon's rebel factions for over a decade. No amount of telling people what to do had actually worked. The Junta was projecting dominance while possessing little real power.

It didn't matter. He was here to *use* Michael Azkon. Respecting him was hardly required.

The shuttle flew toward a large palace in the center of the city. There were four spires on each corner, with a domed ceiling forming the top of the building. Tanner didn't know the ins-and-outs of Enther history, but he figured the palace was a relic of the Theocracy era. But the fact that Michael Azkon hadn't replaced the palace with a more modern government headquarters gave him a clue about the man's temperament.

The shuttle arrived in a hangar bay on the palace's east side. Moonlight bathed the limestone exterior, with the nearby buildings cast in shadows. The shuttle came to a rest in a docking clamp. One of the Junta soldiers grunted and motioned toward the shuttle exit.

Tanner walked down a narrow catwalk, two soldiers on either side of him, and entered the palace interior. The inside was no less opulent than the exterior, with ornate statues made with gold—*gold? Seriously?* Tanner thought, unsure if it was real or fake—and an intricate painting hanging on every wall. Most of them depicted the early settlement years on Enther, although Tanner wasn't surprised to see that none of them explicitly depicted Ashkagi worship. He guessed the Junta must've taken those paintings down after dismantling the old Theocracy.

Everyone knew the planet had been in dire economic straits for a long time. Tanner wondered what the total value of the palace would be if Michael Azkon stripped it down and sold the materials on the solar market. It probably wouldn't turn things around for Enther, but it'd make a dent.

Someone who lords their power over their people was no true leader. Leadership could not be translated into symbols. If you had to rely on opulence and decadence to convey your power, then you had none in the first place. Leadership was a *mindset*, an assumed dominance that drew others to you.

It wasn't hard to test which approach to leadership worked better. Michael Azkon proved utterly incompetent at even securing his own backyard, while Tanner had sent agents out to the far ends of the Natonus System to kill—and, if necessary, die—for him.

The two soldiers led him into a giant hall. Tanner figured it must've been the old Theocracy throne room. Any traces of the old throne had been removed, and the room had instead been converted into a large war room. Uniformed officers huddled in private conferences even in the middle of the night, with a large projector of the planet's surface—its villages, towns, and a scattering of cities—in the middle.

The soldier closest to him held a finger to his earpiece, and then pointed to an antechamber on the right side of the hall. "The chairman will see you now," the soldier said.

"Thanks," Tanner muttered. He walked up a staircase, the one that used to lead to the throne, and his thoughts shifted to his sister back home. What would Rebecca think of him if she could see him now? He was a boy, and then a young man, who'd always kept to himself. He'd never even left Obrigan City. Now he led hundreds on a crusade to save the entire solar system, and he was meeting with a planetary leader.

He liked imagining that she'd be proud of him if she could see him. That she'd forgive him for striking her over a year ago. That's she'd understand the strain he'd been under, and that everything he was doing was to ensure her safety. The tension left his face as memories of his sister raced through his mind, so he forced them from his thoughts. He wasn't about to appear sentimental in front of the general.

Tanner steeled his resolve and pushed open the door to Michael Azkon's office.

It was spacious, almost awkwardly so, as the general only had a disproportionately small desk and three chairs in the room. All the empty space was nauseating.

"Tanner Keltin," Michael Azkon said, gesturing toward one of the chairs facing his desk. The general talked deeper than Tanner guessed he naturally sounded, and had a grizzled face with a scar across his nose. If it was possible to fake a scar convincingly, Tanner wouldn't put it past the general.

"It's an honor to meet you," Tanner said, letting the edge of his mouth curl into a grin. His personal assessment of Michael and his leadership abilities—or lack thereof—aside, he was here to do a job. One that required him to behave as any high-level politician would.

The two shook hands, and Tanner sat down. "You've probably never been in a meeting like this before, so I'll spare you the boring stuff. Let's get down to business," Michael said. "Considering your affiliation with the Offspring, I'm sure the Union would be more than happy to take you off our hands. I'm half-inclined to let you rot in one of our jails and radio the Union to come pick you up. The only reason you're sitting here is because you're offering something I want."

"Brandon Zahem," Tanner said, remaining unfazed despite Michael's threats. Of course the general would try to bluster his way through the start of the negotiations. It was almost sad how predictable he was.

"But I think it's more than that," Tanner said before Michael had the chance to respond. "You're unhappy with the Union. After Brandon's people carried out that attack on Rhavego, they made it look like you couldn't keep a lid on your own planet's problems. And then the Union made it worse by blatantly ignoring your own sovereignty when they launched that drone strike. Just like when they sent their warships to Calimor last year. They have no respect for your own sphere of influence. I get the sense that there's little love lost between you and the Union."

Michael's flinch was obvious. The general composed himself and spoke. "The Union only started caring about Brandon Zahem once their own people were dying. But I've been losing people to the Ashkagi for years, and Tricia Favan couldn't have cared less. And now, instead of giving me the assistance I need to end Brandon Zahem once and for all, she's just made everything worse."

It was subtle, but Tanner heard the general's voice break. His eyes looked glazed over, like he'd been losing sleep for weeks ever since the Rhavego attack. Tanner figured Michael was fatigued enough that he was being more open than he might usually be. Or that he was just underestimating Tanner's savvy. He supposed either worked in his favor.

"Exactly," Tanner said, pressing the advantage. "Brandon Zahem and the Union both made you look weak. But I'm giving you an opportunity—your *only* opportunity—to come out of this looking stronger. To show the whole system that you still have control of your planet. Any questions about your strength will dissipate once Brandon Zahem is dead."

"Politics is complicated," Michael growled. "You're a neophyte thinking you understand everything. Why should I trust you?"

Tanner shrugged. "Maybe I've misjudged you. Maybe you really *are* just some running dog of the Union, of Tricia Favan. Maybe your response to the Union's slights is to grin and hand me over to them, confirming for everyone who holds all the power in this system." He figured playing on the man's ego would be more effective than trying to justify his political advice.

Michael's eyes looked like they could burn a hole through Tanner's face. But the general's shoulders deflated slightly. He knew Tanner was right. "You make a good point," Michael muttered. "But even if it isn't in my interests to turn you over, I don't understand why *you're* here. What could you have to gain from handing your ally over to me?"

Tanner paused, taking in a deep breath and enjoying the feeling of his chest inflate. It was about to be a big ask, and he knew it. "I want you to declare war on the Horde."

Michael just stared at him. A single one of his eyebrows crept up. "What?" the general eventually asked.

"Our interests are aligned," Tanner said. "As long as the status quo on Enther and the outer rim persists, the Union will be free to operate unchecked. They'll be able to slowly hunt down my people. But with a war going on..."

By now, Tanner had the Union prime minister figured out. She was a coward. Tricia Favan would only commit the Union military when they faced no real danger. She'd lost all her resolve in the war with the Horde. The outbreak of an armed conflict among the outer planets would scare the Union fleets and their killer drones away, which would give the Offspring the space they needed to operate.

"And I know you have no love for your Ikkren rivals," Tanner continued. "Calimor should've been *yours*. It would've been, if the damned newars hadn't shown up. But the only reason they succeeded was because of their alliance with the Horde."

"You're correct," Michael said. "Ikkren is growing at my planet's expense. But that doesn't mean a war is the only option."

"I know you've run military simulations," Tanner said. "Your fleet can more than handle the Horde. I know you've been buying up Syndicate weapons in bulk ever since they set up shop on Calimor. If you dispatch ships to blockade Ikkren, and use your well-armed forces to occupy the Horde's cities, you can cut off trade and choke the Horde until you force them to the negotiating table."

Michael rubbed his entire face with one of his palms. "That is, possibly, one of the most insane suggestions I've ever heard."

Tanner smirked. "It would work. The only reason you haven't been able to commit the full force of your military to combatting Horde encroachment is because of the rebels here. And I can turn Brandon's half over to you, while my followers mop up Noah's faction.

"But keep in mind that this is time-sensitive. The arrival of the newars breathed new life into Ikkren's economy, now that the Horde is no longer reliant on importing inner planet products through Enther. And your treasury will only become more and more depleted as time goes on and Calimor out-competes your world for solar trade. You must act now, or your planet's economic malaise will turn to ruin in front of your eyes."

Michael still looked skeptical, but he leaned his head forward slightly. "Let the Offspring defend the home front while you send your forces to Ikkren," Tanner said. "Station another handful of warships along the asteroid belt and announce a full shutdown to all inner planet shipping to the outer rim. It wouldn't be an immediate victory, but the Horde would eventually capitulate. And the Union wouldn't dare intervene."

Michael's eyes drifted up toward the ceiling. The general was clearly contemplating the idea. "Brandon's rebel faction splintered off from Noah's," Tanner continued. "That means, thanks to our alliance, the Offspring are privy to plenty of intel on which towns and villages are sympathetic to Noah. As well as which ones are secretly funneling resources to him. We'd be able to go after him at the source of his strength."

"All this to push the outer rim into war?" Michael asked.

All this for chaos, Tanner wanted to correct him. In reality, he couldn't care less about the Junta's agenda. He wasn't particularly fond of the Horde, but that was only because of their alliance with the invaders. All he really needed was to get the Union off the Offspring's back. The real work could continue then.

"My organization seeks to defend the Natonus System from invasion," Tanner said. "For the foreseeable future, our goals are aligned: stop Union encroachment into the outer rim, and bring the Horde to heel. With the supply lines to the inner planets cut, the newars will suffer. The more they bleed, the more inner planet merchants will return to Enther as a trading hub."

Michael stroked his chin. "Fine. I'll consider it. But first, I want to make sure you're not playing some game with me. Any partnership between us has to be built on *trust*. So, tell me where I can find Brandon Zahem."

Tanner had figured Michael wouldn't make a firm commitment to declaring war on Ikkren until Brandon was dead. Which was fine by Tanner, with Brandon proving to be more of a liability than an asset to the Offspring. Even if he gave up Brandon's location and Michael backed out of the proposed deal, it wouldn't be the worst thing.

He'd still be in the same situation as he was now, minus one loose cannon weighing him down and impeding his own plans. Giving up Brandon either resulted in nothing changing or bringing Michael around to Tanner's proposal. There was no reason not to.

"Brandon is at the abandoned royal retreat at Ruhae," Tanner said. "A coalition of Offspring and Ashkagi forces are holed up there."

Michael's mouth curled into a wide grin. "Well then. I suppose it's time to send a detachment of troops there. What they find may influence the outcome of our negotiations."

"Of course," Tanner said. "But at least let me go back with your forces. I don't want any of my people to be caught in the crossfire."

Michael pondered the idea only briefly. "A fair request. But keep in mind that, if the situation at Ruhae is not what you describe, there will be consequences."

My troops will shoot you, the man might've said. Tanner almost wanted to yawn. So dramatic. Michael's estimation of his own toughness was astronomically higher than it deserved to be, especially after Tanner had manipulated him into doing exactly what he wanted.

"Don't worry," Tanner said, standing up. "Brandon is at Ruhae. And soon, he—and anyone else who gets in our way—will be dead."

CHAPTER 34

Isadora was pretty sure it'd tempt fate to break into the champagne while the election results hadn't been reported yet, but damn if she didn't want something to calm her down. She was possessed with the kind of nervous energy where she felt like she could run a footrace without getting even a little tired.

It'd been a little less than two weeks since the debate between her and Sean, and election results had been streaming in from the outer planets for the last two days. Officials working for Gerald Yellick had collected votes from all three outer rim worlds, as well as the *Preserver*, and dispatched them to Gerald's department on Obrigan. They'd been tabulating everything all day. The official tallies were expected any minute.

That meant there were two ways Isadora's night was about to go:

(1) lose to Sean, write him a concession message where she'd desperately try to avoid telling him to go fuck himself, and retreat to her residence in solemnity. Or (2) win, spend a few minutes toasting her success, and then triumphantly return to her residence to get a hug from Meredith. And then, immediately start packing for a trip to Enther, where she'd promised to visit if she won reelection. She'd link up with Nadia and Russ on the way back.

It didn't help that she was in a conference room at her people's embassy, surrounded by over two dozen aides, staffers, and advisers—including Gabby, Alexander, Katrina, Riley, and Valencia—so they'd all get a front row seat to her shame if she went down in defeat.

They at least had the good graces to leave her alone to fret. Isadora wasn't sure she had the emotional or mental stamina for long, drawn-out small-talk right now. Or for anything, really, other than frantically tapping her foot on the floor.

The screen at the far end of the conference lit up with preliminary results, showing *Satoro: 98%* followed by *Nollam: 2%*. About half the room began cheering wildly, while the other half calmed them down with some variation of "It's just the *Preserver*." Isadora had expected to clean up on the cryo vessel. Unfortunately, they only had a few hundred crew on the ship, so those numbers hardly meant much. Isadora still liked relishing the margin of her victory, even if she knew those numbers were about to get a lot closer.

And so they did.

The numbers on the screen shifted as Gerald's agency began reporting the results from Calimor. Isadora had won the majority of the vote, although it was far closer than it'd been on the *Preserver*. She was leading 54% to 46%, with the few hundred votes from the cryo vessel little more than a dusting on the hundreds of thousands from

Calimor.

"All right, no one jinx it," Valencia shouted loud enough to drown out the other conversations. Then she caught Isadora's eyes and winked at her. They'd expected a dominant win on the *Preserver* and a moderate one on Calimor, meaning that their projections were well-calibrated. Valencia had expected a narrow win at the end of it all, which meant they were still on track. But Isadora wasn't ready to let herself feel optimistic.

While the election agency was continuing to compile the final results from Bitanu and Ikkren, the news feed switched to a graphic displaying demographic trends from Calimor. As expected, Isadora had dominated among colonists brought out of cryo during their first year in the system, while Sean had a moderate edge among those brought out more recently. Ironically, that meant Isadora had won New Arcena by a sizable margin. In hindsight, the fact that the colony Sean personally oversaw supported Isadora over their own mayor would've made for a good campaign talking point. *All the things you think of after the campaigning is already over*, Isadora rued. She supposed if she ended up winning, it wouldn't matter, and if she lost—well, then it wouldn't really matter either, right?

The other demographic results were interesting. Isadora did slightly better among female voters, Sean did better among male ones. Sean outperformed her in the youth vote. The professions most likely to vote for Isadora were crop cultivators, maintenance crew, and security staff. Those most likely to vote for Sean were financial analysts, artisans, and educators.

The demographic data was interrupted as another round of results came in from Bitanu. Isadora tensed up. Bitanu didn't have the same settler population as Calimor, but most of them were more recent colonists, meaning Sean should probably do well. Sure enough, the vote totals shifted to show Sean leading her 53% to 47%. *Surviv-able*, she thought, *if not ideal.* It'd all come down to the votes from Ikkren, which was about evenly divided in terms of first-generation colonists and later ones.

Plenty of others started groaning. "Relax," Valencia shouted again. "It's all good, people. We were expecting a loss on Bitanu. And it's honestly more narrow than I thought." Actually, it was a little bigger than Valencia had predicted, but Isadora liked that her campaign adviser was trying to lift the others' moods.

While they waited for results from Ikkren, a variety of local election results streamed in. Most were mayoral races, where the incumbents had won handily. *Surprise, surprise.* There were a handful of ballot measure results, although most were things like renaming a hydroponics bay after some local hero or something like that.

And then, an announcement from the holo-vision: the final results were in. Isadora turned her head to face the screen. She'd won, the final vote being 51% to 49%.

The next few seconds were a whirlwind for Isadora. The room erupted into the sounds of popping corks and congratulations, an outpouring of glee and joy that made it hard for Isadora to stop and reflect on her own happiness. Or relief, more likely.

Over the next half hour, Isadora entertained dozens of conversations as most of the staffers walked over to shake her hand or give her a hug. Riley offered her personal congratulations before retreating to her office to catch up on work. Alexander, Gabby, and Katrina all did the same. Isadora finally got herself a glass of champagne after most of them had left.

At the end of it all, Valencia walked up to her. "Hey hey hey,"

Valencia said with a sloppy grin, widening her arms to reveal an empty champagne glass. "Guess who called it to a T and doesn't have to go back into cryo?" she said, before sticking both of her thumbs at herself.

Isadora grinned. "As I recall, your final estimate was 52 to 48." Saying it out loud stung a little. After all the campaigning was over, after *everything* she'd done for her people, they'd only returned her to office by a margin of two percentage points.

Valencia waved her hand in dismissal. "Details. Calling the winner is what counts. So, now that we just reelected you for a full ten-year term, mind figuring out something for me to do?"

Isadora's heart dropped at the mention of her remaining time in office. There were days where it felt like emptying the *Preserver* in a decade was feasible, and days when it didn't. Either way, the last two and a half years had been hard enough on her that she wasn't particularly relishing another decade on top of that. But it was her duty now, and she'd demonstrated that she knew what she was doing.

"I'm sure we'll be able to find something appropriate for you," Isadora said.

"Well, if you can't...I've got ideas ready to go," Valencia said.

"Why don't you message them to me," Isadora said with a tired smile. She and her staff had already planned on an Enther trip if she won, which was now her reality. She'd need to leave within a few hours to arrive in the same general time frame as the *Exemplar*.

But there was one important thing she wanted to do first. "All I want to do right now," Isadora said, "is go hug my daughter."

.   .   .

Isadora's wrister was inundated with messages by the time she arrived at her residence. Most messages were congratulatory, plus an official concession from Sean that gave her no small amount of pleasure to read. But she was ready to ignore her inbox for a bit. She opened the door to her residence and called Meredith's name softly.

Inside, her daughter was sitting cross-legged on the couch. "Hey," Meredith said, her voice drawn and low-pitched. She kept her face trained on a datapad reader. "Congrats," she mumbled.

The sudden emotional reversal from the celebration party felt jarring. Isadora shook her head to refocus. "Thank you," she said, "but don't mind that. What's wrong?"

Meredith rested her chin on her index finger, staring at a point on the wall. "I have more reading to catch up on for tomorrow."

Isadora closed her eyes and tried to beat back a tide of impatience. Meredith had never been upfront about negative feelings, and she'd gotten even less so after she turned thirteen. Isadora always had to coax it out of her. It could get frustrating, but she always operated on her own time when it came to verbalizing her fears or anger or grief.

Isadora remembered that she'd gone on a study date with Rebecca earlier in the evening. She couldn't help but fear that something had happened between them—their first fight, perhaps? They were still only a few months into their relationship, but that didn't mean problems couldn't have arisen already. Most teenage relationships had a way of quickly and spectacularly crashing and burning. As much as Isadora wanted the best for her daughter, she wasn't blind to that reality.

Meredith rubbed her chin with her finger and finally spoke up. "Don't worry, nothing happened with Rebecca. Actually, she was really great to talk to tonight. She was the one who encouraged me to bring this up now. She was telling me about this friend she used to have, who started changing. She told me one of her biggest regrets was not talking to him earlier, before everything fell apart." Meredith paused, as though measuring her words. "What I'm saying is, the issue is with *us*."

Any thought, reflection, or joy about the election results slipped away in Isadora's mind. "What do you mean?" she whispered. Part of her wanted to rush over to the couch, but she knew that probably wasn't what Meredith wanted right now. She leaned against the doorframe.

Meredith took in a long breath and exhaled gently. "I feel like you're a different person than you were when we left Earth. And now I'm not sure I'm ever going to get the old you back."

Isadora had no idea how to respond. On one hand, *of course* she was? Spending a sleep-deprived half-year apart from Meredith, where every decision had life-or-death implications for all their people, was inevitably life-changing. And she knew that the more comfortable she got in her job, the more that meant she was adapting to the weight of the office.

But Meredith's tone suggested something else. Isadora considered what it must've been like for her to wake up in the *Preserver*'s cryo bay a year ago. To have to get to know her own mother again, when—from her perspective—they'd only just parted minutes earlier. Meredith had lost her home and many of her friends when they fled Earth, and Isadora was determined to ensure that she wouldn't lose anything else.

"I agree," Isadora said at last. "Part of it is the job. I'm becoming who I have to be to get this job done."

"And who is that?" Meredith said, turning to face Isadora for the first time. "I get that you've had to make hard decisions. And I can't even imagine the stress you're under. But all these things you've done—don't give me that look, I know all the things you've been doing to help your reelection. Denying people voting rights, pressuring your staff to make it as easy as possible for you to win? I'm not *stupid*, I can figure these things out."

Isadora took a deep breath and closed her eyes. "I'm not going to lie to you, Meredith."

"And that *picture*?" Meredith said, her voice rising in pitch. "Of you and Tricia? Right after you sent the drone out to kill those people on Enther?"

Isadora's head fell. "I didn't order that strike. I was just in the room, and—"

"—you *would* have, if it'd been up to you."

Isadora rubbed her lips together. *Probably, yes*, she thought. She couldn't say that out loud. "Those were the same people who attacked us at New Arcena," Isadora said instead. "They were not good people."

Meredith had always been idealistic—more of a Nadia than her own mother, it sometimes seemed. Isadora knew her daughter had no illusions about the kinds of people who joined the Offspring, but she supposed Meredith's philosophical nonviolence might override her distaste for their enemies.

"And pressing buttons to watch people die on the other end of the system *does* make you a good person? But never mind that. The worst part about that whole thing was how you *used* it to help your reelection campaign. How messed up is that? Parading around a photo of you taking other people out to help you keep your job?"

Isadora thought about correcting her that, again, it'd been *Tricia* to order the strike, but that was just semantics at this point.

Meredith looked into Isadora's eyes. "How many people had to die to get your polling numbers up?"

Isadora's heart felt like it was splintering. She'd always counted herself fortunate that she'd never had to deal with a particularly rebellious teenager, but the tradeoff was that she had a perceptive and, frustratingly, morally scrupulous daughter. She hated the old platitudes that adults always used on their children—*it's complicated, you just don't understand* or *you'll see what I mean when you get older*—but she had no idea what else she could say right now.

"Sometimes, things are just...hard," Isadora said, fighting back tears. "When I first got woken up by the *Preserver*'s computer, I knew this job was going to be hard. But I had no idea that there'd be times—long stretches of time, really—where I wouldn't even know if I was doing the right thing. Morally, I mean. It's always been so easy to think I've been doing the *necessary* thing."

Meredith's face softened, but only for an instant. "Why'd you take the job? You could've refused. The computer would've picked someone else."

"I...don't know. I guess I trusted that the computer was right about me."

"Was it because you liked the idea of having power?"

No, Isadora thought immediately. *Maybe,* she thought right after. She'd decided to enter politics in the first place, of course, even though running for city council was nothing like her present job. Still, she'd already made the conscious assessment that she'd be a good politician. Even for those who went into politics for the right reasons, desiring power was foundational to the whole enterprise. Isadora couldn't pretend otherwise.

"I liked the idea of what I could do with the power I was given," she said. "That's still true. Now that I've won reelection, that's exactly what I'm going to do. I'm going to get everyone out of cryo. I'm going to make sure everyone gets a life worth living.

"Sometimes, that means negotiating, signing deals, approving new colonial charters. But other times, that means defending ourselves from people who are trying to hurt us. Like the Offspring. I can't ignore them when they're actively trying to stop us from settling this system. Especially when they resort to violence.

"And the thing is, I don't get to choose. Sometimes—most of the time, really—the job is about making peace. Just not recently. And I couldn't let Sean Nollam win. His ego was going to get lots of our people killed if he'd won." Maybe it was too easy to pretend like her desire to beat Sean was altruistic. Maybe her own political ambitions had morphed into a dark kernel nested in her heart.

"Back when you first asked me if I was okay with you running for city council, I never thought I'd be signing up for *this*," Meredith said. Isadora's heart wept for her daughter. Neither of them had any inkling of the ramifications of that decision. "And now, I guess it's going to be another decade before I can get the old you back. If there's any of her left by then."

"Do you want me to give all this up?" Isadora asked softly. "Do you wish that I'd just resign the position?"

Meredith frowned, put away her datapad, and turned away from Isadora. She sat in silence for what felt like an hour. "No," she said at last. "When I'm being logical, I know you're doing good work. Important work. But sometimes, it's just really *hard*."

"I understand. But I don't know if there's anything I can say that will make it easier." Isadora looked at her feet. "And, look...at the debate, I promised I'd try to negotiate settlement rights on Enther if I was reelected. But it's more than that. I've been working on a plan to finally end the Offspring threat, and it involves cooperating with the Enther government. I have to leave."

"I know," Meredith said sullenly. "There will always be something making you have to leave."

Isadora tried to swallow the lump rising in her throat. "*No*," she said, gritting her teeth to avoid crying. "Not always. Once the threat of the Offspring is over, and once we have more options for colonization, we can bring everyone else out of cryo. And then it can be *over*. I don't have to serve my full ten years if I don't want to."

Isadora would give anything for Meredith to just *look at her*, dammit, but her daughter was busy staring at the walls. "I'm going to go to Enther, but I promise things will be different when I get back. It'll be the beginning of the end of the Offspring threat. Before you know it, the *Preserver* will be empty, and then things will go back to normal.

"Do you remember the day when we left Earth? You were so scared. So was I. Hell, everyone was. Do you remember what I promised you? That before you knew it, we'd be lounging on a beach on some alien world? Well, I meant that. I *meant* that, Meredith. Going to Enther is the first step toward that."

Meredith stayed silent.

"Can you give me a hug, at least?" Isadora pleaded.

Meredith got up and walked over. Isadora grabbed Meredith's shoulders and pulled her close. Isadora wanted to kiss the top of her daughter's head, but she had to stand on her tiptoes to do so. *When did you get so tall?* she thought.

"We'll get through this," Isadora said, rubbing Meredith's back in circles. "This is all temporary. I promise. I love you."

Meredith stirred, as though she wanted to respond but was still resistant. Her arms were still at her side. "I *love* you," Isadora repeated.

"I love you too, mom," Meredith finally mumbled. Isadora hugged her all the tighter.

After what felt like an hour, she let her go. Meredith had to get to sleep and go to school tomorrow. Like a normal girl. One whose mother wasn't traversing the solar system to deal with the threat of a murderous terrorist cell.

Meredith walked to the doorway of her room. Then she turned around, her hand lingering on the doorframe. "Good luck on Enther," she said. She retreated inside and closed the door.

It wasn't what Isadora wanted, but she'd take it. It felt like the universe hadn't let her get what she wanted ever since they'd arrived in the Natonus System. Even winning reelection felt hollow, especially with those margins.

But there was only one road forward. One road to bring all this to an *end*. Because it had to end, for her sake and for Meredith's. So her daughter would stop having to pretend to be a normal girl, so she could just *be* one.

And right now, that one road forward was leading her to Enther.

CHAPTER 35

The first time the green orb of Enther sat in Nadia's viewscreen, she'd been going to the planet as an emissary of peace, a symbol of goodwill. No longer. She was returning to Enther to lead a band of warriors into battle. A single grey speck hovered in orbit of the planet: a transport filled with a spec ops tactical team redeployed from New Arcena to rendezvous with them in orbit.

"We're getting an incoming transmission from the tac team," Derek said. "They're asking for our confirmation codes. Sending them now."

The transponder signature of the *Exemplar* was unique, so Nadia had no idea why they were going through the motions of sending confirmation codes back and forth. But Russ, decked out in a combat suit and standing tall next to her, nodded appreciatively. "Gotta keep up op sec," he said, as if reading Nadia's thoughts. "It's the little stuff that gets good people killed."

Nadia could stomach a few seconds of delay. If everything went right, she'd have Boyd back on the *Exemplar* within the next couple of hours. The Offspring's operations would be destabilized, and Isadora—whose transport should arrive at Enther soon—would have a deal hashed out with the Junta to track down the remnants of the terrorist organization. And Carson would be among their enemies.

She glanced over to the other side of the cockpit, where the former therapist was sitting calmly in his chair. He had his back straight, his hands resting on his knees, and his eyes closed. Nadia's heart ached when she looked at him. They were all about to do something scary, but nothing as frightening as Carson's mission.

"Confirmation codes received," Derek said. "They've also confirmed that the transport vessel we've been tracking has just arrived at Ruhae. They're asking for a go order."

Nadia looked to Russ, expecting him to give the order, since he was technically in charge of the operation. Instead, she saw him looking back at her. "This is your ship. We're here in part to get your man back. You made this whole operation possible, which makes me inclined to think you should be the one to give the order."

Nadia blinked in surprise. If someone had told her she'd be giving the order to commence a military operation when the *Preserver*'s computer pulled her out of cryo—hell, even a few months ago—she'd have looked at them like they were crazy. Russ gave her a reassuring nod and a grim smile.

Nadia stepped up to the comm terminal on the side of the cockpit controls. She reached the terminal and pressed the transmit button. "This is Nadia Jibor," she said, trying to keep her voice from wavering, "you have a go order."

"Copy that," a firm voice said from the other end. The spec ops transport bloomed, its engines suddenly lighting up against a backdrop of black space. Derek fired the *Exemplar*'s thrusters simultaneously. Both ships sped toward the planet.

"We should arrive at Ruhae in fifteen minutes," Derek said, giving Nadia a sudden, intense feeling of deja vu.

Nadia knew Derek wanted to be going in with them. Wanted to be there when they found Boyd. But landing the ship in Offspring territory would be a mistake, so he'd have to keep orbiting the target site until they were ready to leave. Staying on the ship was important, and Derek knew it was necessary, but that didn't make it any easier. She felt for him almost as much as Carson.

"You got things under control up here?" Russ asked Derek, who hesitated for a moment before nodding. "All right. The rest of us should review our plan of attack." Russ headed toward the *Exemplar*'s port wing, where there was a small meeting room with a holo-projector, although not before giving Derek a reassuring pat on the shoulders.

Nadia followed Russ while Carson brought up the rear. He was mostly looking at his feet as they went. "Hey," Nadia said softly, wishing she could've gotten to know the man better. Anyone willing to put everything on the line like that was a hero. "It'll be okay. We're all here because we believe you can succeed."

Carson nodded, but his expression showed how little he actually believed that. The trio walked the rest of the way to the *Exemplar*'s meeting room in silence.

Once they got there, Derek announced over the intercom that they'd breach atmo any second. They all strapped in, and Russ flipped a switch on the underside of the central table. He pressed another few buttons, and a holographic layout of an underground facility shot up above the projector.

"This is our best approximation for the layout of the abandoned retreat," Russ explained. "Unfortunately, all the data I pulled from the net was ten years old, back before the Junta took control of the planet. Most of the sources indicated the facility was abandoned after the Junta took over, but we should be careful in case the Offspring or the Ashkagi have done any redecorating."

Nadia and Carson nodded. Russ pressed another few controls, and the projection zoomed in on a jungle clearing just outside the entrance. Before he could continue, the ship rattled. *Must've just passed into the atmosphere*, Nadia thought. Their plan was to arrive in the middle of a violent storm at Ruhae in the hope that the rain and thunder would drown out the sound of their engines until they were right on top of the facility. That meant they were in for a rough descent.

"We should expect resistance almost as soon as we're on the ground," Russ continued, trying to steady himself. "Most likely, our enemies relocated here because of the Union drone strike on their old headquarters. That means they'll probably have guards posted outside. The landing zone will be hot."

The drone strike was partly why they were making a move now. Russ had hoped that the strike would've thinned out their enemies' numbers, at least enough to give them a real shot. And since they were following a shuttle of new Offspring recruits, they figured they had a pretty small window where they could feasibly mount a direct assault on their enemy's base of operations.

"That means both of you should hang back while the operators clear the LZ," Russ continued. "We'll need to move quickly, immediately neutralizing any hostiles and entering the facility before they get the chance to report on our numbers. Once we're inside, I'll work with the operators to set up a beachhead at the entrance hall."

Russ zoomed in as the ship rocked, causing the projection to shimmer for a second. The schematics didn't give a detailed view of what they could expect to find inside, but Nadia noted that the entrance hallway was *big*. Big enough to make it hard for just eight spec ops troops and Russ to effectively cover the entire space. But Russ seemed unconcerned. She'd trust that he understood the military stakes better than she did.

The projection shifted again, this time to a large rear annex. "This appears to be where the royal family would've stayed back when Ruhae was still online," Russ said. "I'd bet our enemies have turned the entire annex into a dormitory section. The operators and I will punch through the central chambers in a push to reach the annex. Once our enemies know they're under attack, we'd expect them to send all their available forces to protect the dormitories. That's where we'd guess their leadership is."

In reality, Russ and the two fireteams were just a distraction, masking the real objectives. If they could draw more of their enemies out from the other sections of the facility, that'd clear a path for both Nadia and Carson. "You could get caught in a pincer," Nadia realized. If more Offspring and Ashkagi closed in around them, Russ and the commandos would be under fire from all sides.

"Yes," Russ said flatly, his jaw taut. "We will be."

Nadia's eyes flared. The soldiers he'd picked for the operation meant business, clearly.

"Next part of the operation," Russ continued, shifting the projection to focus on the facility's east wing. Another wave of turbulence made him stumble before he continued. "According to one of the reports, this is a new wing. The last king of the Theocracy was power-hungry and ambitious, and apparently kept political prisoners in a newly constructed wing of his royal retreat. We can't know for certain, but our best guess is that they'll be keeping Boyd somewhere in the cell blocks," Russ said.

"Once we secure the main entrance hallway," he continued, pivoting to face Nadia, "you'll split off on your own into the east wing and search for Boyd. Once you find him, head back immediately. It's hard to know what kind of resistance you should expect. If all goes well, my team and I will draw anyone they've got on duty in the east wing to our location. In a best-case scenario, you'll get a clear path to Boyd. More realistically, you can expect to have to fight your way through a handful of Offspring or Ashkagi."

Nadia gulped. Eight soldiers—nine, including Russ—were all putting their lives on the line just to make sure she encountered minimal enemies on the path to Boyd. She wished she could come up with a better way of expressing her gratitude. For now, following Russ' plan to the letter was the only thing she could think of.

Russ had offered to send one or two of the soldiers with her, but Nadia had refused. The plan hopefully meant she'd encounter very minimal resistance, and she knew how to handle herself. Russ was going to be facing down the bulk of the Offspring and Ashkagi forces, which meant he'd need all hands on deck.

"And finally," Russ said, turning to Carson and switching the projection to Ruhae's west wing, "the main hangar. Our schematics show no other points of interest on this side of the facility. The new Offspring recruits will have arrived about half an hour before we touch down, meaning that they should've gotten everyone off the transport.

But you may still encounter a handful of hostiles on your way to the ship."

Carson nodded and grimaced. "Juliet taught me how to handle hostiles," he said. "Once I get to the hangar, I'll enter the transport vessel and add my name to the list of recruits."

On the flight from Rhavego to Enther, Riley had created a fake cover persona for Carson: a disgruntled Obrigan City worker who lost his job to a refugee guest worker. Once Carson entered his information into the transport, it'd link up automatically with all the fake information Riley had seeded onto the net, giving added plausibility to his cover. And since they figured most of the Offspring's weapons and gear would have some kind of bio-locking system, inputting his info would allow Carson to use their devices while undercover.

It was still a risky plan. The new recruits would know that Carson wasn't part of their crew, of course. But they were banking on the hope that the utter sense of chaos introduced by their operation would give Carson a window to seamlessly meld in with the Offspring. Hopefully, with their adversaries distracted by Russ' onslaught, no one would question Carson's story. Maybe it was a fool's errand, but almost every mission Nadia had been on since arriving in Natonus had been a fool's errand. And some of them worked out.

"If you encounter anyone before uploading your information to the transport's databanks—" Russ began.

"—then I take them out. No witnesses," Carson said. The edge in the man's voice elicited a shiver out of Nadia. Russ had only been working with him for about two weeks, but it sounded like he'd brought Carson around to the hard decisions and actions he'd have to take in the field.

"Once you've secured Boyd," Russ said, turning back to face

Nadia, "we'll need to get out quickly. With Derek and the other pilot circling the area, we'll call for an exfil once we're on our way out."

"Three minutes," Derek's voice suddenly boomed over the intercom.

"All right," Russ said. "That's our cue. Let's make this work."

The trio unstrapped and headed back. Just before they reached the cockpit, Carson paused. "In case I don't make it back," he blurted, fixing his eyes on Russ, "I want you to find my brother. His name's Stacy Erlinza. He's a filmmaker at New Arcena." Carson's mouth registered a brief smile at the mention of his brother's name.

"I haven't been able to contact him ever since they brought me out of cryo," Carson continued. "If this...if this is it, I want you to go tell him that I loved him. That I was thinking about him right up to the end. That I was trying to do all of this just to make sure he didn't have to spend his life worrying about the Offspring."

Nadia watched as Russ' face softened—an expression she'd never seen before. He put a hand on Carson's shoulder and locked eyes with the other man. "If the worst happens, I'll relay your message to your brother personally."

"And I'll fly him there," Nadia said. "You have my word."

Carson took a deep breath, and then the trio entered the cockpit together.

The Enther jungles stretched out as far as Nadia could see from the viewscreen. The giant tree leaves looked like they were racing by, with Derek flying just above the canopy. Rain splattered all over the viewscreen. Moonlight danced across the treeline.

Nadia walked over to the co-pilot's station and looked out to their left. The spec ops transport was flying just off their port side, keeping low. A commando was sitting at the edge of the transport, his legs hanging out into thin air, as he surveyed the landscape from the scope of his plasma rifle.

This should've felt just like when she, Boyd, and Derek had flown down and parked themselves between New Arcena and a Union attack group last year. Except everything was different. Last time, Nadia felt like a beacon of hope amid two sides spiraling toward conflict.

No longer. Nadia was a knife in the night, aimed straight at the heart of their enemies. At the people who'd taken Boyd prisoner, who'd sabotaged the peace summit she'd painstakingly organized, who'd butchered thirty-two innocent colonists on New Arcena.

Russ looked at Nadia. "You know we're not coming to give any logical speeches about how everyone should just get along, right?" he asked, casting a wry grin in her direction. "We're here to shoot bad guys."

Nadia nodded. "I know."

In another minute, the treeline gave way to a clearing. "This is it," Russ said. "We can *do* this, people."

And then their ships were right on top of Ruhae.

From their vantage point, the only thing visible was a stone-lined courtyard filled with a pond and several benches. Sure enough, she could make out a handful of guards on patrol in the signature brown enviro-suits of the Offspring.

"Bank hard," Russ said. Derek swerved their ship violently, forcing Nadia to steady herself with her palm on the bulkhead. She glimpsed the spec ops transport doing the same thing.

Derek kept the *Exemplar* hovering a few feet off the ground. "Time to move!" Russ said urgently, storming toward the rear airlock. Nadia and Carson turned to follow him.

"Hey," Derek said before Nadia departed the cockpit. "This is going to go okay. We'll have Boyd back in no time."

"Thanks," Nadia said. "Just keep the engine running." Then she turned and raced after Russ and Carson.

When she reached the airlock, Russ had already forced the door open. The rain was coming down in sheets, its roar making a formidable challenge to the engines of the *Exemplar* and the spec ops transport. "We need to secure the LZ!" Russ said. "Hang back for just a minute!" He jumped out. All eight members of the tac team had already exited their vehicle and were pushing toward the courtyard. Their plan to use the storm to mask their arrival must've worked. They weren't getting shot at yet, at least.

Nadia was surprised at how fast it happened. The New Arcena soldiers moved as a cohesive unit, each one pulling their rifle up to bear, placing their shots, and firing in a single fluid motion. She peeked out at the Offspring patrol. It looked like there were four of them on duty.

None of them even managed to get a shot off. They were cut down almost immediately. The commandos' fire collided with all four bodies, sending them sprawling to the ground. The soldiers fanned out, each one moving toward a separate side of the courtyard perimeter.

"Come on!" Russ shouted back at them. Nadia and Carson exchanged glances, then hopped out of the *Exemplar*.

As Nadia followed Carson toward the center of the courtyard, she looked over her shoulder and saw the *Exemplar*'s engines fire. Both their two vessels ascended back above the treeline seconds later. "Happy hunting," Derek said over their comm channel.

"Stay safe up there," Nadia said. "I'll see you soon."

When Nadia and Carson reached the courtyard, her hair had already turned stringy. Rainwater seeped down her face. One of the soldiers keyed a command into a nearby terminal, which pulled apart a circular grating at the center and revealed an elevator platform. "That's our ride inside," Russ said.

The three of them, alongside the eight members of the spec ops squad, all crowded onto the elevator, rain and mud dripping from all of them. A gear underneath the elevator clicked, and they began their descent into the darkness of the underground facility.

CHAPTER 36

The guards protecting the LZ went down fast, but Russ had a feeling the rest of the facility wouldn't go down as easily. He really wished there was a way to get more accurate intelligence about their opponents' capabilities and numbers. Even with the airstrike on their enemies' old base of operations, they could be about to storm a facility full of a few dozen Offspring and Ashkagi, which would be manageable—or a few hundred, which wouldn't be.

He looked at the eight operators next to him. It was funny to think there'd been a time when he was worried about his people's fighting capabilities. Riley had excelled at her job as defense adviser, and the militia captain on New Arcena had turned a bunch of reservists into deadly competent soldiers. There was a long list of names he'd need to pay his respects to after this was done.

He knew he was putting all their lives on the line, especially considering the lack of intel they had. But he wouldn't be asking them to come here if it wasn't for a greater purpose. He'd met most of the eight soldiers during his last trip to New Arcena. They were some of the reservists who'd been out of cryo for the longest. And he had a good relationship with all of them. There wasn't a team he'd rather be going in with.

Still, he had to admit that the operation was flimsy as all hell. Problem was, this was a massive window of opportunity: the Offspring were probably at a low point in terms of their military strength, and lining up the arrival of the new recruits with an insertion operation for Carson just made too much sense. And with the Offspring already bleeding, any intel Carson could provide might just be the killing blow. The potential payoff for some opportunities was big enough that you just had to ignore the mountain-sized risk that came with them.

Russ turned his gaze to his right, toward Nadia and Carson at the rear of the elevator platform. He was careful not to let either of them see his worries. What they needed was calm reassurance. Russ exchanged glances with both of them and nodded his head. Nadia's mouth twitched into a grin, while Carson seemed lost in his thoughts.

"Looks like we're almost at the bottom, sir," one of the operators to his left said.

"Let's get ready," Russ said, and brought his handgun to bear.

They reached the bottom of the elevator shaft, and no one was there. He figured that was a pretty good sign that they'd taken out the entrance patrol before they got a chance to alert the rest of the base.

It was dark, so nearly everyone immediately pulled on a pair of night-vision goggles. There was a short walkway leading to a large door. Presumably, one that'd lead into the entrance hallway. One of the operators walked up and tested the door. "Looks like it's locked."

"Figures. Let's set some charges," Russ said.

"The commandos brought explosives?" Nadia asked, walking up next to him. Her voice sounded jumpy, having taken on a higher pitch than normal.

"Okay, two things: first, it's 'operators,' not 'commandos,' Nadia. *Operators.* Second, of course we carry breaching devices. We're not rookies." Russ chuckled and flashed Nadia a grin he was only partially sure she could see. The decrepit stone walls looked like they had a few burned-out lamp units, but the facility's new inhabitants hadn't installed any lighting fixtures.

"I guess that was a dumb question," Nadia said, returning the chuckle.

"Don't sweat it," Russ said, moving over to the door. One of the operators had already set an explosive charge. Six troops took position on the left side of the door, while Russ frantically waved at Nadia and Carson to line up behind him on the right side. As soon as the charge went off, the soldier closest to the door tossed a flashbang inside. After the report of the grenade, the soldiers peeled out from cover, one at a time, rifles raised.

"Let us secure the entrance hall," Russ said. "You two stay in cover until then. If things go *real* south, head back to the elevator and get your asses back up to the surface." Both Nadia and Carson nodded in confirmation.

Russ already heard the withering thud of plasma fire as he followed the operator in front of him around the bend in the wall. Russ quickly counted up twelve hostiles: seven Offspring, and five others with tattered outfits that he assumed were Ashkagi. The hall was large, at least twenty feet high, with a mixture of plaster and stone walls. The floor resembled a giant plus sign, with small ponds in all four corners. There was an overhead catwalk.

Luckily, cover was pretty easy. From the looks of it, their enemies had been hauling in a lot of ordnance, since there were crates everywhere. Russ sprinted over to a stack of four crates to his right and removed his goggles. Two plasma bolts landed on the floor right where he'd been standing.

He knew his squad was far deadlier and far better trained than their adversaries. But the problem with plasma weapons was that even some untrained dumbass could be deadly. So the best way to keep his people safe was to move aggressively and quickly, hopefully throwing their enemies off and relying on their own mental discipline.

Russ raised his handgun, quickly identified a hostile on the catwalk overhead, and lined up his shot. He squeezed the trigger, and the enemy combatant staggered and fell. "Move up!" Russ said over his earpiece. "We need to keep them off balance!"

"Copy that," one of the fireteam leaders said. With surgical precision, half the members of the squad popped out from cover to lay down a screen of fire, while the other half took turns closing the distance on their adversaries by moving up to the next row of crates. They moved diagonally, each one on the left side of the room crossing over to the right, and vice versa. Once they were in position, they laid down more fire and the next wave moved forward.

When it was Russ' turn, he sprinted toward the next row of crates on the left. He fired as he went, but he didn't hit anybody. Not that he was expecting to. The more fire they could lay down, the more they'd break their enemies' resolve. As he crossed the last few feet to the next row of crates, he quickly surveyed the battlefield. From his count, it looked like they'd already taken out five hostiles, all while losing no one.

He slammed his back into the crate and caught his breath, wishing he'd kept up his conditioning better during his year with the Syndicate.

The room was already filling with the overpowering smells of ozone and iron. In combat, all corners of your mind were firing at once. The key was to focus only on the most important things. Drown out the unproductive parts of your mind, the parts that were horrified by the brutality of battle and the awful smells and the screams and all the other fucking nightmare fuel around you.

So Russ instead focused on little details. Like the way it was almost lethally beautiful how the spec ops squad moved in tandem, like interconnected parts of a damn efficient machine. Or how everyone's muzzles flashed with brilliant light every time they fired off another salvo. Or the insistent thud-ping of the plasma bolts whizzing every which way.

If Russ could focus on all of that, he could turn control of his mind over to the logical parts. The parts that could focus on the job, focus on making sure everyone got out alive. Raise your arm, line your shots, take out another hostile. Lay down fire for the next wave to move up. Get into position, sprint forward. Rinse and repeat.

In another few seconds, they'd cleared the room. One fireteam member—Sheila, who'd helped him take charge of New Arcena during the Calimor incident—had taken a bolt, but it'd just grazed her shoulder. Everyone else was fine. The soldiers fanned out, taking positions next to each entrance to the central hall. Russ beckoned for Nadia and Carson to join them. His two companions hurried out from behind the entrance doorway.

"Looks like this hallway will take you to the prison block," Russ told Nadia, pointing down the right side of the floor plus sign. "And this will take you to the hangar," Russ said to Carson, pointing toward the opposite direction. "Good luck...both of you," Russ said. "Nadia, I'll see you at the rendezvous point. Carson—well, I'll see you on the other side."

"Here's hoping," Carson said with a solemn nod, and sped off to the west wing.

"Right. See you in just a few minutes," Nadia said, taking a deep breath and checking the handgun strapped to her hip.

She headed in the opposite direction of Carson. Russ watched both of them go, hoping the operators' diversion tactics would work, and that both of them would be able to make it to their destinations safely.

Then he turned around to round up the troops. They were only a distraction team if they managed to cause a serious enough diversion to draw their enemies away from Nadia and Carson. "All right," Russ said, "everyone saddle up. Time to move out."

The eight operators formed up around him, and they proceeded straight ahead. They staggered out in a formation that would've resembled a giant H from above, with Russ and two others in the middle, and three operators lined up on either side of them. If the schematics still held true, they'd hike up a steep rocky cavern that led into a large bath chamber.

That was exactly what they found when the door opened. The nine of them spread out, expecting enemy fire, but it looked like the tunnel was empty. The artificial walls of the entrance hall gave way to jagged, dark, and damp limestone all around them. Russ worked his way up the tunnel, placing his feet carefully. One wrong step and he'd slip on the slick limestone. And in a cavern this steep, a slip could lead to an uncontrolled tumble back down to the entrance door.

Russ and the spec ops squad arrived at the exit without falling. The door slid open, revealing a giant cavern. A bowl-shaped depression ran the length of the chamber. Probably would've been the old royal bath, Russ figured, although there wasn't any water inside now. The ceiling stretched up all the way back to the surface, where glass panes would've given bathers a view of the Enther sky.

There were only four hostiles patrolling the chamber. The resulting firefight was fierce but fast. Plasma fire went everywhere, taking two enemy combatants down before they could even react. The surviving hostiles returned fire, but they were caught off guard, and their shots went wide.

Plasma bolts from their enemies' weapons struck the sides of the natural bath bowl, shattering the rock into pieces. After another salvo from the operators, their two enemies went down. It seemed easy so far: streaming through the retreat, spraying Offspring guts on the walls wherever they went, all while sustaining only a single, non-threatening injury.

Still, Russ figured things were about to get worse. By this point, the entire facility should know they were under attack. He expected they'd be under fire from both sides in minutes. Maybe less.

"Let's spread out, try to hold this chamber," Russ said. The two exits were both natural bottlenecks, and he figured the soldiers could use the bath depression as a form of natural cover.

The operators spread out, one fireteam covering each exit. Within each fireteam, two soldiers took up positions on either side of the exits, while the other two set up firing positions inside the bowl depression.

It was only after everyone had set up that Russ saw the lights in the sky.

He looked up, confused, only to be met with a fierce shower of glass shards. Someone was rappelling in through the glass ceiling far above. His eyes widened as he saw at least a dozen armed individuals lowering down right on top of them.

Before Russ could even wonder who the arrivals were, they were under fire. A barrage of plasma rained down on them, and they were easy targets for an aerial attack. "Get to cover!" Russ shouted over his earpiece. But it was no use. There was no natural protection from above.

Before they could even move, the four operators holed up inside the bowl depression were cut down. The other four turned around and fired up at their attackers. The operators' fire struck two of the rappelling soldiers, but no one else went down. And there were still endless waves of troops coming in. Their enemies returned fire, and three more operators went down.

Russ' emotional half was going haywire, but just like before, he had to suppress those thoughts. His logical side only focused on two words: *run. Survive.*

"Sheila, go!" Russ shouted toward the single operator left standing. The two of them sprinted toward the exit in a mad dash, plasma fire screaming down on both sides. They made it to the entrance and slid down the rocky tunnel back to the entrance hall. A single shot came in from the bath chamber, striking Sheila in the top of her head.

By the time they got to the bottom of the tunnel, she was dead. Her limp body smashed against the cavern wall and lay motionless. Russ' survival instincts got him out the door and back into the entrance hallway before his new attackers could get down the tunnel.

When he got there, a handful of hostiles were waiting for him. Russ ran to his right and hid behind a row of crates as they released a barrage of fire at him. That gave him a better look at the arriving soldiers, who were racing down the rock tunnel at this point. They wore green combat suits with the identifiable emblem of the Junta emblazoned on the shoulder guards. *What the fuck is the Junta military doing here?* he thought. He'd try to contemplate the answer to that question when he wasn't in mortal danger.

The Junta soldiers coming down the tunnel turned their attention to the other enemies in the entrance hall. Now that Russ had a better view, he could tell that they were all Ashkagi, not Offspring. Plasma fire crisscrossed in the open space to Russ' right, but most of the casualties came from the Ashkagi.

While the two sides focused on each other, Russ used the opportunity to bolt for the other side of the room. His boots sloshed through pond water as he traversed the perimeter of the entrance hall.

When he looked back, all the Ashkagi were dead, and the Junta troops were already streaming into the chamber. He trained his handgun on the soldiers and pulled the trigger. One went down, but the others rapidly returned fire. One of the bolts landed right on the barrel of Russ' handgun. Sparks flew out of the weapon, and it snapped in two. Russ cursed, loosed the sole grenade from his belt, and tossed it in his attackers' direction.

As he heard the loud boom echo from wall to wall, his brain went through a series of calculations. Grabbing a dead enemy's weapon was probably a no-go, since they were no doubt bio-locked—part of the reason Carson needed to put his info into the Offspring recruits' transport. And Nadia and Carson were both in danger, but he could only go after one of them.

Carson was more critical to the overall mission, sure, but Russ might blow the man's cover if he went after him. And if he'd already linked up with a group of Offspring, he'd have to treat Russ like an enemy. Better not put him in that kind of position.

Russ looked back, where the grenade had taken the rest of the Junta troops out. Only a few had even followed him out of the bath chamber, meaning that the majority of them had moved elsewhere. *They're here for the Ashkagi*, Russ realized. His people had just gotten caught in the crossfire.

That meant there was still a chance to escape. Now weaponless, Russ ran across the room to the east wing. Time to go save Nadia and get out.

CHAPTER 37

Carson was all on his own now. He didn't have the emotional fortitude to look back at Russ or Nadia as he headed out of the entrance hallway into Ruhae's west wing. He knew that might be the last time he'd ever see any of his people again. Looking back would've sapped the strength he needed to push forward.

If only Juliet could see me now, he thought as the door opened and he worked his way down a stone staircase. He stepped as lightly as possible. Sure, the plan was that Russ and the spec ops team would draw their enemies' attention away from Carson, but he still knew it'd be dangerous to run into any Offspring before he could get to the transport in Ruhae's hangar. He'd need to get there as silently as possible.

The problem with walking quietly and carefully was that it was a slow endeavor, which only gave Carson's brain more time to flash through all the faces he was fairly certain he'd never see again. Juliet. Russ. Nadia, who he hadn't spoken with as often as Russ, but who he'd come to respect and admire. Stacy. *Stacy.*

His brother was why he'd agreed to become a spy in the first place. Every time Carson got to a point where he didn't want to go any further, making sure Stacy didn't have to spend years in fear of Offspring attacks impelled him forward. He'd accept being some martyr in a hopeless mission if it made sure the Offspring couldn't hurt Stacy.

He finally made it to the bottom of the staircase, where he took a right and headed down a hallway with the same plaster-and-stone walls from the entrance hall. The only problem was, he couldn't see the other end. It was buried under a pile of shattered pieces of slab.

It looked like the Offspring had tunneled past the debris, since there was a gaping hole in the left side of the hallway. Carson walked toward the opening, but the sound of voices sent him racing away from the carved-out tunnel almost immediately. It must've been some of the new recruits coming from the shuttle.

His head shot in both directions. There weren't many obvious places to hide, unless...

Carson ran over to the pile of slab debris, pulled one of the stones up, and lay down on the ground. His arms ached under the weight of the stone as he started crawling underneath. The panic started to set in as soon as his legs were underneath the stone. Something about being wedged beneath a large stone slab took his mind back to the rockfall in the Rhavego mining tunnels.

The explosive crack in the mining tunnels' ceiling seeped into his mind. The way it felt like the whole world was collapsing on him. The chill limpness of Juliet's body as she lay on top of him in her final, sacrificial pose. Carson's ribs had fully healed in the time it took the *Exemplar* to reach Enther, but he felt a sharp, phantom pain emanating from his midriff.

He tried to ignore the memories flashing through his mind as he continued to crawl further underneath the rock. He slowly lowered the slab until it was resting on top of him. The piece of stone was heavy, and Carson's breathing was labored, but it wasn't objectively crushing him, no matter what his mind was saying. Now that he was fully beneath the debris, his heart started feeling like it was about to explode. *Do it for Juliet*, he told himself over and over. *Earn her sacrifice.*

Almost as soon as he was in his hiding spot, a group of four individuals walked out of the tunnel. From the thin slit between the edge of the slab and the floor, it looked like all four had on the Offspring's standard brown enviro-suit. Three were carrying themselves with an air of uncertainty, however. Carson guessed they were recruits.

"We're under attack," the one who looked like he was keeping it together said. "This will be your first test. The newars have infiltrated our very home. The reports say they may be somewhere in the bath chamber. We must go there now and reinforce our brothers."

"I...I've never been in a fight before," one of the recruits said. "The recruiter said we'd get plenty of training before we were in the middle of a firefight."

A pair of boots stepped closer to the recruit who'd spoken out. "Sometimes, things don't work out the way we're planning," the Offspring said. "Think about what *Tanner* would do. Or what he'd want you to do. You don't want to let Tanner down, do you?"

Carson had no idea who the hell Tanner was, but he had bigger problems to worry about. His chest felt like it was heaving rapidly, his breath racing so fast and yet still not quick enough. *Please don't let them hear me please don't let them hear me please don't let them hear me* played on repeat in his mind. He was so sure it was over. His breath was running wild, like a horse back on Earth trampling through a wide open plain. They'd pull the slab up and he'd be dead and *just please let it be quick.*

They left instead.

He barely waited for them to round the corner before he pushed himself out from underneath the debris. He placed a hand on the wall to steady himself until he finally got his breath under control. His eyes watered—he was just *so* alone, and *so* hopeless—and he wanted nothing more than to just curl up and wait for someone to find and shoot him.

But there really was no use feeling sorry for himself. He thought back to when he and Juliet first got to Rhavego, when it felt like he couldn't do anything right, and she was constantly berating him and keeping him on a tight, sleepless schedule. He remembered how frustrated and angry he'd felt, cursing her unfair standards. And yet he'd gotten through that. Maybe if he could just find the strength to keep going, he'd make it through this as well. Or maybe not. But there was only one way to find out.

Carson worked his way into the tunnel, composed of recently blasted limestone on all sides. And everything was slick. His right foot slid several inches as soon as he stepped into the tunnel. *At least boots slipping over rock are quiet*, he thought as he fought to regain his balance.

Keeping an arm on the wall to steady himself, he headed down the tunnel. He reemerged in the same hallway as before, except the fallen debris was now behind him. The hallway dead-ended at a glass door.

It was too far to see inside, and Carson worried about someone walking through. There weren't any obvious hiding places between here and the door, which meant he'd have to shoot anyone who came through. And if he encountered a large group, they'd get the best of him for sure.

He drew his handgun nonetheless. He'd keep pressing forward until he couldn't. Slinking down the hallway, keeping his back pressed to the wall, he eventually arrived at the door. There was a turbolift to the left, but it looked like it was defunct. Now that he could see through the glass door, it looked like there was a hangar control room inside. There were two Offspring and two Ashkagi inside, although they hadn't noticed him yet.

Carson assessed his options. He needed to get into the hangar bay proper, but with the turbolift next to him out of service, it seemed like the only way to do that was to go through the control room. But he wasn't sure if he'd stand much of a chance in a firefight with four adversaries. Maybe he could head back to the debris pile and hide for as long as it took the four of them to leave. But he didn't relish the thought of mentally reliving the mining tunnel collapse on Rhavego once more.

As he continued to deliberate, he saw the two Offspring suddenly turn their attention to their wristers. After a few seconds, they looked up and exchanged glances. Then they drew their weapons. Carson furrowed his brow. *Are they heading out to reinforce the rest of their people?* he thought. But then why weren't the Ashkagi reacting?

The two Offspring walked up to their Ashkagi counterparts, levelled the barrels of their plasma guns at the back of their necks, and shot them. The two Ashkagi slumped to the ground.

Carrson's eyes went wide. The key piece of the puzzle that'd led him and his companions to Enther was that Brandon's radical Ash-kagi faction and the Offspring were working together. Had the Off-spring reconsidered that partnership?

He didn't have the luxury of thinking through the problem for long. The two Offspring holstered their weapons and turned toward the door. Carson darted out of view before they could catch a glimpse of him.

What could he do? He could try to shoot them, but he still didn't like his odds. And they were too close for him to head back to the de-bris pile and hide. His gaze returned to the defunct turbolift, and he got an idea. He ran over to the turbolift and tried to pry open the door.

It hardly budged. Gritting his teeth, Carson dug his fingers in the small crack between the two sliding flaps, winced, and pulled as hard as possible. His shoulders and back muscles screamed in a protest far sharper than the dull soreness of doing laps in the *Exemplar*'s pool sphere. Carson bit his lip so he wouldn't grunt.

The door flaps slid open just far enough for Carson to squeeze through. Only a second later, the glass door to the control room swished open, and the two Offspring walked out. "Sounds like the Junta just got here," one of them said. "By now, they'll probably be rounding up the rest of Brandon's people."

"It feels weird, stabbing them in the back like this," the other Off-spring said.

Carson pressed his eye to the slit between the door flaps and watched as the original speaker shrugged. "If Tanner thinks it's a good call, then we should trust that it's a good call. And besides, Bran-don got a bunch of our brothers killed with his stupid attack on Rhavego. Partnering with the Junta can't be any worse."

The two voices continued, but they'd gotten far enough away that

Carson could no longer make out what they were saying. His mind immediately turned to Russ and the spec ops team. *Sounds like the Junta just got here*, one of the Offspring had said. Were there really Junta soldiers inside the facility? He hoped Russ and the others were okay.

Carson thought about dispatching a message to Russ and Nadia on his wrister, but decided against it. It'd be too easy for the Offspring to pick up the message, and he'd already removed himself from the others' comm channel. He just had to hope that the others knew how to handle the unexpected arrival of the Junta. And that they'd relay the information about the Junta apparently working with the Offspring back to Isadora Satoro and the rest of the leadership.

He pushed open the door flaps and entered the control room. His handgun was out, but there was no sign of anyone else in the area. He looked out over the hangar bay, where the transport ship was resting on the floor. It didn't look like there was anyone on patrol.

He walked through the room and arrived at another turbolift. This one looked like it was still functioning, with small strips of neon lights glowing. Carson stepped into the lift and took it down to the hangar level. He looked around when the door opened, but there were still no signs of anyone.

He tiptoed carefully over to the ship, brought his handgun to bear, and opened the shuttle's side door. He stepped inside with his gun at the ready. But the ship's interior was just as empty as the hangar.

Carson holstered his weapon and walked up to the transport cockpit, where he pulled up a crew manifest on the ship's root menu. Sure enough, there were about a dozen names listed. He added *Erlinza, Carson* to the very bottom of the list. Then, he pulled up a holo-recording function, took a picture of his face, and uploaded it to the computer. The computer acknowledged that it'd found a copy of his fake records Riley had set up, and then linked his info to the fake background. He pressed his thumb into a scanner. A green light indicated that the computer had integrated his biometric data with the Offspring's network.

Carson took a few deep breaths, trying to work out a plan to get back to the facility's main area without arousing suspicion. It seemed like the Offspring were breaking the recruits into small orientation groups already, so he figured he could just say he'd gotten lost and link up with one of the groups. If one of the other recruits said anything about not recognizing him, he'd claim he'd been a stowaway on the transport. It was a backstory Russ had helped him invent—something about Russ doing a similar thing to get from Haphis to Rhavego. And he assumed the Offspring would be the kind of people to admire the verve.

As he continued to hash out a plan, he heard the turbolift activate, followed by frantic footsteps.

Someone in an Offspring uniform burst in through the side of the transport. "I can't do this," the man said, in a panicked voice Carson identified. It was the same recruit who had expressed reservation about going into battle back in the first hallway. "The newars are fucking terrifying," the recruit continued. "I can't face them. I can't do it. I just can't. I want to go home." He collapsed to the floor and placed his head in his hands.

Well, Carson thought. *Time to see if the stowaway excuse works.*

"I guess you had the same idea, yeah?" the recruit said, looking up at Carson for the first time. His face registered confusion, then shock. "You're not—I mean, you weren't—"

"—I was stowed away the entire time," Carson said. "I'd heard about the Offspring, but I couldn't find a specific recruiter. So I had to go through back channels."

"Then why don't you have a uniform?" the recruit asked, eyeing him suspiciously. "We had plenty on the ship. You're one of the filthy newars!" the recruit shouted.

Shouting was no good. Carson grimaced. He knew what he had to do.

He walked over and punched the man in the jaw. The recruit spat out blood, pushed himself to his feet, and the two grappled. Carson drew on the sparring sessions he and Juliet used to have, or, hell, even his wrestling experience from back on Earth.

He forced the recruit back into the bulkhead and delivered a series of powerful punches to the man's gut. The recruit winced and staggered. Carson pressed down on his opponent's shoulders until he forced the man to the floor. Then Carson pinned the recruit down, his legs locked around the man's torso, while he wrapped both his arms around the man's neck.

"My name's Carson Erlinza," Carson muttered as the recruit gasped for breath, thrashing from side to side. "Back on Earth, I used to be a therapist. I worked with people like you. And I wanted to let you know that I'm *sorry*."

The recruit tried to say something, but Carson had a hard time figuring out if it was confusion or anger. The emotional tone of suffocation was hard to read.

"If we lived in a better world, we'd be sitting together in some quiet, comfortable room," Carson said, drawing his arms tighter. "You'd tell me about how you never found much meaning in life until the Offspring contacted you. How you felt isolated, like it was you versus the whole damn system. I'd listen to you, because I believe, deep down, that you're a good person. That you could've been saved."

The thrashing suddenly got more intense. Probably not much time left, Carson thought. He pulled his legs tighter to constrict the man and pressed on his neck even harder.

Everyone has a dark side, Juliet's voice echoed through his head, clear enough that it almost felt like she was right next to him. *Might as well start getting real familiar with yours.*

"But we don't live in a better world," Carson continued. "At least, not right now. I just wanted to tell you that so you could know, at the end of everything, that I *understand*. I get it. You're not a monster. And you can rest easy."

The recruit let out a final gasp, and his entire body went limp. Slowly, Carson pushed himself to his feet, gently setting the corpse on the floor. The man had a similar build as Carson, so taking his brown enviro-suit would be all too easy. Hopefully, that'd help him if he had to use the stowaway cover again. Then he figured he could fire up the transport's engines and incinerate the body to leave no evidence. Might as well get rid of his plasma gun too, for good measure.

Those kinds of calculations made him feel a cold numbness. He'd just killed someone, and yet, all he could think about was the mission. Maybe that was for the best.

After he was done disposing of the recruit's body, he'd head back to the main section of the facility. Where he'd meet his new comrades.

CHAPTER 38

*T*rees! was the only thought going through Isadora's head as the shuttle descended through Enther's atmosphere. Sure, she'd occasionally been to the Obrigan wilderness, which still looked alien, but the overwhelming percentage of her time in the Natonus System had either been spent in the capital city, aboard the *Preserver*, or among the barren red deserts of Calimor.

She really had to get out more.

Enjoying the tapestry of jade-green leaves and the steady pitter-patter of the rain on the sides of the shuttle craft made it easier for Isadora to stop dwelling on Meredith. They'd hardly parted on the best of terms. The biggest problem was, Isadora knew her daughter had been right. She'd employed all kinds of dirty tricks to win her election, which meant the hard part was in front of her: justifying it by getting the job done.

And that started on Enther.

She'd set up a meeting with the chairman of the Junta, General Michael Azkon, in the capital city of Caphila. Concurrently, Nadia, Russ, and Carson were heading for the Offspring base camp out in the jungle wilderness. Hopefully, they'd have drawn a noose around the Offspring soon enough. Isadora wanted nothing more than to turn the page on the past chapter of her tenure—the election, the conflict with the Offspring—and to continue with her people's larger settlement project.

And that meant she was about to see Russ again for the first time in almost two years. She'd spent the first day of the shuttle ride writing ten different drafts of an apology, and scrapped all of them. She just couldn't seem to get the words right. All she could do was hope that when the time came, she'd find the right words to say.

"Somehow I'm getting the feeling you haven't been listening to me," Valencia Peizan's voice came from the seat across from Isadora.

Isadora grinned. "That's because I haven't."

She'd naturally assumed that Valencia would take up some other job outside her governing team after the election was over. So she'd been surprised when Valencia had made a forceful case that Isadora could use a chief of staff, and that Valencia was the one for the job.

Isadora remembered from her city council days that making your campaign manager your chief of staff was usually a mistake, even if it was a mistake that politicians made all the time. Isadora had decided to add her name to the list by accepting Valencia's proposal. They had plenty of resources to support her, clearly, and Isadora had seen firsthand the woman's indomitable work ethic.

And she'd grown a fondness for Valencia's bluntness. She needed to command respect from her staff, of course, but she also needed honesty. Valencia seemed more than happy to fulfill the latter requirement.

"We should review our negotiating strategy," Valencia continued. "You know, with the *planetary leader* you're about to meet with in a few moments."

Isadora returned her gaze back to the window, looking out over the canopy and thinking back to a conversation she'd had with Tricia right before departing Obrigan. "Michael Azkon always wears a uniform a couple sizes too big," Tricia had told her, "just so he can have room to fit his fucking ego inside."

This was the same official who'd held a grudge against Nadia for over a year, and had partially sabotaged her own peacemaking process just to get back at her. Isadora didn't need convincing about the general's ego. But she hoped that an official visit from her, not Nadia, might soothe that same ego.

"I'm going to be extremely deferential," Isadora said, sighing. "And apologetic about the fractured relationship between the Junta and our people."

"You can bet he's gonna make a big fuss about the Union drone strike. Especially because of that picture of you in the room."

"I'm going to acknowledge that it was a massive breach of sovereignty and apologize," Isadora said. "And I will note that partnering with the Junta to mop up the remaining Offspring forces is part of our initiative to ensure that their sovereignty remains intact."

"At which point, the general will probably play the skeptic."

"Right. Which is why I'm prepared to offer various forms of assistance: favorable import-export policies with our outer rim settlements, offering to transfer workers from our colonies for paid labor on Enther construction projects, and making land-use payments if he agrees to allow us to colonize Enther."

"And then, it'll just be hashing out the logistics, unless he refuses you outright. But I have a hard time seeing how he'd say no to all that. It's the best way to save face, and we're offering *generous* economic incentives."

"I agree, I have a good feeling about this one." Isadora checked her wrister. They should arrive in Caphila in fifteen minutes.

"I hate to say it, but I do too," Valencia said. "And hopefully, we'll be prepared for the unexpec—"

She was cut off by the deafening sound of an electronic buzz. A wave of blue light flashed by the window next to Isadora. The lights in the shuttle went out, and the entire ship rattled. Isadora's body felt like it was entirely weightless for a fleeting second, and then the vessel swerved violently in a wide circle.

"We've been hit by an EMP blast!" the pilot shouted from the cockpit.

Isadora barely had time to panic. Her hand instinctively reached for the railing overhead, while her other hand wrapped around her seat straps, as though that would somehow help. She looked over to Valencia, whose breathing had become frantic and whose body had started to visibly shake. And then she looked over to her security detail. The four of them looked equal parts grim and stoic.

The shuttle ripped through the treeline, taking down large branches with it. Luckily, they were less than a hundred feet off the ground, and their wings were still intact, which allowed them to glide. Albeit somewhat violently. As the ground looked like it was hurtling toward them in the window, terror at last struck Isadora. *Please just let me see Meredith again* was all she could think. *Please don't let the fight be our last goodbye.*

The vessel slammed into the ground, but stayed intact. At the last second, the pilot had managed to level them out, and they slid across a surface of mud and moss that was soft enough to cushion at least some of the landing. Even still, Isadora's body jerked hard to the left, and the strap sent a searing pain into her shoulder.

She grabbed the bottom of her seat and winced as they continued to slide over the ground. She heard loud, crackling snaps, followed by the ponderous groan of trees falling. When they finally came to a stop, the security guard closest to Isadora unbuckled and immediately ran over to her. "Are you okay, ma'am?" he said, checking her vitals and waving his fingers in front of her eyes.

"I'm okay," Isadora said. She gave the guard the day's date for good measure. "How are the others?"

"I'll check, ma'am."

While the guard checked on the others in the main cabin, including Valencia, Isadora unstrapped and walked into the cockpit to thank the pilot. When she got there, she saw a massive tree branch that'd collapsed the entire front half of the vessel. And crushed the pilot underneath.

"Everyone's okay in here, ma'am!" the guard called from the rear.

Everyone but one, Isadora thought. She closed her eyes and said a silent thank you to the pilot for keeping the rest of them alive. He'd been the same pilot who'd ferried Isadora to Calimor right after the New Arcena attack. She wished he'd lived to see a system not marred by conflict with the Offspring. Isadora resolved to get out of this alive, return to Obrigan, and make up with Meredith in honor of his memory.

She reopened her eyes and turned back around to the main cabin.

Everyone who'd accompanied her—four guards, as well as Valencia—
were now on their feet. "I can't believe that just happened," Valencia
blurted out. "I mean, what was that?"

"The pilot said it was an EMP blast," Isadora said. "I didn't get a
good look at it. But I trust his judgment."

One of the guards gave her an interrogating look. *She alive?* the
guard was asking. Isadora shook her head slightly, and the guard nodded.

"That means someone attacked us," one of the guards said. "We
need to get to safety ASAP."

"We're in the middle of the jungle wilderness," another said. "It's
probably a couple hundred miles left to the capital city."

"Attacked?" Valencia asked, her eyes widening. "You mean—"

"—when someone shoots you with an EMP, that usually qualifies
as an *attack*," the guard said.

Isadora shot the guard a disapproving look. This was, more or
less, Valencia's first real assignment of her new job, and she was
clearly in shock. Antagonizing her wasn't necessary.

One of the guards in the back furrowed his brow. "I don't think
the rebels or the Offspring have access to an EMP device that could
hit a ship midair. And besides, there's only one faction that knew we
were coming in the first place. I think the Junta might've been the
ones who hit us."

"The Junta?" Isadora asked. She knew Michael Azkon clearly
didn't like Nadia, but he'd never made any indication that his grudge
went beyond Isadora's settlement leader. But the guard was right: unlike the Ashkagi or the Offspring, only the Junta knew where they
were.

But trying to figure out who'd shot at them was secondary to getting out alive. Isadora looked down at her wrister, hoping to send a message to Nadia to ask her if she wouldn't mind coming and picking them up after she wrapped things up at the Offspring hideout. But she was out of luck. The EMP blast had made her device go haywire.

"Is anyone else's wrister working?" Isadora asked. One by one, the other five inspected their own devices. One by one, they shook their heads. "Okay then. That means our tracking beacon has gone out too. Which means our colleagues back on Obrigan won't know where to send a rescue team. We should get to work on finding another solution. Let's start by cataloging the resources we have," she said, nodding toward the supply room in the shuttle's rear. One of the guards left to go investigate.

He returned with a frown on his face. "We only have about three days' worth of food left, since the original plan was to leave right after the meeting to return to Obrigan. And if we're still a couple hundred miles from Caphila, that won't last us the whole journey."

She felt a surge of sympathy for her security detail, who'd trained to shield her in crowds, protect their embassy from intruders, or secure physical locations from sabotage. Surviving a crash landing in the middle of a planetary wilderness had never been part of their training.

But Isadora knew they could survive a few days without food, and if their options were (1) go hungry for a few days or (2) die in the middle of the Enther jungles, then the choice was clear.

"There's also a chemical flare gun," the guard continued. "We could use that to signal for help."

"But if someone shot at us, that'd give away our position," another guard countered.

"And who's to say anyone's looking?" a third guard asked. "If we fire up a flare, and no one is in visual range, it'll be as good as useless. And if someone *is* in visual range, we'd have to stay rooted to the spot or they wouldn't be able to find us. Which would delay us in walking to Caphila."

"The flare gun will leave a chemical trace that another vessel could pick up. And I think going to Caphila is dangerous," a guard said—the same one who'd accused the Junta of shooting the EMP. "We may be walking into a trap."

"A trap is still more survivable than starving in the jungle," a different guard said.

"We don't even know anything about the jungles," another said. "What about dangerous plant life, natural obstacles?"

"Still a better option than staying put and starving."

Isadora held up her palm. All discussion ceased. "I appreciate all your advice and the debate, but I've made up my mind," she said. "Using the flare doesn't make sense. We'll gather what food we have and make for Caphila. We may have to go several days without food, but that's okay. We'll make it. And we'll figure out what to do if the Junta means us harm once we get there." One of the guards looked like he disagreed, but all four went to work gathering the shuttle's food stores.

Isadora turned to Valencia, who was still breathing heavily. "Hell of a first day on the job, huh?" Isadora said with a grin.

"Oh, I'm just trying to keep it together," Valencia said.

"Take all the time you need. After all, we'll have a few days of hiking through the woods."

Isadora pushed open the shuttle's side door and stepped out onto the ground. Her work shoes sank into a thick layer of mud. *Better get used to that*, she thought. Every step she took felt like pulling her foot out of a layer of glue. Mud flecked the hem of her leggings every time she raised her foot.

She hardly cared. She'd walk for as long as her body would take her on no food, even knee-deep in mud, just to see Meredith again.

The four guards and Valencia followed her out, each guard sporting a heavy backpack filled with food rations. "Let's start our hike, shall we?" Isadora said, forcing a grin that belied the grim situation.

The guards weren't even looking at her. Their eyes were locked on the sky. Isadora turned around to see another shuttle approaching. "That could be a rescue crew from Caphila," Isadora said, trying to sound more confident than nervous.

The shuttle swerved and the side door opened, revealing two individuals in brown enviro-suits with plasma guns pointed at them. "Offspring!" one of the guards said, only seconds before plasma fire pelted the outside of the shuttle.

"Back inside!" another one shouted. The six of them sprinted back for the shuttle interior. It was the first time anyone had ever shot at Isadora before, and she found herself surprisingly unpanicked. The situation reminded herself of her first year in the system: beset by danger on all sides, where the only way out was to make a series of increasingly desperate decisions. *Keep making choices*, she told herself over and over. *Keep trying to find a way out.* There was little room for fear.

When they returned to the safety of the downed vessel, two guards took position on either side of the open door. They took turns leaning out to return fire at the circling Offspring shuttle. A withering screen of plasma fire nicked at the sides of their craft. "They've got a repeater cannon," one of the guards grimaced.

Isadora's mind went through a series of calculations. Walking to

Caphila no longer seemed feasible. If they went outside, they'd get gunned down for sure. That left only a single, least-bad course of action.

"We're all going to be okay," Isadora said gently, the vicious screams of plasma fire exchanges almost drowning her out. "We're all going to make it through this."

Valencia looked at her like she'd gone insane. Which was almost funny, since Valencia had been training her how to project calm for the entire campaign season. Now, Isadora was using the same practiced demeanor to calm Valencia down. "Valencia," Isadora said, "I want you to go into our supply area and retrieve the flare gun."

Valencia just nodded her head, as though she was too scared to argue at this point.

"Ma'am?" one of the guards asked, just before moving her head to avoid another salvo from their attackers.

"I realize it isn't ideal," Isadora said. "But it is our way out." Which was a much nicer way of saying *it is our only option left*. The guards slowly began to nod as they contemplated the situation and came around to Isadora's view.

Seconds later, Valencia returned with the flare gun and handed it to Isadora. "Thank you," she said, and readied the device. "I'm going to need some cover fire."

The two guards on either side of the door exchanged grim nods, and both of them spun out simultaneously to unleash a furious barrage of fire at the Offspring. Isadora stepped out into view for only a second. Just long enough to pull the trigger on the flare gun, which let out a deafening pop, followed by a luminescent red flare arcing up into the night sky.

All they could do now was hope that someone was watching.

CHAPTER 39

The door closed behind her, and for the first time since arriving in the Natonus System, Nadia felt truly *alone*. She'd been with her crew aboard the *Exemplar* almost every day since arriving, minus a few months where she was working on the *Preserver* alongside Isadora, Russ, and Vincent. Now, the only way to reassemble her crew was to strike out on her own. Carson had left for the west wing of the base on his own mission, and Russ was helping her by distracting their enemies.

Even with the distant thud-pinging of plasma fire, it was quiet in the base's east wing. So quiet that Nadia could hear her own breathing. Or her heart hammering from the nerves. She took a few deep breaths and pulled her handgun out of its holster. Time to go get Boyd.

She took careful steps down a winding spiral path that led to a straight hallway. She kept her weapon trained dead ahead, expecting an Offspring or an Ashkagi radical to jump out at her any second. But nothing happened, and she proceeded down the hallway unimpeded.

When she got to the other end, Nadia noticed a narrow staircase leading up to the right. She strained her neck, hoping she'd hear if anyone was in the connected room. But she couldn't hear anything. Part of her just wanted to move on—from the schematics, she knew the cell blocks were still ahead of her—but if there *were* enemies, it wouldn't be safe to turn her back on them, distraction team or not.

She walked up the narrow staircase, hugging the wall. The farther up she got, the more she smelled the unmistakable scents of battle. Iron and ozone wafted into her nostrils. She paused at a doorway leading into what looked like a control room and peeked out. There was no one inside, but there were two bodies. Both looked like Ashkagi.

She stepped inside and checked each corner of the room, gun raised. No one was there. Which confused her—had whoever killed the two Ashkagi already left? She didn't think any of their people were in the east wing at all. Did that mean the Offspring were responsible for the two Ashkagi's deaths?

She inspected one of the corpses more closely. Specifically, the hole carved by a plasma bolt through his torso. *Who am I kidding,* Nadia thought, *I probably couldn't tell an entry wound from an exit wound.* Still, she had to admit that it looked like the man had probably been shot in the back. Which pointed to a betrayal—and to the Offspring.

She looked around the room to see if she could find any clues why their enemies might've turned on each other. All she could find were depowered consoles, as well as a central terminal station. She headed back to the main hallway.

She passed through a door at the end of the main corridor. The next room widened out dramatically. Nadia's foot slipped almost immediately. The stones making up the floor of the chamber had cracked or eroded, with groundwater seeping in from all sides. There was only a narrow path leading to the other side. Water had submerged everything else. A single metal catwalk ran perpendicular to the path overhead, with a door on the left side that Nadia assumed led back up to the main area.

Nadia cautiously walked over the non-submerged stones. Once she reached the other side, she saw another exit door to the left, this one at ground level. If there were any Offspring in the east annex, she hoped they'd used the two exits to head back up to the entrance hall. She pressed onward.

The next hallway was equally deserted. She almost wished there was an Offspring on patrol, even though it'd mean getting into a firefight. The fear and anticipation of running into an adversary was almost worse than an actual battle.

Exiting the second hallway, Nadia found herself in a small room overseeing the prison block. There were four Offspring on patrol outside the cells, although it didn't look like they'd seen her yet. She hid behind one of the consoles for good measure. She hadn't been able to get a good count of the actual number of cells, but she figured there were at least a dozen. She wasn't sure she'd be able to take four Offspring all by herself, even in the narrow bottleneck of the cell block. Starting a prison break seemed like her best option.

Nadia stayed low and moved quietly to the main console at the front of the room. She pulled up a function that controlled the cell door security. It was all too easy to flip them from locked to open. What she wasn't expecting, however, was for all the block's cell doors to shoot open, abruptly and loudly, which alerted all four Offspring to her presence immediately. One of them immediately shot at the ceiling. "Stay put, or you get a plasma bolt!" he shouted to the prisoners.

The Offspring in front gave hand signals to the others. The four of them split up, two storming up the stairs to the control room and two staying put to guard the prison block. Nadia widened her eyes and frantically looked through the menu's functions to see if she could lock out the incoming Offspring. She found the controls, but only with enough time to lock the leftmost door. The right door slid open before she could press the lock button.

A wave of plasma fire streaked straight toward her, forcing her to leap for cover behind another console. She pulled a smoke grenade out of her belt and dropped it to the floor. Hopefully, it'd allow her to reposition. A second later, the grenade hissed, and black smoke filled the entire room. She couldn't see more than a foot in front of her, and she hoped that meant the two Offspring were just as blind.

But Nadia gave herself away with a cough. "She's over there!" one of the Offspring said. A plasma bolt landed just next to her right hand.

Cursing, she rolled over and crawled toward the exit. Or at least, where she thought the exit was. As she crawled forward, a leg suddenly appeared through the cloud of smoke right in front of her. She looked up and saw one of her adversaries peering down at her.

Nadia rolled to the side just in time to escape a plasma bolt straight to the face. She brought her own weapon to bear and pulled the trigger. The Offspring groaned and fell to the ground. The other clearly heard their exchange, however, because another round of plasma fire came her way from the other side of the room.

Nadia pushed herself to her feet and ran for the exit. The closer she got, the more the smoke cleared. She raced down the steps to the main cell block. Hearing footsteps behind her, she turned and shot the other Offspring square in the chest before he could fire at her.

That still left the other two Offspring, however. She ran to the mouth of the cell block, the clang of the floor grating echoing as she went. "There are only two left!" Nadia shouted as she hid behind the wall for cover. "Together, we can take them!" One of the Offspring fired down the cell block, and none of the prisoners reacted.

Nadia considered her options. She could try to jump out and shoot them, but she doubted she had the reflexes to get both of them before one got a shot off. She had another smoke grenade, but the two Offspring knew exactly where she was this time. They could just fire blindly and still hit her. She also had a standard explosive grenade, but in these close quarters, she'd probably hurt—if not kill—some of the other prisoners as well.

And then, a sudden shout: "Let's get them!" Which was followed by the sounds of feet trampling and a scuffle. Nadia heard a plasma shot go off and rounded the corner. The prisoners had mobbed the two Offspring. One of them managed to wrestle one of the Offspring's rifles away, and then shot him. Another prisoner landed a hard punch to the other Offspring's temple. After the cell guard had dropped to the floor, the same prisoner picked up his rifle and shot the downed man in the face.

"You're free to go," Nadia shouted, anxiously searching the faces of the prisoners for Boyd. "But this facility is under attack. You should get out while you can. There should be plenty of transports in the hangar bay." As the prisoners rushed off, a single man was left standing at the far end of the cell block. He looked up and locked eyes with

Nadia.

It was Boyd.

"Holy *shit*," Nadia said, choking up. She ran forward and embraced the man tightly, her fingers digging into his back. His face looked ashen and drawn, and he felt thinner inside her embrace than she was used to. But he didn't appear wounded. If the Offspring had tortured him, Russ might've had to stop her from glassing the whole fucking facility from orbit.

Boyd pressed his head into her shoulder. "You came back for me," he said.

"It was never even a question," Nadia replied.

They stayed locked in their embrace for another few seconds, before Boyd finally pulled away. "Are you okay?" Nadia asked frantically. "Did they hurt—"

"—I'm okay," Boyd said, flashing her a faint grin. "I really am. All they did was try to convert me. Suffice to say, I told them to fuck off."

"Of course you did," Nadia said, letting out something halfway between a chuckle and a sob. "But we need to hurry. Derek has the ship ready to go, but we need to get out fast."

She tried to wrap her arm around Boyd's shoulder, which only caused the man to laugh. "Really, I'm fine. They didn't hurt me. I can walk."

"Right," Nadia said. "Sorry. It's just hard to—"

She was cut off as her wrister crackled with an incoming message. "Nadia," Russ' frantic voice came from the other end, "Junta soldiers just entered the facility, and they're shooting the Ashkagi. Everyone on my team is dead. We need to exfil *now*."

Dread gripped Nadia's torso. That explained why the two Ashkagi radicals were dead back in the first room she'd investigated. Had the

Offspring struck a deal with the Junta? Isadora was on the way to Caphila right now, and if the Junta was in league with the Offspring, that'd spell trouble for her trip.

But the loss of the entire spec ops team hit her even harder. Those eight men and women had sacrificed everything to give Nadia the opportunity to rescue Boyd. She refused to waste that sacrifice by stalling. "Come on," she said, grabbing Boyd's wrist and racing back for the hallway upstairs. "We need to go now!"

"I'll try to meet you on your way out," Russ said over the comms, and cut his transmission.

By the time Nadia and Boyd had reached the hallway leading out of the cell block, the rest of the prisoners had already cleared out. "Looks like we have a clear path to the exit," Nadia said.

"Sorry for dragging you down," Boyd panted as they ran. "I've mostly been sitting on my ass since I got captured."

They arrived back in the room with the ruined floor. Boyd began the treacherous crossing first. Just before Nadia was about to step on the first patch of rock, she paused. She thought she'd heard a door sliding open nearby. She looked over her shoulder, but there was nothing. Probably just jitters. She proceeded onward.

Their boots sloshed through the seeping groundwater as they worked their way to the other side. Once again, she thought she heard footsteps. She turned around again, her hand resting on the grip of her handgun this time. But still there was nothing. And she had to hurry. She turned around and kept following Boyd.

Boyd reached the other side and turned around to look at Nadia. But his cheeks suddenly turned pale. A shaky finger rose and pointed behind them.

"Tanner," Boyd breathed.

Nadia turned around slowly. On the other side of the room was a muscular man, slightly shorter than Nadia, dressed in Offspring garb. The man must've come in from the exit on the other side of the room. He had faint brown skin and chestnut hair slicked back away from his forehead. Nadia locked eyes with the man. Little else besides smoldering rage greeted her.

The sound of another door sliding open filled the room.

Overhead, Russ burst through the catwalk exit and ran out into the middle of the balcony. "Nadia!" he called down to her. Russ looked back and forth between her and the Offspring. She noticed he didn't have his handgun on him, much less any grenades.

Nadia looked up for only a split second. When she returned to face the Offspring arrival—the one Boyd had called Tanner—she saw that he was already going for his gun. Nadia froze.

"Get down!" Russ shouted. He took a running leap off the catwalk and barreled toward her after landing. Just before Russ collided with her, she saw Tanner draw his handgun. He was aiming it straight at her.

Russ crashed into her, sending her sprawling to the floor. Her own handgun tumbled away from her, toward Boyd. She looked up at Russ just as the shot went off. His eyes were no longer full of malice or suspicion. Just a warm, protective look.

The plasma bolt tore straight through the middle of Russ' chest.

Slowly, the man sank to his knees, his eyes still fixed on Nadia. Until, slowly, they began to glaze over.

Russ' limp body swayed to the side and fell to the floor.

Nadia screamed.

CHAPTER 40

Tanner recognized Nadia Jibor instantly. She was the first newar he'd ever seen in the flesh, and she looked just as grotesque as he'd imagined. Her shoulders were broad and muscular, presumably from the electroshock therapy. She was disgusting.

He was so focused on her that he barely spotted the second newar until he was running straight for Nadia, after Tanner had already trained his weapon on her. He pulled the trigger. The newar male pushed Nadia out of the way, only to take the bolt from Tanner's gun straight through the heart. Nadia screeched when the other newar went down.

Typical pack behavior. The males getting themselves killed over the females.

But the giddiness made it hard to think at all. It was the first time

Tanner had ever killed anyone. He hadn't been the one to assassinate the pro-refugee Parliament member over a year earlier, nor had he ever personally carried out an attack on the newars' colonies. It felt good to pass this final threshold.

He was marveling at his feat for too long, however, and he barely dodged an incoming salvo of plasma fire from the formerly imprisoned Boyd Makrum. He must've picked up the weapon Nadia had dropped. Tanner ran to the nearby staircase, plasma fire pelting his feet the whole time.

"We have to go!" he heard Boyd shout.

"We can't just leave him!" he heard Nadia reply.

Tanner used the opportunity to spin around and unleash another wave of plasma fire at the two of them. His shots went wide. Boyd grabbed Nadia's wrist and nearly pulled her out the exit. "Come on!" he shouted. The door closed behind them.

Tanner kept his gun trained on the other exit, half-expecting the two to return for their fallen comrade. But almost a minute passed, and nothing happened. They weren't coming back.

He holstered his pistol and walked over to the other newar's corpse. His eyes widened once he saw the man's face. It was Russ Kama: Isadora Satoro's old defense adviser until the Calimor crisis. Tanner had almost forgotten about his existence, but killing him was surely a weighty prize.

But he had bigger things on his mind. The Junta had come through on their deal, streaming through Ruhae and picking off the Offspring's erstwhile Ashkagi allies. They should've rounded up Brandon Zahem's inner circle by now.

Tanner picked up Russ' corpse and wrapped him around his shoulders. Then he headed back up to the main level.

When he returned to the entrance hall, he found a coalition of Offspring and Junta soldiers waiting in formation for him. The commander of the Junta forces walked up. "We've secured most of the facility," the other man said. "Soon, we'll have Brandon Zahem in custody."

"Good," Tanner said. "And the newar infiltration team?"

"We've accounted for all but one of the diversion team," the Junta commander said.

"And I took care of the last one." Tanner angled his shoulders and slung Russ' body on the ground. The other Offspring in the entrance hall leaned in. "This is Russ Kama," Tanner explained, one side of his mouth curling into a grin. "He used to be one of the invaders' highest officials. And now he's the first one to fall. Someone take footage of this and upload it to the net."

While the other Offspring gathered around the carcass, Tanner walked deeper into the facility alongside the Junta commander. "Do you have any updates on the rest of Brandon's forces?" Tanner asked. Although the bulk of the Ashkagi radicals were at Ruhae, there were smaller cells across Enther. Tanner had given up their locations to Michael Azkon per their deal.

"Most of our tac teams have reported in," the Junta commander said. "Your intel was good. We're exterminating the Ashkagi terrorists from one end of the planet to the other."

It was strange that hearing news of their deaths caused Tanner a sense of joy. Back when he'd fled Obrigan over a year earlier, he'd figured partnering with them would be a major windfall for the Offspring. It was almost funny how much had changed in a year, how quickly the Ashkagi had outgrown their own usefulness.

They entered the facility's bath chamber, its floor marred by shattered glass, blood, and newar bodies. This must've been where the rest of the diversion team met their end. Stepping over one of the dead, Tanner couldn't help but grin. Today was shaping up to be a major step forward for the Offspring.

The Junta commander led him into the residential annex. The walls changed suddenly, from stone and plaster to elegant paintings. There were still gold statues left in this part of the retreat from the old Theocracy days.

Brandon Zahem had seemed to delight in the ornate design of the residency, having claimed the old royal chamber itself as his private quarters as soon as they'd arrived at Ruhae. The facility's luxuries were all that was left of a dead lineage of kings and the ashes of the Theocracy. The idea that power was something to be flaunted should've died with them. Brandon hadn't learned the lesson.

Tanner didn't need to flaunt his power, it was just *there*. Anyone could see it in the way his people drank in his words. Obeyed him without question. Died for him. Brandon was obsessed with the material demonstration of power. But he was about to die, while Tanner was on the cusp of accomplishing everything he'd set out to do. History was the ultimate vindicator.

They walked down a hallway lined with statues that led to the royal chamber. A half-dozen Ashkagi were lined up on their knees, hands tied behind their backs, facing the wall. One of the soldiers was videoing the whole thing. As they walked by, a squad of Junta soldiers aimed their rifles at the Ashkagi and shot them, one by one. Another spatter of blood appeared on the walls with every footfall Tanner took.

At last, they arrived in the royal bedroom. Even the bedposts were coated in gold, rising toward the ceiling in interlocking spirals. On the other side of the bed, three Junta troops had Brandon at gunpoint. He was still dressed in his pajamas. Tanner suppressed a chuckle.

"*You*," Brandon hissed when Tanner approached.

He shrugged. "What did you expect? Your stupidity was going to get my people killed. The Junta is offering us protection from the Union in ways you simply can't."

"I made you into everything you are!" Brandon raged. He bared his teeth and nearly rose to his feet. One of the soldiers slammed the butt of her rifle into the man's back. Brandon winced and fell back to his knees.

"On the contrary," Tanner said, narrowing his eyes and lowering his voice to just barely above a whisper. "The Offspring gave your failure of a movement a new lease on life. One that we are now retracting."

Brandon growled, and the same soldier struck him in the side of his face. Blood streamed down the man's cheek, making him look like some crazed, desperate animal. Which he was, Tanner supposed.

One of the other soldiers tossed a mobile holo-projector disc on the ground. Seconds later, an image of Michael Azkon snapped to life on the device. When the general saw Brandon kneeling before him, he just arched an eyebrow. "I'm surprised," Michael said at last.

"Didn't think I'd come through?" Tanner asked.

"Surprised it was that *easy*."

"You're blind!" Brandon said, gritting his teeth. "You think Tanner's on your side? He doesn't care about anyone or anything. Nothing but killing refugees. You think he cares about your alliance? You think he's not manipulating you, waiting for the moment to strike and discard you? If he can betray me, he can betray you."

"Lies," Tanner interjected. "Lies from a desperate fool bargaining for his life."

Brandon was entirely correct, of course. Tanner would sell out Michael—hell, *anyone*, if he had to—to bring an end to the newars' invasion. He'd sacrificed so much and come so far. Nothing would stop him. If Michael ever proved as useless to Tanner as Brandon had, he wouldn't hesitate to discard the general. But his new allies didn't need to know that.

"I think I've heard enough," Michael said. He lifted his hand, and the three Junta soldiers raised their rifles.

Tanner cleared his throat. "I was hoping you might let me have the honors," he said.

The holographic image of the general turned to face him. "Very well," he said, and motioned for his troops to lower their weapons. Tanner walked over to face the kneeling form of Brandon Zahem and drew his plasma weapon.

"You fucking bastard," Brandon spat at his feet. "You'll see. I'll make it out of this and then I'll come for you. I'll even rejoin up with Noah's rebels if that's what it takes. Don't think for a second that—"

He really doesn't get that he's about to die, does he? Tanner mused, baffled. The man was delusional up to the very end. No matter. Tanner raised his arm, pulled the trigger on his gun, and silenced Brandon's invectives permanently.

Tanner holstered his weapon and turned to face the Junta general. "I've followed through on my end of our deal," Tanner said.

"Yes," Michael said, stroking his chin. "Even now, Brandon's forces are going down across the planet. And I have your intelligence to thank."

"I think I've proved that I am a reliable partner," Tanner pressed.

"True," Michael nodded. "It will take some time to mobilize the fleet for a deployment to Ikkren. I will announce a formal declaration of war soon, however, as a sign of good faith. In the meantime, I expect your forces to continue with your end of the bargain."

"I'll redeploy the majority of my forces to cull the remaining rebels. Noah Tasano will be in our sights soon, and you won't have to worry about the home front."

"Good. And one last thing: the refugee leader herself is coming to Enther. Ostensibly, to meet with me and propose a new security arrangement. I wanted to let you know that I have ordered my forces to cripple her shuttle with an EMP blast. Even now, it should be sitting helpless in the jungles."

Tanner arched an eyebrow. *Isadora Satoro* was coming to Enther? It was almost like all his enemies were lining up, eager for him to knock them down. "I'm sending you the coordinates for her shuttle's location now," Michael continued.

Tanner's wrist terminal chirped. He had a team relatively close to the downed shuttle. "I'll dispatch forces immediately," he said, keying in a series of commands into his terminal. If they could take out the newar leader in addition to Russ, today might be the most glorious day in the Offspring's history.

"Good," Michael said. "I look forward to a productive partnership. I'll send you more information in the coming days so we can coordinate our efforts."

"I look forward to it," Tanner said. The holographic image fizzled and disappeared, and the soldier picked up the transmitter.

"We're going to continue mopping up the last of the Ashkagi," the Junta commander said.

"Yes. Good. I'm going to go talk to my people and explain our new objectives. I'll let you get back to work."

Tanner left the royal bedchamber, leaving behind the corpse of his former mentor still bleeding out on the floor. He walked through the connecting hallway—now nothing more than a graveyard of executed Ashkagi radicals—and returned to the reception area. The Junta soldiers had rounded up more prisoners since. Every few seconds, another plasma round went off, and another lifeless Ashkagi slumped to the ground.

Tanner couldn't care. It was time to move on to bigger and better things.

He returned to the bath chamber and paused. So much had happened in just the past few hours that he almost felt dizzy. He figured he'd crash soon, but for now, the surging adrenaline made it difficult to relax. Tanner had finally made his first kill. And after the first, the second hadn't been particularly hard. If two weren't that bad, four should be manageable, and so on.

Deciding to catch his breath before returning to his people in the facility's entrance hall, he walked out into the middle of the bowl-shaped rock depression. His boots sullied with the blood of his enemies, Tanner stared up at the sky. Enther's sole moon gazed down at him past the jagged edges of shattered glass far above. Part of him hardly even cared about the prospect of neutralizing Isadora Satoro. Just like he hardly cared that Nadia Jibor had escaped. Individuals by themselves were weak. Insignificant. The real danger in the newars' colonial enterprise was their overwhelming numbers. People like Isadora or Nadia would be powerless to stop him soon enough.

The entire time he'd been waging his campaign against them, he'd been thinking too small. To think he'd celebrated bombing New Arcena just months earlier. Was taking thirty-two newars off the board really an accomplishment? As long as there was a bottomless source of replacements up there in the night sky, the invasion would never end.

He'd never have been able to imagine doing anything about *that* problem so long as he was working with Brandon. But things were going to be different. Once the Junta declared war on the Horde, they'd force the Union back. Tricia Favan was a spineless coward, who could probably end the looming conflict if she had the guts. But she wouldn't. Her own timidity had rendered her impotent.

And that was the real victory. He didn't care about the Horde, the Junta, or even the Union, beyond its ability to thwart his goals. There was only one thing he cared about, and it was up there in the night sky.

It was time to think bigger. And that meant moving beyond Brandon's ineffective guerrilla tactics. Tanner clenched his teeth. He was going to stop the newar invasion at its source.

He was going to destroy the *Preserver*.

CHAPTER 41

"Are you almost done in there?" a voice called from out in the hallway.

"Sorry," Carson said. "I'll be right there." It'd only been about fifteen minutes since he'd killed the Offspring recruit, taken his enviro-suit, and linked up with another group. Luckily, none of them had been recent arrivals, so Carson didn't even have to worry about his cover story. They'd simply accepted that he was one of the new recruits.

Carson turned back to the mirror. He hardly recognized himself, and it wasn't just because of the brown Offspring enviro-suit he was wearing. His eyes looked sunken, with dark circles underneath. *A killer's eyes*, he thought. Eyes belonging to someone who could strangle a defenseless opponent. Eyes belonging to a man who'd embraced his dark side, who'd do what was necessary to accomplish his objective.

He might've been a therapist once, but that was another life.

Carson splashed water on his face and left his dorm, stepping over the plasma-riddled body of an Ashkagi radical on the way out. The new Offspring recruits had each been assigned an orientation guide, and Carson's had brought him to a room in Ruhae's residential annex. Only problem was, it'd only recently been cleared by the Junta. The blood was still drying on the dead Ashkagi's body.

Carson exited the room and found his guide leaning against the wall. The man's name was Emil Gurtrin, and he said he'd been with the Offspring for a few months. He had dark hair, and his features looked drawn, like they were just a little too small for the size of the man's face.

"I promise, you just happened to show up on an exciting day," Emil said. "The newar raid took everyone by surprise. And I knew that Tanner was reevaluating our relationship with the Ashkagi, but I didn't think the Junta would come in just like that." Emil had already mentioned someone named Tanner a handful of times. Carson had surmised that he was the Offspring's leader, though he didn't seem to have any official title. It was just "Tanner." That was usually how different cell leaders had operated back in Primordial, but Carson knew that some violent organizations preferred made-up titles and ranks.

It was easy enough for Carson to play the part of a shell-shocked recruit. He was new to war and death as well, and the images of his fight with the dead recruit had forced him into a state of cold detachment. Lying to the Offspring was surprisingly easy, as though he was just going through the motions in a dream.

Emil lowered his brow and stared at him, a look of concern

flashing across his face. "You'll be okay, brother. You are strong. Capable. That's why you're here."

"Maybe it'll hit me harder later," Carson said. "Right now, it feels good just to finally be around people who *get* it."

"I hear you, brother," Emil said. "We're a community here. We look after each other, keep each other safe. Not like in the core worlds. Everyone just cares about two things in Union space: money and status. Things are different out here."

"I look forward to becoming a part of that community," Carson said, falling into step behind the other man and stepping past a seemingly unending array of carnage from where the Junta had executed the rest of the Ashkagi. Carson and Emil were about to enter the bath chamber when a squad of Junta soldiers hauled in another round of Ashkagi prisoners.

Emil smirked. "I have a good feeling about you, brother. But come. I hear there is a surprise waiting for us in the main entrance hall."

He hated it when Emil called him "brother." *I have a brother*, Carson thought. *His name is Stacy Erlinza*. Already, it felt like there was a great distance between Carson and his old life. *I have a brother, his name is Stacy Erlinza*, he repeated to himself, getting a feeling that the phrase was about to become a mantra. A small, thin thread connecting him to his old life. To who he really was.

They entered the bath chamber. Carson had already been here earlier, as Emil had led him to the residence annex, but it hadn't gotten easier to look at. Seven members of the team that'd flown in with them lay dead on the floor. They'd all died because they believed in him, in his ability to find something of worth—some key piece of intelligence—while embedded in the Offspring.

Carson felt miserable every time they passed one of the soldier's corpses. Most likely, they'd died for nothing. "They're savages," Emil said. "They attacked like vicious animals. And even still, we beat them back." There was a certain mechanicalness to Emil's voice as he called Carson's people *savages*. As though he was just repeating the same phrases he'd been told hundreds of times already.

It squared with Carson's understanding of radicalization. Manipulators had always found it easy enough to convince the hopeless and the miserable to do whatever they wanted. Often, it could be as simple as interspersing memorable phrases and sayings with expressions of sympathy and understanding. *Which is what I'm doing now*, Carson realized. He and this Tanner character were both trying to manipulate the same kind of people.

"Are you holding up okay? I know this was a lot," Emil said, his voice softening. "I'm lucky—when I first got to Enther, it was uneventful. You and your cohort have already gone through incredible circumstances."

"I'm...okay," Carson said: a multilayered lie. "When I was recruited, I knew danger was gonna be involved. I welcome it."

Emil nodded sympathetically. "That was most of our experience. Still, it's different when you're living it as opposed to just imagining it." His expressions of sympathy and warmth just made Carson angrier. If he knew Carson's real identity, he'd probably just shoot him on the spot. His sentimentality was a lie, a cloak around the darkness growing inside him.

The two of them arrived in the main entrance hallway, where about a dozen Offspring were standing in a semicircle. A few of them turned around to face Carson and Emil with wide-eyed, giddy expressions on their faces. *What are they looking at?* Carson thought.

He almost broke down when he saw.

At the center of the semicircle was Russ Kama's still form, a deep plasma wound right through his heart. Carson's mind immediately flashed back to the Rhavego mining tunnels, where Russ had helped him get back on his feet after Juliet's death. Or how he'd reassured Carson the entire flight to Enther. He'd barely known the man, and yet, he was immeasurably grateful to him.

And now he was dead. Just like Juliet. Everyone who'd tried to help him, to protect him, ended up getting killed. Like Carson was cursed.

He felt his jaw wavering and bit his tongue until he tasted blood. He wanted to scream, punch the wall, or maybe curl up on the ground and cry. He'd left Earth with Stacy to avoid the hardships of Hegemony rule, but he'd woken up to a harsh, uncaring, fucked up world.

"I recognize him," Emil said. "He's one of the newar leaders, right?"

It enraged Carson that he didn't even *know* Russ' name. They saw him as a trophy, not as a real person.

"Used to be," one of the Offspring said. "His name's Russ Kama," he added, pronouncing *Kama* all wrong, making the first syllable all nasally. And only making Carson angrier. "I think he was their military guy a year back. Heard he got replaced."

One of the other Offspring kicked the body and flashed a cruel grin. "One thing's for sure: he definitely isn't their military guy anymore." Not clawing the speaker's eyes out was one of the hardest exercises of self-restraint Carson had ever experienced.

That was when he heard a door open on the far side of the entrance hall. His eyes shot up, and he saw Nadia's face appear. She was flanked by a man who Carson recognized as Boyd Makrum, even though he'd never met him. Two thoughts immediately entered Carson's mind: *I'm glad Nadia got Boyd, at least* and *What the hell are they doing here?* Based on the timing of his own endeavor, he figured Nadia must've just rescued Boyd. That meant they'd regrouped fast.

The two of them looked surprised to see how many Offspring had gathered in the main hall. But they reacted faster, raising their handguns before any of the Offspring could draw their own weapons. They unleashed a barrage of fire at their position. Two Offspring in front of Carson went down immediately. Everyone dove for cover.

As he ran for one of the nearby crates, he locked eyes with Nadia for a second. They exchanged an unspoken, mutual acknowledgement. Carson could see the pain—and the rage—in the woman's eyes. *She must be coming for Russ' body*, he realized. He thought about how mad it'd make Russ that Nadia and Boyd were risking themselves like this to get his body back, and he had to stifle a laugh. Still, trying not to laugh was better than trying not to cry.

One of the Offspring nearby popped out of cover, but received a plasma bolt in the head before he could fire off his own weapon. He fell to the ground with a heavy thud right next to Carson.

He couldn't help but notice a smoke grenade in the dead Offspring's utility belt. If Carson used it, he could give Nadia and Boyd a clear path to the body, allowing them to retrieve Russ and get out before the Offspring could regroup. But he didn't want to give away his cover.

When he looked up, however, everyone else was totally focused on Nadia and Boyd. Carson's fingers reached for the dead Offspring's belt and wrapped around the grenade. Holding his breath, Carson searched around in case anyone else shot him a stray glance. He waited until everyone was back in cover so it'd look like either Nadia or Boyd had tossed the grenade. And then he threw the device between the Offspring firing line and Russ' body.

Smoke filled the gap, and most everyone around him started coughing. A few fired blindly at where Nadia and Boyd had been, but it didn't sound like they hit either of them.

When the smoke cleared, Nadia and Boyd had disappeared. Along with Russ' body. Carson suppressed a grin. It was a small accomplishment, but it was his first undercover success. He'd cherish the moment for as long as he could.

He experienced a confusing mix of emotions. On one hand, Carson was happy that Nadia had found Boyd and that they were safe for now. At least the operation hadn't been a complete disaster. On the other, he envied them. Nadia was going to hop back in the *Exemplar* and return to civilized society. She wasn't stuck with the Offspring for the indefinite future.

Emil worked his way back to Carson. "Are you okay?" the other man asked.

Before he could respond, he heard another door swish open, this one behind him. He turned around and saw a single individual emerge. He was clearly Offspring, with pale brown skin, slicked-back, deep brown hair, and intense eyes. Carson looked around him and saw every other Offspring's demeanor change. The arriving man didn't have to do anything. He already had a captive audience.

"That's Tanner Keltin," Emil whispered in awe.

Carson didn't need the clarification. He could tell by everyone else's body language that Tanner was their leader, official or no. Carson focused on the man, wondering what kind of leader Tanner would prove to be. Maybe a little bit of psychoanalysis would help distract him from the grief at Russ' death.

It usually went one of two ways in violent organizations like the Offspring, steeped in machismo. Carson suspected Tanner would either act aggressively dominant—potentially even physically threatening—or calming and reassuring. A gentle, encouraging leader. Someone who could comfort the terminally insecure, then turn that into maniacal devotion.

"What happened?" Tanner said, eyeing the three Offspring bodies on the floor.

"The newars regrouped and took Russ' body," one of the Offspring reported. "They took us completely by surprise. We let you down. I'm sorry." The speaker hung his head in shame.

Tanner walked over to the Offspring who'd spoken. It looked like an effort at physical intimidation—a reminder of who held all the power—and Carson wondered if he might end up being the first kind of leader. But when "None of you have ever let me down" were the gentle words he used, Carson reassessed his assumptions.

Tanner placed a hand on the speaker's shoulder. "We are all brothers here," he continued: an obvious contradiction—if they were a fraternal organization, why did Tanner seem to have all the power? "What matters is that he is dead. And we don't need to worry about Nadia Jibor anymore. Soon, she will be irrelevant to our cause."

Tanner walked around, comforting and shaking everyone's hand. Carson found it revolting, but it took little effort to see why it was effective. Most everyone susceptible to radicalization never had a healthy home life. Tanner was the older brother or the father everyone wished they'd had.

At last, Tanner reached Carson. "You must be one of our new recruits," he said, extending his hand.

"I'm Carson Erlinza," he said, shaking Tanner's hand. "One of the newars took my job back on Obrigan. I'm here because I'm ready to do something about it."

Tanner had a twinkle in his eyes. "Good. I promise that you'll have an opportunity to do just that. Soon."

Tanner walked to the center of the room and stepped on top of one of the crates. "I know tonight has been trying, my brothers," he said. "But I promise, everything is about to change. Brandon Zahem is dead, and soon, the rest of his people will be as well. I've partnered us with the Junta, who can keep us safe from the Union.

"Per our arrangement, the Junta will soon declare war on the Ikkren Horde. And they will work to establish a blockade around the system's asteroid belt, cutting off trade and military assistance from the Union to the newars. Under the cover of their war with the Horde, we will strike at will.

"I know that you all have questions. And, I promise, I will answer all of them in the coming days. I only ask that you trust me for a little while longer. We will get through this, and—I swear to you all—we will be victorious."

"We will follow you forever," Emil blurted out. A handful of others echoed him.

Carson, meanwhile, had counted three different usages of the word *promise*. If anyone else had noticed, they didn't react to the repetition. Carson was already building a working impression of Tanner: someone who relied on implicit reminders of his own physical prowess, but generally acted comforting and even inspiring. And someone who sold his followers on a vague vision where specifics were few and far between.

Tanner grinned. "I never doubted it. I need to return to the residence annex and discuss our partnership with the Junta further. I may even need to return to Caphila for an extended period of time. But for now, it'd be wise to pack your things. I promise you this: living in squalor under constant danger ends today. Our partnership with the Junta will turn everything around."

Scratch that. Make it four *times*, Carson thought. Watching how easily everyone else accepted Tanner's words was almost surreal, however, now that Carson was seeing it firsthand as opposed to hearing it secondhand from a patient. Tanner's actions were obvious manipulation—how could they trust that he had a plan if he wasn't giving them any information? But all the other Offspring seemed afraid, and Tanner knew how to use that fear to control them.

"Natonus for the Natonese," Tanner said, waving his hand at the gathered Offspring.

"Natonus for the Natonese!" they echoed. Tanner departed.

"He's a genius," Emil said to Carson almost as soon as he left. "You should consider yourself incredibly lucky that you got to meet him on your first day."

"It's my understanding that he helped turn the Offspring around," Carson said guardedly.

"We were nothing before Tanner took charge," Emil said. "I'd follow him to the ends of the universe. Just like everyone else. But come, brother. Tanner said we should pack our things and get ready to move out. Let's work on getting this ordnance up to the surface," Emil said, tilting his head toward one of the crates nearby.

Carson squatted down, and the two men lifted up simultaneously. They carried the crate over to the elevator that led back to the surface. As they walked across the room, Carson studied the other man's eyes.

It was now his job to figure out what Tanner was planning. That meant either figuring it out himself, or somehow convincing one of the others to feed him information. But how could he get any of the other Offspring to second-guess Tanner? All of them had the same starry-eyed expression when he'd been talking.

All Carson could do was keep forging ahead, hoping that there was a vulnerability deep enough in the Offspring's organization that he'd be able to exploit. And that he'd manage to do so before Tanner accomplished whatever he was planning.

CHAPTER 42

When Nadia had pictured what it'd be like to be back on the *Exemplar* with Boyd and Derek again, it was nothing like how things were now. After taking off and getting out of range of Ruhae, Derek had met Nadia and Boyd at the airlock. Even the two men's first hug was solemn and silent. Nadia and Boyd had then taken Russ' body to a cargo area in the port wing after telling Derek what'd happened. Boyd had fashioned a makeshift coffin out of an unused gear locker.

Nadia leaned against the wall and watched Boyd lower Russ into the locker. His final resting place. She wished she could react, but she just felt empty. Hollow. Trying to cry felt like drawing water out of a well that'd dried up long ago.

"Are you okay?" she said finally.

Boyd nodded, closing the locker. "Glad to be back. I just wish it was under better circumstances."

"Me too," Nadia whispered. All she'd wanted was a triumphal reunion with her best friend, but fate had been far crueler.

"You should get to the cockpit," Boyd said, walking over and resting a palm on Nadia's shoulder. *We just rescued him from Offspring imprisonment, and he's the one comforting me?* she thought. "I'll make sure the engines are ready for a hard burn to break atmo," he said, making for the engine room.

Nadia nodded and followed him out. Her steps were slow and plodding as she made her way for the cockpit.

"The troop transport pilot's been trying to get a hold of us," Derek said solemnly as soon as Nadia entered. "Do you want to tell him, or should I?"

"I will," Nadia muttered. She sat in the co-pilot's chair. It felt larger today, like it was threatening to swallow her whole. She glanced over at the nearby console and flipped a button.

"I haven't heard anything from the distraction team," the transport pilot said, panicked. "What happened?"

Nadia cleared her throat, but she wasn't sure if it made her voice sound any less scratchy. "Everyone is dead," she said. "All members of your team, as well as Russ Kama."

There was nothing but silence on the other end for several seconds. "...copy," the pilot finally said, his voice sounding as deflated as Nadia felt. "And the rest of the operation?"

"The ship's in port," Nadia said: their agreed-upon code phrase to indicate that Carson had been inserted successfully, in case the Offspring had somehow hacked their comms. Although they were probably far enough from Ruhae by now that it didn't matter. Still, she figured being careful couldn't hurt. "And I got Boyd out. Those were the only things that went right."

"I understand," the pilot said, his voice cracking for a moment. "I'll follow you out."

Derek turned to Nadia. "Wasn't Isadora supposed to meet with the Junta chairman?" he said. "You told me the Junta is now in bed with the Offspring. Doesn't that mean she's in danger?"

Nadia turned her head slowly. Everything still felt dreamlike—a waking nightmare, more like—so the realization was far more surreal than it should've been. Nadia had even thought the same thing back at Ruhae, after she'd encountered evidence that the Offspring had turned on the Ashkagi, before the encounter with Tanner and Russ' death had forced any thoughts about Isadora from her mind.

But Derek was right: she was probably about to reach the planetary capital right now. And even though diplomatic immunity *should* be a thing, in theory, Nadia had learned that the Junta simply couldn't be trusted. And the time lag meant sending a message to Obrigan was a nonstarter. The *Exemplar* was the only other refugee vessel close enough to mobilize a rapid response if Isadora was in danger.

But Nadia's body still reacted slowly. Logically, she knew they had to do something. But she'd figured she'd feel more horrified, like she had when she was racing to Calimor to end the near-conflict between the Union and their people. Now, there was a void inside her where acute emotions couldn't escape.

Eventually, she brought herself to message Isadora on her wrister. Sure enough, Isadora didn't respond. They had to act. She turned back to the console and flipped the dispatch switch again. "Actually, we may still have another stop to make," Nadia said. Her own voice sounded strange to her—too slow, too monotone, too quiet. "We're heading to Caphila. Hopefully to intercept Isadora's transport before she gets there. We have reason to believe that the Offspring may be allied with the Junta, which means they could be planning a trap for her."

"Copy," the pilot said. The *Exemplar* swerved slightly as Derek veered them to the left. Out the viewscreen, Nadia looked back and watched the troop transport swerve to follow them.

Nadia sank into her chair. Time seemed to stretch out—or contract, she couldn't really be sure—as they sailed over the canopy. The planet was mostly undeveloped, which meant that flying over Enther was like looking out over a never-ending sea of trees. "How much farther to the capital?" Nadia asked eventually.

"We should be there in a little under ten minutes," Derek said, although she wouldn't have been surprised if he'd told her they still had hours left.

Nadia returned her attention to the scanner, which was when she saw the obvious markers of a chemical flare. "What's this?" she asked.

Derek looked over at his scanner station. "That could be Isadora," he said. "Should I go investigate?"

Nadia's mind still felt like it was lagging. Sure, maybe Derek was right, but what if it was someone else lost in the jungles, and they lost valuable time investigating the source of the flare? But if it really was Isadora, she wouldn't send up a flare unless something was seriously wrong.

"Nadia," Derek said gently. "We need to make a decision."

"I..."

"I think we should investigate the flare."

"I...agree," she said finally. Derek gave her a sympathetic look and radioed the new destination over to the troop transport.

If Isadora and her staff were in danger, that meant they should come in hot. That finally kicked Nadia into action. She'd already watched one of the original four die in front of her today. She wasn't about to watch Isadora go too.

"Boyd," she said into the ship's intercom system, "do you think you're fit for a shootout?"

"More Offspring?" Boyd's voice came over the comms. "Always."

Nadia's mouth twitched into as much as a grin as she could muster, which wasn't very much at all. "Meet me at the aft airlock."

Derek locked eyes with her and gave her an encouraging nod as she left. She returned to the posterior section of the *Exemplar* and linked up with Boyd, who was descending the engine room staircase. Nadia explained the situation as quickly as possible.

Boyd pulled a handgun out of his hip holster and led the way to the airlock. "You made the right choice, I think," he said. "I'd have gone after the flare too." Nadia wished she could've felt more comforted by the assurance as she took position on one side of the airlock door.

"I'm getting a visual on the source of the flare now," Derek's voice came over the intercom. "Sure enough, it's a downed shuttle. Looks like one of ours. And they're under attack from an Offspring gunship."

Nadia and Boyd exchanged glances, and Nadia drew her own weapon. "I'm going to do a flyby," Derek said. "Both of you might want to hang on."

No sooner had Nadia wrapped her other hand around a vertical railing next to the airlock door when it slid open, revealing a jungle clearing. It'd started raining even harder since they left Ruhae, with flashes of thunder off in the distance.

Her body tumbled to the left wildly as Derek executed a sharp change in direction. Her shoulder protested violently, like it was about to rip right out of its socket. As they leveled out on their new trajectory, Nadia eventually steadied herself and refocused her attention on the clearing.

A dozen Offspring were closing in on a downed shuttle. Plasma bolts were coming out of the craft, which meant there had to be at least *someone* alive inside. But Nadia couldn't get a good visual.

She and Boyd both aimed their handguns out the open airlock simultaneously. Plasma bolts shot out from both of their barrels, joining the violent frenzy of fire below. Two Offspring at the edge of their offensive line went down immediately.

The others turned their attention to the arriving *Exemplar* too late. Boyd took out another one as their vessel raced by. A few harmless bolts pelted the *Exemplar*'s underbelly, going well wide of either of them.

"Hold on," Derek said. "I'm going to land directly between the two sides, airlock pointed to the downed shuttle. Our hull can take a few hits from the Offspring while we load up with the crash survivors."

"Plus," Boyd muttered, "it's an extremely on-brand maneuver for us."

Nadia wished Derek had given them just a *little* more forewarning, since she barely had time to tighten her grip on the railing when she felt herself falling back in the opposite direction. Her back collided hard against the wall, a biting pain working its way up her spine.

They were on the ground by the time she'd steadied herself. Boyd made it outside first and set up alongside the edge of the vessel. He fired at the Offspring from cover. Nadia followed him out, beckoning furiously toward the shuttle. "We're here to rescue you!" she shouted.

"But we need to leave now!"

A handful of security guards Nadia was pretty sure she recognized filed out, shooting at the Offspring line as they went. And then she saw Isadora. It'd been over a year since the two had seen each other in person, and Nadia almost didn't recognize her. She looked like she'd aged at least a half-decade since. Although Nadia figured she might be thinking the same thing about her. An unspoken conversation commenced between the two, communicated only through their eyes. A dialogue of mutual hardship, of pain, of loss—and of warmth and acceptance.

Isadora stepped out into the rain, plasma bolts whizzing by. She somehow managed to look regal, even if her hair was wet and stringy and she was dashing desperately for safety aboard the *Exemplar*. Nadia caught her and pulled her inside. Once Isadora was in, the rest of her protection detail filed in, along with a young woman Nadia didn't recognize.

The airlock slammed shut. The engines fired. They were airborne sooner than any of the crash survivors had the chance to steady themselves, and the airlock corridor turned into a frantic mess of eight bodies staggering in every direction.

In time, they leveled out. "I knew you'd come," Isadora said. "I just had a feeling when I fired off the flare."

"Always," Nadia whispered.

Boyd led the way back to the main deck and helped the guards and the young woman strap in before they breached atmo. Nadia and Isadora brought up the rear, leaving faint specks of mud everywhere they walked.

"You must be coming back from Ruhae," Isadora said. "Did you manage to get Carson Erlinza inside?"

Nadia nodded. "He's with the Offspring now."

"Well, that's something, at least," Isadora said. Then, she flattened the ends of her blouse and chuckled. "I guess that means Russ is somewhere onboard," she said. "This reunion's been a long time coming. I have a lot to say. A lot to *apologize* for, really," she added. "So," she turned to face Nadia, "where's Russ?"

Nadia couldn't maintain eye contact. She bit her lip and looked at the floor.

"Nadia," Isadora repeated, more slowly and more seriously, "...where's Russ?"

·   ·   ·

They'd made it to space, where they'd linked up with the troop transport and transferred Isadora's security guards, plus the other woman—Nadia had learned her name was Valencia Peizan—to the other vessel, since the *Exemplar* only had four cabins.

And in all that time, Nadia was pretty sure Isadora hadn't moved.

She was standing in the cargo room, staring at the makeshift coffin with Russ inside. Nadia had visited her to ask if she needed anything, and Isadora had responded in the negative without moving so much as a muscle. Her eyes had stayed locked on the casket.

Nadia had then returned to the canteen, where she met Derek and Boyd. The *Exemplar* was back on autopilot, a course logged for Obrigan. It'd only take a few days to get there, but Nadia had no idea what'd happen when they did. She tried to summon excitement about finally seeing the Natonese capital world, but found herself empty.

"We need to get a better sense of what's about to happen," Boyd said. "I just checked the news feeds: the Junta has issued a formal war declaration on the Horde. They're mobilizing their fleet as we speak."

"They're coming after my planet, my *people*," Derek said, his jaw tightening. "We can't do nothing."

He was right, but doing nothing sounded too damn good for the immediate future. Nadia appreciated that Boyd and Derek were keeping everything on track, but she wished she could just hibernate and forget the world for the next few weeks. It was foolish thinking—her troubles would still be there when she woke up—but it was tempting.

"We aren't going to abandon our allies," Nadia forced herself to say. "Our *friends*. I'll go talk to Isadora."

She left the canteen and headed for the port wing, where Isadora still hadn't moved. Her face looked stricken beyond grief. There was no pained expression. Just flat, crushing misery.

Nadia lingered at the doorway, trying to figure out the right words. "I know this is the worst time to think about what comes next, but we need to start planning," she said. "Boyd just told me that the Junta—"

"—declared war on Ikkren. Yes, I saw," Isadora said. So she *had* moved.

"I was thinking about it, and it makes sense on a surface level," Nadia said. "But I'm worried we can't just think about the surface. From the little Boyd's told me about Tanner, he seems like he's one of the few Offspring who thinks strategically. Which makes him even more dangerous."

Just mentioning Tanner quickened Nadia's heartbeat. She could still picture the man's eyes, burning with sheer hate and malice, as he'd fired the shot that killed Russ. Nadia had already fantasized about encountering Tanner again. Next time, she'd be ready: ready to meet malice with malice. Ready to do what had to be done.

But wallowing in her hatred for the Offspring leader did nothing to help them in the short term. "I'd bet Tanner manipulated the Junta into war."

"I'm sorry," Isadora said, still facing Russ' coffin, "can you backtrack a little? Who's this 'Tanner' individual?"

"Right. Sorry. Tanner Keltin. I know we've been wondering whether we've been dealing with a bunch of scattered Offspring cells, or one unified organization. According to Boyd, Tanner's been behind everything. He brought the entire organization under his heel after the Calimor crisis."

Isadora nodded, but her attention was still directed on the coffin, as though she hadn't really heard Nadia. And then, suddenly, her neck snapped up, and she swiveled her head to face Nadia. The color had drained from her cheeks.

"Tanner *Keltin*?" Isadora asked. "Is that...is that a common surname here?"

CHAPTER 43

The coffin floated by the viewscreen in Isadora's guest room aboard the *Exemplar*. Inside was Russ Kama, her erstwhile security adviser, who she'd fired because she was too ashamed to admit that the near-war with the Union had been her fault just as much as it'd been Russ'. And now he was dead. Her firing him was the last interaction they'd ever have.

Despite that, Isadora's attention was elsewhere. Union security forces had just taken her daughter's girlfriend into custody, following a transmission from Isadora to Tricia Favan about the identity of the Offspring leader. Tanner Keltin. *Keltin*. Rebecca had already admitted that he was her brother, according to the police file Isadora had received on her wrister.

But she didn't need the police report to know what'd happened.

Alongside the file were almost a dozen messages from Meredith, all unread. It was the first time Isadora had felt like she didn't have the emotional strength to hear her daughter out. What was there to say? *Your girlfriend could be a major security risk, and we need to assess that before you can go back to spending time with her* was all she could say. And it sounded as hollow and empty as she felt.

So Isadora returned her attention to the viewscreen, where Russ' coffin was receding beyond visible distance. There was grief no matter where her mind went. If she went back and forth between her two sources of misery quickly enough, neither would have time to completely overwhelm her.

She'd felt that Russ deserved better. Deserved a hero's funeral, whatever that meant in their circumstances. But they had no plots available to them on Obrigan, and Russ had come to Natonus without any other family members. So they'd decided on a simple means of disposing the body. A soldier's funeral. She figured Russ might've liked that. It was more than the other soldiers she'd sent in would get.

Isadora pressed her palm to the viewscreen, as though she was waving goodbye to her old security adviser. Her mind played their final parting on repeat, the memory crystalline in its clarity. *You deserve better* was the last thing Russ had told her before leaving her life forever.

"I'm not sure I *do* deserve better," Isadora whispered. The fault for pushing their people toward conflict with the Union last year was not Russ' alone. She'd sacrificed him like he was some game piece instead of a real, living human being.

At the time, she'd thought she was finally taking initiative, finally accepting the weight of her position's responsibility. And now? If she hadn't fired Russ, he might very well still be alive. Tanner had been the one to put a plasma bolt in him, but Isadora couldn't help but think that she was the one who'd killed him.

Was there any humanity still left inside her? Or was she just an empty vessel of political ambition, emotionally stunted by her own decisions? Tricia had told her not to be so hard on herself, that what you did with political power was more important than how you got it in the first place. But what'd Isadora even accomplished? There was a holographic number in her office that went down every time she brought more people out of cryo, sure, but that was just photons of light on a screen. The image of Russ' coffin floating away was the only real, visible effect of her decisions she'd seen in a long time.

She wished so desperately that there was someone else—*anyone* else—who could be trusted with her job. She was never even supposed to have this position. Why did she ever think she'd possibly be *good* at it? Maybe everyone would just be better off if she stuck herself back in cryo. She could come out years later, when there were no murderous Offspring thwarting her every move.

She collected herself and departed her cabin. She walked to the *Exemplar*'s canteen, where Nadia was sitting in one of the seats, her feet propped up on the edge. One of Nadia's arms was wrapped around her knees, the other grasping a coffee tumbler. She barely looked up to acknowledge Isadora when she walked in.

Isadora sat down across from Nadia, folded her arms on the table, and buried her head on her forearms. She remembered the time she and Nadia had seen each other right after the Calimor crisis, when it felt like nothing could stop them. When it seemed like everything was just going to get better and better. Isadora would've given anything to go back to that moment. But time, *damn* time, only moved in one direction.

"I don't think I can do this," she whispered.

Nadia took a deep breath but stayed silent. Isadora berated herself—was she just looking for sympathy? Fishing for Nadia to embrace her and tell her that everything was okay? She was nothing more than a creature of politics. All she wanted was to feed off other's flattery. *You're pathetic*, she told herself.

"I dunno if I can do this either," Nadia finally said. "I can't stop thinking about how everything would've probably worked out better if someone else had my job. If I was still in cryo." Isadora found it oddly comforting that both of them struggled with feelings of inadequacy.

"I was just so *stupid*," Nadia continued. "I wish I could go back in time and shake my previous self. I dunno if I ever told you this, but there was a time, a few months back, where I had the opportunity to shoot Michael Azkon. I didn't, of course. But what if I had? Would his successor have still partnered with the Offspring? Would all those soldiers still be alive? Would *Russ*?"

The logical side of Isadora wanted to tell Nadia that she'd accomplished so much. Her colonization efforts had given literally *millions* an opportunity to live their lives. And trusting others was a strength, not a weakness.

But how could Isadora express any of that in a way that didn't sound empty? "I've had similar thoughts," she said. "About Russ, that is. I keep thinking of all the forks in the road that led to his death. And I keep thinking, 'What if I'd made that decision differently? Or that other one?' I swear, Nadia, I feel like I'm going mad."

"That's exactly what I've been thinking. Every few minutes, I think of something else, some small thing that might've kept him alive."

There was no comfort to be had, nothing Isadora or Nadia could say to each other that'd fix things—except for solidarity. Like they were trapped in a dark tunnel together, no light visible at either end, and all they could appreciate was that at least they were together.

"Have you thought about the future anymore?" Nadia asked. "About what's going to happen when we get back to the capital?"

"I still haven't figured that out," Isadora sighed.

"We're going to need to go after them," Nadia said, an edge of anger in her voice. "So far, we've been focused on settlement. But that's going to have to change. We can't bring more people out of cryo while our enemies are on the prowl. Our priority has to be ending the Offspring threat."

Isadora felt cold hearing Nadia speak. Things had to be bad if her settlement leader—and not just *any* settlement leader, Nadia Jibor of all people—was telling her that making war had to take precedence over further colonization.

But even that seemed impossible. The Offspring had powerful allies in the Junta, and Isadora knew Tricia well enough to know that the prime minister wouldn't risk the outbreak of a solar war by interfering. Just a week earlier—hell, *days*—Isadora had thought they were drawing a noose around the Offspring. And now, they seemed more unstoppable than ever.

She'd promised Meredith that the Offspring threat would be over soon when she'd left Obrigan. It was just another way she'd let her daughter down.

"We still have Carson," Nadia continued. "I have no idea what the plan is with him, but he could still give us a major edge."

The plan was to have his handler, Juliet Lessitor, collect the intel he found and dispatch it back to Riley and Isadora. But Juliet was dead, and Carson was truly on his own. It was just another thing that'd gone wrong: what use was a spy who didn't have any way to send information along? It'd be too risky for Carson to send them messages directly from his wrister.

"And I think it's time we stop pretending we can make nice with the Junta," Nadia said. "They shot at us back when we were setting New Arcena up. They tried to capture me, and they shot your shuttle down."

Isadora wanted to protest that they didn't *know* it was the Junta who'd fired the EMP at her shuttle, but those words would ring hollow. The Junta was working with the Offspring, and they had the capability to bring down her vessel. Who else could it have been?

"They're our *enemies*," Nadia pressed. "We should treat them as such."

Isadora regarded the lines in Nadia's face, or the way her pupils smoldered when she talked about the Junta, or the hard line of her jaw. Where had the Nadia she knew gone—the woman who always saw the good in everyone, even to a fault? Writing off anyone as unredeemable had never been her style.

But it was more complicated than that. Isadora had no illusions about the Junta, but they had warships that could destroy the *Preserver*. Menacing her or Nadia was one thing, but threatening millions of lives was another. She couldn't risk worsening the relationship between their people and the Junta.

But when she looked at Nadia and saw the rage simmering beneath the surface, Isadora wasn't sure she was ready to have a conversation about the harsh limitations of solar politics.

"We can figure all of that out in time. For now, I actually have a...question to ask you," Isadora said, searching for some topic, *any* other topic, to switch to.

The wrath dissipated from Nadia's face, and curiosity took hold instead. "What's going on?"

"It's...Meredith." Isadora explained the conversation they'd had before she left, ending with an update on Rebecca. She'd already had to explain why she knew the Keltin name.

Nadia snorted. "You must be the only person in human history who's ever been in this situation."

Despite herself, Isadora suppressed a chuckle. It felt good to ignore everything and just focus on the universe's cruel humor.

When she returned her gaze to Nadia, she saw that she'd adopted a thoughtful expression. "You know, just a few weeks ago, Russ and I were having a conversation in this very room that took me by surprise. We talked about our lives before fleeing Earth, about our frustrations and our failures. We even acknowledged that the other made some reasonable points."

Isadora felt a fleeting warmth in her heart. After the bitter arguments between Nadia and Russ in the early days of their settlement efforts, she never could've imagined them being able to sit down, talk about things maturely, and get along. But the warmth disappeared when Isadora remembered that, now, she'd never get to witness anything like that at all.

"I know you're probably thinking about the way things used to be," Nadia said. "Back when we were still on the *Preserver*, and it was just me, you, Russ, and Vincent. But the point I'm trying to make is: things can always change between people. We forgive and forget. And if it could happen between me and Russ of all people, I guarantee it can happen between you and your daughter. You'll get past this, and Meredith will understand. I promise."

Isadora closed her eyes, letting the tension ease for the first time since she'd left Obrigan. Nadia had never been a parent, but that was *exactly* what she needed to hear right now.

But it also made for an interesting contrast to Nadia's diatribe against the Junta earlier. *People can forgive, forget, and move on* seemed diametrically opposite to writing off the entire Junta as irredeemably antagonistic.

That was how Russ would still live on. The old debates between Nadia and Russ hadn't disappeared with his death, they'd simply *moved*. Now, their competing philosophies waged war inside Nadia. The more Isadora paid attention, the more she could see the signs of mental battle written across the woman's face. Wrath and mercy were locked in a fierce competition for dominance in her headspace.

Maybe Nadia wasn't the same woman Isadora used to know. Time only moved in one direction, after all. Everything and everyone was changing all around her: Nadia was carrying on Russ' torch, her people's settlement efforts had transformed the entire Natonese outer rim, she'd solidified her leadership position, the Offspring had risen to challenge them...and Meredith. Meredith was growing up, developing the confidence to confront her mother, and figuring out her place in her new home as she moved into adulthood.

Everywhere Isadora looked, she saw chaos. Impermanence. Maybe that was the extent of the comfort she'd be able to draw out of the present situation: that this too would, in fact, pass. That the Offspring could still be defeated. That not all was lost, that Russ' sacrifice wouldn't be in vain.

In the past, whenever the world felt too unbearable for her, she'd always turned to her daughter. It felt strange to delay reading Meredith's messages, even if only for a few hours. That had to be the first step. Meredith was the core of everything, Isadora's reason for being.

How could she be bothered by a cold, uncaring universe when her daughter *was* her entire universe?

It was time to face the music. And then the next step, and the next step after that. The chips would fall where they may. Isadora pulled up her wrister and opened the first message from her daughter.

ACKNOWLEDGEMENTS

I started drafting this book in the very last days of 2019. I always knew it was going to be darker than the first book in the trilogy, which ended up being some pretty unfortunate foreshadowing for how 2020 was going to go. But as much as the world looks different now from when I started this book, one thing hasn't changed: the tremendous support network that has made this book possible. As always, Sarah stands at the top of that list. She still found time to read the earliest drafts of this book while figuring out how to manage a research lab from home and baking bread. *Lots* of bread. I hope my monthslong quest to find yeast was a suitable way of expressing gratitude. Enormous credit also goes to Angela, Brian, Joe, and Tiffany, who read and provided amazing comments for this book at an astounding pace (the original Operation Warp Speed?), and made it immeasurably better. Natasha Snow (Natasha Snow Designs; www.natashasnow-designs.com) delivered the perfect cover for this book, much as she did for the first one. It brings me no small amount of smugness to know, already, what the third book's cover will look like—and I can promise it's just as good as the first two. In stressful times, I have often turned toward cardiovascular exercise to help relax. As such, I would like to thank both the entire sport of running as well as the Pennsylvania Election Commission for providing some top-notch cardio workouts during this book's production. Lastly, I'd like to thank you, the reader, for making it through a dark book during dark times. I hope that the novel's closing takeaway—that this too shall pass—can provide some degree of comfort. Here's to a better world in time for the third book.

ABOUT THE AUTHOR

Matt Levin lives in Texas with his wife and two dogs. He enjoys running, swimming, and backpacking while not writing. As well as staying approximately six feet away from everyone. Join him on Facebook at @mattlevinwriter, or follow his work at mattlevinwriter.wordpress.com.

Made in the USA
Middletown, DE
03 July 2023